Scribe Publications

THE MANDRAKE FILE

Cédric Bannel, 45, began his career as a French foreign diplomat and as a senior public official working on financial sanctions against Iraq. He has gone on to found and head one of France's biggest Internet companies.

Polly McLean, born in South Africa in 1974, is an award-winning freelance translator based in Oxford, England. Her previous translations include *The Patience Stone* by Atiq Rahimi, *Lobster* by Guillaume Lecasble, and *Secret* by Philippe Grimbert.

By the same author

Le Huitième Fléau (1999)
La Menace Mercure (2000)
Élixir (2004)

THE MANDRAKE FILE

CÉDRIC BANNEL

Translated by Polly McLean

SCRIBE
Melbourne

Scribe Publications Pty Ltd
18–20 Edward St, Brunswick, Victoria, Australia 3056
Email: info@scribepub.com.au

First published by Robert Laffont as *L'Homme de Kaboul* 2011
First published by Scribe 2012

This work was published with the support of the *Centre national du livre*.

Typeset in 12/15 pt Granjon by the publishers
Printed and bound in Australia by Griffin Press

FSC www.fsc.org MIX Paper from responsible sources FSC® C009448

The paper this book is printed on is certified against the Forest Stewardship Council® Standards. Griffin Press holds FSC chain of custody certification SGS-COC-005088. FSC promotes environmentally responsible, socially beneficial and economically viable management of the world's forests.

National Library of Australia
Cataloguing-in-Publication data

Bannel, Cédric.

The Mandrake File.

9781921844867 (pbk.)

840

www.scribepublications.com.au

Part I

1.

'WHAT WERE YOU THINKING ABOUT, when you pulled the trigger?' asked Osama.

'Pulling the trigger.'

'Did it not occur to you that your bullets would be destroying an entire family? Both Abdul's wives died alongside him. His eight kids are in hospital, two of them in a critical condition.'

'That bastard stole my fabric,' pleaded the prisoner. 'The whole stock. Eight thousand afghanis' worth!'

Osama Kandar, commander-in-chief of Kabul's Murder Squad, leapt up in a fit of rage. The prisoner, who was securely cuffed to his chair, flinched and nearly toppled backwards. Osama paid no attention. It had been a long time since he'd noticed the impact of his unusual physique. Osama was a little over fifty years old, and six foot five tall. He was lean (barely 89 kilogrammes) and imposing, with a short, grey-flecked beard and crew-cut hair. His flinty green eyes tended to have a hypnotic effect on his enemies.

'You're an idiot, and a murderer! You shot at a whole family with your Kalashnikov while they were sitting eating. For fabric. Do you realise the damage you've done? For nothing!'

'Not for nothing. He took me for eight thousand afghanis,' repeated the prisoner stubbornly.

Osama shook his head in disgust. Most of Kabul's murders were committed with Kalashnikovs — usually for unpaid debts, thefts, or honour killings. The guilty didn't realise that they might end up hanged. Osama had had enough of talking to such a stupid prisoner. He was about to call one of his deputies to take over when an orderly walked into his office. He was young, with the slanting eyes of the Hazara people. A long scar ran across his left cheek.

'*Qomaandaan*, we've just been informed that the security minister has turned up at the site of a suicide.'

'A suicide bombing, you mean?'

'*Na,* an actual suicide.'

Osama stared at the policeman, surprised. Kabul had one of the highest death rates in the world, so he always had plenty of work, but not many people killed themselves. If you were lucky enough to escape bombings, gangs, score settling, domestic murders, and the fatwas imposed by the Taliban, you were unlikely to commit suicide. In Afghanistan, staying in one piece every day was a gift from God.

'What can the minister be doing there?' muttered Osama to himself. 'Do you know who it was who died?'

'Na.'

'What about where it happened?'

'At some businessman's house, not far from the Serai Shomali bus station. It looks as if he killed his night watchman first, and then himself. His other servants found him this morning.'

'Do you have his name?'

'Na, qomaandaan.'

Intrigued, Osama opened a drawer of his small, rickety desk and took out the brand-new mobile phone he'd been given by the Coalition. Like many Afghanis, Osama was losing patience with the Coalition, and the blunders and humiliations it kept enforcing on the populace. But he was a man of the law, and the NATO forces were in his country with a UN mandate and the blessing of the authorities. Thanks to them, he had new technical resources and, more importantly, enough money to pay his men, who were no longer forced to take bribes to make a living.

He put the phone in his jacket pocket. It was the beginning of March and still very cold, so he also pulled on his thick wool *chakman* and an astrakhan fur hat. Osama always wore Afghan-style clothes — today a baggy dark-red *shalwar* that narrowed at the ankle, and a loose-fitting *kurta* worn outside the shalwar.

'I'll go now,' he said to the young policeman.

In the corridor he greeted his deputy, Babrak Khan Wardak, a highly educated young academic who had somehow ended up in the police force. Like many young men, Babrak was clean-shaven and wore jeans, with his kurta tucked into his belt western-style. Under the Taliban, that would have been enough to send you to prison. Which isn't to say that the Islamists weren't regaining influence — for a while now, more and more men had been leaving their shirts untucked.

Osama's 4x4 was ready and waiting, with a policeman at the wheel. Behind it idled a dark-green American pick-up, with three men sitting on improvised seats in the back, wearing immaculate uniforms and safari helmets, and carrying assault rifles. Both vehicles were new — gifts from the UN, like almost all the official vehicles driving around Kabul. Osama had heard people saying that a 30 per cent backhander had been given to the transport ministry, but he didn't know if it was true. In Kabul, everything could be bought, starting with President Karzaï's family and inner circle, many of whom had made fortunes worth hundreds of millions of dollars. As if the Afghans needed widespread corruption on top of poverty, war, and millions of deaths and disappearances.

The driver took off at top speed. Osama settled down into his seat to think. As head of the Murder Squad, he was informed of every death in the city. Hundreds of people died of non-natural causes every year, but three-quarters of those were linked to terrorism and therefore not part of police statistics. Osama was smart enough to keep his distance and to let the Coalition authorities handle those cases. The Americans seemed friendly enough, but they were suspicious of Osama — as of all Afghans — and all the more so because of his name. How to explain that when he'd been named by his father, Mohamed Kandar III, Baloch shepherd and son of a shepherd, Sheikh Osama Bin Laden was merely an obscure Saudi child, whose only claim to fame was being born with a silver spoon in his mouth? But that's how it was — being called Osama wasn't exactly an asset when you were police commander in a country occupied by NATO forces.

Babrak leaned forward to talk to him, grinning.

'It must be important, if a minister has bothered to go. And in any case, this is my first male suicide! Until now, it's just been women refusing arranged marriages.'

'Perhaps it's a member of his family. I've been wondering why he was told before us. But I better warn you, you'll be disappointed.'

'Why?'

'Suicides are pretty dull, from a police point of view. Sad, mundane stories of broken lives. Hard for the families to recover.'

'I didn't know you'd already handled one.'

'I saw quite a few in Moscow.'

Osama had a rare gift for languages. On top of Dari, he spoke fluent English and a bit of Turkish. He had also learnt Russian as a young inspector doing professional training in Moscow, shortly before the Russian occupation. On his return, he was immediately appointed to the brand new Murder Squad.

The driver braked sharply, catapulting Osama towards the windscreen, and interrupting his train of thought.

'Boķ Soyun!'

The Turkmen driver was swearing at the minibus that had cut in front of them. Osama tensed instinctively. Many lives ended like this: a car cutting you up, men leaping out and firing their Kalashnikovs — or, worse, the driver detonating his belt of explosives for a free ride to paradise upon hitting his target. Osama was known for his piety, but he was still a target for the Taliban on account of being a government official. The Afghan people's hatred for the Coalition increased with every day that passed, with every new gaffe and affront. Loyal civil servants were often thought of as collaborators, which obviously increased their chances of succumbing to the next suicide bomb. But for Osama there was no other choice: he was deeply anti-Taliban, having seen what they'd done to his country during the five years of their 'reign'.

Half an hour later, the 4x4 stopped in front of a narrow alley.

'We'll have to walk the rest of the way,' said the driver.

He got out, Kalashnikov in hand, followed by Osama and his

deputy. Two more men jumped out of the pickup to bring up the rear, carrying German weapons that had been a 'present' from the Coalition to the Kabul police force.

Women in blue burqas or brightly coloured headscarves were hurrying along with their shopping. Children were leaving school — the girls in black uniforms with white veils, the boys all in blue. A few raggedy kids were hawking cheap goods in the hope of making a few afghanis.

After about a hundred metres, the alley narrowed further and they had to elbow their way through. The neighbourhood was teeming with activity: men transporting bundles, parcels, and boxes on their shoulders; scooters carrying three people, weaving through in a belch of smoke. A pleasant smell of grilled meat and spices hung in the air. As they passed a small mosque, a hostile-looking man wearing the bushy beard of the Taliban spat at Osama's feet. He pretended not to notice. Civil servants — especially policemen — were not welcome in this part of Kabul.

The driver stopped in front of a big wooden door at the end of the alley. Several men were stationed there, shouldering weapons including an RPG7. Osama was surprised to see two bearded Westerners. They were wearing black fatigues, earpieces, and transmission equipment, and packing heavy weaponry — the standard gear of the Blackwater mercenaries used by the Coalition on sensitive missions. The company had responded to scandal by rebranding itself as the less sinister-sounding Xe, but it was still the same outfit. No one was fooled; people still called them Blackwater.

One of the Westerners made as if to bar Osama's way. He produced his laminated ID, which the other Westerner examined carefully before waving him through. Osama repressed a surge of fury. In theory, Blackwater didn't have any rank in Afghanistan, still less over the head of Kabul's Murder Squad. But, in fact, they ran the city, and no one could do anything about it. Osama wondered what they were doing at a suicide.

'The dead man wasn't a Westerner, was he?' Osama asked Babrak.

'No, Afghan.'

Behind the plain brown walls, Osama found not the usual ruin, but an impressive home. He walked through a marble-walled courtyard and an empty room furnished only with expensive rugs.

A corpse was laid out on a sofa with a bullet in its head. A bored-looking man in a threadbare coat squatted next to it, chewing a stick of liquorice. A pistol butt showed from under his *Kiyepanak*.

'Is this him?' asked Osama.

The cop took the liquorice out of his mouth to reply: 'No, this is the night watchman. The owner killed him and then himself.'

Drawn by the murmur of voices, they continued through a Western-style drawing room with wooden floorboards: something few Afghans could afford, given the price and rarity of wood. Osama wondered why the owner had built such a luxurious home in this run-down area. Why the need for privacy? Intrigued, he noticed several paintings on the walls, unlike anything he'd seen before. He walked through another reception room, this one furnished Afghan-style, and into a vast study. Four men, including a Westerner in battle fatigues, were standing around a body lying on the floor in a pool of its own blood. Among them, Osama recognised his stupid, corrupt, and despised Pashtun boss, Security Minister Burhanuddin Khan Durrani.

He saw a flash of repressed annoyance cross Durrani's face as he greeted him.

'Ah, Kandar! We were expecting a local inspector — you needn't have bothered coming all this way.'

In that case, what was he, a government minister and clan chief, doing here, thought Osama — not that he said anything of the sort. As he walked towards them, he tried to take a mental photograph of the scene. The man on the floor was about fifty years old, plump, wearing a traditional *pankan*. He was still holding a pistol, which Osama could see was an automatic Beretta. The bullet had entered through the mouth, exploding the whole back of the head but leaving the face intact. Blood and sticky grey matter had spurted all over the walls and the ceiling. The man's eyes were wide open. He looked surprised. Osama noticed a dark stain on the front of his trousers — he had urinated on himself.

'Who was he?'

He had recognised the man, but wanted to hear it from his boss.

'Wali Wadi,' replied Durrani, with a contemptuous laugh.

Wadi was a small-time intermediary, known for various kinds of trade with the occupying forces. He specialised in obtaining petrol from the military depots and selling it on to the service station companies. He had been involved in commandeering trucks and food-aid deliveries, and trafficking light weapons, but nothing bad enough to land him in serious trouble. Osama knew him by reputation. Wadi was Uzbek, which had kept him out of the bloody fighting between the Pashtun and Tajik clans. He was also a careful man, appreciated by Russians, Westerners, and Taliban alike for the way he kept his word. He was a rather ordinary middleman, hardly the type to commit suicide.

'Are there witnesses?'

'He killed his night watchman before turning the gun on himself. The rest of his staff doesn't sleep here. So, Kandar, what do they call it in Russia when you kill your family members and then yourself?'

The final part of Durrani's statement had been in English. This reference to Osama's training in the USSR was purely to render him suspicious in the eyes of the Westerner, and it seemed to do the trick.

'Altruistic suicide,' replied Osama. 'But this was a servant, not a family member'.

'Wadi lived alone. It seems that he preferred boys to women. Perhaps that's why he killed himself.'

'Perhaps. But I would like to talk to the other members of staff.'

'You're wasting your time, Kandar.'

Osama didn't reply. He had understood. For some reason, the government wanted to bury this case. Khan Durrani was there to persuade his own police force not to do its job.

'You will allow me to conduct my investigation according to normal proceedings, Minister,' replied Osama with an emphasis on the 'my'. 'I will, of course, make sure not to waste police time.'

Khan Durrani softened immediately.

'Of course, do your work. Keep me in the loop. And let me know as soon as you've closed the file.'

He marched out with the other visitors at his heels, leaving Osama and his officers alone in the room. As the group passed by, Osama spotted a discreet logo on the Westerner's fatigues: not Xe but DynCorp, the company responsible for the security of President Karzaï, and him alone.

One of Osama's team approached him.

'What should we do, *hajji*?'

Osama had earned the title 'hajji', or 'holy man', by twice making the pilgrimage to Mecca, as all good Muslims must do at least once in their lives. The more religious of his thirty-odd staff used 'hajji', while the handful of secular officers, including his deputy, simply called him 'boss' or 'qomaandaan'.

Osama didn't reply; he just pulled a pair of latex gloves from his pocket. It was nothing like the West, in Kabul: no paper bootees, no preservation of the crime scene, no laser rangefinder, no samples analysed in a mass spectrometer or under an electronic microscope. Osama worked in the old way, dependent on his own brain, minimal technical support, and what he could remember from the Moscow Murder Squad manual. The Russians had their faults, but they were thorough. They had taught him everything he knew, and he considered himself the equal of any Westerner.

An ankle holster was poking out from the dead man's trouser leg. He carefully pulled the weapon free, and inspected it with interest. It was a compact, lightweight pistol made of composite materials. He'd never seen anything like it.

'Babrak!'

His deputy rushed over.

'What is this pistol?'

'A Russian GSH-18,' replied Babrak immediately. 'An automatic designed for the Special Forces.'

Osama noticed that there was no safety catch. He pulled back the slide. A live round flew out with a click.

'He was ready, with the cartridge all set to go. He was carrying two weapons, including this concealed one. He was feeling under threat,' remarked Osama quietly.

His deputy pulled on gloves and frisked the body. He immediately came across a third weapon — a small revolver — hidden in one of the trouser pockets.

'What can this mean?' asked Babrak, amazed.

'See if you can find any other weapons in the house.'

Osama sat down on the sofa. This whole business unsettled him. Fifteen minutes later, Babrak returned with three more pistols, two Kalashnikovs, a shotgun, and several grenades. Not so excessive. Osama examined them intently.

'Strange.'

'What's bothering you, boss?'

'Wadi was a communist. He started trafficking in the early 1980s, with the help of the Russians. He owed them everything. Both the pistols he was packing are Russian. And all these weapons, too. Even the shotgun. And the grenades. So why did he kill himself with an Italian Beretta?'

Babrak shrugged, out of his depth.

Alert now, Osama sniffed the dead man's hands. He couldn't detect any gunpowder on the left hand, which had held the pistol. There was a slight burn on the man's lip, where the weapon had detonated. He gently unbuttoned the shirt, looking for signs of struggle. There was not the slightest bruise.

'Did you find anything else in the house?'

'Nothing.'

Osama noticed his deputy's discomfort.

'Are you sure?'

Babrak blushed, and awkwardly produced a little bag from his pocket. Osama recognised a lump of the base opium used to make heroin. It must have weighed about half a kilo, and would be worth around fifty thousand afghanis, or eight months' salary.

'He won't be needing it any more,' pleaded Babrak, 'and my TV is on thc blink.'

Osama shrugged. Another officer would soon steal it, so why shouldn't his deputy's young family benefit?

'Keep it, but try to establish the source and the quality. Wadi wasn't involved in the drug trade, as far as I know. Did you find any other narcotics?'

'No. Perhaps it's an old stash. It seems more like a sample than anything.'

Osama took the trouble to look around the house himself. Just in case. The bedroom was massive, with a gold-plated four-poster bed, and a pile of gay Western porn magazines next to it. He flicked through one, and put it down uneasily. These would soon be filched, too, and sold on for a fortune — for all their moralising tirades, the Taliban were known to be particularly partial to that kind of thing.

In the bathroom, he found masses of French beauty products. He noticed an uncapped deodorant and an open tube of toothpaste. The paste hadn't had time to dry. He touched the toothbrush; it was still slightly damp. He continued his investigation. In the kitchen he found several packs of cat food. It was a real trend in Kabul these days: owning a pet, especially a cat, was the hot new thing among the Afghan bourgeoisie, and every little shop stocked their food. There was also a tray on the table, loaded with a dirty plate, a crystal glass, and an open bottle of cognac, as well as the remains of a pistachio cake. It was officially forbidden for Afghans to stock as well as drink alcohol, but it wasn't unusual for rich businessmen to drink it in private. You could even get alcohol in Kabul under the Taliban, when simple possession was punishable by maiming or death.

Osama wandered around the empty house for a while longer, and then returned to the body. He undid the shirt again. There were traces of deodorant under the armpits. Despite the encroaching smell of death, he could still make out the subtle French eau de toilette on the dead man's skin. Once he was sure he wouldn't find anything else of interest, Osama stood up.

'Let's go back to the police station. Summon the other servants there, and we'll question them in the basement.'

The windowless basement interrogation rooms, with their creepily stained walls, were enough to make even the most recalcitrant witnesses talk.

As they left, Babrak asked, 'What do you think?'

'And you?'

'It's hardly the case of the century. He committed suicide. I mean, it's obvious that he blew his own brains out.'

'I'm not so sure.'

'But the weapon, the place ... it all hangs together. Why don't you think so?'

'Wali Wadi had dinner, ate half a pistachio cake, washed, put on deodorant and eau de toilette, brushed his teeth, picked up two automatic weapons and secreted them on his body, and then shot himself in the head with the only non-Russian gun in the house?'

'You did say that suicides are often rather sad.'

'Sad, perhaps, but not implausible.'

Berne was home to a clandestine organisation that carried out secret missions for various governments and large multinational corporations. It was fronted by several companies and NGOs, with evocative names like the Office of Strategic Affairs, the Institute of Economic Risk, the International Investigation Company, etc. All these cover outfits were Swiss, but they had foreign subsidiaries, enabling them to operate throughout the world. The organisation itself had no name. Those who worked there or commissioned its services knew it simply as the Entity. A few days previously, the Entity had been tasked with finding the financial director of Willard Consulting, an influential lobbying group based in Lausanne. The man had disappeared, along with some data that absolutely had to be kept private. It was 10.00 pm; but, like most of his colleagues, a young analyst called Nick Snee was still hard at work, studying a database from the Swiss Transport Ministry. The case had been accorded the highest urgency ranking, 'Priority Level Ruby'.

The first intimation of the storm that would throw Nick's life into the most unimaginable chaos couldn't have been more ordinary: a phone call. Nick's colleague Werner — a highly strung thirty-year-old with a body builder's physique and a heavy German accent — had just thrown down his files in exhaustion and was surfing the web in an effort to relax.

'Answer for me?' he asked. 'I'm buying a boat.'

'You've been buying a boat for the last six months,' countered Nick, 'and I haven't seen so much as a keel.'

'Exactly — I've got to get a move on if I want to live this dream.

Come on, do me a favour.'

Nick picked up the mobile phone and put it on loudspeaker.

'Lucas?' asked an unfamiliar voice.

At the Entity, it was standard procedure to give a false name. To the outside world, Werner — if that was his real name — was Lucas.

'Hey, Mickey!' shouted Werner, from the other side of the room.

Mickey was a drug dealer named for his outsize ears. He was one of the informers put on the case by Werner, who had spent six years in the Zurich police Drugs Squad, and reasoned that a man on the run might be in touch with all sorts of shady characters.

'It's Christmas, my friend! Father Mickey is here with his sledge.'

Nick felt his heart begin to race. He would never have believed that this classy, rich, well-respected fugitive would cross the path of one of his colleague's dodgy informers.

'I've found someone who fits your description,' said the dealer. 'A posh, well-to-do banker type. He's holed up in a squat outside Zurich. He's got a gun and a bag full of papers. Sounds like the guy you're looking for. Interested?'

'You betcha! Can you tell us more about this squat where he's hiding, Mickey?'

'Yeah. It's an old disused factory. In an industrial area north of the city. Used to be called Chimic Cystine. The junkies call it The Factory.'

Werner gave Nick the thumbs up. He swapped a bit more information with Mickey and put the phone down, having promised to pay him his bonus the very next day.

'I'll tell the general,' said Werner excitedly.

The general was the founder of the Entity. His English, French, German, and Russian were all fluent and accentless, and no one knew quite who he was or where he came from. A few minutes later Werner returned, looking disappointed.

'He's crazy! He's sending a whole K team out there to track the guy down, and didn't even suggest I go along. We've been sidelined, mate.'

'How come?'

'You know the general. Since when did that bastard ever tell you anything about his reasons?'

'This whole thing is weird,' said Nick. 'I'd like to know why the case has been ranked so urgent. I think this is the first Flash Ruby ever.'

'Every question has an answer. Let's go and find out what's happening for ourselves.'

Nick put his feet on the table.

'I think we'd better stay out of it. I don't like this case. I don't know why — it's a hunch.'

'Come on, man, stop getting so worked up. It was me who found the guy, and it's my right to see what's happening. Let's go.'

Werner put on his jacket without waiting for Nick to reply. Grumbling, Nick did the same, and a few minutes later they were speeding towards Zurich. In theory, the Entity wasn't supposed to carry out missions on Swiss territory, which was the exclusive domain of the official counter-intelligence services, but it often did. The Entity didn't really respect any laws, starting with the subtle and complex division of missions between Swiss governmental organisations.

'Christ, that hangdog look of yours is driving me nuts. What's wrong with you? Are you scared?' asked Werner.

'This whole thing stinks. We'd do better to keep out of it, that's all. I'm telling you, we're analysts, not Ks.'

K was the Entity's shock troop — twenty-or-so men who lived even more secret lives than the rest of the company. Nick had bumped into a few of them at headquarters during missions, and also heard a lot of stories about the demented things they were supposed to have done. If those stories were true, the Ks deserved respect. They were overseen by the Entity's second-in-command, Joseph, a quiet man who gave off an aura of mystery and danger.

Nick glanced at his own face in the rear-view mirror: he didn't look anything like a K, and that was putting it mildly. He was of average height, and although he did a lot of outdoor sports, he still looked more like a perennial student than a secret agent. His curly light-brown hair reached just below his shirt collar. His laughing blue eyes sparkled with intelligence, and his mother's high cheekbones lit up his face every time he smiled.

The urban landscape changed as soon as they entered the Zurich suburbs. Old buildings, warehouses, creepy figures lurking in the dusk.

'I'm lost. Did you download a map from Google?'

'Don't worry,' said Werner, tapping at the satnav on his knees. 'I'll navigate.'

Mickey had told them that the fugitive was hiding on the first floor of an abandoned factory, in 'the honeymoon suite'.

Nick had asked, 'The honeymoon suite?'

'Yeah, that's what they call it. Junkies in need of cash use it to see clients. You know — selling their bodies for a bit of gear.'

The surroundings were becoming more and more bleak as they approached the factory. Abandoned buildings and warehouses, and burnt-out cars sitting on their axles.

'It looks like Beirut or something,' said Nick. 'What the hell is this place?'

'The underbelly of the Swiss dream, mate.'

The atmosphere in the car was tense, and Nick was starting to sweat. The streetlights weren't working, and it was very dark. But there were lots of cars on the road, making the whole place seem even more bizarre.

'Who are all these people?' asked Nick.

'Clients,' said Werner, who seemed totally at ease. 'Looking for whores, or drugs, or sometimes both.'

After a while, a massive, ghostly shape loomed up in front of them. A rain-soaked urban ruin. The brick chimneys at either end of the building resembled the strange and pointless prows of a boat. Nick slowed to walking pace. The car's tyres crunched over needles and empty beer cans. Nick parked next to a skip, and killed the engine.

'This place gives me the creeps.'

'Young Nick Snee discovers, at the age of thirty, that Switzerland isn't all leafy residential suburbs like where he grew up with mummy,' jeered Werner. 'Jesus! It's a squat, that's all. Just a dump full of wasted losers.'

'Wasted and probably dangerous losers.'

'Yeah, right! As soon as they see us, they'll scarper like the cockroaches they are.'

'What do we do now? Wait for the shock troops?'

'Don't you want to find out why the general has sent fifteen K troops after just one guy?' replied Werner. 'You said yourself that the case stinks.'

Nick picked up the night-vision binoculars.

'It's mad,' he murmured. 'The whole building is full of people. I can see a few lights.'

'They must be pirating an electric cable. They always do that in squats.'

'No, it's flickering too much to be electricity. Must be either little gas lamps, or candles.'

They waited an hour, without the slightest sign of a commando unit. Then Werner reached behind the seat and picked up a pump-action shotgun wrapped in a blanket. The breech clicked loudly open as he loaded it.

'What the hell are you doing with that? We're not supposed to use weapons without permission!'

'Are you taking the piss?'

'We can't go in there alone, Werner. The dealers will finish us off in an instant.'

'We're going in, my friend — ex-cop's honour. There's a pistol in the glove compartment — just grab it, will you?'

'Let me tell you one more time. I'm an a-n-a-l-y-s-t. And you know I'm a useless shot. There's no way I'm taking a weapon.'

'We'll park the car over on the far side of the building. There's a blind spot under the south tower, where no one will see us. Stop moaning and drive, you lump.'

Against his better judgement, Nick drove slowly over to the building with his lights off. Close up, the disused factory was more sinister than ever. Werner sniggered.

'Welcome to the cathedral of junk ...'

They parked under one of the chimneys, and waited another few minutes in total silence.

'Right, let's go!' Werner was suddenly impatient. 'In any case, those K troops are masters of the quiet approach. We could hang around all night, only to find they've already left with our guy.'

They slipped into the building through a hole in the wall. They had gone about thirty metres when a foul smell stopped Nick in his tracks. Werner had frozen, too, white as a sheet.

'Fuck, Werner, what's that smell?' muttered Nick. 'It reeks of piss!'

He turned away and threw up, followed by his friend a couple of seconds later. The stench of urine was so overpowering that they were suffocating like fish out of water, with their mouths gaping open. Suddenly, Werner remembered something.

'Oh shit! I'm sure I read an article about this factory. It closed down a couple of years ago. It used to produce cystine, a medicine made from pork or cow piss, bird feathers, and other gross stuff. That's why it stinks in here. The council shut down the factory; they want to make this a residential area.

'We can't stay,' pleaded Nick, about to pass out. 'We need masks! We'd better go back to the office.'

For a moment, his colleague was tempted to agree. Then he remembered the man they were looking for. Usually, finding missing people was a job for the national police. This must be one explosive case, for the Entity to pull out all the stops for something so seemingly banal.

'I found the guy, and I'm going to bring him to the general myself,' said Werner, in a tone that brooked no argument.

Covering their mouths and noses with handkerchiefs, they moved deeper into the building. The ground floor was massive, more than two hundred metres long and about twenty high. It was cluttered with half-full stills of yellowish liquid. The smell was strongest here. Big drops fell at regular intervals. *Plop. Plop. Plop.* Nick and Werner staggered forward, their steps taking on the rhythm of the drops of repulsive liquid hitting the floor with clockwork regularity.

There were dozens of people in the central nave: the living dead, all horribly thin, mostly crashed out on mattresses. Each mattress had a candle or two burning in front of it. What must once have been a pretty girl turned her ravaged face towards Werner and Nick as they passed. She couldn't have been more than thirty years old, but was missing half her teeth. Yellowish liquid dripped on to her from one of the stills, and she did nothing to stop it. Nick felt a pang of anguish, but walked on quickly. There was nothing to be done for her, or at least nothing that *he* could do.

They walked through a doorway and found themselves in a second, smaller nave, with barely any candles. The residents here were at death's door, and too poor to afford light. The drains were blocked by the most repulsive filth. They splashed through yellowish puddles, getting their trousers wet. Two or three men approached them, but, put off by the sight of the shotgun, scattered like birds. Then Nick pointed out some concrete stairs on his right. Mickey had said the fugitive was hiding on the first floor. They paused when they reached the top of the stairs; at least here they could breathe.

'My god, clean air!' said Nick rapturously.

A voice surged out of the darkness: 'You don't notice, after a while.'

They span around to see an emaciated figure step out of the gloom. It was a woman, her head covered in scabs. She could have been any age between thirty and sixty. She was wearing groin-hugging pink cycle shorts, a stained bridal corset made out of white lace, a green windcheater, and battered yellow trainers. She looked like something out of a horror film.

'What don't you notice?' asked Werner, once he'd recovered the power of speech.

'The smell. Deadly down there in the Zone. The zombies is the only ones that can take it. It's gonna be another two years before the vats of piss is empty. You forget the smell up here. The piss don't rain on your head, fresh air comes through the roof. First class, innit?'

She wasn't joking. There was a first class even in hell.

'Who you lookin' for?'

'A fugitive. A rich banker, not a junkie.'

'Yeah,' she said scornfully. 'Got in yesterday, don't do nothing but puke. Can't get used to the smell. Don't even want to fuck the girls. Must be waitin' for something. Don't look like no junkie I ever saw.'

'Do you know where he is?'

The woman held out her hand. She grabbed the notes off Werner and stashed them inside her windcheater.

'Come on then.'

After the downstairs nave, the first floor was a different world. A hive for tramps, junkies, and dealers; for shady, underworld people. There was a momentary burst of murmuring as they walked through. When they came to a landing, the woman tugged at Nick's arm and took them down a narrow corridor. Easily recognisable sounds filled the air, interspersed with the odd cry.

'Thought I'd take you this way,' she said with a horrible grin. 'Never know, might give you a taste for it.'

They were in a long, thin room, split into several alcoves. The alcove doors had been stolen, but they were kept private by curtains — some open, some closed. Candles had been placed in hollows notched out of the walls. On mattresses, they could make out both boys and girls. Some of them looked healthy enough; others were already destroyed, with their arms, legs, and whole bodies covered in blackish marks. Clients were moving on top of some of them, in a cacophony of obscene grunts and groans.

'The honeymoon suite,' murmured the woman.

Nick felt as if he were inside a Hieronymus Bosh painting. Another corridor, more rooms. Then a closed door — the first since they'd arrived.

'Behind there,' said the woman. And she was gone, down a hidden staircase.

'Wait!' cried Nick.

But the woman had disappeared ... Werner opened the door, which was several metres high and made of reinforced steel. An empty corridor went off at a right angle. Werner crouched down to take a peek.

'What can you see?' whispered Nick.

'A very long corridor. Two armed men sitting at a table set crossways, about thirty metres away. They must be guarding the supply of drugs. There's no way we could get through.'

Nick poked his head around. At exactly that moment, two red spots appeared on the men's heads.

'Laser guns. Must be the K troops,' murmured Werner.

There was a brief burst of silenced gunfire. The dealers collapsed, killed outright.

'They shot without warning!' cried Werner to Nick, stunned.

Just then, several men ran in from a different set of stairs — all in black, wearing cagoules, guns out in front. One of them saw Werner and Nick, and span around. Werner straightened and put his hands up.

'It's me.'

A hail of bullets tore through the air and hit him in the chest. He fell to the ground.

'Werner!' screamed Nick.

It was like a nightmare. He saw the gun swing towards him, the black barrel point at his head, and the man's finger hover on the trigger. Then, suddenly, the barrel lifted. The K signalled to Nick that he had recognised him, and muttered a few words into his mic. Nick bent over Werner. His colleague's eyes were wide open. Blood was spurting from a horrific wound in his chest. Nick took hold of his hand, shattered.

'Werner, please. Come back. Come back.'

The commando walked over.

'You're crazy!' screamed Nick. 'You've killed him. He's dead!'

'You should have identified yourselves,' replied the K coldly. 'You'd been ordered to stay outside. Everyone inside this building is a potential target.'

The cagoule hid everything except the man's eyes. But Nick recognised him anyway. He only knew him by his first name: Wilfrid. There wasn't the slightest trace of shame or regret in Wilfrid's eyes. As if he had just crushed an insect.

'There's no signal in here,' shouted Nick.

'You shouldn't even have been inside. Our instructions were to catch the fugitive at any price. We eliminate anything between him and us.'

'But why, goddammit? Who is this guy?'

' "The capture of this fugitive is a government priority, and takes precedence over every other consideration," ' recited the commando.

He picked Nick up by the collar, carried him to the corridor, and sent him flying. Nick felt himself sail through the air, before landing painfully on the concrete floor. The commando came back a few moments later with the pistol, which he threw at him.

'You don't belong here. You're not fit. Go back to the office. We'll take care of the fugitive, and Werner's body.'

He disappeared. Nick lay on the floor for a few moments, getting his breath back, and then stood up with tears in his eyes. What was happening? His world was falling apart. He started staggering towards the exit. The honeymoon suite was deathly silent. Most of the junkies had scarpered, and the others were lurking in their cells. As he passed a mattress shoved into the corner of a sort of hole in the wall, he noticed that the curtain was now open; when they'd come past just a few moments earlier, it had been closed. An expensive overcoat was lying over a box next to the mattress. Overcoming his terror, Nick entered the alcove. There was a leather travelling bag by the wall. He tore it open. Polo shirts, suit shirts, underwear … all of it new designer stuff. No junkie could afford things like this. Not here, anyway.

'That's where your guy was,' said a voice behind Nick.

He span around. It was the woman.

'Ain't my fault,' she said. 'The bloke you're looking for gave me two hundred francs to send anyone lookin' for him off the wrong way. Your mate only gave me fifty.'

'Where is he now?'

'Gone. Took the other stairs. Forget it, you'll never catch him! And not your mates, neither.'

Nick collapsed on the mattress, overwhelmed.

'Don't know who that bloke is,' said the woman. 'Must be pretty big, cos your mates is butcherin' everyone down that end, tryin' to find him.'

Nick suddenly noticed a CD case next to the mattress. The cover was half out, as if the fugitive had opened it in a hurry before he left. On the back was a long series of letters: *RD. JK. GN. AD. LP. OK. BR. TG. RR. OL. TA. SW. PM. ER. WAJ. GT. JKO. KL. PP. MK. JH. DF. GHJ. KLP.*

He turned the case over. On the front, in felt-tip pen, someone had written *The Mandrake File.*

2.

OSAMA GOT HOME SLIGHTLY LATER than usual, around 9.00 pm. Even with their combined salaries, he and his wife could only afford to live far out of town, in the working-class suburb of Khair Khana. Things would obviously have been different if he'd taken bribes, or if his wife had worked in the private sector. But he enjoyed the laughter and liveliness of his family-friendly neighbourhood, where most people knew each other and spent time together — the men and women separately, of course. His favourite thing to do on a Saturday was to walk to the nearby Panjsad Family market and wander aimlessly among the bird traders there. The traders knew Osama, and enjoyed showing him their latest treasures. Once in a while he would buy one. He wouldn't have been able to explain why, but he found it terribly moving to hold the small, defenceless ball of silky feathers in his large hand.

Osama greeted the duty policemen in front of his house, and opened the front door. It was the kind of modest, flat-roofed brick-and-cob house found in working-class areas all over Afghanistan: single-storey, with three bedrooms, a large living room and a kitchen, all of it with bare wiring trailing out of the walls. At least it had running water, which wasn't the case in the Postakacho slum a mile away. Their women were forced to walk kilometres every day, in the freezing winter and the fiercely hot summer, to fetch a jar or two of water for their families. The line of women seemed to grow longer every day, and it broke Osama's heart.

He put his briefcase on the sofa, and opened a window to air the room. The goat-wool rugs were simple but in good condition, and he owned a few items of furniture, and some brightly coloured hand-painted boxes for his most precious things. Best of all was the ancient Russian hot-water tank in the bathroom. On the down side, he'd never been able to save enough money for a central-heating system, and so they had to make do with an old stove.

He heard noises in the kitchen. His wife was home from the hospital. She walked into the living room wearing an orange housecoat, with her long red hair rippling over her shoulders, and a Western magazine in her hand.

Malalai Kandar was a gynaecologist. An independent, freethinking feminist who had done most of her medical training in Baku, when it was part of the Soviet Union. She endured the country's moral strictures as best she could — helped by the fact that all her patients were women. Life had become impossible for the other medics: women were no longer allowed to treat men, or to work alongside male doctors, students, or nurses. Since the Russians had left, the fundamentalist net was slowly but surely closing around Afghan women, reducing them to a state of total subjection.

'How was your day?' she asked.

'Interesting. I've just picked up the weirdest case.'

Despite having been married for thirty years, and having two grown children and another who had died in the war against the Russians, their bond was as strong as ever. Osama had never been tempted to cheat on Malalai, or to take a second, younger wife. He was entitled to up to four wives, under Islamic law, as long as he provided them all with the same standard of living. But Malalai had warned him that she would leave with his privates in her pocket if he ever so much as suggested it. He hadn't argued. Lots of his 'pick n mix' colleagues secretly took the piss out of him and his wife's supposed upper hand in their relationship. He knew that didn't do much for his professional reputation, but he was happy like this. He didn't need four wives.

'Want to tell me about it?'

He hesitated for a moment, and then told her about Wali Wadi's apparent suicide, his own doubts, and the presence of the minister and the American DynCorp guy.

'That Khan Durrani's a piece of crap,' erupted Malalai. 'He's stupid and he's corrupt. He was all matey with the Russians, and then the Taliban, and now the Coalition. He'd sell dates to Martians if he had half a chance. It's because of men like him that we're stuck in the dark ages!'

'He's no worse than a lot of other people.'

'Don't say things you don't mean.'

'Things are improving,' soothed Osama. 'President Karzaï was re-elected, despite Taliban pressure. The schools have re-opened, and the economy is getting going again.'

'And younger and younger girls are being made to wear the burqa ... At least when the Russians were here, I could go about my life wearing normal clothes, I could go to a café, see a film, eat out with my friends, buy silly magazines like this, rather than having to hide myself away. Now I feel like a prisoner. This city is becoming more and more like a prison every day.'

Since his re-election, President Karzaï had been playing a dangerous game. Under the guise of national reconciliation with former members of the Taliban, he was surreptitiously allowing them a hand in state affairs, and thus preparing the way for their more-or-less overt return to power. Ministers, MPs, and other staunch anti-Taliban figures, such as the head of the secret service, had been sidelined and replaced by hard-line Islamists. The pressure on women was increasing all the time. The fear was in the process of moving sides.

'Careful,' said Osama, 'you could be accused of being a communist.'

'I liked the communists better than the Taliban. At least, under them, women had rights.'

Osama didn't reply; he agreed with his wife. And, anyway, he'd never been much good at debating, and there was no point arguing with Malalai — she always ended up with the last word.

'How are you going to stop that stupid minister from getting you in trouble?'

'I'm not sure yet. I'll have to be careful — there's something fishy about this case.'

'Don't take any risks.'

'I've got to finish my investigation. If the man was assassinated, it's up to me to find the culprit.'

'My poor darling,' said Malalai, putting her arms around him. 'You're the only man in this country who actually does his job. Come and eat — I've made *qabali palaw* and spicy *mantu,* just how you like it.'

Seeing the worried look on his wife's face, Osama stood up.

'I'll be careful, I promise,' he said firmly. 'I'll pray now, and then we can eat.'

NICK KEPT TRYING to call his superiors as he drove back to the office, but to no avail. Every time he got through, an anonymous operator trotted out the same sentence: 'There will be no telephone communication on this subject, not even in code. Return to the office.'

The Entity headquarters was frenetically busy. The main open-plan office was packed, given the time of night. Nick saw men he'd never set eyes on before. There were K officers in the briefing room, still taking off their gear: bulletproof vests, helmets, transmission equipment, and assault rifles fitted with silencers. Wilfrid, the one who had killed Werner, saw Nick and ambled over.

'Sorry about your mate,' he drawled.

'That was a monstrous fuck-up!'

'It was you who fucked up, Nick. You and Werner. You were told not to enter the building. What the hell were you doing in there?'

'It's illegal to shoot without warning! If you'd paused to think before pressing the trigger, Werner would still be alive.'

'I simply applied our usual procedure. You and Werner were behaving like dangerous amateurs.'

Nick was about to go for him when the general strode up.

'Stop this childish nonsense, right now!'

His furious tone spoke for itself. This was the Entity's first bungle since its inception, and it was a big one. He stared at Wilfrid, and then at Nick. Because of the time pressure, he had decided to send his K troops out without their boss, Joseph, who was on assignment in France. He had allowed the less-experienced Wilfrid to lead the assault. The team had studied plans of the factory before going in, but the plans were incomplete and didn't feature various wastewater pipes — and so the fugitive had escaped.

The general turned towards Nick.

'Snee, in my office. Now.'

Nick followed him, mortified. The general's office was that of a powerful man: seventy square metres, with a gorgeous view through three massive bombproof windows. It was furnished in a slightly pompous, English traditional style, cheered up by a few models of propeller-driven bombers from the Second World War. An enormous oil painting of a B52 dropping its bombs on a rice paddy covered one whole wall — the influence of a youth in the air force, some people said. Nick, on the other hand, had the distinct impression that the general simply preferred planes to people.

'Sit down,' he said, curtly.

Even in civilian clothes, the general gave off an air of natural authority reinforced by years of military command.

'You fucked up, Snee. You entered that factory without notifying our teams. Then you exposed yourselves just as the intervention was taking place. These are beginners' mistakes. It's your fault that Werner is dead.'

'Our men shouldn't have opened fire without warning.'

'Warning? Where do you think you are? There are no warnings. We're not cops, Snee. We might wear civvies, but we're soldiers at war.'

'But …'

'We'll tell your colleague's family that he died on a training exercise. Werner was divorced, and had no kids. There won't be an enquiry, and I'm asking you to keep your big mouth shut about this incident. I'm telling you, in fact. If you give us a moment's trouble, I'll have you crushed. Do I make myself clear?'

Werner's death didn't mean anything to the general. To him, it was just an 'incident'. Nick nodded, despite himself.

'Snee, say, "Yes, general!"' shouted the big man.

'Yes, general.'

He felt like a child being humiliated by its teacher in front of the class. His friend was dead, the general was treating him like a kid, and he wasn't saying a word. Why couldn't he stand up and tell this psychopath a few home truths, for God's sake? Suddenly, the general's face lit up with a smile.

'You'll see, Snee, you'll forget. In a war, there are always casualties. That's sad, but it's life. We're working to protect Civilisation, the West with a capital W, and we have to take risks. Now, give me one reason, one single reason, not to fire you from the Entity right now for failing to carry out the orders of your superiors.'

Nick was astonished by his boss's change of subject. He'd already written off Werner's death.

'I haven't got a reason. I did what I thought was right, and bear absolutely no responsibility for Werner's death, whatever you might think. And I have a question for you, too. Are you looking for a document called *The Mandrake File*?

The general almost choked.

'What kind of a question is that! Christ, what are you talking about?'

'This.'

Nick put the CD case he'd taken from the factory onto the general's desk. After a moment's hesitation, the general picked it up and examined it from every angle. Then he looked hard at Nick, and said: 'Go home.'

'Do we know what this Mandrake report is all about?'

'Nick, I am formally forbidding you from discussing any of this with anyone whatsoever, including anyone from the Entity.'

Nick realised that he wasn't going to be told anything further. He stood up. As he was walking out of the door, the general added: 'The existence of that file is classified. Even its name is confidential. Do we understand each other?'

AFTER A RATHER TEDIOUS morning, Osama's other deputy, Gulbudin, handed him a first draft of his report on Wali Wadi's suicide.

Gulbudin was forty-five years old and had been a chief inspector for ten years. A few years ago, he had lost a foot to a Russian landmine in the Khawak Mountains, but this infirmity didn't stop him from whizzing around on his United Nations-donated prosthesis. He had also lost an eye, a 'souvenir' from a 1996 shell explosion when Massoud's troops had shelled Kabul, causing a massacre and earning themselves the permanent hatred of most inhabitants. Gulbudin had been seriously injured, and Osama had taken him to hospital himself, despite the shells exploding all around. This had earned him Gulbudin's unending loyalty. Another point in his favour was that he was Hazara, not Pashtun.

Having read Gulbudin's report carefully, Osama put it back in its cardboard folder. The report was perfect — it didn't prioritise any one avenue, but didn't close any down, either. Gulbudin's writing was a brilliant example of its kind, and a great help to Osama, who sometimes struggled to navigate the security minister's convoluted and bureaucratic world. Most of his young policemen were of a generation educated exclusively in the Koranic schools — the Taliban having closed the secular universities — and it showed in the quality of their written work. Over and above their loyalty and intelligence, Gulbudin and Babrak were indispensable to Osama because they were intellectuals as well as cops. He was proud of having deputies who were better educated than him, and never missed an opportunity to show them off to his superiors.

Osama walked into the corridor and called together the other members of his core team. There was Abdul, a promising young policeman who'd spent two years training with the German Murder Squad, as well as Jihad and Rangin, two impressive officers in their thirties. Jihad had once been a bomb-disposal expert for the Northern Alliance; he was one of the few Pashtuns to have joined Massoud's Tajik troops. His family were fervent followers of wahhabism, one of the most rigid branches of Islam. All four of his brothers were called Jihad, and all five of his sisters, Palestine. But Jihad worshipped hard rock, America, and the movies. He carried out his daily prayers, but only as a matter of form, because Islam was the state religion. As far as Osama could tell, he didn't have the slightest religious conviction. He was always clean-shaven, and dressed like a Western student, in jeans and trainers. Rangin, on the other hand, was the son of a strongly secular, communist man who had worked for the Khad or secret services during the Russian era. Rangin's father had been assassinated by the Taliban as soon as they came to power. Rangin's red hair and green eyes were fairly common in northern Afghanistan, but his Slavic features were the cause of much intrigue and gossip among the police force, especially as he'd been conceived a few months after the Russian invasion. He, too, wore European clothes and was clean-shaven, but, in contrast to Jihad, was rather strait-laced. Rangin and Jihad were the best of friends, and always worked as a pair. They were the only Pashtuns on Osama's team that he trusted completely.

'Gulbudin's report is superb,' began Osama. 'It should allow us to continue investigating for a few more days without interference. Bravo!'

Gulbudin looked down modestly.

'What should we make of the minister's presence at Wali Wadi's home?' asked Jihad.

'What should we make of a man who wears a Rolex worth a million afghanis? Be suspicious of him, anyone who works for him, and anyone from his clan. From now on, we'll be operating in isolation, so don't say anything to your colleagues, and don't let anything slip. This investigation is top secret. OK?'

'Yes, qomaandaan.'

Osama turned towards Babrak.

'The body?'

'I asked for the autopsy to be done today. *Daktar* Mimouda was on duty, but I know what you think of him, so I asked daktar Katoun to do it instead. He was willing because it's you. I promised you would buy him a basket of his favourite strawberries as soon as they hit the markets.'

Osama groaned. Fruit from the Panjshir valley was famous throughout the area — especially the first strawberries of spring. They would cost him at least fifty afghanis, but it was for a good cause. Katoun was a well-respected and honest surgeon who had interned in Azerbaijan, whereas Osama suspected that Mimouda, the head university doctor, hadn't even passed his school exams. Mimouda was one of the scheming and uneducated men who had emerged during the Taliban era, but whom no one had dared remove from office when they left, just in case ...

'Ask the daktar to check the corpse's neck. I couldn't see any marks, but if he was strangled, his glottis might have been damaged. He should also check for traces of skin under the nails.'

'You think someone was holding him as he committed suicide?'

'Something like that. I'll need his hands testing for powder — I couldn't smell anything. He should also pay attention to his armpits, his skin, the content of his stomach, and his gums. If we can prove that he brushed his teeth just before dying, we will have a pretty invincible argument. Most importantly, make sure he sends the report to the justice minister at the same time as he sends it to me.'

Babrak nodded knowingly. Since 2002, it had been necessary to obtain the public prosecutor's permission before embarking on a criminal investigation. Despite many efforts, the police had been unable to block this strange, Italian-inspired reform. Fortunately the justice minister, a Russian-educated Tajik, loathed Khan Durrani with a passion. If he had the report, it would be very hard for the security minister to demand it be rewritten or, worse, lean on the prosecutor's office to prevent an official investigation.

'What do we do now?' asked Gulbudin.

'We need to visit Wadi's offices,' said Osama. 'Just Gulbudin and Babrak — the rest of you, keep working on the file.'

His 4x4 was already waiting outside, tailed by the usual pickup full of fierce-looking policemen.

Wali Wadi's offices were in the old district of Murad Khane, not far from police headquarters. Osama ignored security protocol to roll down his window and let in the smells of the city. Reconstruction was in full spate, so Kabul was packed with building sites. The Coalition was raining dollars on the capital. Most of it had been hijacked by the various clans milling around President Karzaï, but there was enough left over to create a boom the city hadn't seen since the arrival of the Russians. On top of that, billions of dollars of drug money were feeding rampant property speculation. If the war were to start up again, it would all be destroyed for the nth time by Katyusha rockets fired by the Taliban from the nearby mountains, and the city would start on another downward spiral. It was depressing, but Osama just had to put up with it. Kabul was his city, and he didn't want to leave.

Suddenly, they heard the boom of an explosion, in the distance. A fraction of a second later, the car windows trembled. Osama exchanged glances with Gulbudin. Another suicide bomb. In just the last ten days, two lots of Taliban had blown themselves up in public — the first, as a convoy of Western contractors was driving past; the second, to wipe out some big shot in the security services. These unexpected and devastating attacks had become the heartbeat of Kabul, crushing the atmosphere, despite the fatalism of the inhabitants.

'We'll soon find out where it went off,' said Babrak excitedly. 'Sounded like a big one.'

After half an hour's inching through heavy traffic, the driver double-parked in front of a shabby-looking modern building. In the hall, a listless guard didn't even ask who they had come to see — although the three Kalashnikov-wielding plainclothes cops surrounding Osama may have put him off. Next to the reception booth, a bronze plaque announced 'Wali Wadi Holdings, 3rd floor.' The lift wasn't working, so they took the narrow stairs to the third-floor landing. They found a single door, sporting an identical plaque. Osama entered without knocking. Inside, things were radically different: a massive, freshly painted reception area with wooden floorboards, and modern art on the walls that resembled the paintings Osama had already seen at Wali Wadi's home. A young man was sitting behind a desk, talking on the phone. As soon as he saw the armed men, he paled and hung up hastily. Osama presented his card.

'You work with Wali Wadi?'

'Yes, *sahib,* I was his personal secretary,' replied the young man quietly. 'I was expecting you.'

Up close, Osama noticed that the young man's eyes had been outlined in khol, giving him a rather feminine, doe-like appearance.

Although that didn't mean a thing — young Taliban men liked to make *them*selves up, too.

'May I see his office?'

The room was enormous, and kept in semi-darkness by lined curtains. There was no street noise at all. Bulletproof windows, thought Osama. A large, modern hardwood desk, several overly ornate armchairs that looked as if they were Lebanese, and a sofa. Wadi had done better than Osama had realised.

'Have my colleagues already been?' asked Osama.

'No one,' replied the young man. 'I heard about sahib Wadi's death on the radio this morning.'

So they had the lead on the security minister's henchmen, thought Osama with satisfaction.

'Was everything as it should be? Any signs of breaking and entering?'

'The alarm was on, and the office was tidy. I didn't notice anything out of the ordinary. No one had touched the safe.'

'You have a safe here?'

'Behind the painting.'

The young man took down a lithograph, revealing the door of a rather large safe with a numerical keyboard and built-in screen. Osama noticed a Western logo on the front: 'Hartmann'. It was the first time he'd come across such a modern safe — usually, only old Russian models made it to Kabul. He looked closer. It had a very deep keyhole. The safe looked new, and invulnerable.

'Sahib Wali Wadi got it last month,' offered the young man. 'It's a European model — he had it sent over specially. It's the only one in the whole of Afghanistan,' he added, proudly.

Osama wondered whether Wali Wadi had had a bunch of keys on him when the body was found. He turned towards Gulbudin, who had been thinking the same thing and shook his head slowly.

'I didn't notice, boss. I'll check when we get back.'

Osama spent a few minutes examining the desk. There were some dull-looking files on it — market analysis by Western banks, and few old papers — and an unmarked plastic case. It was empty, apart from some English-language instructions, which he handed to the young man.

'What is this?'

'Specialised software for encrypting documents, Sahib. It's called PGP; top of the range. Wali Wadi had it sent over from Dubai three days ago.'

'What did he want to encrypt?'

The young man gestured helplessly.

'I don't know, Sahib.'

'Did your boss seem different lately? Anxious, or depressed?'

'He didn't tell me much. Business seemed good — great, in fact.'

'Why did he buy this safe?'

'Sahib Wadi told me that he needed to step up his security systems, now he was playing with the big boys.'

'He said that — "with the big boys"?'

'Yes. He bought another one for himself.'

Osama looked at his deputy again, and Gulbudin shook his head. Their search had not revealed the safe. Osama cursed his lack of thoroughness. They would have to start again, and be a lot more rigorous.

'We changed the locks of the office three months ago,' continued the young man, 'and installed a camera over the front door.'

'I didn't see it.'

'It's well hidden in the ceiling, with only the lens poking out. It's European, too.'

Osama felt his pulse begin to race.

'Do you know where the recordings are kept?'

The young man nodded. He took Osama into a little room adjoining the kitchen. A state-of-the-art computer sat on a table, purring.

'It's all on the hard drive.'

'Perfect.'

Osama asked for the data to be retrieved. The search of the office didn't throw up anything much, except for a few bottles of alcohol — whisky, vodka, French wines — and an impressive pile of brand-new porn magazines. Osama let Babrak and Gulbudin take the bottles. They were delighted. They'd sell them on to journalists and NGO workers for a good price. This was their lucky day.

By the time his men came back with the surveillance computer monitor, it was time for morning prayers. Osama unfurled his mat in the middle of the office, and made the ritual prayer invoking Allah's mercy as his deputies looked on. Neither Gulbudin nor Babrak were devout, but for different reasons — Gulbudin because, deep down, he was a committed atheist, nostalgic for communist rule, and Babrak because, like many of his generation, he would rather listen to Western music, hang out with his friends, and surf the Internet than pray to a God who had abandoned his country many years ago. Osama accepted it; his faith was deep.

3.

THE GENERAL RE-READ THE LATEST MESSAGES from Kabul. He wasn't sure what Kandar was up to, and that made him very anxious. But the real problem was right here, in Berne. He took Nick's personal file out of the safe and started reading. Twenty-nine years old. Mother, Swiss, a nurse; father, criminal lawyer in one of the top London chambers and previously a diplomat; one brother, four years his senior, a banker in Singapore. The parents' divorce had caused long-term damage — the brothers barely spoke to each other, the parents even less so. The mother had remarried some sort of crank, a beekeeper by trade, and lived with him in eastern France. As for Nick: nondescript school career, boarding school from the age of fourteen, very respectable double degree in maths and oriental languages at the University of Geneva. Nick's passion for extreme sports — an odd fit with his reserved demeanour and thinker's physique — had been pronounced even then. A way of escaping the trials of living with divorced and distracted parents, perhaps? After that, one of his language professors had encouraged him to apply to the FSS (Swiss Federal Security Services), where he was soon identified as 'exceptional'. He always came top of his cohort of analysts. Three years later, he was taken on by the Entity's strategic-analysis unit, on the personal recommendation of the head of the FSS.

Since then, Nick had made a real name for himself in the organisation with two operations. The first, 'Air Kamikaze', was carried out entirely by the Entity on behalf of the CIA. The idea — to set up a network of travel agencies to be used by Jihad trainees but controlled by the West — had been Nick's, and he had implemented it from start to finish. A Gulf bank with a big presence in Switzerland had enabled the speedy growth of the selected agencies by offering credit and support at just the right time. These agencies were headed by hard-line, wanted Islamists from Palestine and the Middle East. They obviously had no idea that their work was being organised and financed by the CIA, or that every last detail of their activities was under surveillance, thanks to the most sophisticated electronic equipment available in the West. The network, comprising forty-two agencies, had supplied hundreds of plane tickets to trainee terrorists, who were then put under surveillance as soon as they arrived in friendly countries. This had enabled the foiling of several planned attacks in Europe and the US, without anyone working out what was going on. The agencies were still in business.

Nick's second operation was even more famous. It was known as operation 'halal pig'. It all began when a certain Imam Sadar issued a well-researched fatwa claiming that, contrary to popular Islamic opinion, the pig was not in itself impure: pigs could be eaten, and even kept as pets, as long as they were purebred Persian Gulf pigs, a breed dating back to the time of the prophet and known as the halal pig. An anti-halal pig website immediately popped up (in Arabic, Persian, Dari, English, French, and then a dozen other languages), calling for an insurgency against Imam Sadar, who was accused of being an unbeliever and a Zionist agent. The controversy snowballed, creating massive amounts of Internet traffic as the anti-halal pig website became a popular gathering place for Muslims all over the world. The faithful rushed to Internet cafés in the Middle East and elsewhere to pledge their support to *fatwas* ranked from one (rebuking Imam Sadar) to seven (beheading him). The faithful could also text their support to the brothers planning to pursue Sadar to the ends of the earth, and assassinate him. Hundreds of thousands of Muslims registered their support of the fatal fatwa, and even greater numbers sent SMS support.

The whole farcical thing — a product of Nick's fertile imagination

— had grown beyond his wildest dreams. Imam Sadar didn't exist, and the website calling for the insurgency had been designed by a pair of Lebanese freelancers. Every time someone voted in support of the fatal fatwa, the website released a secret cookie allowing the user's IP address to be registered. The text messages sent by gullible believers were also registered. Once the hugely powerful Echelon computer network had confirmed the data, the Entity was able to offer the best imaginable (and totally illegal, of course) global database of Islamist sympathisers to the various Western intelligence services. Almost nine hundred thousand people considered to be high-risk Muslims were listed, without their knowledge. For the few Western officials who knew about it, operation halal pig had become — with its blend of daring, cunning, and technology — a prime example of 21st-century espionage.

The general carried on reading.

As far as the Entity knew, Nick had had several flings over the last few years. He'd also had a secret liaison with a slightly older, 32-year-old Entity analyst, Margaret Hoffman. It had lasted a few months. Romantic relationships between agents were officially forbidden, but, given the success of operation 'halal pig', the internal security services had turned a blind eye. According to the file, Nick and Margaret had split up the previous September, so no action had been taken against them. The former operations director of the FSS evaluated Nick as follows:

Nick Snee: Poor combat skills. Poor shooting skills. Poor ability in field operations. An extremely clever boy, certainly, but rather spoilt, and has never known hardship or suffering. His emotionality and insufficient ability to handle pain mean that he could never make a top-level operative.

On the other hand, the former head of FSS Intelligence commented:

Nick Snee's boy scout demeanour may hinder his career, but he is of quite exceptional intelligence, with a remarkable capacity for elaboration, and the imagination and spark of originality characteristic of the very greatest spies. He is the best analyst I have ever had under me. Despite his young age, it is my opinion that he should be given greater levels of operational responsibility in the immediate term.

The general snapped the file shut. Nick was a brilliant, promising individual, one of those rare people able to subvert the course of things on his own initiative. The halal pig case had proven that. What a shame he'd noticed the CD case, with its twenty-four pairs of initials. Twenty-four names that should never have featured in a report like this, but now did. And that changed everything.

He sighed, and walked over to the secure meeting room. Joseph was waiting for him, sitting at the other end of the long table. He was of medium height, and wearing dockers and a black polo-neck jumper that emphasised his narrow hips and powerful shoulders. It was impossible to tell his age. His hair was grey, and combed back. He had a strange face, with the smooth cheeks of a child. His pale-blue eyes were as cold as death; there was no feeling when you looked into them, no warmth, nothing. Eye-contact with Joseph was enough to give most people goose bumps.

In intelligence agencies throughout the world, the mix of civilians and military men is a delicate matter. The soldiers have rigour, stamina, training, and total obedience on their side. Civilians, on the other hand, are often more imaginative and innovative, and generally more effective in urban operations. Civilian and military spies have always rubbed along without really understanding each other; but with the general and Joseph, things were different. The general had total confidence in his head of operations, even if he was a civilian, for the simple reason that he knew Joseph was the best of his kind. For his part, Joseph was no more capable of feeling empathy for the general than for anyone else, but he appreciated his professionalism, his nose for strategy, and his ability to handle setbacks. He saw his boss — with his rustic, old-fashioned manners and highly sophisticated brain — as one of the great warriors occasionally produced by the West.

'How's the manhunt going?' asked the general. 'It's been four days. The client is starting to get restless.'

'If Willard Consulting hadn't fucked up, we wouldn't be in this mess. Give me the time I need.'

'The time? What time?'

'The time it takes. These things can't be forced.'

'They don't see it quite like that.'

'They need to calm down, given the chaos they've created.'

That's true, thought the general sourly. The directors of Willard Consulting had found out that there were two copies of the Mandrake report — one in Zurich and the other in Kabul — and in their panic had launched two operations at the same time. The assassination of the company's own financial director had failed, and the man had sensibly fled. Plus the hit man charged with assassinating Wali Wadi had not managed to get his hands on the report, which was still hidden somewhere in Kabul.

A right mess.

'How do we get this under control?' demanded the general.

'By cleaning things up. Here and in Kabul.'

Joseph's thin lips were pulled back, emphasising the strangeness of his smooth face. He looked like a dead man, which in a certain sense he was. He had no family, no friends, no one he could count on. No one loved him, and he didn't love anyone. No one slept in his bed, and if he slept with anyone, it was a prostitute. He had killed more than a hundred times, and he would kill again. Right now, even though nothing about him gave it away, he was feeling something akin to rage, on account of his team's failure at the Factory.

'Does Nick have the slightest notion of what's in the Mandrake report?' he asked, calmly.

'No. But he's clever enough to put two and two together. If he happens to guess some of the names that those initials stand for, we'll have a problem. A big one.'

'Should I take action?'

'Not right now. First, I'd like to give him a more active role in our search for the fugitive.'

'Why?'

'He's already implicated in the case, whether we like it or not. Also, he and Werner found the fugitive before anyone else; that shows he's got something to offer. We need him — he's our best analyst. He might come up with an approach that no one else has thought of.'

'And if he does? I'm happy to wipe out all the traitors or Taliban you like. But Nick is different. He's one of ours, and that's not what I do, even if he is a pain.'

The general sighed. He liked Nick, but there was no room for emotion here.

'We'll decide whether to unleash your guys when and if that happens. It would depend on a lot of things. But we have no right to be weak, or even conscience-stricken — this case is too important. Can I count on you, Joseph, whatever the cost?'

Joseph shrugged magnanimously.

'I'll do what needs to be done.'

'When do you leave for Kabul?'

'In a minute.'

'Good. Cut off all leads, by any means necessary, whatever the consequences. Nobody must ever link Wali Wadi's death to the report. Not ever.'

'You are aware that the official investigation is continuing? The minister seems worried. He's not sure he can muzzle the cop in charge.'

But he would have to, whatever the price. The Entity's IT guys had proven that Wali Wadi had made a CD copy of the Mandrake report. He'd encrypted it, but that wouldn't matter to the Entity's specialists, who had access to the most powerful computers in the world. If they found the CD, they would soon be able to read it. The investigating cop was the problem. He might happen to find it — the ultimate nightmare for Willard Consulting and the few handpicked Western officials who were in on the case.

'Our instructions are clear. Stop him. We have carte blanche.'

THAT AFTERNOON, Osama started his search for someone to open Wali Wadi's safes. He called his friend Reza, the head of the Kabul police intelligence department, which was a small service compared to the powerful Afghan secret service, the NDS.

'So,' began his friend, 'I hear you're caught up in a suicide? What was going on? Did Wadi have AIDS?'

'I'm not sure yet,' replied Osama, realising that Katoun had better do a serology. 'The case is looking complicated.'

'I hear that the boss is keeping a close eye on it. Do you think they were in business together?'

'For the moment I'm floundering,' admitted Osama. 'Just trying to do my job without taking a stray bullet.'

'More like a stray grenade, in your case,' laughed Reza nervously. 'Take good care. Right, now what can I do for you?'

'I'm looking for someone to open a safe. A state-of-the-art European safe. No one in the science department can help me. Do you know anyone?'

'Hmmm ... not easy. I used to have a guy like that, who'd spent twenty years in Germany, but I don't know where he is these days. I heard he joined Al-Qaeda, and died in Tora Bora in late 2001. Unless he's hiding out in the tribal areas. In which case, he might as well be on the moon ... '

'What do you do when you need to open a reinforced door?'

'This isn't Moscow, Osama! That hasn't happened for at least two years. The last time I couldn't get into somewhere through the door, the Americans bulldozed the wall for me.'

'OK, I get it,' said Osama, disappointed.

'Hang on ... I've just thought of someone who could help you. A kid who spent several years in an Italian prison for burglary. Word is, he's a genius with safes.'

'Where is he?'

'That's the rub. He's in Pul-e-Charkhi. Block 7.'

Osama felt his body sag. Pul-e-Charkhi was Kabul's main prison, and block 7 was a prison within the prison, known for its violence and terrible conditions. Only the most dangerous inmates were detained there.

'Do you know what he's in for?'

'He killed a Coalition soldier. A Canadian.'

Osama paused. In this country, that was the most heinous crime imaginable. But it was also the sort of thing that would attract the admiration of Al-Qaeda supporters. Pul-e-Charkhi had been a Taliban stronghold; there must still be a few of them quietly occupying important posts.

'Don't tell me you're thinking what I'm thinking,' said Reza.

'I am.'

'You won't be able to get him out, not even for an official investigation. Not even for a few hours.'

'I need him. Who could help me?'

His friend thought about it.

'Do you remember the prison governor?'

'Yes,' groaned Osama. 'We met in the North as mujahedeen. He shot himself in the hand to avoid returning to the front. I punished him severely. He should have been shot, but he managed to escape.'

'I'd heard that story, but I didn't know if it was true. He still can't stand you, I suppose?'

'I wouldn't have thought so … '

'OK, we'll have to find another way — an unofficial route.' Reza thought for a moment. 'We could try Mullah Bakir. He was the prison Imam until they fired him after the June 2008 escape attempt. I think he wanted the job because it gave him direct access to top Taliban members serving time. I'm sure he still has plenty of contacts in there. Do you know him?'

'I've heard of him, obviously.'

Mullah Bakir was quite a celebrity. He had hosted a very popular show on national radio under the Taliban, until they shut the media down for obscure religious reasons. Every Afghan was familiar with his distinctive nasal drawl. He was an erudite imam, considered sophisticated and intellectual, and he led prayers at the Shah-e Do Shamsera mosque in central Kabul. He had been on the Taliban's secret council from 1996 to 2001. He had not been investigated since — a token of good faith by some of President Karzaï's inner circle to the other side, just in case … Mullah Bakir was also known as the most westernised of the Taliban, to the extent that the word could ever apply to anyone who preached a return to the most antiquated form of Islam.

'Do you think a former Taliban chief would be up for helping me? I've killed quite a few of them.'

'Mullah Bakir is different. He's someone you can talk to. The Taliban kept very quiet about any disputes between members of their council, but they were sometimes pretty major, I can tell you. I've got a whole file on him. He was definitely the leader of the moderates. He was against the stoning of women, corporal punishment, and the forbidding of westernised leisure activities. He was the only senior Taliban to oppose Mullah Omar on the asylum given to bin Laden and Al-Qaeda. He was also against the Al-Qaeda strategy of aggression toward the West, because he knew the risks it posed to the Taliban regime.'

And how painfully right history had shown him to be … a man like that would definitely be under surveillance by the secret services, thought Osama. He would have to be careful if he wanted to contact him without the government knowing.

'How could he help me?'

'He has lots of influence with the governor. If you can convince him to 'lend' you the prisoner for a few hours, I'm sure it will be possible.'

'How do we stop the NDS from finding out?'

Reza burst out laughing.

'Amrullah Saleh got him the job!'

The former head of the NDS! An ex-mujahedeen Tajik and friend of Massoud's who had himself killed dozens of Taliban …

'Don't get yourself all worked up,' said Reza. 'I'll vouch for him. Will that do?'

'OK. I'll go and see him after five o'clock prayers.'

He hung up and unfurled his mat. He needed to pray before such a delicate task.

SHAH-E DO SHAMSERA MOSQUE had been a civic building before it became a place of worship. It looked like a quirky old European palace, with its pale-yellow walls, sloping roof, rounded windows, and columns embellishing a façade topped by a single tiny minaret. The inside smelled musty, of feet. A few of the faithful were praying on threadbare mats. Osama headed towards the mullah's quarters at the back. He had come alone, by taxi, having first made sure to lose anyone on his tail, in case the security minister's henchmen were already following him. He was wearing a turban as well as a scarf wrapped around the lower part of his face, so he wouldn't be recognised. His only protection was a pistol and two grenades in the pocket of his *jelak*. Not much use, to be honest — there wasn't a great deal you could do against a *shahid* willing to blow himself up.

A one-legged man was standing in front of the mullah's office, leaning on a stick. One of the faithful, a spy for the extremist fringe of the Taliban, an NDS informer … or perhaps all three. Osama had come prepared: he handed over a brown envelope stuck down with sellotape, containing his badge.

'Give the closed envelope to mullah Bakir, and tell him I want to speak to him.'

The man bowed and withdrew. He returned a few moments later.

'The mullah will see you now, sir.'

He led Osama into a tiny waiting room, and then a huge room that served as office, living room, kitchen, and bedroom. There was a narrow bed in one corner. The floor was beaten earth, the furniture old and rickety, and the cob walls and cracked ceilings dirty, but a huge bookcase took up the whole of one wall, and several flat screen computers sat imposingly on the mullah's desk. The piles of English and American magazines scattered around the place — *Newsweek*, *Time*, *Foreign Affairs* — were even more of a surprise. The one-legged servant withdrew, leaving the two men alone.

Mullah Bakir was sitting with a steaming glass of tea. He was a short, fat man with laughing eyes. He lumbered to his feet, held out a limp hand — good manners in Afghanistan — and embarked on a series of traditional Afghan greetings: 'How are your family, is your body strong? *Manda na Bashi.* May your family prosper. May you live a long life.' He still spoke in that strange, slow, nasal way, enunciating each syllable and pausing between sentences as if addressing a crowd. Osama sat down opposite the mullah, who poured him a glass of mint tea and pushed a dish of biscuits towards him. Osama was struck by how wily the man seemed, and by his innate elegance, despite the simple clothes. He felt even more inclined to be cautious.

'So, to what do I owe this visit, qomaandaan? I hear all sorts of things about you. Some of it very good — you're one of the few men at police headquarters to carry out your daily prayers. But I also hear that your wife has communist sympathies and supports the infidels. Is that the influence of your training in Moscow?'

'Seeing as you're so well informed, you must know that my training took place before the invasion. I was a young officer of twenty. In those days, plenty of civil servants completed their training in Russia. You know the rest.'

'Meaning that you then joined the troops of that dog Massoud? I'm aware of that, yes. I know the role you played in the battalion that killed more than thirty Russians in one day during the battle of Taloqan. I even know that you killed lots of our men with your precious Dragunov. How many, exactly?

'I will not abide anyone referring to qomaandaan Massoud as a "dog". The Taliban disgraced themselves by killing him. He was one of the finest men our country has ever produced,' retorted Osama, reeling from the mullah's knowledge of his life.

'He was killed by Al-Qaeda, not the Taliban,' replied the mullah. 'It's not the same thing at all. But don't let's argue, brother Osama.' He sipped his tea. 'I don't like arguing with honest men. To what do I owe your visit?'

Osama regained his composure.

'I'm investigating the suicide of a businessman. I need to open his safes, and the only man who can do it is in Pul-e-Charkhi. I need to get him out for a few hours, without my superiors getting in the way.'

'Which part of the prison is he in?'

'Block 7. He killed a Coalition soldier.'

'I know the man,' said the mullah. 'His name is Afouk Ak Tikrini. The Canadian soldier he killed had raped his sister; he was acting in self-defence. Those NATO dogs had no right to put him in prison. Once we've got rid of them, Ak Tikrini will be released to a hero's welcome, *Insha'Allah*. You say he knows how to open safes?'

'That's what I'm told. I need to know if he's able to open a European model.'

'I'll ask him myself. What make is it?'

'It's a top-of-the-range, latest-model Hartmann.'

The mullah wrote 'Hartmann' on a piece of paper. 'Is that a Jewish name?'

'I don't know — and I don't see why it matters.'

'Hmm. Did you know that two of your guys from the Murder Squad were part of the team that arrested Ak Tikrini? You were on assignment in Herat that week.'

Osama couldn't remember the exact situation, but he replied: 'My men were doing their work. If Ak Tikrini is innocent, the court will release him. Nobody has the right to take the law into their own hands. I may not have been there, but I stand by his arrest completely.'

'Would you stand by it in a Taliban court?' asked the mullah, bluntly.

'I'm the boss, so I stand by my acts and those of my staff. And don't forget that if you threaten me I have the power to arrest you, whatever friends you may have in the Taliban or the NDS,' replied Osama, alluding to Bakir's ambiguous links with the security services.

The mullah burst out laughing.

'No need to lose your temper, brother Osama. I'll see what I can do. Come back tomorrow morning.'

4.

NICK WAS LOOKING AT A THICK PILE of papers stamped 'Top Secret': the fugitive's file. The general had suddenly called him in and ordered him to carry out his own search. He would be working alone, with no assistants and outside the hierarchy. The general's sole instruction to him had been to think, and think outside the box. Nick was only half surprised. His moments of brilliance had earned him a unique status at the Entity, and much leeway in his work. But this isolated role was perplexing in its total separateness from the rest of the team. The general had also refused to answer his queries about why the Mandrake report was classified information, and who was trying to find the fugitive ... reasonable questions to which he would have liked an answer before starting his search. He put these concerns aside for a moment, and flicked through the fugitive's file. It was in three sections: the first described his childhood and personal life; the second, his career; the third was made up of various documents that didn't fit either category. Nick settled into his armchair and began to read.

The fugitive had been born in a small town in the Vaud canton. He was named for his uncle Leonard, a baker by trade and the most successful man in the family. His father was a second-rate mechanic who had left when Leonard was eight months old. His mother had brought him up until she died in an accident at the spring-making factory where she worked. Leonard, who was six at the time, was put into care until the age of eighteen. According to the file, he never spoke about that period of his life, suggesting that it hadn't been easy. Photos showed a small boy, and then a sickly adolescent, with curly hair and glasses almost as big as his face.

His schoolwork was excellent. He attended the University of Geneva, and then Princeton in the United States, where he acquired a brilliant doctorate in business management. He was recruited by Ernst & Young consulting, and became one of their youngest European partners at the tender age of thirty-two. He was already earning 350,000 Swiss francs a year, and then Willard Consulting headhunted him for a salary of 450,000. He had been at Willard ever since, and on the board of directors for ten years. At the time of his disappearance he was the company's financial director, which gave him access to everything. His basic salary was a million Swiss francs, plus an equivalent bonus. Certain individual transactions yielded further bonuses, sometimes hitting seven figures. He was a rich man.

In terms of personal life, he was very solitary — obsessed with his work, and incapable of attachment. This difficult personality was probably explained by the premature death of so many people he had cared about. As a young man, he'd fallen madly in love with a girl on holiday in Tunisia, only for her to be killed in a car crash. The people who knew him best said that he never discussed his personal life with colleagues, and that this girl who died seemed to have been the only person he had ever loved. He lived in a small, expensively furnished house on Zurich's exclusive Gold Coast. He always drove a Mercedes, most recently a C 63 AMG. The car described him well: a rich, powerful, discreet man who didn't like to draw attention to himself. The Entity had turned his house inside out, without finding anything remotely compromising: no drugs, no cigarettes, no porn. The fugitive's life was smooth and uncontroversial. The only weakness was a 'subscription' to the Zurich escort service Romance. Sometime between the 25th and 30th of every month, he would order an escort. She would arrive at his house around 6.00 pm, and would never be invited to stay the night. For the last nine years it had been the same girl, a brunette by the name of Jacqueline. Nick looked at the enclosed photo — she was a stunning woman, with very dark hair, plucked eyebrows, and small round glasses that gave her a rather serious look. Josephine had described the fugitive as a distant lover, who wasn't much interested in sex. The scenario had never changed over the nine years (one hundred and three meetings, to be precise); it followed the same predictable path every time. Once his business was done, the fugitive would kiss the girl on the forehead and send her home with a hundred Swiss francs on top of the official fee.

Aside from Jacqueline, he didn't seem to have any real relationships. He would occasionally go for a drink with a work colleague, but he didn't have any friends — not at the gym where he ran on the treadmill twice a week, and not at the resort where he went fishing three times a year, always in the third week of March, the first week of September, and the second week of December. He had a licence for a Sig Sauer pistol, which had not been found at his home.

Nick stopped reading to make himself some lunch. He hadn't had much appetite since Werner died. He took a piece of goat's cheese, a slice of ham, and a vanilla yoghurt out of the fridge, and brought the file over to the dining-room table so he could read while he ate.

He spent the afternoon reading the section about the fugitive's career. This seemingly drab man was an extremely talented, confident, high-flying professional working at an international level. All his former colleagues and associates praised his exceptional memory and analytical skills. He was someone who could attend to the most technical details while still keeping the big picture in mind, as befits top directors. Two former associates had stated that Willard Consulting owed him a great deal, and would never have grown to its present size without him.

Nick wrote his notes on the file itself, as he carefully read through each of the appraisals. They were strikingly consistent: the fugitive was both obsessed with detail and extremely perceptive; he prepared his financial deals like a battle plan; he was always a step or two ahead of the game. Nick went back to the personal file to check if he was a chess player, but it didn't seem so. That was a surprise.

He moved on to the final section. The police report on the shoot-out in the Zurich squat was the only interesting document. That situation puzzled Nick. Why would such a rich man hide himself away in a sordid place like that, to which he had no prior links? How had he even known it existed? Finally, and most importantly, why had he gone to ground in Zurich, rather than fleeing Switzerland?

Osama decided to drop in on Katoun on his way home, to check how Wali Wadi's autopsy was progressing. His wife was on duty that night, so there was no need to rush home.

He told his driver to take him to Shafakhana Emergency Hospital in central Kabul. The hospital specialised in the treatment of bomb victims, and had been renovated by the UN after it was almost completely destroyed in the most recent Kabul fighting. The entrance to the hospital was, as usual, crowded with families, traders, and security. He passed a man with his two burqa-clad wives and multiple offspring, cleared the security checks intended to prevent suicide bombs, and started looking for Katoun. He spent fifteen minutes wandering around before finding him in a small, windowless basement office. It was freezing, despite the heating being on full blast. Katoun was a mischievous-looking bald man with a bushy moustache. He was tapping away on his computer at great speed.

'Ah, Osama, *khosh amadin.* I was just writing your report.'

'I couldn't wait.'

'I understand. That's why I rushed over here — I don't even have a computer at the medico-legal institute. You can't imagine the conditions I work in there; it's a real butcher's shop, and getting worse all the time. Coffee?'

'Na. Tea would be nice, though.'

The doctor picked up the phone and ordered two teas. The men chatted pleasantly as they waited. In Afghanistan, it's rude to talk business immediately, and Katoun was a cultured man who respected the rules of traditional hospitality. He glanced at the old clock hanging from the ceiling.

'It's time for prayers,' he said. 'Would you care to join me? There's a room next door.'

'I'd be delighted.'

On their return, they found a tray loaded with a plate of pastries, a battered teapot, and two glasses. Katoun devoured a couple of honey-drenched pastries while Osama stuck to tea. Eventually, after ten minutes or so, Katoun decided to broach the subject that Osama had come for.

'About Wali Wadi. My report will say that the deceased died as a result of a single bullet fired at point-blank range into the mouth, from a 9mm calibre parabellum. The bullet destroyed the cortex and part of the brain stem, causing immediate death, probably without attendant reflex movements. The entry angle of the missile was consistent with suicide, as long as the person was left-handed, as was the case with Wali Wadi. There was a burn on the bottom lip, and a certain amount of powder in the nose, implying that the barrel had been inserted quite deeply into the mouth when the shot was fired; the burn comes from the gas seeping out of the breech. The blast also destroyed the palate, which contributed to the massive bleeding — there was blood in the throat as well as externally.'

'Did you find any signs of a struggle, or any other indication that someone apart from Wali Wadi might have fired the gun?'

'I didn't find anything like that, but if the attackers were wearing silk or latex gloves they wouldn't have made any marks on the skin.'

'I see. So you have nothing for me,' said Osama, disappointed.

'Wait, I haven't finished. I found residues of deodorant on the dead man's armpits, and traces of alcohol on his chest, wrists, and neck. He had applied cologne just before he died, as you thought. Analysis of his stomach revealed an undigested meal of lamb, rice, and pistachio cake. He had a blood-alcohol level of 0.045 per cent.'

'Is that high?'

'No. He'd had a drink, but not enough to be drunk. He certainly didn't inebriate himself before committing suicide, if that's what you're asking.'

'Sounds more like a casual glass. Did you do the serology?'

'Negative for HIV and Hepatitis A. The results for Hep B and C will take three days, but his liver looked normal, and I would guess he was in perfect health.'

'What will you say in your report?'

'What do you want me to say?'

'The truth, as long as it allows me to continue my enquiry.'

'I'll say that the man died from a bullet to the head. I won't mention there being no evidence of a struggle, and I'll focus on the signs that are inconsistent with a suicide.'

'Did you test the hand for gunpowder?' asked Osama, suddenly.

'I don't have the reagent, and I can't get hold of it. The lab has used up the supplies donated by the English.'

Osama wasn't surprised. In 2002, Scotland Yard had given the scientific police a lot of modern equipment, but the collaboration had ceased after a few months; since then, hardly any new materials had been bought. The French had renovated the old buildings, trained new technicians, and built a modern lab, but they were still lacking all the small consumable items.

'If you want me to do the test, you'll have to find me a kit overseas,' continued Katoun. 'And you'd better get a move on — I won't be able to keep the body in the morgue for long.'

'I'll do my best.'

'God is with you, Osama Kandar,' said Katoun as he hugged him.

As he reached the end of the corridor, Osama heard the doctor call out: 'And when you come back, don't forget that basket of strawberries. Your deputy promised me a nice one.'

ZURICH, RUE KLEIN. Nick's heart was beating fast as he bounded up the steps to an austere-looking redbrick-and-stone house. It had a slate roof, huge lattice windows, and an alarm box set into the wall just above a first-floor window. There was nothing suspicious around the fugitive's house, and no dubious-looking cars. He went around to the little garden at the back. The shutters here were painted grey. There was a French window to the kitchen. A few moments later, he was inside.

The house was expensively furnished in a strange mix of wood, metal, and modern rugs in shimmering colours. It seemed peculiar, given the fugitive's ascetic personality.

Nick took off his coat. He might be considered the Entity's best analyst, but he didn't know much about criminal investigation. Had it been arrogant to accept his boss's mission?

He started by searching the ground floor — the large sitting room where he'd left his stuff, an ultra-modern panelled dining room, and a vast kitchen whose walls and ceiling were painted the same dark grey as the shutters. Nick noticed that the appliances were made by Boffi; they must have cost a packet.

He opened the fridge: a bottle of champagne, and a few goodies from Fauchon that were nearly past their sell-by date. He wondered whether the Entity guys had helped themselves. He spent an hour searching every possible hiding place, but found nothing.

He moved on to the study, which took up most of the first floor. The stairs had been papered with banknotes from around the world — euros, yens, and more exotic currency like escudos, dinars, and yuans. He smiled to see one featuring Saddam Hussein. The room was impressively furnished, like the rest of the house. A six-or-seven-metre-long bookcase covered one entire wall. The only sign of the Entity's previous search was the open safe on the wall opposite. It was empty. Nick flicked through the search report. The Entity men had found the fugitive's passport, thirty thousand dollars, various original certificates, and details of a numbered UBS account with a balance of seven million dollars.

He was still in Europe, thought Nick. Or else somewhere he could drive to without a passport, or catch a boat to and bribe the officials on arrival ... somewhere in Africa, perhaps. Unless he had another passport, but that seemed unlikely — he wouldn't have known the right kind of people.

Nick rummaged through the desk drawers. There were notes and reports, which he examined minutely, but nothing that linked the fugitive to any dubious schemes or transactions. Modern art adorned the walls. The painting that usually concealed the safe had been left on the floor. He put it back up, noticing that the safe had been positioned facing the desk. This painting was different from the others — it was an impressionist landscape, in the 19th-century European style, of two women emerging from a lake at sunset, their damp towels clinging to their creamy, curvaceous bodies. Other women, swathed in lengths of brightly coloured fabric, waited on the banks with a picnic basket.

The painting had a very soft, soothing effect.

He looked at his watch. Another hour had passed. He went up to the bedroom, on the second floor. The room was about eighty square metres in size, with exposed beams and six windows looking out on either side of the house. It was painted almond-green. The bed was huge — two metres square — and there was also a sofa and a low table. The thick wool carpet invited touch. In a drawer of the bedside table, he found an unopened pack of condoms and a credit-card receipt.

The fugitive had bought the condoms in October the previous year, but hadn't used them since. Strange, thought Nick.

The dressing room was reminiscent of an upmarket shop: twenty square metres, oak panelled, with identical black suits hanging at precise intervals. One shelf for white shirts, another for blue, all bearing the same French logo as the suits. White boxers and black socks each in their own drawer. Sportswear in a separate cupboard: three pairs of trainers, four pairs of black shorts, eight white T-shirts.

Nick sprawled on the bed. This house was too perfect. It didn't tell any kind of story. It reminded him of a stage set. He had a fleeting sense of having missed something important in the study, but the thought (if you could call it that) was immediately forgotten.

JOSEPH WOKE with a start. Beige roughcast walls, greyish ceiling … he pushed back the covers as his brain processed the information. He was in Kabul. On his journey from the airport around 10.00 pm, the flat, unlit city had looked like something out of olden times: unpaved roads, 1960s buildings still bearing the scars of war, long lines of tottering, shanty-type dwellings. He took a scalding shower, wrapped a towel around his waist, and returned to the living room of the apartment he had rented for his stay. His body was covered in scars, accumulated on his violent assignments. When Joseph was a new recruit, his teacher's motto was 'often wounded, never down'. He drew the curtains. The sky was turquoise, with magnificent snowy mountains on the horizon in every direction. His 'residence' was surrounded by squat, ugly prefab buildings that had been hastily put up on muddy ground to house Western military and civilians.

He could just make out a mob of heavily armed private guards and ANA soldiers patrolling the edges of the compound. His close-cropped hair was still damp from the shower as he dialled the number of an Afghan cop who worked undercover for the BND, the German secret service. This man would, he hoped, become his main contact. The mole picked up on the second ring.

'Baléh?'

'Hamid Dostom?'

'Speaking.'

'I'm a friend of your German friends. Do you know who I mean?'

'I think so,' replied the Afghan cautiously, in German.

'Our mutual friends spoke very warmly of you. I've just arrived in Kabul, and I think we could have an interesting time together. Would you be able to spare me a moment, today?'

'No problem,' said the cop immediately. 'We could meet at a guest house.'

'I'd prefer somewhere discreet, with no Westerners.'

'In that case, come to the city centre. Go two blocks past police headquarters and you'll find a café called Kabul & Kandahar, on Charahi Ansari.'

'I'll see you there in half an hour.'

He hung up. The mole would never know that he wasn't from the BND. The compartmentalisation of the various services allowed the Entity — which didn't have its own network of informers — to get away with this kind of manoeuvre. He dressed quickly, in khaki dockers and jacket, white shirt, blue tie, ankle boots. Several holsters bearing automatic weapons were hanging on the back of a chair. He put them on carefully — hip, shoulder, right ankle, and finally a dagger for his wrist. He completed the outfit with his padded jacket, and a chitrali on his head. The stairwell was freezing, and smelled strongly of detergent. Outside, a 4x4 was purring gently, with Amin, one of his favourite Ks, at the wheel.

'To the office?'

'No. Head towards police headquarters.'

They stopped for the tense soldiers at the security-zone checkpoint.

'No particular alerts this morning?'

'We've been told to avoid the area around the presidential palace; apparently someone might blow themselves up there.'

They drove through a second ANA checkpoint without stopping. Joseph barely glanced at these Afghans trying to do their hundred-dollar-a-month job while the entire country descended into chaos. They eventually left the protected area and joined the traffic. It was Joseph's first time in Kabul, and he was amazed at the city's dynamism, despite the poverty. Buildings were going up all over the place, and people were rushing around in the most indescribable tumult. The presence of the NATO forces was less oppressive than he'd anticipated, but there were bulletproof civil vehicles everywhere.

'Do you speak the language at all?'

'Can't understand a word, boss. I'm from Northern Algeria, as you know, and they speak Persian here … '

'Well, at least you're all Muslim … '

'Fucking religion! I don't believe in anything. I saw too many awful things back home to believe in God. If he does exist, he must be a real bastard, sitting up there laughing at the sight of us killing each other.'

'I don't see it that way,' replied Joseph, coldly.

No one knew that he was a sanctimonious man who attended confession every week. They stopped at some lights, behind a convoy of Turkish tanks with soldiers standing on top staring fiercely out at the street. Next they passed a lorry on its side. A large pothole had completely bent and swallowed up the axle. Smoke was coming out of the radiator where it had hit the tarmac.

'Funny country, eh?' commented Amin, glancing at a bearded man and his two burqa-clad wives piled on to a moped. 'These bastards really fucked up the Russians. Let's hope they don't do the same to us.'

Joseph nodded. But it was looking likely. And how was he supposed to find the missing CD in this bloody shambles?

Osama hadn't slept well, disturbed by all his worries about the investigation. He'd woken at 3.00 am, obsessing about how to get the fingerprint tests done without arousing his boss's suspicions. As often happened, his restless sleep had given him an idea. He jumped up, full of excitement. As soon as he got to work, he started looking for Galina Bosnikova's number. Galina was a feisty young cop who had impressed him greatly when they'd worked together in Moscow. That was many years ago, but she was still at the same police station, so he was able to find her number in less than an hour. He gave thanks for his luck, and for God's help.

Galina liked him. He'd always suspected she had a bit of a crush on him, too, but he'd never succumbed — in his religion it was a crime to be unfaithful.

'Osama!' she cried when he announced who he was. 'I was wondering what had become of you. September 11th must have made your life hell. How come you haven't changed your name?'

'I haven't tried. I just put up with it. It would be harder if I lived in the United States, obviously … '

Galina told him that she'd been promoted to the highest level of chief inspector, and would be taking superintendent exams in the next few weeks. She was studying for them day and night. She had been appointed to the Rape Squad, which was particularly traumatic because the economic crisis and the rise in alcoholism had been decreasing the age of the victims.

'So, Osama, to what do I owe the pleasure?'

'I need help,' he admitted. 'I'm investigating a supposed suicide, and I'd like to test the victim's hands for gunpowder, but I don't have the right kits, and the official avenues will take too long. Do you think you could get me some?'

Galina thought for a moment. 'I should think so. A friend of mine works in the Murder Squad, and they've definitely got those kits. I could ask her for a few and send them over to you. Stay on the line, and I'll call her from another phone.'

Osama settled deeper into his chair. The Coalition's help was a miracle. Before, he would never have been able to make an international call from his own office, but now any investigating officer could phone anywhere in the world. A few moments later, Galina was back on the line.

'I spoke to her, and she's up for it. The only thing is that the expiry dates on her kits are for the end of this week — but she says that's absolutely fine, they'll work for at least another six months. With the bureaucracy here, it might take her several weeks to get hold of new ones ...'

'They sound great,' said Osama. 'I'll give you my address at the station. Please make sure to write "personal" on the envelope.'

'But is the post working in Kabul? Wouldn't you rather I tried to send it by diplomatic bag?'

'The post arrives fine. There are several flights a week from Moscow — I'll definitely get it.'

Osama put the phone down. He still wasn't used to the return of normal life: phones not being tapped, post arriving on the day it was supposed to almost everywhere in the city, the fact that he could walk around wherever he wanted, the lack of bombings. It was a new experience, completely different from what he had lived through all his life. All Afghans had become used to their freedom being partial, restricted, and contingent, and to constant violence. Normality felt like a fog, a strange sense of the unknown and of déjà-vu, a fragile equilibrium that could vanish at any moment.

He looked at his watch. It was time to hear what his men had managed to find out. He gathered them all into the scruffy meeting room next to his office, whose only luxuries were a coffee machine and a wood-burning stove.

'Let's have an update on the latest developments. Why don't you go first, Babrak,' suggested Osama, taking a sip of his scalding coffee.

'Our interrogation of the domestic staff and the personal assistant didn't yield much. It seems that Wali Wadi had been up to something big over the past few weeks, and was rather on edge.'

'Do you have any idea what that was?'

'Not yet, although I'm sure it involved foreigners. His maid said that he often spoke English on the phone, and used to make foreign calls very late, after midnight.'

'He must have been calling a different time-zone, to the west of us. So, in Europe or America. Interesting,' said Osama, stroking his beard. 'And was that new?'

'We don't know. Another thing is that Wadi had beefed up his security systems at home and at work. But on the night he died, he sent his bodyguards home and retained only his night watchman, an Uzbek like him, who had worked for him for twenty years. It seems he was expecting someone he absolutely didn't want recognised. A government official, perhaps?'

'Or a foreigner,' concluded Osama. 'Was the night watchman posted inside the house, or outside?'

'I don't know. I'll find out. Why do you ask, boss?'

'I'd like to know if he could have seen the visitor's number plates. If Wali Wadi had posted him inside, it might suggest he didn't want his servant to see the visitor's car.'

'A car with government plates?'

'Or diplomatic. What did the surveillance hard drive reveal?'

'It had been erased,' said Gulbudin. 'Actually, better than that: reformatted. The drive was blank.'

'How do you explain that?'

'I asked my cousin, who works in computers. According to him, when a hard drive has been erased you can still recover the data, unless special software has been used to totally wipe and overwrite it. Which is what has happened in this instance.'

'Afghans can do that?'

Babrak, Jihad, and Rangin all smiled at once.

'This isn't the Middle Ages, boss. My cousin could do it, and I'm sure hundreds of other computer programmers in Kabul, too.'

'All right, all right,' snapped Osama, annoyed that his deputy was speaking to him like his wife. 'Anything else?'

'Yes,' said Jihad. 'Something that seemed important to me. Wali Wadi's mobile phone hasn't been found, either at his house or at his office. Someone must have taken it when he died.'

'Which means that we can't trace his calls ... If he was killed, the phone was probably taken by the murderer, perhaps to cut off a lead. Unless it was stolen by a policeman or a member of the house staff the morning the body was discovered.' Osama was musing aloud. 'Do you know which network he used?'

'*Baléh.* We found Etisalat bills at his office. I phoned the number on the bill, and it went through to voicemail. I had one of Wali Wadi's domestic staff listen to the message, and he confirmed that it was his voice.'

'Good work, and fast, too,' said Osama. 'Do we know anyone at Etisalat?'

'You don't want to make an official request?' asked Babrak.

'No. It would have to be approved higher up, and the minister would block it. I'd rather continue on the quiet. What was the bill like?'

'Nothing out of the ordinary. One of our guys is on his way back to the office to look for an itemised bill or anything else we might have missed.'

'What about the Beretta he killed himself with? What do you have on that?'

'Nothing, qomaandaan,' replied Rangin. 'It's not a new model, maybe fifteen or twenty years old, very standard. The series number has been filed off.'

'Have you ever come across a gun with its number filed off before?' asked Osama.

'Never,' admitted Rangin.

'So, try to find out more. Does the filing look as if it was done professionally?'

Rangin blushed.

'No, actually ... it looked pretty rough.'

'In that case, you should be able to see the number through a microscope. I saw that done in Moscow, years ago — and it even solved the case. Send someone to the science department; they might be able to look at it on the spot.'

'No problem, boss. Anything else?'

'You're not doing badly,' said Osama with a smile. 'My theory, at this point, is murder disguised as suicide. Wali Wadi must have been murdered either for information that he had, or business he had done. We need to discover the motive. So, you're going to search Wadi's house and office again, and look into his business more thoroughly. Discreetly, of course.'

'What are we looking for, boss?'

'Anything that explains our own minister putting a spanner in the works.'

Joseph found his contact sitting at the back of the café, with a steaming *chai siah* in front of him. He was short and plump, with a thick moustache, trimmed beard, and grey, crew-cut hair. He looked happy to be there. Meetings with BND spies were probably always followed by a fat envelope, for little or no risk.

Joseph took off his chitrali. 'My name is Helmut. Your friend in Berlin is a colleague of mine. I'm working on a very particular case. Your usual contact is not aware that I'm seeing you, and it is crucial that you say nothing at all about our meeting.'

'No problem,' said the informer with a smile. 'I'm at your service.'

He spoke German with a strong Pakistani accent, so he probably came from one of the tribal areas. He ordered more tea with a click of his fingers. The café owner took the opportunity to put a basket of flatbread and butter on their table, and the contact leapt on them as if he hadn't eaten for days. Joseph tasted a piece of bread. It was delicious, and melted in the mouth, but the butter was too strong and slightly rancid. He put his piece of bread down on the old newspaper that served as a plate, and wondered how many people had handled it before it reached him.

'How are things going at the station these days?' he asked, to get the ball rolling.

The cop wiped the melting butter off his chin.

'Good. We have lots of equipment now — radios, computers, cars for tailing suspects … I've arrested several traffickers myself, and been well rewarded for it. We're making good progress in the fight against drugs.'

Joseph stopped himself sniggering. President Karzaï's own brother trafficked drugs, and the police only ever arrested the little guys, leaving the big shots in peace. The informer started talking about the political situation in the country, and then the Coalition. Joseph listened attentively, despite his growing frustration; he didn't want the man to feel rushed. After quarter of an hour, the cop paused, and looked at Joseph questioningly. It was time to talk business. Joseph pushed his bag under the table.

'There are two things in the bag that might be of interest to you.'

The Afghan hesitated for a fraction of a second, but his curiosity got the better of him. He opened the bag.

'The mini tape recorder is a highly sophisticated device. The microphone is so sensitive that even when it's in your pocket, you can record a conversation up to three metres away.'

'You want me to tape someone?'

'A cop at police headquarters. I need to know the sound of his voice. You can just make up a reason to talk to him with that machine in your pocket. He won't suspect a thing.'

The man hesitated a moment. 'OK. Who is it?'

'Osama Kandar.'

'Commandant Kandar? The head of the Murder Squad?' The policeman looked horrified.

'The very same. I thought he was a colonel, not a commandant?'

'Kandar was in charge of Massoud's sniper teams during the war. He's a hero. That's why everyone calls him by his title — qomaandaan — and not by his rank. It's a tribute to his life as a mujahedeen commander.'

Joseph took it in. What else didn't they know about this guy?

'I'll pay you well.'

The informer looked thunderstruck.

'I'll pay you more than you think,' continued Joseph. 'Have a look at the other object.'

The cop took the metal sheet out of the bag and inspected it curiously.

'It's heavy. What is it? A bomb?'

'A tag.'

'A tag? Like in *Enemy of the State*?'

'Exactly. It gives off a continuous signal on a particular frequency that can only be picked up by a satellite. It allows us to track a car — you stick it under the chassis, right in the middle, under the prop-shaft. The colour and shape stop it from being picked up by standard security checks. You can't see it with the simple mirror-on-a-stick that they use at the checkpoints; the car has to be on a ramp for it to become visible. We want you to stick it under Kandar's vehicle.'

'That's dangerous, sahib!'

'For someone like you, it'll be child's play.'

'Tags can set off drone fire,' said the informer, faintly. 'Do you want to kill him?'

'We don't want to kill Commandant Kandar. We just want to know what he's up to.'

Joseph took a bulging envelope out of his pocket and put it on the table.

'Go on, open it,' he said, in a more friendly tone, with an encouraging smile.

The policeman's eyes widened when he saw the amount of money in the envelope.

'We hear you're after a second wife. We'd be happy to help you acquire her, in exchange for your help. There's a thousand dollars in that envelope. And another four thousand waiting for you when you complete the mission. That's exactly what you need for the dowry — and with that kind of money, you'll be marrying a beautiful young virgin. It's a good offer. A decent offer, but I will of course understand if you're not brave enough to do what we're asking. We would still be friends. And we would just visit one of your colleagues, who will definitely accept.'

The Afghan opened his mouth to reply, and shut it again. He resealed the envelope and put it in his pocket, red-faced.

'Once you've positioned the tag, press the commutation switch, which is here on the left. The diode will stay alight for five seconds and then go off. That means the tag is working. The battery lasts for two weeks. And that's all you have to do. If we need to prolong the mission, I'll give you a new battery.'

He pushed a piece of paper towards the cop.

'That's my Afghan mobile-phone number. Call me or send me an SMS as soon as you have the voice recording. It's very urgent. I need it in the next forty-eight hours, max. The same for the tag — it must be put on immediately. Do you understand?'

'Yes. I'll do as you have asked me.'

5.

THE REST OF OSAMA'S DAY passed slowly, in a wealth of unimportant investigations. He received several requests for reports, as if his superiors were trying to inundate him with work so he couldn't devote himself to the Wali Wadi case. He wasn't paranoid — far from it — but he could feel the pressure increasing, as if an invisible noose were being tightened around his neck. He did what was asked of him as professionally as he could. When he finished, he realised it was nearly 7.00pm and that the tasks had taken him all day.

He told Gulbudin and Babrak that he was going home, and left in his filthy 4x4. When he arrived home, Malalai was cleaning the living room. She noticed him at the door and switched off the ancient Russian vacuum cleaner that roared like a Tupolev taking off. Their meagre salaries didn't allow for a new one — never mind a cleaning lady for more than a few hours a week. Their elderly house was always dusty. Malalai had swapped her heavy street-dress for a brightly coloured silk-and-cotton tunic that left her arms bare, and revealed rather than concealed her breasts. Osama's throat tightened.

'Don't look at me like that,' she teased. 'You remind me of that American cartoon fox with its tongue hanging out.'

'It's not a fox, it's a wolf.' Osama took off his *chakman*. 'You're living proof that Allah created woman as temptation for man.'

'Am I supposed to be charmed, that my husband still takes pleasure in looking at me after all these years?'

'As long as it's only me. It's a good thing other men don't get to see you like this,' he replied, regretting the last sentence as soon as it came out of his mouth.

'Stop!' she spat angrily, shoving the vacuum cleaner against the wall. 'I know you secretly approve of the Taliban rules on the burqa. Deep down, you probably think it's for our own good!'

'We've discussed this a million times. The burqa is oppressive to wear, yes, but you can't deny that it protects you from male lust. I spoke to one of my old colleagues from Moscow today, and she told me that the number of rapes in the city has gone through the roof. You should see what Muscovite women wear in the summer, or when they go out in the evening. No wonder the number of rapes is constantly on the increase.'

'That's not the fault of the women,' exploded Malalai. 'It's because you men are animals. You think of nothing but what's between your legs! If women turn you on, that's your problem. You should walk around town blindfolded, rather than making us go out in that vile blue bag.'

'You've always lived in the city, but Afghan culture is mostly rural. No one in the countryside criticises the burqa. It's traditional. The Koran requires it.'

'The Koran doesn't require anything of the sort. That's a misreading. This country is just obsessed with enslaving us. The Koran says this; the Koran says that — all of it with one end, of course. Humiliating women. Putting them down. Enslaving them. I suppose it's the Koran that requires women to vacuum, rather than men? In America, men do their own vacuuming.'

'Now you're being silly, Malalai. No man vacuums!'

'They do. I read it in a magazine.'

'It's a lie.'

'No, that's what it said, and there was a photo.'

'It must have been a homosexual, then, not a real man.'

'Great, another smart remark. You're going from strength to strength, aren't you? Come on, Osama, don't you see we have to resist these narrow-minded fundamentalists? I so want you to be different from men like that.'

'I'm not like them,' protested Osama. 'And you know it.'

'Unless you do everything in your power to fight those trying to keep us in the dark ages, your passivity is a form of support.'

'I do not support them.' Osama lost his temper. 'I've killed enough Taliban not to be accused of cowardice towards them. Right, that's enough — this conversation is pointless. You read too many foreign magazines, that's your problem. Where's my mat? I'm going to pray.'

'No way,' she said, barring his passage. She lowered her voice. 'Don't let yourself be infected by these backward ideas, Osama. Women have the right to choose how we live, behave, and dress, without men telling us what to do. We are not objects that must be protected against our will. Women are equal to men. Take the case of my work — would a male obstetrician be better at his job than me? No. We have to work to improve the mindset in this country so that we can have more rights. And that's exactly what I decided to do today.'

'What are you saying?' asked Osama anxiously.

'I spent the day at a women's meeting hosted by the cultural attaché to the French embassy.'

'That pig? He's a pervert and an unbeliever! He crashed his armoured 4x4 into a bus last month; the traffic police were sure he'd been drinking alcohol and was drunk.'

'He is not a pervert. We discussed an international support programme for Afghan women. I'm going to sign up, especially as I've been co-opted onto RAWA's secret council.'

'You've what?' cried Osama, taken aback.

RAWA, the Revolutionary Association of the Women of Afghanistan, was a secret organisation made up entirely of women, whose mission was to stand up for women's rights in Afghanistan and Pakistan. It functioned like a resistance movement, divided into cells whose members didn't know one another, and so couldn't denounce each other in the event of an arrest or kidnapping. The founder, Meena, had been assassinated under President Najibullah, without anyone knowing whether the Afghan secret services or the Islamists were responsible.

'France, Italy, and Japan are going to help us raise more money from UNESCO, and perhaps other international organisations as well. Then we can train new educators to travel the country increasing women's awareness that they've got to say 'no' to male tyranny. We will stand up for our rights and ways of thinking in our everyday lives. And we've decided to wage war so that girls can freely attend school and college in the rural areas.'

'You're crazy. Totally nuts! The Taliban will kill you, like Meena. You'll get yourself stabbed. Or worse, raped.'

'Another intelligent statement, from a modern, highly evolved man: being raped is worse than being killed. Are you being reactionary on purpose, today?'

'Don't play around with words. You can't do this!'

'Are you asking me to accept the unacceptable?'

'This is our culture, our way of life. The way things are. Women have always worn the burqa and the tchador in Afghanistan.'

'That's not true. It has not always been like this. It wasn't when Zahir was Shah. Or under Khalq rule.'

'You were young. That's enough about the communists — they destroyed our country. All this is their fault.'

'It's opposition to the spread of knowledge that has destroyed our country, Osama. Afghan women have no right to allow ourselves to continue to be humiliated by ignorant men. As an educated woman, it's my responsibility to stand up and fight. If I didn't, I wouldn't be able to look myself in the face.'

'What you're doing is insane. You're taking huge risks. Plotting with unbelievers will bring you nothing but misfortune. And Allah might take offence.'

'Allah? Do you really think God cares about our fate? He has no interest in us, my dear Osama. Look at the state of our country — nothing but poverty, violence, corruption, and despair.'

'Allah's intentions are known by Him alone. He has his reasons for making us suffer. It is not our place to try and understand Him.'

'Now you're talking rubbish. You should work less, and think more.'

THE NEXT MORNING, Osama rose even earlier than usual, to make sure Malalai didn't leave before him. They'd started arguing again just as they were going to bed, although he had managed to obtain a goodnight kiss, in line with their agreement never to go to sleep without making peace. Around 6.00am, he saw her emerging from the bathroom. She was wearing her usual outfit — a long, baggy tunic of simple blue cotton *karbaz,* and a shawl over her hair.

'I've made coffee, and warmed up the bean stew, if you'd like some.'

'Thanks. I'll just have the coffee.'

'Have you thought about last night's conversation, Malalai?'

'Which one? I don't remember us talking about anything particularly interesting.'

'For the love of God, just listen to me, for once. Don't do it, I'm begging you. Don't join RAWA.'

'Otherwise what? You're going to lock me in the house like a bad wife, with one of your cousins keeping watch? Or beat me, perhaps?' she said defiantly.

'It's you that's talking rubbish now. Just don't do it, that's all. RAWA is the Taliban's main target. If they get into power, even I won't be able to protect you. We'd have to flee the country.'

'If I don't stand up for our rights, who will? NATO? My decision is made.'

She strode out. A few seconds later, he heard her moped roar to life, followed by the screech of tires on the stony lane, and then silence. He went out, too. His driver was waiting by the car, looking embarrassed. He'd probably heard them shouting. Marital disputes were usually resolved by some kind of correction of the uppity wife. Osama knew that by the end of the morning the whole police station would have heard what had happened. They'd be sniggering about how weak he was, again. How he must have offended God, to fall for a woman like that!

His entire team was in the meeting room waiting for him, but his row with Malalai had made him so angry that he just stalked past and shut himself away in his office. He spent half the morning in there, nursing his fury. Malalai had underestimated the determination of the Taliban. Apprentice martyrs were begging for the honour of blowing themselves up in the middle of a RAWA meeting. Not to mention the possible betrayals: police were arresting more and more women intent on the status of *shahid* or martyr.

He was glancing distractedly through his mail when an orderly came to say that a messenger was asking for him. It was a young boy of no more than eleven or twelve, wearing a long, stained, cotton tunic, battered trainers with no socks, and the white cap of a Koranic school. He seemed rather intimidated at finding himself in the heart of police headquarters, whose reputation amongst most Kabulis was sinister, to say the least. The child held out an envelope to Osama, who opened it immediately, despite security guidelines: he knew who it was from. The envelope contained a single sheet of heavy, good-quality paper, with the message: *Come as soon as possible. I'm expecting you. I can get your man out.* Osama thanked the boy with a ten-afghani note. To allay suspicion, he remained in his office for another half-hour, dealing with everyday business, then picked up his pistol and grenade, and slipped out the back door. He walked aimlessly through the streets for about twenty minutes. Once he was sure no one was following him, he hailed a cab. At the mullah's office, the same one-legged man let him in. The mullah was eating, with a napkin tied around his neck.

'Ah, qomaandaan! This lamb and candied fruit stew is delicious. Would you care to join me?'

'Thank you — a drink would be fine,' replied Osama.

The mullah looked disappointed. His belly was so large that he had to eat at quite a distance from the table, with his arms stretched out. While he stuffed himself like a gluttonous cat, they chatted about the weather, government business, and the latest Coalition blunder. Then Mullah Bakir wiped his beard with his napkin and pushed back his plate.

'Most excellent! You really should have partaken with me. Before she died, my wife used to cook the best stew in Kabul. She would blend all kinds of spices — cumin, massaman, and other herbs whose names I don't even know. Luckily, one of my devotees managed to track down the recipe.'

'Do you feast like this every day?'

'Every chance that Allah gives me. And Allah, may he be blessed, knows that those chances are many. I was supposed to be working on my computer this morning, but when they brought me this stew I couldn't resist.'

Osama hadn't known that Mullah Bakir's wife was dead. He looked around for a photo of a woman or child, but there were none to be seen. His eyes paused for a moment on the Internet router purring on the desk, bristling with wires.

'For a man who wishes to return to the Islam of the founding fathers, I'm intrigued to see that you're not opposed to the most modern American technology,' he teased.

'Do not confuse me with my Taliban colleagues, brother Osama. We are not all inclined to live as we did in the Middle Ages. We aspire to an Islamic state, certainly, but I for one intend a *modern* Islamic state, in line with the current century. Why flout twelve hundred years' of progress to return to the olden days? Why make use of the Kalashnikov, but not the computer? Of electricity, but not changes in lifestyle? As for the United States, it's well known that I was in favour of a good relationship with them. As was, in fact, the case for a number of years.'

The mullah took a sip of tea, his pinkie in the air. 'I've managed to arrange a short excursion from prison for the man you mentioned. The prison director's deputy will personally accompany him to the southern gate, at half past six this evening. He must be returned before midnight. Between those times, he's all yours; do with him as you will.'

'Thank you. I am much indebted to you.'

'I'm aware of that,' said the mullah, pouring himself more tea. 'In fact, that's why I organised this excursion. What do your Western friends call that, in financial terms? An option, isn't it? I'm betting heavily on you, qomaandaan.'

'I don't understand what you're talking about.'

'Don't pretend to be less intelligent than you really are. Being a little rustic isn't incompatible with intelligence, is it — otherwise how would you have become the great mujahedeen that you were?'

'You needn't hope that I can be persuaded to cover up criminal activities on the part of your Taliban friends. I need this man for an official investigation, not a personal favour.'

Mullah Bakir shook his head, putting on a sorry face.

'In this world, all favours are personal. I'm doing this favour for you, brother Osama, not for the head of police of an ungodly regime that is rotten to the core. I'd like to take this opportunity to let you know that you'll have to sign a temporary-release licence for the director. This will make you responsible to the prison management for the timely return of his prisoner.'

'The prison director …'

'Hates you, I know. But, luckily, his fear of me is even more powerful than his hatred of you. He will comply like the little doggie that he is.'

'I see,' said Osama. 'Is this a way for you to have one over on me if things go wrong?'

'You see, you're much less naïve than you try to make out. One could see it like that. Or as a form of security … the prison director isn't the most courageous man in Kabul. If you run into any problems, he could sell the signed document to anyone who might want to use it to blackmail you. Me, for instance. Or even that ass of a security minister, whom they tell me you can't stand. What do you expect? No one in this country has much sense of honour these days. The war was been going on too long, and the Afghans have hocked themselves to too many people, in too short a time: the communists, the Russians, the Northern Alliance, us, and now the Americans … You should be happy — I could have presented you with a done deal at the prison gates tonight. It's no mean thing to be forewarned.'

'That's true,' said Osama. 'And I'm grateful. Why are you taking the risk of helping me? It can only cause you trouble. The simple fact that I've realised the extent of your influence puts you in danger.'

'People more powerful than you have known that for a long time, brother Osama, and I'm still here. Things are sometimes more complex than they seem. And Wali Wadi had his fingers in some peculiar pies. Whatever you find out will be interesting information — and, as you must have realised, information is my passion. My life blood, even. Good luck, qomaandaan.'

After another careful read of the file, Nick decided it was time to meet the fugitive's regular prostitute, Jacqueline. The Entity's official investigation team hadn't thought her at all important as a witness. To Nick, this was a serious mistake.

Jacqueline was the only woman whom the fugitive saw regularly, and he'd been seeing her for nine years. Leonard was a man of rules and regulations. A man like him lived a very ordered life. This meeting would allow Nick to discover anything at all unusual — anything that had changed before Leonard's disappearance. The same girl for nine years: had he confided in her? Nick was convinced she'd be able to shed some light on the fugitive's personality. He was also pretty sure there'd been another prostitute, before her, and again for a long time. Why had Leonard left her? A man like him would only change if there was a good reason to do so.

He dialled the escort service. It went straight through to muzak, and then a woman picked up.

'Hello, Romance.'

'Hello, I'd like to book an appointment, please.'

'Are you an existing client of ours?'

'No, but a friend of mine is.'

'Excellent. Did you have a particular type in mind? We have a wide variety of girls and boys. Europe, Asia, Africa — whatever age and body type you would prefer.'

'I'd like to see Jacqueline. This afternoon, if possible.'

The woman consulted her list.

'She's not working this afternoon. I'll see if she's free. Are you aware of our fees?'

'Yes, that won't be a problem.'

'What's your first name?'

'Martin,' said Nick.

'Please hold.'

More muzak. Two minutes later, the woman came back on the line.

'Jacqueline can meet you later, but she'll only be able to stay for two hours. Will that be OK?'

'Perfect. Do you entertain clients at your offices?'

'I'm afraid not; we don't have the space. How about a hotel? Our ladies are often invited to The Winston.'

'That's the hotel next to Citronelle restaurant? Certainly.'

Nick knew of The Winston. It was an attractive, family-run hotel on a quiet road off the Bahnhofstrasse, one of the most expensive streets in the world, and next door to one of the swankiest restaurants in Zurich. He arranged to meet Jacqueline there.

At the end of the afternoon, Osama gave the signal to leave for the prison. He couldn't have risked tackling such a sensitive mission alone, so he'd selected ten of his most reliable staff to keep watch over the prisoner. As well as Babrak, Gulbudin, Jihad, Rangin, and Abdul, he'd chosen five Northern Alliance old-timers — all Tajiks from the same village. They piled into his 4x4 and a pick-up, with a minibus driven by two 'regular' policemen bringing up the rear. At a certain point in their journey, the minibus stopped in the middle of the road, and the two other vehicles sped off ahead. Osama leant out of the window to check whether they'd successfully shaken their tail, while his deputies scanned the road, their Kalashnikovs at the ready, for suspect cars or two-wheelers. Osama calmly closed his window.

'It's OK. No one is following us.'

'You're taking a big risk with this operation, boss. Who got him out of prison for you?' asked Gulbudin.

'It's better that you don't know, for your own safety. This case is dangerous. Speaking of which, I'd like to say that if you want to keep out of this, Babrak, you still can. You have young children, and I would be sympathetic.'

'And let Gulbudin have all the kudos on a case like this? No way, boss. I'm with you,' his deputy said. 'I'm sure I'll be learning some interesting stuff.'

'In Kabul, the interesting stuff is always the most dangerous.'

They were outside the built-up area now, speeding along the tarred road to Pul-e-Charkhi, thirty kilometres from the city centre. The driver turned onto a heavily potholed road. They went through an initial ANA roadblock, then another, reinforced by a dozen light-armoured vehicles and a couple of T-72 tanks. Security had become much tighter since the prison had been attacked by thirty Taliban troops.

'While we're at it, why don't you tell me the latest gossip about me?'

'Well, I don't know if I ought to say ...' began Babrak cautiously. Encouraged by a wave of Osama's hand, he continued, 'They say that your wife has set up a women's organisation. That she talks like a communist or a *kafir,* and openly criticises the mullahs. One of the police drivers said that she's supported by a Western diplomat, an unbeliever who drinks alcohol and visits ungodly establishments.'

'News travels fast!'

'Yes. Actually, there's something I want to tell you, about me. I don't want you to hear it from someone else, so I'd better tell you myself: I've decided to take a second wife.'

'You?' exclaimed Osama, stunned.

'Yes. I know I don't attend prayers as often as you, and I could be a better Muslim ...'

'So why take a second wife?'

'Well, my first is starting to give me grief,' admitted Babrak. 'She's criticising the amount of time I spend at work, she doesn't want to visit my parents, and she keeps complaining about the electricity cuts in our area. The local mullah told me that taking a second wife is the best way to ensure the first behaves, *Al Hamdullilah*. My family will pay for the dowry, so I won't have to contribute anything.'

'I thought you loved her.'

'But I do!'

'Your reasoning is a little hasty. Put yourself in her shoes for a moment: if you were a woman, wouldn't you be deeply hurt if your husband wed another woman?'

'Of course!' replied Babrak, bursting out laughing.

When he saw his boss's face, he stopped.

'Have you considered what your kids will think?'

'No,' admitted Babrak.

'Well, you should.'

Their conversation was interrupted by their arrival at the prison. The massive, sprawling edifice stood in the middle of a property of several hectares, without a single tree or place to hide. The high ochre walls were dotted with rickety watchtowers every hundred metres or so. A perfect example of Soviet architecture. Since the fall of the Taliban, the Americans had installed many new things, including cameras and volumetric detection systems. Armed soldiers were dozing on the flatbeds of various old trucks parked near the gates, which were themselves blocked by a pick-up equipped with a Dushka machine gun. Osama turned towards Gulbudin.

'You'd better go — I'm too well known.'

Gulbudin obeyed, followed by a few of their men. In front of the prison gates he had a lively chat with a man wearing a filthy uniform and a beige skullcap. After several minutes he returned, a piece of paper in his hand.

'They want you to sign this, boss.'

Osama signed. A few minutes later, Gulbudin emerged from the building with a man in a tattered *shalwar kameez,* hands cuffed behind his back. He seemed in shock at finding himself in the open air. Osama's men surrounded him immediately, in case he tried to escape. Babrak motioned him into the car next to him, with a policeman on the other side. Osama turned around.

'Are you Afouk Ak Tikrini?'

'Yes.'

'Do you know why you're here?'

'No. They didn't tell me anything, just that they were taking me out of my cell.'

'I need you to open two safes for me. I've been told you're an expert — is that right?'

'Yes,' admitted the man.

'Would you be able to open a European safe, a Hartmann?'

'I'd need my tools. They're at home.'

'You keep burglar's tools at your house?'

'I took them with me when I was thrown out of Italy. They're expensive tools, and I thought I might be able to sell them for a profit here.'

'OK, let's go and get them.'

The convict lived in a tiny house in the eastern part of Kabul.

Four policemen, Osama himself, and the two deputies went inside with him, to make sure he didn't try to escape or pick up a weapon. He came out with two Delsey suitcases, which they helped him carry to the 4x4.

'Where did you buy suitcases like this?' asked Babrak, amazed.

'Actually, I picked them up on one of my "excursions", in Rome. The Italian cops thought they were mine, so they said I could keep them.'

Once they were at Wali Wadi's house, Ak Tikrini seemed to relax. He opened the two cases, and slowly and carefully set out his tools on a piece of red felt — a drill, several kinds of pliers, levers, and metal rods, and a laptop computer that he plugged into the mains.

'It's important to set your tools out right, and always in the same order,' he said. 'Then you can pick them up as and when you need them, and not leave anything behind if you have to get out quickly.'

'How many burglaries did you commit?' asked Osama.

'Two hundred and thirty-seven, with about twenty on high-security safes. I was only caught five times, and sentenced twice. I made a fortune, but sadly the Italian cops found and froze all my bank accounts, and I was thrown out with the equivalent of a thousand euros.' He smiled at Osama. 'I'm not trying to boast, but you are lucky to have found me — there's no one with my level of expertise within two thousand square kilometres.'

He put on a helmet fitted with a powerful torch and a pair of unusual magnifying goggles that covered half his face.

'Strange,' he said.

Osama walked up behind him.

'What's strange?'

'Look at these marks next to the keyhole. They're invisible to the naked eye, but with my goggles you can see them.'

'Do you mean these tiny scratches? They're barely visible.'

'That's right.'

'What does it mean?'

'Someone has already opened this safe. He used a very sophisticated machine that inserts minuscule metal rods into the keyhole. I've never seen one, but I know that some of my colleagues use them. They can impersonate a key for any keyhole. As for the code, you plug in a powerful computer like mine, with a special programme that tries every combination. No safe can withstand it.'

'How long would it take to open this safe with that kind of equipment?'

'An hour, or perhaps a little less.'

'What about you — how long will it take you?'

'About the same, but I'll have to break the door.'

'Take some close-up photos of the keyhole,' Osama instructed one of his men. 'We may need proof of what we've seen.'

It took Ak Tikrini an hour to open the safe. Osama rushed over as the door came off with a screeching of metal. The safe was empty, but he couldn't help reaching into it and feeling around. There was nothing there — not even a speck of dust.

'Let's go over to his office and open the second safe.'

They went through the same procedure at the office, with the same result: an empty safe.

'Apart from you, what Afghan would be able to open these safes without leaving tracks?' Osama asked Ak Tikrini.

'No one. The equipment I told you about is rare, and I'm certain that there's neither the equipment nor the people to use it anywhere in Afghanistan.'

'Would you be able to?'

'Not straight away, and not as cleanly. This guy left barely any tracks. He must be very experienced — a pro.'

'I see,' said Osama. 'You've helped us a great deal. I'll make sure to have a word with the prosecutor handling your case.'

'My lawyer has never visited me, and one of the guards told me I might be extradited to Canada and sentenced to life imprisonment there. All I did was defend my sister's honour!'

'The Coalition countries are more and more sensitive to the blunders and problems caused by their troops. I'll see to it that you're able to present your case to a member of the Canadian legal profession or military police.' Osama put his hand on the man's shoulder. 'You know, those Western countries don't operate like ours: over there, the courts are honest and independent. If things really happened as you say they did, the Canadians will be the first to insist that mitigating circumstances are taken into account. You've a decent chance of going free.'

They dropped him at the prison around 11.00pm. As he watched Ak Tikrini enter the sinister building, Osama couldn't help registering a sense of foreboding. He asked his driver to travel in the pick-up so he could talk to his deputies in confidence on the way back to the office. He roared off, the pick-up following.

'So, what do you think?' asked Babrak almost immediately. 'Is that the end of the trail?'

'We've just made some major progress. This has been an excellent evening.'

'Why? We don't have anything. The safes were empty!'

'We have a crucial piece of information: we know that someone opened those safes, and that they were not Afghans. They used technical resources that don't exist here, and were therefore imported. This supports an idea that's been running through my mind since I first visited the scene of the crime. Suicide as cover is an idea that would never have occurred to an Afghan. It's a terrible ruse: murder or assassination would have been far more plausible. To recap, we have a murder disguised as a suicide, which could only have been organised by a Westerner; a safe that could only have been opened by a Westerner; and a minister that only very powerful people would be able to manipulate.'

'Who?'

'That, my dear Babrak, is what we have to work out.'

Joseph put down his night-vision glasses. He'd decided to swing by the police station, to get a sense of the place in case he had to intervene. He had seen the superintendent getting into his 4x4, followed by a pack of men who divided themselves into two protective vehicles. He'd recognised Kandar as soon as he set eyes on him, without even having to check the photos he'd received from Berne: an austere giant, well over six foot, as thin as a rake, with a three-day-old beard and an astrakhan hat. They had started following the superintendent and his entourage immediately, keeping a reasonable distance throughout their bizarre trip to the prison, an as-yet-unidentified house and, finally, an office building.

He turned towards his K. Amin was trying to find out the identity of the prisoner that the superintendent had sprung from prison. Joseph couldn't work out what Kandar was brewing, and he didn't like it.

'Do you have the name of the owner of the house they've just been to?'

'I'm waiting. We'll have it in a couple of minutes.'

Amin had been tapping at the laptop on his knees for more than half an hour. Joseph sighed, and slumped into the car seat. He was used to waiting around: his job was 99 per cent waiting for 1 per cent action. A few seconds later, a beep informed them that an email had arrived. He sat up immediately.

'Well?'

'This is Wali Wadi's office address.'

Joseph didn't comment. It was what he'd suspected from the beginning.

'Any news about the guy they sprang?'

'Not yet, boss. Sorry.'

Joseph looked at his silent phone. He'd called his informer at the police station as soon as they'd seen the convict climb into Kandar's car. The mole had promised to go to the prison immediately to find out what was going on, but he hadn't been in touch since. Suddenly, a movement caught Joseph's attention. Several armed men were leaving the office building. The tall figure of commandant Kandar towered above the rest. He stepped into his 4x4 as the men bustled around him. The two vehicles drove off at once.

'Let's go. Follow them!' ordered Joseph.

The ancient, peeling Peykan darted off in pursuit. A double-turbo engine had replaced the anaemic four cylinders of the Iranian original, and state-of-the-art shock absorbers now provided the suspension. The bodywork and armoured windows could deflect Kalashnikov bullets. This car was a great cover against being spotted. It was night time, but the traffic was still heavy: trucks, military vehicles, and also plenty of civilian cars. The whole city was plunged in darkness. It felt very strange and oppressive, like being in a horror film.

'Mad, isn't it — this unlit city,' commented Amin at the same moment.

They sped along. The cars coming the other way posed a problem, as they were mostly driven on full beam, without a thought for the other vehicles.

'Everyone's terrified,' murmured Amin. 'I haven't seen anyone doing less than 45mph.'

'They're afraid of being kidnapped. It's dangerous at night here — anything could happen, and does. Do you recognise this road? We're on our way back to the prison.'

'Looks like it, boss.'

'He's returning the prisoner. There's no point following them. Let's go.'

Amin span the car around in the middle of the road with a gnashing of tortured gears. Joseph put a hand on his thigh.

'Chill.'

Probably best to avoid getting shot at by some trigger-happy soldier. A car like this cost a lot of money, especially to repair the armouring, and he'd be needing it in the days to come.

They were speeding towards the compound when Joseph's mobile phone rang. It was his mole at the police station. Joseph listened silently as the man explained how he'd identified the prisoner with the help of one of his distant cousins, a warder at the prison. When Joseph heard that the man — a certain Ak Tikrini — had killed a coalition soldier, he realised that this case was still full of surprises. He hung up thoughtfully.

'What are we doing?' asked Amin.

'I don't understand what this is all about, but it's important. We should inform Berne.'

'Shit! Back to the office, you mean?'

'I'd rather call the general than send an email, even an encrypted one. I'll have to use the cube. We'll sleep there.'

The Entity had rented temporary offices in an area near the airport, thought to be one of the most secure places in the whole of

Afghanistan. But then the same had been said of Bagram, until it was attacked by a dozen explosive-laden martyrs. The Entity offices were on the first floor of a prefab building, with little heating and barely any furniture, but a specialised company — Swiss, of course — had already set them up with the latest IT equipment and satellite connections. The technicians had also installed an encrypted communication room, a ten-metre-square cube tiled in metal sheets covered with electric cables. The cube was supposed to deflect any electromagnetic interception, thus allowing Joseph to communicate safely with Berne.

'Why is Kandar springing a guy like that from the nick?'

'I don't know, Amin. That's exactly what's worrying me.'

NICK'S SUITE at The Winston consisted of a large bedroom with a mirror opposite the bed, and an adjoining living room furnished with a sofa, two armchairs, and a leather-topped desk, of a style he couldn't quite pinpoint. French, probably. The walls were adorned with elegant lithographs and old paintings, all featuring women in varying states of undress. One of them depicted courtesans in eastern clothing, and was called *In the Sultan of Peshawar's Harem, around 1875.* The Winston looked more like an upmarket brothel than a luxury hotel. Nick stretched out on the bed, and allowed his mind to empty.

By the time the doorbell rang, he felt rested and in top form. He opened the door to the woman whose photo he had seen in the Entity's case file. She was athletic, fortyish, with laughing eyes, dusky skin, and very long black hair. Taller than he'd imagined — probably five foot eight. Very classy. He'd rarely come across such a beautiful woman.

'Hello, I'm Jacqueline,' she said naturally, holding out her hand. 'And you must be Martin?'

Nick was speechless, unable to respond. Jacqueline smiled charmingly.

'You're shy, or perhaps you've changed your mind? May I come in?'

She spoke German with a light French accent. Nick moved out of the way.

'Please.'

Jacqueline confidently slipped off her coat and let it fall to the sofa, revealing a navy-blue dress cut above the knee to show off her legs and make the most of her slim hips and large, probably remodelled breasts. The outfit didn't really go with her respectable, teacherly glasses. As far as Nick could tell, she was wearing a black bra, whose fine lace could just be made out beneath the flimsy fabric of her dress. She looked like something out of a fashion magazine. He blushed again, gesturing for her to sit down in front of him. She crossed her legs elegantly, and burst out laughing. A fresh laugh.

'I'm met some shy men in my time, but this takes the biscuit! You're cute; I like you. Are you a sportsman?'

'I like skiing and mountain climbing.'

'I addoorre mountain climbing. Where are you from?'

'Geneva, but I live in Berne.'

They sat facing each other for a few moments, not speaking.

'You seem like an unusual young man. Do you have any specific wishes with regards to us?' She leant towards him, allowing him to smell her subtle but potent perfume. 'Any particular fantasies? I could teach you some new … climbing techniques.'

She laughed deep in her throat, like a respectable woman slightly shocked by her own saucy joke.

'Actually, I didn't call you for … relations. I would like to talk to you.'

'What about?'

She was still smiling, but her attitude had changed slightly. He sensed that she was on her guard. He wasn't surprised — it was like this for every prostitute the world over, whether they worked in luxury hotels or squalid back alleys. In their profession, the new clients who didn't want the merchandise were often the ones who caused trouble. Strangely, this insight freed him up. He rested his chin on his hands, and let Jacqueline look at him.

'About one of your regular clients. His first name is Leonard.'

She stood up, her face closed.

'I don't know any Leonard. And, in any case, the rule is that you never talk to any client about another client. I'm surprised you don't know that.'

'The rule no longer stands when the client's life is in danger,' responded Nick gently. 'Leonard is on the run, from people who want to kill him. If I don't find him before they do, he's dead.'

He hated himself for lying, but what else could he do? Jacqueline sat back down, stunned.

'Are you a friend of his?'

'Look at me. Do I look as if I would mean him any harm?'

She looked at him carefully. He seemed to pass the test.

'You look like a cop, but you're not. Who are you?'

Prostitutes have an uncanny ability to recognise cops and, more generally, anyone who might wish to harm them. A call girl like Jacqueline wouldn't have lasted ten years in the profession, even in this luxurious environment, without that ability.

'I'm a sort of investigator, a friendly investigator. Are you willing to help me, Jacqueline?'

'Why would I want to do that?'

'Neither you nor I have anything to gain from a financial point of view — it's a matter of principle. Or morality, if you prefer. You've been seeing Leonard for nine years. I can't believe that you're completely indifferent to his fate.'

This was a cop trick that Werner had often mentioned: 'If you want a prostitute to help you,' he would say, 'always treat her with respect, like a lady; no one ever treats prostitutes like ladies, least of all the police.'

'I'd be happy to help you. But I'm warning you, I barely know anything. When I didn't hear from him, I did wonder if he'd disappeared.'

'Did he seem anxious, before that?'

'Not at all.'

She told him what he'd already read in the case file. He took notes, stopping her from time to time to ask a question.

'Did he ever try to see you outside of one of your ... sessions?'

'Never.'

'When he was with you, did he behave like the man he seemed to be? Any pet crazes or weird tics?'

'It sometimes seemed to me that he didn't much enjoy what we were doing. When we made love, he seemed … focussed. As if he were working. I don't think he felt a great deal of pleasure.'

'Why did he pay so much, then?'

'He's rich; money isn't an issue for people like him.'

'Your reply seems a little simplistic, if you'll forgive me for saying so.'

Jacqueline thought for a moment.

'I think I reassured him. I come across quite serious, and initially presented myself as a teacher looking to make a bit of cash. I don't think he ever believed me, but the idea seemed to excite him.'

'Excite him, or please him?'

'Same thing, isn't it?'

'You said yourself that he didn't seem to get very excited,' replied Nick, looking down at his notebook.

'You're right. What I told him didn't excite him — it pleased him.' She looked into his eyes. 'Only cops ask questions like that.'

'I'm trying to ask questions that will help me get to know him better,' said Nick, to decrease the tension. 'There are many things about Leonard's behaviour that I don't understand. A shrink would be just as likely as a cop to ask these questions.'

'I doubt a shrink would be too thrilled with the comparison.'

'You've been his mistress for nine years. What do you know about who Leonard was seeing before he met you?'

'You think that's important?'

'Leonard has disappeared. Everything is important.'

'Hmm, let me think. Yes, he did mention a girl. It was when we first started seeing each other. Six or seven years ago. One Christmas. He seemed a little depressed. He told me that what he liked about me was my class, just like the girl he was seeing before. I asked him why he'd stopped seeing her, if he liked her so much. I was a bit cross, and worried, too: Leonard was already a good client — faithful and generous, never hit me — and I didn't want him replacing me with anyone else. He laughed and told me that he'd never see Yasmina again, despite her being so beautiful, because she was on drugs. He was scared of AIDS, and didn't want to run any risks.'

'Yasmina? Did she have Arabic blood?'

'I suppose so. We never talked about it again.'

Nick stared at Jacqueline. Something had just occurred to him.

'Forgive me the personal question, but you seem slightly Middle Eastern, despite your French name. Where are you from?'

'I'm Lebanese.'

The rest of the conversation didn't yield anything of interest. Nick took a thousand Swiss francs from his wallet — the price for two hours with Jacqueline, and enough to support a family in the developing world for a year. She took the notes delicately, putting them in her bag with doe-like grace. He warned her to be careful, and let her go.

6.

When Osama woke up the next morning, his head was pounding as if in a vice. Putting his thoughts into words had made him aware of the enormity of the situation. He was used to challenging cases, to threats and work pressure, but he could sense that the risks here were of a different order entirely. The hot-water cylinder wasn't working, so he took a cold shower. Outside, the wind was howling. He opened the curtains. Kabul had been hit by icy wind and flurries of snow, dropping the temperature by twenty degrees in just a few hours — fairly normal for this time of year. It wasn't yet dawn, and the lane he lived in lay in darkness, with a few lit windows and the occasional motorbike headlights providing the only sources of light. He could just make out the policeman who watched over his house at night, Nafouz, with his Kalashnikov at his side and his *panchol* soaked by the snow. Osama himself was shivering, despite the toughness he'd acquired in the mountains: the house was barely heated, so it couldn't have been more than six or seven degrees.

He put on a thick, quilted *shalwar* instead of his usual trousers, and replaced his usual ankle boots with fur-lined Russian ones. He breakfasted quickly on dates, goats' cheese, and coffee — alone, as Malalai was on three-day duty at the hospital. Being alone got him down, especially after their fight a couple of days earlier. He drank another coffee. He was washing his tin cup at the kitchen sink when he heard a single knock on the door, followed by two more. This knock from Nafouz meant that someone was here to see him and that there was no danger. He unlocked the door. A man was standing there, wrapped in a black *kalpan,* his face obscured by a woollen scarf, a hat on his head. He took off the scarf. Osama was stunned to see Mullah Bakir.

'Good morning, brother Osama. May I come in for a moment?'

Osama opened the door, speechless. Mullah Bakir brushed the snow off his coat and hung it on a peg in the hall.

'A glorious house, brother Osama!' he mocked. 'A real palace! I'm glad to see there's at least one cop in this country who lives off no more than what he's paid by the government. You're a real *Al Gaida!'*

It was a fashionable joke to classify people into three groups: the *Al Faidas,* who got rich; the *Al Qaida,* who fought; and the *Al Gaida,* who got done …

'I didn't know you had such a sense of humour. I've nothing proper to eat, I'm afraid, but if you'd like a coffee, follow me,' grumbled Osama. 'I've just made some.'

He took out a second tin cup exactly like the first, and filled it with steaming coffee. The mullah held it up for a moment.

'Standard Russian-army issue. Doesn't your delicious wife have anything better to offer you, or is this nostalgia for your early years as a mujahedeen?'

'These cups do indeed date from the Northern Alliance,' said Osama. 'They were initially stolen from the bodies of Russian soldiers, and we bought them after that. They didn't cost much — five afghanis. And they last a lifetime.'

'Lots of sugar in my coffee,' said the mullah.

Osama bought his coffee in the souk, from an Azerbaijani merchant who ground it as fine as flour and added cardamom. He boiled it in a pot of water, as they did in Turkmenistan. His father had always done it that way. Osama was a traditional man, and he hoped that both his children would continue to make their coffee like this — although he doubted it.

'I thought it best to come and see you myself,' began the mullah as he breathed in the aroma of the coffee, 'as the minister has got wind of your little jaunt — some Westerners told him that you'd taken

Afouk Ak Tikrini out of the prison for a few hours.'

'Westerners? What Westerners could have known about our excursion?'

'I don't know exactly who, but I do know they were unbelievers — Christians, not NDS guys.'

'Are you sure the minister isn't the source of the information himself?' asked Osama tonelessly.

'He heard it from Westerners, and not the other way around. I'm absolutely sure. I have an informer high up in Khan Durrani's office.'

'If he gets hold of a copy of the temporary-release licence I signed, he'll use it to suspend me from office. Which would allow him to take me off the case.'

Mullah Bakir smiled, and took the licence out of his pocket.

'Here it is. I personally went to fetch it from the prison director half an hour after you drove off with Ak Tikrini.'

'Why?' asked Osama, stunned.

'Because I'm suspicious of him, and because it could do you a great deal of harm. And also, I admit, to consolidate my power over him.'

'Do you think it was he who called? Out of revenge?'

'The leak didn't come from the prison, I'm sure of that. As I told you last time, the director is too afraid of me.'

If that was true, it meant that he was already being tailed, despite the care he had taken. The people who had found out what he was up to were experienced professionals. He thought back to the Westerner in the minister's entourage at Wali Wadi's home.

'You've been spotted by an unofficial outfit,' added the mullah, as if reading Osama's thoughts. 'Professionals.'

'Who?'

'I don't know — there are so many of them. But not, according to my contact, the official part of the CIA, or a big European secret service. Maybe the Russians, or the SAD, or some agency like that, or worse. And pretty powerful, to be able to get straight through to the minister.'

Osama had heard of the Special Activities Division. He knew it was the paramilitary branch of the CIA, and that it ran the most sensitive, violent missions in his country.

'The security minister reacted fast, and brutally, when the Westerners called him. Two men came to the prison. They had a release licence signed by the minister himself. They've just taken Ak Tikrini. I don't know where they went. As soon as I heard, I came to see you.'

'The safes at Wali Wadi's home and office were both empty. Ak Tikrini didn't help me at all, so the minister is getting his knickers in a twist over nothing,' said Osama.

'Maybe, but he now knows that your investigation is serious.' The mullah pointed a finger at him. 'He knows that you had no hesitation in taking a man convicted for murder out of his cell. He cannot use that information against you, as you brought Ak Tikrini back to his cell that same evening, but his suspicion of you will have grown even stronger.'

'I'll be careful. I'm used to it.'

'Also, I seem to have heard that you've been waiting for a parcel from Russia. The man who told me mentioned that the minister knows about it, and has asked that the packet be intercepted and sent to him. One of his men gave the order to the postal services minister yesterday afternoon.'

This time, Osama was rendered speechless. The news meant that not only was he being followed, but his phone was being tapped — he'd been alone when he called Moscow. He had told no one in his team, not even his deputies. He had made the call in Russian, so a team with bilingual technicians must have done the tapping. Again, this pointed to an organisation, or at the very least an outfit able to call on significant resources.

'You're dealing with powerful people,' commented Mullah Bakir smoothly. 'May I know what is in this famous parcel from Russia?'

Osama sized him up for a moment. It would be hard to hide the truth from him.

'Chemical kits intended to establish whether Wali Wadi had gunpowder on his hands.'

'Oh, so you don't think Wadi committed suicide? What a surprise!' joked the mullah, before becoming serious again. 'I can try to intercept the parcel before the minister does. But, in order to do that, I would be forced to ask the help of individuals whose methods you may not approve of. The purging of Taliban members from the postal and telecommunications services has been … incomplete, shall we say, and we still have a lot of people there. Did you know that there are as many Taliban staff in the censorship office as there were under Mullah Omar?'

Osama was lost in thought, and didn't reply immediately. There were lots of Tajiks in the postal service, as in all government departments, and he was sure he could find old Northern Alliance people to counter the minister's henchmen. That would be much less dangerous for him than relying on Mullah Bakir's more-or-less clandestine networks. He still didn't understand what the imam stood to gain by helping him, given that he'd put everything he had into fighting the Taliban; until he did, he needed to keep his guard up.

'I am grateful for the information you've given me, Mullah. It is very valuable. But I will deal with intercepting the parcel myself.'

The mullah smiled kindly.

'Of course, do as you think best. I quite understand.' He put on his coat, and bowed slightly. 'Good day, brother Osama. I wish you luck.'

JOSEPH WATCHED THE TANKS driving by beneath his window. He was in one of the warehouses at the massive Bagram military base, far from the temporary offices rented by the Entity. He was waiting for extra surveillance equipment and more sophisticated weaponry for his team, outraged that it had taken him more than two hours to drive the fifty kilometres to the base.

The Taliban had been targeting the narrow strip of tarmac leading to Bagram for several months now. They'd already exploded several IEDs — bombs powerful enough to make mincemeat of the Coalition's hefty tanks. And the military traffic that day had been so heavy that he'd spent half the journey sandwiched between a French and an American convoy, with no overtaking permitted. They'd been perfect targets, crawling along at a snail's pace.

'We're done,' announced Amin as he entered the small glass

office. 'I'm just waiting for a receipt from the customs people.'

Amin passed his encrypted BlackBerry to his boss.

'A first summary of our recordings.'

A team of four translators from Tajikistan had been hard at work since the day before. The police informer had gathered the necessary voiceprints in record time, on the pretext of meeting with Osama and his two deputies to discuss an investigation he was working on. Since then, the Echelon network had been listening in to everything they'd said, wherever they'd said it. Joseph glanced through the summary. No conversations of any interest — except one. He suddenly became very excited. This was just what he'd been waiting for: a golden opportunity to solve his problems by doing away with the cop who was making their lives a misery. He never would have dreamt the chance would come so soon.

'Amin,' he called. 'I need to see the security minister immediately. Let's go. You can call his office on the way, to arrange a meeting.'

'What about the receipt?'

'I couldn't care less. Let's go.'

Joseph took the wheel himself, roaring off in a cloud of dust down a narrow side street with warehouses on either side, some giving off a strong smell of food. Amin pointed to one.

'A marine told me earlier that that's a secret interrogation centre for the Special Activities Division.'

The SAD was one of the CIA's many paramilitary shock units, and specialised in dirty tricks.

'It'll be gone soon.'

These days, the Afghans did the dirty work themselves, as far from official Western bases as possible, in buildings not subject to American law. The new anti-torture laws tended to deter American officers, especially as subcontracting had become just as dangerous, in legal terms, as direct activity. In fact, the existence of outfits such as the Entity was itself a response to these increasingly restrictive regulations.

Joseph swung the jeep on to one of the main roads criss-crossing the military base. They passed a line of the massive beetle-like Buffalo mine-protected vehicles that were the latest must-have equipment. The American army had just ordered ten thousand.

They drove straight through a special checkpoint as they left one of the protected zones within the base itself. Various American services based their outposts there, with the notable exception of the CIA, which had its own building in the centre of Kabul — opposite the president's residence, naturally.

When they eventually reached the gate out of the base, it was blocked by dozens of tanks staffed by jumpy, trigger-happy marines. Ever since a *shahid* had blown up the pride of the CIA's presence in Afghanistan, NATO's already draconian security precautions had become even tighter, with the result that Coalition officers spent less time out in the field, and relied instead on Afghan officers of uncertain loyalty. It wasn't surprising, under these circumstances, that the Coalition drones regularly hit marriages and other civil events instead of Taliban gatherings. In this war, anything was fair game, and the Taliban demonstrated daily their ability to destroy, and even infiltrate, the Allies' security systems.

After an hour's drive, they entered Kabul. Joseph was champing at the bit. The recording had provided them with a unique window of opportunity to dispense with Kandar and his deputies in one fell swoop.

'Why don't you go through the commercial district,' suggested Amin. 'The presidential area looks jammed.'

They drove down a narrow street. Joseph, fully focussed, drove fast and well, skilfully weaving his way between the vehicles. Soon they were passing a row of shops.

'We're near Chicken Street,' announced Amin.

Kabul's main tourist street looked pretty pathetic. A crowd of bearded men and burqa'd women were scurrying around, with not a foreigner in sight. Music was pouring out of different boom boxes in a cacophony of noise. Joseph leant towards Amin.

'Do …'

He didn't have time to finish his sentence. There was a loud blast, and what followed it was like a nightmare: about one hundred metres ahead, a massive mushroom of flames and black smoke burst upwards, flinging bodies in the air above it. It was as if time had stopped, as if they were human puppets held still for a moment.

Two seconds later, the fragments hit the 4x4, sending it careening into a stall. Several pieces of metal lodged into the windscreen, but didn't shatter it. Joseph reacted fast. He braked, shoved the jeep into reverse, ran over a greengrocer's cart, and span the wheel with the handbrake on. The vehicle turned 180 degrees, and he screeched off down a side street. After eight hundred metres he braked sharply. There were flames all over the bonnet.

'We're on fire,' said Amin.

Joseph switched off the engine. His eyes were surprisingly calm.

'It's nothing — petrol that landed on the bonnet during the explosion. There's nothing wrong with the vehicle. That was a narrow escape.'

He opened the jeep door, holding a submachine gun in one hand and a fire extinguisher in the other. He sprayed the extinguisher all over the bonnet and front wheel. Amin joined him, somewhat shaken despite his extensive training. The air smelled acrid, and was dark with smoke.

'My God, that was quite an attack! They must have used at least 50 kilos of explosives.'

Joseph had a faraway look in his eyes as he ran his hand over the shrapnel-riddled windscreen.

'Bolts. Good techniques travel fast, it seems. The Iraqis stuff their IEDs with bolts. I've been hit in two attacks like that — one in Baqubah and the other in Baghdad.'

'Do you think they were targeting us?'

'Can't have been — we were too far away, and there were at least 20 vehicles in front of us. And anyway, no one knows we're here. But we were lucky, that's for sure. If we'd left Bagram three or four minutes earlier, we would have been next to the bomb when it went off and we'd still be there, armoured car or not.'

People were running around in a great panic. Emergency sirens were blaring so loudly that it seemed as if all of Kabul's ambulances were heading for the area.

Their brand new 4x4 now looked like an old banger from a scrap heap. Dozens of fragments had become lodged all over the bodywork. One of the tyres had burst. Most of the paintwork had melted in the heat, turning into a kind of blistered, murky mess.

'Change the wheel,' ordered Joseph. 'We've a meeting to attend.'

It was around midday when the Ariana plane from Moscow rumbled down at Kabul airport. It was an old 727 with flaking paintwork and, like every plane owned by the Afghan airline, had been forbidden from flying in EU airspace. Several machines belonging to local airlines were parked on the tarmac, each more decrepit than the last: a DC-8, an ancient Tupolev, an Antonov 24, and even a DC-3, a plane that dated back to 1945 ... all of them making the brand-new Safi Airways Airbus A340 look like something out of science fiction.

The 727 passed a private jet protected by ANA soldiers huddled into their parkas — a drug baron's expensive toy. While the ground crew were attaching the airstairs, several staff opened the hold and started pulling out the postbags. One of them was looking for something. He was young, with a moustache, and a sheep wool chitrali on the back of his head. He grabbed the first bag, took a pair of cutters out of his pocket, and clipped off the security tie. He rummaged quickly through the bag. Without a word, he passed it to his neighbour, who pulled a new tie out of his pocket and refastened the bag. In the fifth bag, the man found what he was looking for: a small parcel weighing no more than a kilo, addressed to Qomaandaan Kandar at Kabul police headquarters. He opened it with a knife, took out the contents, and replaced them with a Koran. Once the postbag had been retied like the others, he clicked his fingers, and the tractor took them slowly towards the airport building.

Osama was in the middle of eating a kebab with his fingers when Gulbudin walked into his office.

'I've taken the powder kits to Katoun. He'll do it straight away.'

'Good.'

'I'd like a word while we're alone, Qomaandaan. There's something on my mind.'

'What is it?'

'You told me that you were notified of the minister's presence at

Wali Wadi's house by an orderly. I've spent two days trying to track him down, but I can't. I've been around all the policemen on duty that day.'

'How could that be? I didn't invent it, you know.'

'Of course you didn't. I've been wondering if he wasn't someone from outside.'

'He was in uniform. He came into my office very naturally. He didn't ask my name, so he must have known what I look like.'

'Qomaandaan, I'm almost certain it wasn't someone from police headquarters.'

'That's strange. What do you think is going on?'

'I'm not sure yet. It's such an … unexpected type of situation. Can you remember anything about the way he looked that might help me find him?'

'He was young, about thirty, with slightly slanting eyes like a Hazara. A long scar on his cheek — his left cheek.'

'Great. That's very specific. I'll see if anyone knows of someone who fits that description.'

'Do you think somebody wanted me on the case? And sent a false messenger for that very purpose?'

'That would be a logical conclusion …'

'But who could that be? An opponent of the security minister who didn't want the investigation brushed under the carpet? If that's the case, there must be a conspiracy.'

'Or a counter-conspiracy. People know how honest you are, qomaandaan. Whoever it was that sent you would know that once you started investigating, you wouldn't let go.'

Osama didn't like the feeling of having been manipulated or exploited by unknown forces. But he had to admit that Gulbudin's theory made sense, even if it presupposed a kind of paranoid thinking foreign to him.

'You must find this man, whatever the cost. I can't continue working if I don't know what's going on in the wings.'

'I'll try, qomaandaan.'

'Don't try. Find him.'

THE SECURITY MINISTER waved Joseph into his office with a big smile.

'How are you, my dear friend!' he exclaimed, his enthusiasm so pronounced it had to be forced. 'My secretary saw your vehicle — apparently it's been rather bashed up. You weren't near Chicken Street when the last bomb went off, I hope?'

'Actually, we were.'

'You're lucky to have emerged unscathed. In this country, luck plays as big a part as skill, when it comes to staying alive.'

With a great show of courtesy, the minister brought Joseph right into his office and invited him to join him on the sofa, an honour reserved for only the most important guests. A massive, over-ornate silver tray bearing two glasses and a steaming teapot sat on the low table. The minister indicated that Joseph should pour the drinks. When this was done, he held his glass in both hands and inhaled the aroma deeply. Then he leant towards Joseph.

'So? You say you have new information that will help us to stop Kandar? I'm impatient to hear your news.'

'We recorded a conversation between Kandar and his deputies. Apparently, the three of them always meet up for a drink on the anniversary of one of them joining the team.'

'Which one? Babrak or Gulbudin?'

'Babrak.'

'That's the young one. A piece of filth, he won't pass on the tiniest sliver of information. That team behaves like some kind of cult.'

Joseph took a sip of tea.

'They talked about meeting, and I quote, "at the usual café." Do you see what I'm getting at? We'll have all three of them in a public place at the same time. It's a chance in a million.'

'You want to eliminate all three of them at once?'

'Don't you think? One commando, with a powerful machine gun. Fifteen seconds, and our problem is solved.'

The minister drained his cup with an enigmatic smile. His dilemma was not at all a moral one — he lived in a country that had been at war for thirty years, and in which millions of people had died or disappeared. A few bodies more or less wouldn't make the slightest difference.

'It's a good idea.'

'I have a complete team with me. We can act on very short notice, but I will need logistical help with the approach route and the getaway. We don't know Kabul well enough to carry out an operation like this on our own.'

'I'll supply you with reliable men to back you up. Men from my home village. But you can't kill three policemen without taking a few precautions, even in Kabul. The qomaandaan is better known than you might think, and his difficult relationship with me is no secret either. There's no way we can gun them down — it might draw attention to the investigation.'

'Do you have a better idea?'

'Yes. I'm thinking of a shahid. A suicide bomb, by a martyr, at this same café. Plenty of other people will die alongside them, so there won't be any way to prove they were the intended targets.'

The minister stood up. He was a strategic man, not remotely impulsive, which explained his success in politics. He was clever, with a sharp sense of what was going on. He didn't leave anything out of his deliberations, and never took a decision lightly.

'I'll ask for a detailed report on Babrak's habits. I'll soon know where they've been celebrating this anniversary.' He looked at his watch. 'Now here's a jolly thing — I've just sent some men to fetch Kandar, so I can put a bit of pressure on him. He'll be at my place later. Isn't that funny?'

'Afghan humour, I take it?'

'English, my dear sir, English. I did my schooling at Eton. And it was there, from an old political history professor, that I learnt the great principle that has made me the man I am.'

'May one know this principle?'

'If you can't buy someone, crush him.'

Osama was in his office reading a report on the murder of a young girl by her mother-in-law — a mainstay of domestic violence cases, sadly — when he was interrupted by two men in civilian clothes, followed by a stressed-looking Gulbudin. The only thing that set them apart from the other officers at police headquarters was their slightly condescending manner. 'Secret police,' he thought immediately, putting the report down. One of the men confirmed his fears by presenting the little red, white, and green laminated card carried by NDS officers.

'Good day, qomaandaan. Our apologies for disturbing you. We are from the ministry of security.'

'I don't like to be visited without an appointment. What do you want?' asked Osama coldly, inspecting the photo and the hologram on the card.

'His Excellency Burhanuddin Khan Durrani, Minister and Clan Chief, may God be praised, would like to see you immediately. He awaits you at home.'

Osama hesitated, then stood up. The minister was his hierarchical superior and an influential member of Karzaï's government, and he had no choice but to obey.

'I'm off,' he said to Gulbudin. 'Keep working on what we were just discussing.'

In the corridor he called out to Babrak.

'Come with me. And bring your Kalashnikov.'

There was no question of attending the meeting alone: an ambush or kidnapping could happen in seconds … In the street, he politely declined the two secret agents' offer of a ride and stepped into his own 4x4, with the usual protective pick-up parked behind.

'What's going on?' asked his young deputy anxiously. 'Why has the NDS summoned you?'

'His Excellency Burhanuddin Khan Durrani must have received my Koran from Moscow …'

'A Russian Koran? What are you saying?'

Osama told him how he had received the powder kits from under the nose of the NDS at Kabul airport. Babrak burst out laughing.

'Not only did you get one over on him; he now knows that you know. Why didn't you just have the packet stolen?'

'It was a little arrogant,' admitted Osama. 'But I have to admit that all day I've been imagining his face as he opened the parcel, and it's cheered me up no end.'

'Why did he call in the NDS? The ministry of security doesn't have any power over the secret services — they only answer to the president.'

'To put pressure on me. To demonstrate that he controls everything. These guys are Pashtun; they must be from his clan.'

'Do you think he can get you taken off the case?'

'No, not any more. Look at this.'

He took an envelope out of his pocket. Babrak unfolded the document inside, and read it avidly.

'Clearly,' he said thoughtfully, 'this changes everything.'

They sped over to the smart neighbourhood of Chair Poor, where the smallest house sold for more than three million dollars. Other drivers kept making way for them — the small-lettered black number plates exclusive to the NDS clearly had a great effect on the traffic. The convoy passed through a mobile checkpoint before turning on to a wide street kept free of traffic by mobile chicanes and concrete blocks strong enough to stop a suicide truck. Osama's driver made sure their police pass was visible on the dashboard. Fifty metres later, they passed a second checkpoint, much more rigorous than the first. South Americans — Salvadorians or Nicaraguans — in tattered uniforms were mounting a lively guard alongside the Afghan soldiers. Ex *contras* were particularly prized by the mercenary companies for their counter-guerrilla techniques, their modest salary demands, and because no one cared when they died.

The NDS henchmen's car finally came to a stop in front of the minister's residence — an enormous, ugly house built in Soviet times, and formerly home to President Najibullah's brother. One of the secret police officers solemnly held the door open for Osama. A few moments later, he found himself in a gloomy anteroom with damp stains on the walls. A naked bulb in the lamp stand on the flashy pedestal table lent a pale light to the disproportionately high room. Sure that the minister intended to humiliate him by making him wait as long as possible, Osama knelt down to pray, then took his Koran out of his pocket. To his great surprise, he'd barely had time to open it when a servant came to find him. He was taken down a long corridor, whose threadbare carpet came unstuck at almost every step, and delivered into his enemy's lair. Durrani's study was vast. It was fitted out with gilt furniture and a chandelier on which only half the bulbs were working. The cream walls were still discoloured where paintings had been removed — by the Taliban, presumably — and not replaced. An Apple computer sat on a table, next to a battery of phones, a pile of signature books, and an assault rifle. The minister gestured to Osama to sit down. A huge gold Rolex glittered on his wrist, and he wore a solitaire diamond on the little finger of his other hand.

'My respects, Minister, Sir,' said Osama.

With a wave of his hand, the minister dismissed excessive courtesy as inappropriate between them. The politician's spinelessness seemed even more glaring than usual to Osama in this old-fashioned setting. The man was clever, and cunning, but he had been massively enriching himself ever since Karzaï came to power, buying buildings and land to build on in Kabul, and farmland in the north, near Mazar-i-Sharif. Osama had also heard rumours that he'd bought some impressive properties in the south of France and London. A tray with a teapot and two glasses was placed in front of Osama — a clear invitation for him to be the one to pour. Osama did nothing of the sort, contenting himself with looking coldly at the minister. In Afghanistan, relationships are highly codified: the powerful person does not bestir himself in the presence of a subordinate; he has the tea poured for him and he drinks first. But Osama had no intention of serving tea to his boss. He would happily — and against all protocol — serve his men, or people he respected such as Dr Katoun, but not a snake like the minister.

'I hear that your investigation of Wali Wadi's suicide is taking some wild turns,' began the minister acidly. 'There have been some dangerous initiatives. Pulling a man accused of a crime against a Coalition soldier out of prison is an extremely serious thing to do. I haven't told President Karzaï of this regrettable action of yours, but I can assure you that he would be furious.'

'I did what I had to do to move my investigation forward. I'm afraid it wasn't much use, as you know, because both Wali Wadi's safes were empty.'

'Why are you so set on thinking of this as a criminal case?'

'It seems obvious to me.' Osama opened the old leather satchel he'd brought with him and took out two documents that he placed on the table. 'The first,' he said, 'is a new report from the pathologist, Dr Katoun. The second contains my initial conclusions.'

The minister drew back, as if scared of being contaminated by the documents. Then he took hold of them, hesitantly, and began reading. By the time he put them down, his pinched lips left no doubt as to his fury.

'Your hypotheses are each more specious than the last! This report is no more than a litany of implausible and groundless suggestions.'

Osama didn't flinch. 'The powder test on the dead man's hands proves irrefutably that Wali Wadi did not fire the gun he was holding. From that, the only possible conclusion is that someone else held the weapon, and killed Wali Wadi, before putting it into his hand after his death. To me, that is a murder.'

'You used tests whose origins and reliability are completely unproven.'

'The tests are Russian, and used by the Moscow Murder Squad, which can supply all necessary proof.'

The minister waited a few seconds, in order to increase the effect of what he was about to say, and then asked conclusively, 'And when is the expiry date for those tests?'

Osama suddenly remembered the warning from his Russian colleague. He cursed himself for failing to foresee this manoeuvre.

'I'll check but, according to my colleague, they are valid for six months after the expiry date.'

'In that case, why doesn't the manufacturer put off the expiry date for six months? If the expiry date is past I will consider the results of these tests null and void, and ask you to take any conclusion linked to them out of your final report.'

He emphasised the word *final*.

'We'll just have to import some new tests.'

'There's no point.' The minister suddenly turned on the charm: 'You're a very determined investigator, qomaandaan Kandar, but it's important not to confuse determination and relentlessness. Unless you find some tangible proof for your pseudo-murder thesis, I would ask you to please close this investigation. In the immediate term.'

The minister stood up and took Osama by the arm to walk him back to the door. In the anteroom he came right up close, as if they were best friends. So close that Osama could smell his garlicky breath.

'I assume you used your old Northern Alliance mujahedeen buddies to intercept the tests at the airport. You know that national reconciliation between Pashtuns and Tajiks is one of the president's most cherished projects. You mustn't give the impression that you're employing clan members, qomaandaan. Do that, and you're taking a serious risk with your career. Not to mention your security, and that of your family.'

With these threatening words, he dismissed a dumbfounded Osama.

THE POLICEMAN CONTRACTED to place the tag under Osama's car slipped into the garage at police headquarters, carrying his bag. He'd checked out the garage several times already, but had been put off by the number of witnesses. Today, for the first time, it was empty, apart from three members of staff. He headed for one of the mechanics, to whom he had already spoken. He frowned as he tried to remember his name, but it was no good — they hadn't spoken for long enough. He walked over, affecting a smile.

'*Salaam alaikum.* May your family thrive, your body be strong, and your household live in peace.'

The conversation started up easily. The mechanic was a real chatterbox, and they talked animatedly of the decision made by the Taliban in one of the eastern provinces to put an upper limit on dowries — a thousand dollars for a first wife, and seven hundred for a second. This decision had provoked much debate; it was all people talked about. The mechanic thought that there should be a greater discount for a second-hand wife as compared to a virgin; in Kabul, five thousand dollars for a virgin and three thousand for a second-hand woman didn't seem enough of a discrepancy. The policeman agreed loudly, confiding to his new friend that he was on the point of acquiring a second wife himself — and a fresh one at that.

'But how can you afford five thousand dollars?' asked the astounded mechanic.

'I manage,' said the cop, with an air of mystery.

They spent the next few minutes discussing the merits of possessing a second wife as compared to just one, reckoning that one of the real perks was being able to accomplish your conjugal duty with one, *Insha'Allah,* if the other was unavailable. But what if both were unavailable at the same time, exclaimed the mechanic. Take a third, suggested the cop, and they both burst out laughing. Once he felt sure of the mechanic's trust, the policeman said casually, 'I'm up shit creek — my old Land Cruiser broke down again last week. The bosses have all the luck, with their good-quality new cars. I'm told commandant Kandar has a GMC, same as the ministers.'

'No,' said the mechanic. 'He has a Land Cruiser, like all the section heads. What's more, the aircon is messed up and the passenger door creaks — something to do with the hinge that I haven't been able to fix.'

'I don't believe a word of it,' said the policeman. 'My friend at the NDS told me he drives a GMC.'

'He's winding you up, and I can prove it. The car's here — I'll show it to you.'

They walked over to the back of the garage, where several dusty 4x4s were parked next to a couple of ramps. The mechanic pointed at one of them.

'Look, it's that one. A Land Cruiser, definitely!'

The 4x4 had white civilian plates rather than red police ones. The cop made a mental note of the number: *KBL 97744 SH*. He chatted with the mechanic for a while longer, and then took his leave. But he didn't actually leave; he just slipped into the stairwell and hid behind an inner door that happened to be open, next to the ramp. A few minutes later he heard the mechanics walking to the other end of the garage to pray. He rushed to Osama's jeep and slipped beneath it. The magnet was so strong that the chassis tore the tag out of his hands. He checked, and it seemed stuck to the car. He pressed the release mechanism. A green light appeared, and went off again. The tag was undetectable, being partly hidden by the transmission, as well as camouflaged to the chassis. The cop eased himself out from under the vehicle, happy to have earned enough for a new wife from such an easy job. No one had seen him.

7.

Ever since he'd met her, Nick had been thinking about the implications of his conversation with Jacqueline. One particular sentence intrigued him. Jacqueline had said that the fugitive dropped the prostitute he'd been seeing before because she was on drugs. This news resonated with something he'd been wondering about ever since he first became involved with the case: why had the fugitive chosen that junky-filled squat? A rich man like him could have hidden anywhere. What if the fugitive had simply been trying to find Yasmina, his old call girl, to ask her for help?

It was an attractive idea, although at this stage he couldn't see quite where it might lead. Everything in the fugitive's life was immaculate, ordered to the highest degree. Suddenly he was being pursued by killers sent by the company to which he had devoted his life. He had managed to escape, miraculously. His world was falling apart. He had had to go on the run. Where could he turn? He remembered Yasmina. He had formed a financial relationship with her that lasted several years. She took drugs and lived in squats, in a shady world, a world apart. A squat. Wouldn't that be the perfect place to hide? Surely no one would look for a financier like him in a place like that …

Nick stopped at a café and ordered a decaf. His theory was good. The issue was how to find Yasmina. The squat had closed down — too many deaths on a single day. The cops had sealed off the building, and the council had walled up the doors and windows. He finished his coffee and ordered another. This woman was already a prostitute ten years ago. There was no way the Swiss police's Vice Squad wouldn't have a file on her. He looked at his watch. It was too late tonight — he'd work on it tomorrow.

Osama's house felt sad and empty without his wife, who was still on duty at the hospital. He put on an Ahmad Zahir CD and cooked up some eggs with the leftover rice. He kept thinking about the conversation he'd had with the minister a few hours earlier. He felt repulsed by the way that Khan Durrani had threatened him — in a roundabout and indirect way, yes, but threatened him nonetheless. He thought of himself as a loyal servant of his country, whatever the political situation. When the mujahedeen took Kabul in 1992 he returned, wreathed in military glory, to his job as police superintendent of the 11th district. He refused to take part in the witch-hunt against former Khalq members. Many of those who'd collaborated with the Russians, and lived very comfortably from it, recovered their reputations at that point by taking part in the lynching. Houses, shops, and businesses were seized as part of a supposed 'purification'. Unscrupulous individuals became rich over a period of weeks by dishonestly appropriating other peoples' belongings, while others were hung or stoned for no other reason than their oppressors' greed.

Later on, in 1996, when the Taliban invaded Kabul and lynched president Najibullah, Osama stayed on the sidelines, doing his best to apply the old secular penal code. When a new Islamic-inspired code was announced, Osama reluctantly left his job, and once again — as he had twenty years before — joined his friends in the Northern Alliance, this time to fight the Taliban. When the Taliban fell and he returned to Kabul, he was welcomed as a hero. The new regime was short of experienced policemen, and he was named head of the Murder Squad the same day his predecessor was hung for having taken part in various atrocities. He sighed. What a life! He had lost a brother and a son in the war, half his family was still in exile, and he'd lost count of the cousins and uncles who'd died in the fighting. Had any other country been as turbulent as Afghanistan over these last thirty years?

When Osama had finished his dinner, he washed up his plate and cutlery, and started thinking about the minister again. He'd managed to avoid compromising his conscience so far, and he wasn't going to start now. He walked into the bedroom. The concrete floor was freezing, and the bedcovers as cold and hard as stone. For the first time in ages, he placed a loaded automatic rifle next to his bedside table, and two grenades within easy reach.

JOSEPH WALKED into the minister's brightly lit drawing room. It was almost midnight. The minister bade him sit down on the sofa opposite his comfortable armchair. An enormous silver teapot was on the table, as well as two glasses embellished with gold trim. There was also a bottle of whisky — a great luxury in Kabul. Joseph sat down, refusing the alcohol. He never touched a drop.

'We agree with your plan,' he said simply.

'Excellent. And I have made a lot of progress. My men have established where they have their anniversary get-together. Babrak is a regular at a popular café for young Kabulis called the Hamad Café. It's been hosting DJ nights every Friday for the past two years. That's where the three of them have met the last three times. I don't think it's quite Kandar's cup of tea, but he's so keen on his deputy that he must never have said so.

'Do we know if they stayed a long time?'

'Apparently, last year, Kandar only stayed an hour. Gulbudin, a bit longer. And Babrak, until the early hours.'

'That's long enough for our purposes. Can we get a bomb in there?'

'Security at the door is pretty lax. It could be done.'

'Good. Are we confident about who frequents the café? My superiors are only willing to go ahead with this if we're absolutely sure that no Westerner could possibly die in the explosion.'

'Oh, so you don't want to massacre any whites? Only Afghans?' asked the minister with a hint of irony.

'It's not that. The people we're working for don't want expatriate or humanitarian-agency blood on their hands, that's all.'

'I can assure you there's no danger of that. As you'll realise if you spend a bit longer in Kabul, most of the places open to Westerners are closed to Afghans, and vice versa. Because of alcohol. This place is patronised by Afghans, and Afghans only.'

'That's the first problem solved. There's a second: my superiors will not allow me personally to participate. Too dangerous, should anything go wrong. But I will provide the material. The detonator and radio transmitter will be Russian or Czech, to help confuse things. Not state of the art, but certainly good enough to achieve our ends. The explosive will be top quality — C5, which is ten times more powerful than C4. A batch from the Indian army. No way it can be traced back to us, just in case.'

'I'm taking notes. So you'd like my men to take care of the operational aspect? That can be done, but ...'

'To tell you the truth, I'm thinking of the team that took care of Wali Wadi. Our file on them is very positive, even though they didn't get their hands on this report. With our support, they certainly have the resources to carry out this operation.'

'Excellent idea,' agreed the minister.

'Do you already know who the actual martyr will be?'

Khan Durrani pushed a cardboard folder over to Joseph.

'I've the perfect candidate — far too stupid to realise he's being tricked. Some men from my clan have already approached him. He'll do what we need him to do, when we need him to do it, without suspecting a thing.'

'Perfect,' said Joseph, putting the folder in his bag. 'The bomb will make him famous. In an enclosed space, three kilos of C5 is enough to kill fifteen or twenty people, maybe more. Are you sure you can handle the consequences?'

'Suicide bombs go off every day,' said the minister lightly. 'This one won't draw any more attention than any other. And I'll take care of the investigation. There might be a bit of a fuss for a day or two, but it'll soon die down.'

'I trust you.'

Joseph stood up. He glanced at the minister's almost-empty bookshelf. The Taliban would have decreed the books it once held irreligious, and burned them. There were barely any books left in the city, apart from copies of the Koran.

'It's Wednesday. Kandar and his two deputies are meeting tomorrow evening. Will you be ready?'

'Yes.'

By the following morning, the southern wind had chased away the area of low pressure that had been hanging over Kabul for the last few days as a result of the icy rain and snow. The late-winter sun shone brightly in the sky, and the temperature was once again mild. Osama made the most of the lack of pollution on his way to work, opening the car window and breathing in the fresh morning air. Once it got to April, the temperature would soar and Kabul would be bathed in a cloud of acrid dust until autumn.

Shahabuddin Watt was blocked because of a collision between a minibus and a cart of watermelons towed by a donkey. The driver turned sharply into Jade Kolola Pushtha, adding almost a mile to their journey. By the time Osama arrived at the police station, most of his team were already there. Babrak was waiting at his office door in a state of great excitement. Osama tossed his hat onto a peg.

'You seem happy,' he said.

'I've had good news. One of our men sometimes plays Buzkashi with a friend who works for Etisalat. He's in the IT department, and has access to every client's itemised calls.'

'Do you have his name?'

'Better than that. I've arranged to have lunch with him.'

'Good work!'

'We'll have to give him a reason to help us. Cash,' said Babrak, rubbing his thumb and forefinger. 'How much is left in the informers' box, qomaandaan?'

The informers' box was a little tin box into which all the Murder Squad officers put a small contribution — usually a 'levy' from the people they'd arrested. This money allowed them to pay informers and any civilians who helped with their investigations.

'Almost nothing,' admitted Osama. 'Less than five hundred afghanis. We spent it all on the Babur gang case.'

The Babur gang was an organised crew that specialised in

kidnapping Kabuli civilians and holding them to ransom. It mainly operated in and around one of Kabul's few tourist attractions, the Babur Gardens. The gang tortured its victims until they confessed where they'd hidden their savings, then killed them and looted their house. Following an eight-month investigation, Osama had arrested the whole gang. Four were sentenced to death and shot, and the others were rotting in Pul-e-Charkhi.

'He's a young guy, who apparently wants to move abroad. He won't tell us anything unless we pay him.'

'Let's find a way around it. Have you sold the bottles of alcohol we found at Wadi's place?'

'Not yet. I'm supposed to be meeting an expat at the Serena Hotel tomorrow, but we wouldn't make enough.'

'We'll have to think of something else, then.'

Babrak smiled craftily.

'I've had an idea, qomaandaan. Do you remember all those porn magazines that Wali Wadi had at his home and office? There were almost fifty of them. I went and picked them up last night, as no one had dared steal them.'

'But they're gay magazines!'

'So? They're worth a lot of money. We could make tens of thousands!'

Osama was deeply shocked at the idea of making money from those degrading magazines. But he had to admit that the end justified the means. His deputy waited, smiling, sure of Osama's response.

'It's a good idea,' admitted Osama eventually. 'You've been very clever.'

'Can you help me get a good price for them?'

'Contact Superintendent Abdullah Kratin Balla at the Vice Squad, and tell him that I told you to call. He'll find a middleman for you.'

'I'll do it right away.'

'You can keep the money from the alcohol for yourself.'

'Thanks, qomaandaan. I thought I'd share it with Gulbudin. He needs a new back wheel for his motorbike.'

'Be careful,' warned Osama. 'The possession of magazines like that could put you in prison, or even get you killed. Make absolutely sure you're not followed by the NDS. Take someone reliable with you, and arrange a way to shake off your tail when you leave the station.'

'Sure thing, boss.'

'Also, make sure to wipe off all the magazines you've touched. Use ether, rather than just a cloth, or some of the fingerprints will remain. Come and collect me when you've sold them, and we'll go to this lunch together.'

NICK HAD DECIDED to drive to Zurich police station in his own Mazda convertible, rather than the work Peugeot. It was barely an hour's drive from Berne, and there wasn't much traffic at this time of the morning. Usually, he loved the feeling of speeding down an empty motorway in a low-slung car. But not today. He was feeling more and more gloomy, despite the excitement of his investigation. As if things were no longer fitting together as they should. As if his perspective on life was undergoing a major shift. He wondered how his future might turn out. Could he become a winter sports professional? Or use his talent for foreign languages to work for an international organisation? One thing he knew, for sure, was that he'd had enough of intelligence. The death of his friend Werner had made him suddenly grow up. It had opened his eyes. He'd lost the excitement of the early years, and also the intoxicating sense of working for a noble and important cause. He'd lost his faith. He was experiencing a generalised sense of disgust.

But how did one leave an outfit like the Entity? How did you tell a man like the general that you'd had enough? Would Nick be entitled to a full and proper redundancy complete with references, or would he be the victim of a sudden, secret death in a car crash, or by falling off a bridge? Officially, he worked for one of the Entity's numerous cover outfits, an international-relations research institute. Maybe he would be able to leave on good terms. Or maybe not.

One thing was for sure. The Entity was not what he'd previously thought. Analysts and their dirty tricks against Islamic fundamentalists were just one facet. The other was a dark, even more secret, organisation. The K troops. They were not a romantic concept intended to attract people like him who never left the air-conditioned Entity headquarters. He had realised that the K troops were at the heart of the Entity. Which meant that for years he'd been working for an organisation completely different from what he had thought — an outfit whose very DNA was geared towards violence rather than intelligence.

He didn't like it. It wasn't how he wanted to live his life.

This train of thought was interrupted by his arrival in Zurich. He parked easily, near the police station. It was a huge old building famous for its Augusto Giacometti entrance hall. The Vice Squad was on the second floor. In the corridor he greeted an inspector just leaving on a job, wearing a bulletproof vest and carrying a shotgun.

'Who is your most recent recruit?'

'Inspector Binterchrüp. In the last office, by the loos.'

Binterchrüp was a young policeman with an open face, a few days' stubble, and clothes that immediately marked him out as a beat cop. He shared his tiny, windowless office with three colleagues who weren't around at this early hour. Nick had chosen the most recent arrival because new cops tended to cooperate better than experienced ones. He produced his fake federal justice department card, and introduced himself as the person in charge of an investigation into a network of heroin traffickers. Binterchrüp didn't seem particularly impressed, but did ask him to sit down.

'How can I help you?'

'I've been told there's a prostitute who'd be able to give me information on someone in the network. A certain Yasmina. She was a regular at the Langstrasse squat where there was a shoot-out last month.'

'The junky squat? I'll see what we have on her,' said Binterchrüp, suddenly excited.

He tapped her name into the computer.

'We have 185 Yasminas on file.'

'I didn't think there would be so many,' admitted Nick, disappointed.

'Zurich might be one of the safest cities in the world, but prostitutes flock to cash like bees to honey. We keep them out of sight, but that doesn't mean we don't face the same problems as every city. Is your girl black, or Arab?'

'Arab.'

He didn't actually know, but Jacqueline was Lebanese, and he couldn't imagine the fugitive with a black prostitute. Perhaps he had a penchant for Middle Eastern girls.

'How old is she?'

Nick counted in his head. The fugitive had stopped seeing Yasmina ten years previously. Her replacement, Jacqueline, was already a real woman then, no longer a girl. If there was a pattern, then Yasmina was probably no spring chicken.

'She must be at least forty, but I wouldn't be surprised if she's older.'

'Let's see what we've got ... OK, I've three names. Yasmina Hat Yaha, thirty-four, HIV positive, hustles next to the Fluntern cemetery, arrived in Zurich five years ago.'

'No, it isn't her. My girl was already working here ten years ago.'

'Yasmina Sitruk. Good family. Now forty-six years old. Raped by a neighbour at the age of eight. Parents brought charges. Orphaned as a result of a car crash. Lived with an uncle and aunt. Started using drugs at sixteen; on the game at nineteen. These days she's on the vodka — several litres a day.'

The cop swung his computer screen around so that Nick could see a photo. The woman was obese, her ravaged face half hidden by straggly, greasy hair. Nick knew drugs destroyed their users, and she would of course have looked different when she was young, but he couldn't imagine the man he was pursuing sleeping with this monster, even ten years ago.

'It's not her.'

'So, the last filly in my little stable?' said the inspector, flicking to a new file. 'Yasmina Fatma, forty-six. Arrived from Algeria at the age of eighteen, lived in a hostel. Successfully studied accounting. First arrested for prostitution in 1988. Then nothing until 2000, when she was collared during an investigation of one of her Russian clients.

At the time, she was top of her game, part of a call-girl network, five hundred dollars a pop. She caught hepatitis C, the company kicked her out, and she found herself on the street. From there it was downhill. High on speed, grass, a bit of smack — snorted first and then injected – crack. These days, she hustles for twenty francs a time.'

The cop showed Nick a photo. The girl looked out of it, with the haggard face of a junky, but there was still something from *before* that was visible. From the look of it, she must have been gorgeous.

'That could be her. The girl I'm looking for was once a call girl. Could you print it out for me?'

'Of course.'

'Where can I find her?'

'She used to solicit quite discreetly behind Limatplatz. But her file shows she was recently arrested near Letten.'

Nick was aware of the area's reputation. At the start of the 1990s, the government had allowed a sort of drug-amnesty to develop in Letten, and junkies had flocked there from all over Europe. The government was horrified by the media coverage of their doomed experiment — the entire world press carrying photos of junkies in the 'Swiss paradise' getting high in broad daylight on needle-strewn pavements — and abruptly shut it down.

'Is it still a druggy area?'

'Yes. Nothing like before, but there are still a fair amount of dealers and all kinds of prostitution under the Kornhausbrücke bridge. A word of warning: if you turn up there with that pretty little face, you'll run into trouble. Take two guns rather than one, and keep your car doors locked. It's one of the few really scary places in Zurich.'

Babrak drove down the cluttered lane. One of his men was discreetly following him, one hundred metres behind, to make sure that he wasn't being tailed. He'd taken a very circuitous route, and carried out a classic de-tailing manoeuvre near Salang Watt: a friendly car suddenly blocking the little side street he'd taken. He checked the instructions he'd noted on a piece of paper. The man he was meeting, Dost Muhar, was a middleman well known under the Taliban to anyone looking for either pornographic material or access to forthcoming young men. People murmured that many of the top Taliban were partial to *bacha bazi,* the traditional dancing boys whose lascivious moves left little doubt as to their sexual role. Not that this stopped the destroyers of vice from insisting that sodomites be punished by stoning or amputation ... Babrak had endured Taliban rule for almost five years, but he still struggled to understand the contradictions inherent in their highly unusual ways of thinking and behaving.

As if in response to his thoughts, he passed a stall selling traditional remedies. There was a banner across the entire shop-front announcing an attractive price on rhinoceros horn powder. 'Be strong, be a real Afghan man!' screamed the advert. Sex — whether licit or illicit — was actually very present in Afghan culture. Babrak knew that for the last few months the Americans had been ingratiating themselves with village chiefs by handing out Viagra, which was much more effective in eliciting the chiefs' friendliness than were the traditional financial donations. The blue pills enabled them to regularly fulfil their conjugal duties with each of their four wives, ensuring that the whole village was aware of its chief's potent virility, which in turn did wonders for his authority ... Babrak asked the way a couple of times, and finally stopped in front of a little stall with nothing to distinguish it from all the others. The shop window was empty, apart from a few musical instruments and an old concert poster. It was squashed between a mechanic's workshop and a tyre-repair place. No one took any notice of him. He walked in, and a small bell rang. A man stood up from the stool he'd been sitting on. He wore a turban and a long, unkempt beard. Babrak noticed that he was missing all the fingers of his left hand. There was any number of amputees in Afghanistan — people who'd either been wounded in the war, or punished by the Taliban for diverging from Islamic rules.

'*Salaam Alaykum*', said the man softly. He'd spoken in Pashtun rather than Dari, like most uneducated Taliban. 'May you be in good health.'

'*Wa-Alaykum as-Salam,*' replied Babrak. 'May your body be strong and your family be well; blessings for a long life.'

The man ogled the bag that Babrak had put down.

'May I offer you some tea?' he suggested.

'With pleasure.'

The man clapped his hands, and a boy of about 12 appeared from behind the curtain at the back of the shop. He was wearing baggy trousers and a low-cut top that revealed his hairless chest. Babrak wondered if he was a *bacha bazi.* The man curtly ordered two *chai siaa.* While they were waiting for their tea, they discussed business, and how it had never been this good in Kabul, *Insha'Allah.* Once the black tea was served, Babrak began.

'I'm a policeman,' he said. 'Your name was given to me by a work colleague. During one of our operations, I came across a certain number of rather interesting Western magazines. It seems to me that they are very valuable.'

'I'd like to see them.'

Babrak opened his bag and took out the pile of magazines. His companion's eyes widened momentarily as Babrak laid them out on the table. The he flicked through them unhurriedly, one by one, using his good hand to turn the pages, and his stump to hold them still. Babrak soon realised that he was making two piles — one of the magazines featuring only men, and one of those depicting both men and women. There were three focussing on sado-masochism, and he put those aside. Almost fifteen minutes had passed by the time the middleman put down the last magazine.

'It's a good collection,' he said. 'The models are young and Western, the magazines are new — it's obvious they were flown in. I'd be happy to buy it from you. How much do you want?'

'How much will you give me?'

'I could offer you a hundred afghanis for each of the Russian and European magazines, and two hundred for the American ones. For the three leather magazines, my price would likewise be two hundred afghanis.' He took out his calculator. 'There are 56 magazines here, so I'm offering you fifteen thousand afghanis.'

'You must be joking,' cried Babrak. 'They're worth five times that!'

This was the usual start to a negotiation of this scale. They haggled for about twenty minutes, and finally settled on a price of twenty-five thousand two hundred afghanis. The middleman pulled a wad of dirty notes from his tunic like a magician. He laboriously counted out the amount, and then Babrak carefully counted it, too.

'*Allahu Akbar,* God wanted us to do business together, my brother. May Allah be with you,' said the middleman as Babrak walked out of the door. 'May He guide your steps back to my door, with many more lovely magazines!'

Babrak took his leave, astonished as much by the Taliban's welcome as by the amount he had paid.

Osama had arranged to meet the Etisalat technician at the central Kabul restaurant Herat, near Cinema Park, a popular gathering place for families. It was a much more luxurious establishment than he usually frequented. He walked through the main restaurant into the garden at the back. A few makeshift tents had been erected among the leafless trees; each was heated by a brazier and contained a beautifully laid table. Chickens cackled in cages stacked along the wall. In the middle of the garden, another cage contained a small deer and a goat kid, nibbling at grain as they waited to be barbecued. He sat down at a table, hoping that the environment would put the technician at ease. He had the twenty five thousand two hundred afghanis that Babrak had returned with in his pocket, along with the five hundred from the informers' box. That would come to at least three times, maybe four times, their guest's monthly salary, so he felt confident that they'd be able to close the deal. Babrak joined him once he'd parked the car, putting his folding-stock Kalashnikov on the table as half the other guests had done, and greedily falling on the upmarket menu. A few minutes after noon, a young man appeared. He had long hair and a moustache, and was wearing a worn shirt tucked into Western-style trousers, and a brown leather jacket. The jacket had a massive 'Nike by Adidas' logo on it — a typical fake from the Peshawar or Islamabad markets.

'That's him,' said Babrak.

When he noticed Osama and Babrak, the young man smiled

shyly and walked slowly towards them. Osama stood up.

'I am qomaandaan Osama Kandar.'

The young man smiled awkwardly at finding himself with Murder Squad policemen.

'Thank you for accepting our invitation,' began Osama. 'If God wills it, your assistance may help Babrak and me solve the murder investigation we are currently working on.'

'I would be very happy to help the police catch a criminal, with the help of God.'

'Do you have the information we need?'

'Yes, I brought it all with me.'

Realising that the young man was waiting for him to produce the cash, Osama got down to business.

'I have the money in my pocket. We'd like to wait and see what you're offering before we give it to you.'

'I want to emigrate to Canada,' apologised the young man. 'I need a lot of money for the plane ticket and my first few months there.' He took a brown envelope out of his jacket. 'This is what I have. We only keep the data for two months; we don't have the I.T. capacity to store it for longer.'

Osama glanced through the printout. It was eight pages long; Wali Wadi seemed to make calls day and night. He would need an entire team of people to check all these numbers. He soon saw that certain numbers featured frequently. Three of them were Afghan numbers starting with the (079) Kabul code. He continued reading. When he saw the international numbers, his heart started racing. There were only two. The first started with 4122, and the other with 964. He swung the piece of paper around so the young man could read it.

'What countries are these for?'

'The first is Switzerland — 22 is the Geneva code. The second is Iraq — it's a Baghdad number.'

'Can we find out whose?'

The young man shrugged.

'I've looked. It's for the Ministry of Reconstruction.'

'And the Swiss number?'

'It's on the red list.'

Osama didn't know what to make of this surprising news. Switzerland was an important financial location, and home to lots of sensitive business deals, so it wasn't surprising that a middleman should have business contacts there. But Iraq? He took the wad of notes out of his pocket.

'You've done well. Here's your money. It goes without saying that you should keep this deal quiet. Would you like to have lunch with us?'

'I'd rather not,' stammered the young man. 'If I was seen …'

He stood up hurriedly and rushed off as if the devil was on his heels. Osama shrugged his shoulders.

'Are you hungry?'

'Yes!' exclaimed Babrak.

'Don't eat too much. Remember, we're eating at the Hamad café this evening.'

'How could I forget?' replied Babrak, laughing. 'But I've every faith in Gulbudin; I know he'll finish anything I might leave on my plate. It's as if he still thinks he's in the mountains being a mujahedeen.'

'We didn't have anything to eat,' replied Osama, with a faraway look in his eyes. 'Lots of us were very affected by that. Some have been frugal ever since. And others …'

They ordered. Pilau rice with grilled chicken and lamb ravioli for Babrak; lentil salad with lamb kidneys and spinach for Osama. The meal was brought with Afghan bread and delicious homemade yoghurt. There was no cutlery — you ate with your hands in this luxurious setting, as you did everywhere else.

'So, what do you think?' asked Babrak with his mouth full. 'Iraq, Switzerland … we're moving off our usual patch.'

Osama finished chewing a stubborn piece of lamb before replying.

'There were at least thirty calls over a period of two months — so about one every other day. Maybe the two countries were involved in a joint deal, with the same supplier and the same middleman.'

'Could Wali Wadi have been trying to get information on a deal that had taken place in Iraq, so he could copy it?'

'I don't think so: he wouldn't have called that often — he would just have gone there a couple of times.'

They stopped talking to concentrate on their meal. It was spicy and delicious; the grains of rice were unusually long. Osama had never eaten such refined food — there were advantages to having money. Babrak was thrilled, and gobbled it all up noisily and messily. Osama smiled. The young man came from a Shiite family that was even poorer than his own, and completely illiterate. The fact that he'd done so well in his studies, coming from a family like that, was a miracle in itself.

'Who might be able to help us?' asked Babrak, once they'd finished their meal and he'd wiped his dripping hands.

'Logically, I should ask the Swiss embassy or, in the case of Iraq, the FBI. It has a branch at the American embassy that is part of the International Contract Corruption Task Force.'

'Are you going to contact them?'

'No, it's too soon. I'd like to have a clearer idea of what we're getting into first. There are powerful foreign interests behind this case. People who are doing everything in their power to stop us progressing with our investigation.'

Babrak wiped his chin again — it was still covered in sauce — and burst out laughing.

'Those Westerners aren't that bright, boss!'

'Actually, you're wrong; they're very bright, in fact. Everyone who's underestimated them has come to regret it. Look at the Taliban — they were swept out of office in three weeks.'

Babrak stood up. It had taken Osama a while to get used to this young generation who spoke differently from him, and dressed (and often thought) like Westerners. Initially, he'd been shocked. Then he'd started appreciating their keen intelligence, their naturalness, and even their casual manners. These young people might be selfish, but they were in favour of peace, and would rather spend their money on electronic gadgets than go to war. Even the violent game of buzkashi was on the wane; the young preferred more civilised sports like football and baseball. These young people were the only thing protecting the future from a generation of uneducated and violent young Taliban.

THE FORMER TALIBAN MEMBER chosen by the minister to blow up the Hamad Café wiped away the sweat dripping into his eyes. Abdul Hakat, for that was his name, still couldn't believe his good fortune in being selected for this mission. He was a little afraid that he might fail. What if they didn't let him in to the café — would he still be paid what they'd promised?

Since spending two years in prison, the slightest stress gave Abdul panic attacks. He hadn't been an important-enough member of the Taliban to be sent to Guantanamo, but he had been severely tortured before his imprisonment, and still bore the scars of his brutal treatment at the hands of the NDS. Since then, he had occasionally earned a handful of afghanis by denouncing someone — usually someone who had done no wrong, and then found it very hard to prove to government officers that he was innocent. The mission Abdul had been given was to establish formal proof that the manager of the Hamad Café's security arrangements were inadequate. In order to do so, he'd been given a fake bomb-belt. His job was to enter the bar and leave the belt in the toilets; a policeman would then collect it and present it to the owner as proof.

Abdul Hakat had been called into NDS headquarters by an important policeman who had introduced himself as a friend of the owner of the Hamad Café, who was in conflict with his manager over security arrangements. Abdul wasn't worried — security arrangements were an everyday subject of conversation in Kabul: when they were too rigorous, they created endless queues that put off the punters, but when they were too lax, people went elsewhere … Abdul took off his motorbike helmet and slipped into a recess between two houses. He was very early — the café didn't open until 8.00pm — and he didn't want to spend money sitting in some other establishment. He wrapped himself in a blanket as protection from the cold, and waited.

TOWARDS THE END of the afternoon, having spent three hours on everyday business, Osama discreetly left the police station.

After wandering around the area's narrow lanes for about twenty minutes, carrying out various manoeuvres he'd been taught in Moscow to shake off anyone following him, he hailed a cab. In the taxi he wrapped a scarf around the lower part of his face and crammed a *pakol* on his head. It wasn't a sophisticated disguise, but he was convinced he wasn't being followed, and just wanted to avoid being recognised. He hopped out of the taxi in the middle of a traffic jam, and took another going in the opposite direction.

'The old royal palace,' he told the driver.

The journey took longer than he'd hoped, on account of all the road works. A few poorly paid labourers were breaking up the soil using only hand tools, without the benefit of any modern machinery. The American contractor who'd won the job would make tens of thousands of dollars per hundred metres, for the cost of a few expatriates hunkered down in the city centre.

Once the taxi had passed the still impressive ruins of the old palace, it turned in front of the museum — a pathetic building with, bizarrely, the remains of a steam engine in its garden. Next, the driver turned down an unpaved lane.

'Are you sure this is right?' asked Osama anxiously.

'Absolutely.'

Chilstone was one of Kabul's poorest areas — no running water, no refuse collection, no public services at all. Osama got out next to a small corner-shop and walked down a stinking lane, doing his best to avoid the filth all over the ground. The squat cob houses were crammed up against each other, or separated by wasteland that had been turned into makeshift cemeteries. The inhabitants were too poor to afford proper gravestones, so they'd used simple pieces of bevelled stone. There were a few green flags draped over the graves of those who'd died a violent death, victim to bombs or the Taliban. Approximately half the graves were decorated in this way. A cemetery, a block of houses, a cemetery, a block of houses … Osama walked through the squalid lanes for about fifteen minutes. The people living in this deprived neighbourhood were almost all Aimaqs, an ethnic group of Mongol nomads who lived mainly in central and western Afghanistan, and tended to be very poor. Osama was Baloch, an ethnic group with Persian origins, whose members lived almost exclusively in the southwest. But when he was growing up in Chahar Borjak, he'd become friendly with some boys from the small Aimaq community, and their fate had touched him deeply. He was still close to a few of them, including the man he had come to see.

He walked deeper into the neighbourhood, trying not to focus on the overwhelming stink. The area housed two tanneries, a rubbish dump covering several hectares, and an abattoir. Sheep and cow carcasses were allowed to rot in open pits without the council doing anything about it. He wondered how people managed to breathe in the summertime, when the heat rose to 40 degrees. After a few hundred metres, he stopped to ask a child for directions.

'Do you know where I can find the public scribe, sahib Kalkana's office?'

The child pointed to a side street barely visible in the dusk. Night was starting to fall.

'Nazdik.'

Not far, which didn't mean much — the office might be a hundred metres away, or two kilometres. Osama finally came to a dilapidated house with the door open. Two oil lamps lit a dark room in which a dozen men were waiting. The door was so low that he had to stoop to enter. Inside, the smell was even stronger. Osama greeted the men, and continued down a narrow corridor. An old man sat at a rickety desk with a trembling candle on top of it. He was so thin that his skin seemed stuck to his bones. Osama bent towards him.

'I'm a friend of sahib Kalkana. Tell him that Osama would like to see him.'

The secretary couldn't hear a word. Osama had to repeat his message twice in the old man's ear. When he finally understood, he struggled painfully to his feet and disappeared behind a curtain. A moment later, he came back with a man as short as Osama was tall. Abdul Kalkana was very dark-skinned, with a bushy beard and the characteristic almond-shaped eyes of the Aimaq. He embraced Osama warmly.

'You? You're lucky — I'm just between jobs, and have a few

minutes to spare. I'm happy to see you. Come inside for a moment.'

Kalkana showed him into a small office furnished simply with a desk, two chairs, and an overflowing bookcase. Kalkana's professional materials, a computer and laser printer, occupied pride of place on the desk. They were switched off. In this part of Kabul, there was only electricity for an hour or two a day. Osama noticed lots of different knick-knacks on the shelves — old writing cases, goose quills, different kinds of inkstands. Kalkana had always been a collector. Alongside these work-related objects were other, stranger items, among which he recognised several kinds of dolls. Malalai had told him what they were for. In the old days, they were used in the treatment of women, who would point at the affected part of the body on the doll so that the daktar didn't have to touch them. Since the rise of the Taliban, there had been no need for these dolls, as male doctors were not allowed to treat female patients — even with recourse to a doll. They were now just relics of a bygone time.

'I see that you haven't moved, or had any improvements done,' commented Osama. 'Why don't you leave this place?'

'Rent is expensive,' said his friend. 'And also, I don't want to leave my brothers. I like it here.'

As a public scribe, Kalkana wrote all kinds of documents for the illiterate people who required his services: letters of complaint to the government, marriage contracts, job applications, wills, letters to far-flung family … Sometimes, the requests were a little more exotic: Kalkana had once boasted to Osama that he wrote the most beautiful love letters in the whole of Afghanistan. Sadly, there were fewer and fewer requests for this kind of thing: the young people phoned rather than wrote, unless you counted the horribly misspelt SMS messages that didn't seem to put off their recipients. Despite being clever enough to be a teacher or even a university lecturer, Kalkana had chosen to devote his life to the Aimaq, and never wavered from his vocation as a public scribe. It was a very pure state of mind, for which Osama admired him greatly.

'What would you like to drink?' Kalkana asked.

'A *chai sabz*.'

Kalkana walked over to a gas ring.

'There's no point asking my secretary to make it — I have to tell him everything three times. He used to be a great musician, and your friends have made him almost deaf.'

'I noticed that. What happened to him?'

'He lost an eardrum in a shell fired by your Northern Alliance chums in 1996. Direct fire on this neighbourhood, where everyone knew there wasn't a single combatant! Then, in 1999, the Taliban arrested him because his beard wasn't bushy enough. When he couldn't hear what they were saying, they beat him so hard with an electric cable that he lost his hearing in the other ear, as well as his sight in one eye. That's this country for you: an innocent, talented man, whose music was once well known, is tortured by both camps without the slightest respect for his human dignity. This country is insane, Osama. I don't think the war will ever cease.'

'And you will never cease being outraged. You're proof that there's still hope for our country.'

His friend came back with the teapot.

'Leave it,' said Osama. 'I'll pour.'

'I couldn't.'

'Allow me, please — it's an honour to serve you.'

'You're my guest — let me.'

They haggled like this for a moment, arguing over the symbolic teapot. In the end, Osama took the glass that his friend held out to him.

'It's time for prayers,' he said. 'Can I leave you for a moment?'

'Please.'

Osama took off his shoes, unfurled a rug that had been rolled up against a wall, and prayed. When he stood up, he felt calmer.

'I've come to ask you a favour.'

'The mighty qomaandaan Kandar needs help from a humble Aimaq scribe? What's going on, Osama? Are you in trouble?'

'Let's just say that I'm working on a difficult investigation and that certain people, including my boss, would prefer that it came to nothing. Do you understand?'

'What do you need me to do?'

'You told me that one of your cousins was a pathologist in Turkey.

Is that still the case?'

'Qassam? Yes, I think so. I spoke to him in January; he was still working in Istanbul, in one of the city's biggest hospitals. What do you need from him?'

'I'd like you to call him as soon as possible. I need a kit that tests for the remains of powder on a person's hands. He must use them all the time. I need a well-known brand, within the expiry date. If possible, two.'

'OK, I'll ask him. Should I have them delivered to your office?'

'No, here. I need them as soon as possible.'

'The post doesn't come here, Osama,' said his friend. 'But I have a PO box at the central post office — I could go and collect the parcel from there.'

'Ask your cousin to send it express. I don't yet know how or when I'll make it up to you, but I will.'

Osama hugged him.

'*Lotfan,* my friend. It's very important.'

He departed with a slightly lighter heart.

Around eight in the evening, Babrak left his house, excited to be meeting up with his boss and Gulbudin. He'd just had a big row with his wife, who'd been making his life hell ever since he'd told her he was intending to take a second wife. She'd threatened to leave with his two children, which had led to a bigger and more explosive fight than they'd ever had before. It was a theoretical threat, of course, because the law categorically forbade women from abandoning the family home. And yet he'd left under a torrent of abuse. Babrak could feel his beliefs wobbling. Was it really fair to take a second wife if the first was so against it? He loved her and didn't want her to be unhappy, but it was hard to know how to behave with women when there were so many contradictory messages. Having decreed that women should benefit from new, if not equal rights, the Karzaï government had recently introduced a law that allowed a husband to renounce his wives without any financial compensation if they refused to carry out their conjugal duties. The law had entered a couple's private life, controlling what they could and could not do, even in bed. No one really understood what rights women could claim these days. So what was he supposed to think, when he was just a simple policeman?

He got on his motorbike and slipped into the traffic.

OSAMA AND GULBUDIN were waiting for Babrak at a table in the 'VIP' box they'd been given when they arrived at the Hamad Café. They both had a glass of mango juice in front of them, but Gulbudin hadn't touched his. He looked tense, and was grimacing with pain.

'No better?' asked Osama, anxiously.

'No, qomaandaan. I'm sorry.'

The explosion that had taken off Gulbudin's leg several years before had left several shell fragments in his body. One of them was near the spinal column, and he suffered awful nerve pain whenever it shifted a few millimetres. In those moments, Gulbudin was in agony. And it could happen at any time, without the slightest warning.

'Do you have any morphine with you?'

'No, it's at my place.'

He was white as a sheet, with big beads of sweat appearing on his forehead. Osama wiped them off with his napkin.

'You can't carry on like this. I'll take you home in my car.'

'But … Babrak …'

'He'll understand. We can do it tomorrow night instead.'

These bouts of pain were as short-lived as they were sudden. They were usually over in a few hours.

'OK,' murmured Gulbudin. 'I'll call him on his mobile to explain.'

'I'll help you walk.'

'Qomaandaan, I saw one of our policemen near the entrance. Can we go out the back? I wouldn't like any of our men to see me in this state.'

'No problem. My 4x4 is parked around the back, anyway. I'll ask security to let us out.'

IT TOOK BABRAK less than half an hour to reach his favourite music café. He quietly stashed his pistol and two grenades under the saddle.

It wasn't that he was frightened, exactly, but Osama's warnings had put him vaguely on edge. It was the first time he'd worked on an investigation implicating a member of government — and a powerful one at that. The invisible involvement of Westerners in the case also added to his anxiety. Like many of his countrymen, Babrak jeered at them in public, but secretly feared their power.

Bicycles and mopeds were parked all around the café, though at a certain distance on account of the security barriers. He avoided the security search by flashing his police card, and walked into the bar. The clientele was, of course, entirely male. The atmosphere was happy and relaxed, even though people were only drinking fruit juice and fizzy drinks. An uncensored Lady Gaga video was showing. The singer was strutting her obscene stuff to the noisy delight of the crowd. Babrak started looking for Osama and Gulbudin.

Abdul Hakat looked at his watch. It was time. He put on the belt. It was heavy — much heavier than he'd expected, maybe three kilos. It looked very like a real one, as described in the popular press. There was no manual detonator on his, of course, but … he was suddenly seized by a horrible doubt. He unpicked the hem: the belt was stuffed with a sort of grey putty. Suspicious, he took out his knife, cut some off, and pulled out his lighter.

The contractor who'd assassinated Wali Wadi was watching Abdul Hakat through binoculars, from the back of a big armoured 4x4 parked about one hundred metres away. He was with one of his men, a Spaniard who'd been in the Engineers. He had seen Osama and Gulbudin enter the bar, and then Babrak, and was waiting for the shahid to get a move on.

'What's that bloody idiot doing?' he grumbled.

'What do you reckon?' asked the Spaniard. 'Guess!'

'I don't feel like guessing.'

'It looks to me as if he's trying to set light to the C5 with his lighter.' He sniggered. '*Maricon!* He can try, but that C5 won't blow up, not even if he uses a flamethrower. No detonator, no boom, *nada.*'

Hakat suddenly let go of the piece of semtex and rubbed his hand in pain.

'Fucking idiot burnt himself,' said the Spaniard.

'Oh well, we chose the right candidate. What a loser! I wish he'd just get in there so we could be done with it. I've had enough.'

They saw Abdul Hakat readjust his coat and walk out of the shadows towards the café.

'Hang on a minute. We told him to wear Western clothes!'

'He is wearing Western clothes. Jeans, trainers, and a T-shirt, just like you said.'

'They might be Western, but they're all scuzzy! Look at him — he looks like a tramp. He'll never get through security dressed like that. What's wrong with you? Why didn't you check what he was wearing?'

'Those guys could wear Prada and still look like shit. What'll we do?' asked the Spaniard, horrified.

'Go get him! Quick. I'll stash the transmission equipment.'

The Spaniard returned a few moments later with the Taliban guy in tow. He seemed stunned by the presence of the 4x4. The contractor wound down his window.

'Do you speak English?'

The man only understood Dari.

'Shoes. T-Shirt. No good,' the Spaniard jabbered, pointing at the clothes.

The contractor soon lost patience with Hakat's confusion.

'Shit! What size shoes do you wear?' he asked the Spaniard.

'11.'

The contractor looked at Hakat. Then he sighed and took off his own trainers and T-shirt, and held them out to him.

'He'll have to wear them. With the jacket open so the T-shirt is visible.'

Abdul Hakat put on the new clothes. Wearing the immaculate, crimson New Balance trainers and an Abercrombie T-shirt, he finally looked like a Westernised young Kabuli — the best style for getting through security. He gave the thumbs up, thrilled.

'Goot goot!'

'That's right, good. Dickhead! Right, get him out of here,' instructed the contractor, furious at having had to give up his new shoes.

Hakat trotted off towards the café entrance.

'Lucky he didn't understand what the hell was going on,' said the Spaniard. 'Westerners run everything in Kabul — he must think we're testing the security arrangements because we want to buy the Hamad Café. Anyway, it's cool. His jacket is perfect — it hides the bomb.'

'Yeah.'

The bomb belt was attached by two straps hidden underneath the T-shirt, and just a narrow strip at the belt. The three kilos of explosives sat in the middle of the back, along the spine, and would get through the search as long as the security guard, reassured by Hakat's appearance, made do with frisking his legs, belt, chest, and hips. The Spaniard pulled the remote control out from underneath his seat and pushed a lever. A green light came on with a beep. The contractor ground his teeth.

'Christ, only the Russians would invent such a noisy remote for a detonator!'

Abdul Hakat had reached the security guards. He held his breath. Less than ten seconds later, he was in. The contractor started his stopwatch. Abdul had been told to order a drink and keep the receipt as further proof of his presence in the bar. The contractor counted forty seconds — time enough for Hakat to reach the bar, which was in the middle of the café. Wherever they were sitting, Kandar and his men would be hit by the full force of the bomb. The contractor looked at the Spaniard, who nodded. He pushed the button on the remote control. The roof and walls of the café vanished in a flurry of flames and a rumbling of hell.

He drove off. Mission accomplished.

8.

OSAMA WOKE WITH A START at about one o'clock in the morning. He sat up in bed. His wife was shaking him.

'What's the matter, *Habibi?*'

'Your phone — it keeps ringing. It must be important.'

Osama felt his way out of bed. The bedside lamp was broken, and neither he nor Malalai had had time to buy a new bulb. He accidentally kicked a chair, which hurt. He swore, and ran to the living room, where he'd left his mobile phone.

'Yes?'

'Qomaandaan Kandar?'

It was a woman's voice — an unknown woman. Osama could hear the panic in her voice.

'Speaking. Who are you?'

'I'm Babrak's wife. Your deputy.'

'What's going on?'

'Babrak was having a drink with you and Gulbudin at the Hamad Café this evening, wasn't he?'

'Yes, but we had to leave earlier than expected. We left without seeing Babrak. Why, hasn't he come home?'

The woman burst into tears.

'It said on the radio there's been an explosion at the Hamad Café.'

Usually, explosions resonated throughout the city, sometimes shaking windows several kilometres away. Osama hadn't heard anything that night, but then Kabul was a big city of three million people, and it went on for kilometres.

'I'll find out,' said Osama, his heart hammering.

He immediately turned on his police radio.

'Central?'

'Good evening, sir, how may I help you?'

Osama recognised the slightly upper-class voice of Nouora, a Tajik woman who was the night-shift radio operator. Her rich businessman husband had been killed by the Taliban, and all his assets stolen by regime collaborators. His wife had never been able to get her house back, and she survived as best she could on this difficult job. She was famous at police headquarters because, chic Kabuli that she was, she spoke a sophisticated Dari that some of the policemen who only spoke basic Pashtun didn't understand.

'It's Osama Kandar.'

'Oh, good evening, qomaandaan. Delighted to hear your voice — it's been a long time. What can I do for you?'

'It seems there's been a bomb?'

'Yes, at the Hamad Café, two hours ago. A man blew himself up in the middle of all those young people. Total carnage. At the first count, there were twenty-five dead and eighty wounded. Another of those deranged Taliban!'

'Do you know if any of our men were among the victims?'

'I don't have any details. Would you like me to put you through to someone on site? The intelligence service is there.'

'No, thank you. I'll go myself.'

He dressed quickly, watched by his anxious wife. She had never met Babrak, but knew how fond Osama was of him. He took his usual weapons, as well as his rifle, as he hadn't arranged an escort for this unexpected outing. For a moment, he wondered if this might be a ruse to get him out of the house without protection, but he had no choice. The night watchman, all muffled up in a double-thick coat, greeted him with surprise.

'You're going out, hajji?

'Yes, there's been a bomb in town. No one's touched my car?'

'No one.' The watchman spat on the floor. 'I've been watching it all night.'

Osama roared off. He soon came across an ambulance with its sirens blaring, and decided to follow it. Another soon joined them. A bad sign: it implied that the building had collapsed on the victims, who were still being pulled out two hours after the explosion. He passed Charahi Haji Yaqoob and then drove down a series of roads with modern buildings on either side. Most had been hit in the 1996 bombing of Kabul, and some were still open to the elements, with families living in them. These disembowelled, lit-up buildings were a sight you never forgot.

Osama soon saw a knot of flashing lights up ahead. Jumpy soldiers were blocking the road, fingers on their triggers. He abandoned his car and continued on foot, flashing his police card to pass through a second roadblock. The true scope of the disaster became more and more apparent as he drew nearer to the site. Rescue teams and police were running about all over the place as the lights flashed. He was stopped at a final roadblock fifty metres from the Hamad Café. At this one, American and Turkish Coalition soldiers were backing up the ANA. Plainclothes NDS officers were everywhere, recognisable by their well-displayed pistols. One of them saw Osama and let him through without asking for his card.

Osama was familiar with suicide bombs, and the sight was tragically ordinary. The front of the building had been ripped open, and blackened by flames. Debris had scattered everywhere, along with bits of bodies that had not yet been collected by the emergency services. On one car bonnet he noticed a hand that had been cleanly removed from the rest of the body; it was a pale hand, with smooth fingers, clearly the hand of a young man. He carried on walking through the rubble. The usual smell was in the air. It wasn't the gunpowder used by amateur terrorists, but C5. The Pakistanis gave it out to various terrorist groups, while denying this to the Americans. Only the most organised Taliban groups used it because it required a proper detonator, whereas gunpowder only needed a fuse. Osama saw his counterpart Reza, head of the intelligence department. Reza looked surprised to see him.

'What are you doing here?'

'I was here with Gulbudin earlier. My deputy Babrak was

supposed to meet us, but we left before he arrived. And he hasn't been home.'

The intelligence man looked upset, but not terribly. He'd seen so much death these last thirty years.

'We haven't started the identification process yet. We've put the bodies in that alley, behind the main building, if you want to have a look. Er … Osama, I don't need to paint a picture of the state they're in, do I?'

It was even worse there. Rescue teams were working on a few of the wounded who hadn't yet been evacuated. Most seemed seriously burned, or crippled, with their limbs torn off. Several wore bloody bandages around their eyes, which had been blinded by the blast or by fragments. The air was filled with their groans. A little further on, a large number of bodies had been simply laid out on the ground, hurriedly wrapped in old, bloodstained sheets. Osama saw plainclothes policemen gathered around a headless body, slightly apart from the others. The head, which was in a shocking state, had been put down a little further away. The head of a shahid always became separated from the body in the blast, flung away from it semi-intact. That was how they were so easily identified. But that wasn't the case here. Osama had never seen such a badly destroyed face.

He started walking down the rows of bodies, bending over each corpse, pulling back the sheet covering it. Each was a horror show. At the eighth body, his heart missed a beat. An arm was protruding from the sheet, encased in a torn, blue leather jacket oddly like Babrak's. The sheet was at a strange angle, as if covering only half a body. He pulled it gently aside, already knowing what he would see. Babrak was lying on his back. The top part of his body was in reasonable shape, but the entire bottom half had been blown off at the pelvis. A fragment of glass had hit his right eye and gone straight through the skull. He looked calm, rested, with only the terrible injuries testifying to the violence of his death. Osama took his hand. He felt paralysed, unable to breathe, his heart in a vise. Babrak was like his son. And now he was dead. Who could have done something like this?

He slowly recited the prayer of the dead, and then stood up in a cold fury. The intelligence department head was busy yelling at one of his deputies for not having started the identification of the martyr.

'Do you have a moment, Reza?'

'Well?'

Seeing Osama's pale face, he went quiet.

'Your deputy? He's one of the dead?'

Osama nodded.

'Killed outright — a fragment through the eye. He wouldn't have felt a thing. Do you have anything yet?'

'A little.' Reza took Osama aside. 'He blew himself up, that's for sure. At first sight, it seems he acted alone. The security guard who let him in has miraculously survived. He recognised the body from its clothes. The man was wearing a pair of jeans, a jacket, a tight T-shirt, and red trainers … Western clothes, in short — not what a Taliban shahid would wear. The security guard said he frisked him as usual.'

'Do you believe him?'

The cop spat on the floor.

'Yes. He's too shaken up to invent it.'

'It's weird,' said Osama. 'The head is extremely damaged.'

'Ah, you noticed that, too? What do you think?'

'He wasn't wearing the bomb around his waist. He must have had it around his legs, or against his back. The trajectory of the head being torn off wasn't that of a typical bomb.'

'I thought the same thing,' said Reza. 'Which would explain why the security guard didn't find anything.'

'Has he been identified?'

'He had his papers on him, but they were torn to pieces in the explosion. I'm going to ask the scientific department to try to put them back together, but it won't be any good — they're too damaged. I'd rather use his fingerprints and what's left of his face.'

'There's probably a file on him already, on account of being a Taliban,' said Osama. 'Will you let me know as soon as you have any news?'

'Of course.'

'Can I ask you a favour? Use the best pathologist for the autopsy.'

'I see who you want to avoid … but who would you like me to use?'

'Daktar Katoun. Can you do that for me?'

'OK. I'll call him now.'

'I'm going to look at the shahid's body,' said Osama by way of farewell.

He went back to the corpse. With a wave of his hand, he dismissed the policemen gathered around it. He looked so grave that even the NDS men left. Osama pulled on a pair of gloves and crouched down. The martyr had been cut in two by the explosion. The bottom part of his body was in a decent state up to the pelvis, but the chest had disappeared, as if it had been crushed. Without the head he was impossible to identify; and even with it, there would be difficulties. Osama looked at the trousers — a tattered pair of holey jeans — and then at the shoes. They were almost new, the same bright red as the blood all around. He gently pulled one off. The martyr wasn't wearing any socks, despite the cold, and his foot was black with dirt. Osama stood up and went home without greeting anyone.

OSAMA SLEPT BADLY that night, haunted by images of Babrak's disfigured face, so calm in death. In the early hours, Malalai pulled him close.

'It'll never end. It's not fair.'

'He was only thirty. A clever, likeable boy. A brilliant police officer. I thought of him as our son.'

Osama had tears in his eyes, but he managed to control himself. His anger was turning to rage.

'No one is safe. They're blowing themselves up all over the place. What can we do against maniacs like them, Osama? Shut ourselves up at home?'

'It is a funny coincidence, though.'

'You think his death is linked to your investigation?'

'I'm wondering. It looked like an indiscriminate attack, but I do think it's strange that some guy would blow himself up exactly where Babrak, Gulbudin, and I were meeting.'

'You're frightening me,' said Malalai, her face pale.

Osama stood up. The tiles were cold, even though Malalai had put logs in the stove. He could hear the rain pouring down, which was quite rare even at this time of year. As he took his shower, he thought of how Babrak's wife reacted when he dropped by to give her the news at four o'clock in the morning. She had collapsed without a sound — not crying, just trembling all over, which was more upsetting than if she'd started to scream. Her two children were awake, despite the late hour, and he could see the fear in their eyes, as if they'd understood that they would never see their father again. The little girl was feverishly clutching a kind of stuffed donkey.

Dismissing these dark thoughts, Osama put on a new shirt and a tie — something he hadn't worn for ten years. Malalai wept as she watched him dress, pick up his gun, and check the cartridge.

'I'm going to try and find out what happened,' he said simply.

His car and the protective pick-up were waiting outside, motors idling. The men were serious and tense. The news of his deputy's death had already been around police headquarters. Babrak had been very popular. It was barely dawn when Osama arrived at the office. He walked over to the intelligence department. Reza was there, unshaven, his hair a mess.

'Hello, Osama.' He pushed a glass of steaming tea towards him. 'I have slept, on the camp bed. Not much, as you can imagine.'

'Do you have any more news?'

'We've identified the shahid. His name was Abdul Hakat. He was a former Taliban who spent two years in prison after the fall of the regime.'

'Was he well known?'

'Yes and no, *bale, na.* Enough to be on file, but not enough to be under serious surveillance. He was a little guy. He'd been keeping his nose clean since his spell in prison. He sometimes worked as an NDS informer — he'd denounced a dozen-or-so people.'

'What do the NDS say?'

'You know them. Those bastards don't tell me *anything*. They'll never admit that the guy worked for them when he came out of prison. Hakat might have been bluffing or double bluffing. Or maybe his old Taliban friends re-converted him.'

'Have you begun the local investigation?'

'The entire family is downstairs in the cells. We're putting pressure on the brother — he's another of those bloody Taliban. He'll spit it all out, I promise. We've got three days!'

The penal code was a strange mixture of Western law and Afghan tradition: police custody was limited to seventy-two hours by law, but nothing prevented police from torturing suspects during that time, and in terrorism cases they rarely failed to do so.

'Has he started talking?'

'He swears that his brother was no longer a real Taliban, and would never have blown himself up. Yeah, right. Do you want to see him?'

'Yes.'

They made their way down to the basement. A narrow staircase led to a long, wide corridor made from raw concrete and lit at ten-metre intervals by a neon strip. The atmosphere was gloomy, and the smell almost unbearable. There was a row of doors on either side — some completely solid, some with a small grill. These were the interrogation rooms and the cells. They walked into one of them, a windowless room measuring about twenty square metres. There was a heavy wooden table in the middle, with hooks at each corner to enable a man to be spread-eagled, and a few rickety chairs scattered around. A naked man was bound to one of the chairs, with his arms behind his back. Two cops stood over him. The man's nose was broken, he had blood all over his face, and one eye was swollen shut from a particularly harsh blow. His feet were purple from being beaten with a cosh. He was covered in vomit, urine, and faeces. The cops in the intelligence section were not soft. One of them lifted the cosh he was holding and brought it down hard on the prisoner's face. Blood spurted as the man screamed.

Reza took one of the policemen by the arm.

'So, what's he producing?' he whispered.

'Same thing. This bastard swears his brother was no longer a Taliban — he'd only joined them to get ahead, not out of conviction. This man is listed as dangerous, too. We've had cause to watch him every now and then.'

'Is he hiding something?'

'I don't think so. But we'll keep working on him anyway.'

They went back upstairs.

'Let's go to his house. You come, too,' said Reza.

Abdul Hakat lived in a Pashtun shantytown to the south of the city. Fierce-looking cops were guarding his house, a cob hovel with mounds of stinking rubbish piled out front. A crowd of hostile, bushy-bearded men were prowling around, periodically yelling threatening curses. The atmosphere was electric.

'This is a Taliban neighbourhood,' remarked Osama.

'I don't give a damn. If those bastards think we're going to ask permission to do our job, they've got another think coming,' said Reza.

Osama was the first to walk into the house. In the corner, a cluster of women sat enveloped in their burqas. Five blue shapes of similar size and weight. No way of telling who was in there, on account of the mesh hiding their eyes. An armed soldier was guarding them, with a finger on the trigger of his Kalashnikov.

'Who are these women?'

'Abdul Hakat's mother, plus his father's other two wives, and his brother's two wives.'

'Abdul wasn't married?'

'No.'

'Where is the father?'

'His heart packed up during the interrogation; my men may have been a little heavy-handed. He's in hospital.'

'How's he doing?'

'Badly. The daktar who examined him thinks he's going to die.'

Great. Osama spotted a letter on a sort of wooden workbench.

'Is that the farewell letter?'

'Yes. His mother said that someone else wrote it for him — he couldn't read or write.'

Osama read it. It was a short letter written in Pashtun, full of references to Allah, and explaining that kafirs and bad Muslims must die. The letter concluded with the certainty that Abdul would end up in paradise, surrounded by virgins. There was nothing unusual about it, nothing to distinguish it from any other farewell letter he'd read. When the bomber was illiterate, which was nearly always the case, a mullah would write the letter for him.

'The grammar is perfect. Whoever wrote it is very well educated,' said Osama.

'Not all Taliban are uneducated,' replied Reza. 'That won't help us find out who wrote it. Perhaps the brother will give us a name. And we'll ask the neighbours which mosque he attended.'

'Can I see his room?'

It was minuscule. The intelligence police had already turned it upside down.

'Have we found anything?' asked Reza curtly.

'Nothing, qomaandaan,' replied one of his men. 'No Taliban propaganda.'

'Obviously. He couldn't read,' grumbled his boss.

Osama rummaged through the dead man's things. They were all in very poor condition. He looked for shoes, and found a pair of crumbling Pakistani-made rangers. All the clothing was dirty, and had been worn a great deal, to judge by its stench.

'You've been looking through those clothes for ten minutes,' said Reza. 'Something suspicious?'

'There are only Afghan clothes here, yet Hakat was dressed in Western gear. His shoes looked new and well made, whereas all this stuff is old and filthy. Smell this — it stinks.'

'Perhaps he wore his best clothes to go out?'

'What money would he have bought them with? American shoes like the ones he was wearing cost thousands of afghanis. There's something funny going on.'

'I'm not following you.'

Osama looked around the room.

'Let's go to the hospital. Katoun must have started his autopsy by now.'

DAKTAR KATOUN was in the office where Osama had found him on his previous visit. They shook hands for a long time.

'I'm sorry about your deputy.'

'Any news?'

'I've finished. For the sake of time, I did the autopsy here rather than at the Medico-Legal Institute. The public prosecutor's office won't like it, but I think they'll forgive me.'

Osama and Reza sat down opposite the doctor, who pulled a piece of paper from the printer behind his desk.

'I didn't have much — only a lower half of the body and a head. The individual died immediately following the detonation of two to three kilograms of powerful high explosives that he was wearing on his body. The smell is indicative of penthrite, and in my opinion it was C5, as you already suspected. I think he was wearing it against his back, which would explain the effect on the body, and the fact that part of the belly skin remained attached and was hanging down in front of his thighs like an apron. Instead of flying up vertically and then falling back down, the head was blasted off at an angle of about 45 degrees. It smashed violently into a wall, which explains the terrible damage.

'The security guard has confirmed that he wasn't in the habit of frisking people's spines. Which means the explosives were strapped on outside the usual frisking area.'

'This is a first, then. Have you seen it before?' asked Osama.

'No. I've looked on the Internet, and I haven't seen anything like it in Iraq or Pakistan either.'

'A new operating procedure,' said Reza. 'They're improving all the time.'

'Please note that I haven't had any organs to examine, on account of the state of the torso. You might be interested to know that the body was particularly dirty. Hakat hadn't taken a bath for at least three or four weeks.'

'Strange,' said Osama. 'They usually make a big deal of washing and perfuming themselves before the attack, don't they?'

'Not always,' replied Reza. 'I've seen two shahids that hadn't prepared their bodies. Had he shaved his pubic hair, Doctor?'

'No.'

Osama thought back to his examination of the body, and said, 'It seemed to me that his jeans were rather tight. Was he wearing any protective bandages or layers of underpants?'

'No particular protection, just a single pair of pants, as filthy as everything else.'

'Strange.'

Osama and his colleague looked at each other. As a general rule, shahids protected their genitals with tight bandages or several layers of pants worn on top of each other, to safeguard their virility for life 'afterwards', when they would meet the seventy-two virgins in paradise.

'He referred to the virgins in his letter but didn't protect his penis,' said Osama.

'The guy was a real dickhead,' said Reza. 'A loser. You can't draw any conclusions from this.'

Not so sure, thought Osama.

LATER ON, in his office, Osama looked through the series of photos of Abdul Hakat that he'd taken before leaving the pathologist's office. He imagined the head flying through the air like a football when the bomb exploded. He had once seen a DVD of a member of the Israeli FBI, Shin Beth, interrogating a Palestinian martyr whose bomb had failed to explode. When the man was shown photos of other martyrs — of their intact heads and the pulp that remained of the rest of their bodies, including the genitals — he seemed stunned. As if suddenly realising the consequences of the act for his own body. Osama looked at the close-up photo of one of Abdul Hakat's shoes. The same thing still bothered him. How could such a poor man, and a dirty one at that, have bought shoes like this? It was obvious from the fabric and the brilliant colour that they were expensive, rather than cheap copies imported from Pakistan. He used an old magnifying glass to look at the brand more closely. New Balance. He'd never heard of it. He called over one of his drivers, a young man of about twenty who'd spent a dozen years as a refugee in Turkmenistan with his parents, and was known for being up to date with the latest trends.

'Ahmad, have you heard of a brand of shoes called New Balance?'

The young man shook his head.

'No, qomaandaan.'

'Ask around other people your age, and let me know if anyone's heard of them.'

Two hours later, the driver came to tell him that no one had ever heard of New Balance. Osama was about to go and ask around himself, when the same young boy that Mullah Bakir had sent before appeared in his office. Understanding the message, Osama put on his coat.

IT WAS SNOWING in Berne, but from the secure meeting room at Entity headquarters there was no way of discerning the weather outside. It was a blind room, the walls covered with leather and precious metal sheeting, and protected from electronic interception by a complex network of electromagnetic waves. The general was giving an update on the search for the fugitive. On the other side of the world, in Kabul, Joseph sat in his secure cube. The news wasn't good. The two men spoke quietly, leaning towards their cameras. They were tense and anxious.

'It's been too long since he gave us the slip. He vanished in Geneva, and we've no serious leads. I don't think we're going to be able to find him now.'

'I can't understand how something like this could happen.'

'Me neither. Our men have checked every flight minutely. His name doesn't feature. He wasn't well connected enough to obtain a fake passport, so I think he must still be in Switzerland. Or a neighbouring country that can be reached by land — France, Italy, Austria … there's no lack of them. If he reached the coast, he could rent a boat and slip off to somewhere else, Africa even, and we would have lost him.'

'What about private flights?'

'We've studied them all, one by one. There have been several hundred since he vanished. Ten men have been working full time on that. Most private flights are chartered by companies based in tax havens. It's not easy to get a precise list of the passengers, or the actual destinations. Private flights are still a black hole in the security of all our countries. And if he managed to take one from a neighbouring country, our chances of finding him are even slimmer. The man is clever, rich, and well organised.'

'I'm still hoping that Nick will find a trail that has escaped us.'

'Are you joking? He won't find anything.'

'What's your conclusion? I want to know what you think.'

'Let's stop beating around the bush and look at things straight. The man has totally slipped out of our hands. It's fucked.'

The closeness between Joseph and the general meant that they never minced words. They talked freely to one another. With anyone else on his team, the general would have exploded — but not here, with Joseph.

'Statistics show that when you don't catch a fugitive within the first seventy-two hours, your chances of finding him any time soon become almost nil,' continued Joseph. 'A new window of opportunity usually occurs after twenty-four months, when the fugitive starts to feel homesick: at that time, he begins to make mistakes and is more easily caught.'

'Twenty-four months? You must be out of your mind! We're not going to wait *two years* to catch him!'

'Why not? The fact that nothing has been leaked confirms our hypothesis that the fugitive is not interested in publicising the report. The two psychiatrists who drew up his profile think that he would only make the report public as a last resort, if he were cornered. He's a proud man and a perfectionist. He thinks he can dupe us. What's more, he'd have a lot to lose from disclosure of the report.'

'That's too big a risk to take.'

'It's a limited risk. As long as the fugitive is in control of the situation, he will keep the report in his possession. And that's our priority, isn't it?'

'Our priority is to find it. And you, my senior expert, are suggesting that we simply give up.'

'We're not the only ones looking for it, if I'm not mistaken. Why should we succeed where all the official services have failed? I can't make miracles happen. Let's retain a surveillance team of a dozen men. If he makes a mistake, as he inevitably will, we'll jump on him. In the meantime, we stop our active investigations, which aren't getting us anywhere.'

'That's not my brief.'

'There's no other option. He'll make himself known by screwing up, sooner or later. It's just a matter of time.'

The general nodded his head. Joseph's solution did seem to be the most rational, but he didn't want to admit defeat.

'Our clients are worried about the situation in Afghanistan,' he continued. 'What's the likelihood that that cop will find out the truth?'

'He's the best policeman in the country. He was trained by the Russians, and he's incorruptible. He's unravelling the story millimetre by millimetre. I think we're at tipping point.'

'I've had enough of this whole business; we're not on top of it. You have to stop him, once and for all.'

'You want to have your cake and eat it. How can I promise you the work will be done properly, if you make me rely on shitty external consultants every time someone has to pull a trigger?'

'I don't want you exposed to any more risk than necessary.'

'Well, the consequence is that things go wrong.'

'Start again. He has to die. But not at your hands. Find the right team.'

Mullah Bakir used the traditional litany of greetings, pouring out the whole extended version in Dari, holding Osama's hand in his own. His eyes expressed genuine pain as he explained to Osama how sad he felt for him.

'Would you like us to say a few *hadiths* together in memory of the boy?'

'Gladly.'

The mullah took a rug that was propped against the wall and unrolled it to face Mecca.

'This rug is from Jerusalem,' he said, 'I only use it for special occasions.'

By the time they stood up again, more than a few minutes had passed.

'What do you think of the attack?' asked Osama.

'I haven't received much news yet, brother. The first questions that I asked have not yet yielded any response. Nobody knew this Abdul Hakat. He didn't make much impression in prison. The Taliban were slightly suspicious of him.'

'Had he been processed by a Kabul Taliban cell?'

'I haven't had time to be sure of that yet. The security systems your friends have put in place require the rebels to work in a different way, using independent cells. It takes a long time to acquire information. There's no way one can use the phone. It'll be a few more days before I've spoken to everyone.'

'So you don't have any reliable information at all?'

'The very fact that I don't is in itself information, brother Osama. This Abdul Hakat wasn't processed by any of the main cells of the Taliban movement.'

'And yet he used a sophisticated device and the very latest type of explosive, C5.'

Mullah Bakir swept the argument aside with a wave of his hand.

'You can buy that anywhere; it doesn't mean a thing. He could even have got it from the tribal areas.'

'How? He didn't have a penny.'

'You're the policeman. Keep looking before you come to any conclusions.'

'When will you know the truth?'

'Perhaps never. People don't tell me everything. Some of my brothers in the revolution know that I absolutely disapprove of suicide bombing. Not only does it cheapen our combatants' lives, I also see it as contrary to the precepts of Islam, because the Koran forbids the murder of innocent civilians.'

'Even Christians? Your men weren't so particular when you were in power,' Osama couldn't help retorting.

"The unbeliever must have a genuine opportunity to convert; killing him in a crowd does not give him that chance," recited the mullah. 'I have written several fatwas on the subject, one of which, *Allah U Akhbar,* was taken up by my Egyptian brothers at Cairo's central mosque. It has now become the standard position for Egyptian Imams, and that gives me great joy. Have you noticed that the Muslim Brotherhood has never organised a suicide bombing? What I'm trying to say is that some radical members of our revolutionary movement will not be so keen to talk to my messengers.' The mullah settled himself into his armchair. 'Having said that, even if we don't know the *whole* truth, we can arrive at an approximation. We'll soon have some kind of view on the source of this attack.'

'And right now, in this room, what is your view, Mullah — your personal intuition, given the little information that you have?'

Mullah Bakir turned his deep, dark eyes on Osama. All the joy had gone out of them. The two men stared at each other silently for a few moments, and then the mullah said, 'I don't think this attack was one of ours. I find it unlikely that a man who doesn't seem to be part of any secret group could suddenly decide to blow himself up, acquire the necessary equipment, and carry out his plan in such a high-security environment. Your colleagues are questioning the imam of his mosque as we speak; they are torturing him to make him admit whatever they want to hear. I know that imam: he's a moderate man, opposed to any kind of violence, and would never have trained up a shahid. In any case, he's not clever enough. Training a martyr takes a lot of time and a complete intellectual hold over the person. You have to gradually take over their will, to the point of controlling the deepest instinct in us all: the desire to live. That imam isn't up to it.'

'Was Abdul Hakat seeing another imam?'

'I'm told he wasn't. Although I should add that my messenger didn't have time for a more in-depth discussion, because he was interrupted by your henchmen breaking down the door of the mosque, with their usual finesse. They dragged the imam away before the end of the conversation …'

Osama stood up and bowed slightly.

'Thank you for the information you've given me, Mullah. I value it greatly.'

As Osama reached the door, the mullah said, 'The fact that you were in that café with your two deputies just before the bombing was no accident. If Gulbudin hadn't had that sciatic crisis, all three of you would have been dead. I don't think it can be a coincidence.'

Osama turned around.

'Me neither.'

'Are you going to continue with your investigation?'

'What do you think?'

'Our Arab friends have a wonderful proverb. It says, I believe, that it's better to be an alive dog than a dead lion.'

'The case behind Wadi Wali's death must be hugely important, to drive those who want to prevent my investigation to such monstrous lengths.'

The mullah sighed.

'You're a brave man, brother Osama. Try to stay alive for a few more days. Your investigation interests me.'

Osama walked back towards him.

'But why, damnit?'

'Because, like you, I sense that the Christians are involved, and I'd like to know if we're dealing with the Russians, NATO, or someone else. Because this puppet government and the ill-assorted military Coalition that props it up will sooner or later be pushed out by a new and, hopefully, moderate Taliban movement. At that point, we'll need the UN to both allow us to take power and help us negotiate with the Tajiks and Hazara to prevent a civil war. We can obtain this blank cheque in many ways. Through negotiation. Through terror. Or through the building of common interests.'

'Or through blackmail ...'

The mullah smiled thinly.

'Blackmail is such an ugly word. We will soon be in power, brother Osama — that much is for sure. The only thing still in the balance is how we acquire it. I want to save lives, to prevent more massacres, and to re-launch our movement on a decent basis, cutting the links it is trying to establish with Al Qaida, and signing a non-aggression pact with the Northern Alliance. Only the western Coalition can help me do that.'

'I don't understand your strategy.'

The mullah gazed dreamily into the distance.

'The art of politics is one of execution, and requires a hefty dose of complexity. Simplistic strategies never work. Good luck, brother

Osama. My thoughts are with you.'

Osama returned to the hospital. Daktar Katoun was seeing a patient, but Osama insisted he be disturbed. He arrived running, in white coat and bloodstained gloves.

'I need your services again,' said Osama.

'Of course, but hurry up. I was busy taking a lemon-sized cyst out of a patient.'

'I need you to give me one of the shahid's shoes. I'll bring it back later.'

'What if they ask me for the dead man's belongings?'

'If it's the NDS, tell them you've given them to the intelligence department; if it's the police, say the opposite.'

'OK, OK,' grumbled the doctor. 'Wait here.'

He came back a few moments later, holding a sterile bag containing the shoe.

'I took this one because it was intact.'

'Thank you. I owe you for this.'

Letten lived up to its reputation as a marketplace for cheap sex. The prostitutes stood in a line as the cars — shiny as new pins, according to Swiss tradition — drove slowly past, checking out the merchandise. It was extremely busy, during the day as well as at night. Nick had been driving up and down since his conversation with the Vice Squad policeman, but to no avail. He'd already had more than enough of the seedy atmosphere, but each time he wanted to stop and go home, he thought of Werner. This was the least he could do.

The place was teeming with people. Nick felt uncomfortable in his small, low-slung convertible — the hood hindered his view, and he had to twist around to check out the pavement pros.

There was a semblance of order: first the prettiest prostitutes, of all hues, then the less attractive ones, who'd been doing it too long. And finally the transvestites, pathetic under thick layers of make-up that barely concealed the stubble of a beard or moustache. He drove slowly, with Yasmina's photo in his hand. None of the girls looked like her, either up close or far away. At the end of the street were the women no one should have wanted, but who still attracted a few clients in search of extreme experience. He could just make out furtive shadows creeping along the pavement or slipping towards the thicket surrounding the old train station. He parked up on the verge, checking nervously that his pistol was strapped to his hip as it was supposed to be. Outside, the tension was palpable. Negotiations were whispered: 'Twenty-five francs a time', 'No, twenty', 'I'll pay you thirty, but no condom.'

He noticed a girl in a recess. She was rather pretty, but seemed high as a kite, rocking back and forth, her eyes half shut.

'Come, darling, thirty francs.'

'Sorry, no.'

He walked past her towards another, much older, woman a little further on.

'Alright, twenty,' pressed the first. 'I'll suck you — you can make love to me.'

'Sorry,' said Nick.

The girl caught up with him.

'Come on, ten, no condom. I need a rock.'

A rock of crack. As if she wasn't wasted enough already. Nick kept walking, and the girl grabbed hold of him, sobbing.

'Christ, I need a rock, I need it. One franc, I'll do you for one, one franc right now.'

Terrified that she might scratch him, Nick shook her off. He held out a five-franc note, which she grabbed from his hands. Her face was gaunt and her eyes were red. She was still pretty, but she'd soon be a wreck. She ran off with her five francs. The woman he'd come to talk to sniggered.

'That poor Marilyn, she's totally wasted. Five francs will buy her half a rock, and last her about half an hour.'

Nick took out a twenty-franc note, and waved it in front of the woman's nose.

'I need some information.'

'Tell me, chicken. You're cute, I like you.'

The woman moved out of the bushes. She was heavy, and her

leather trousers and jacket were too tight. They must have been elegant once, but now they were old and misshapen. She seemed healthy enough, though, and clean. As Nick had guessed from far away, she was at least sixty, if not more. She might know Yasmina as a fellow old-timer. He took the photo out of his pocket.

'Does this remind you of anyone?'

The woman moved closer. Nick could smell her cheap perfume. She pouted.

'Maybe. What will you give me, on top of the twenty francs?'

Nick put the note back in his pocket.

'Give me the info, and I'll give you twenty francs. Otherwise, I'm out of here.'

'Hang on a minute, don't be cross, chicken.'

She licked her too-red lips with her too-long tongue. Nick felt pretty shaky, and wondered how convincing he was as a hard man. Not very, he reckoned.

'Your lady's name is Yasmina. She's one of the old-timers here.'

Nick felt a surge of hope.

'Do you know where I can find her?'

'The last time I saw her, she was hustling down by the river, behind the cheese factory, in the 10th district, near the Limmat. It's a huge factory — you'll see and smell it from kilometres away. There's a row of squatted buildings and a big waste ground with corrugated iron shelters that the tramps use. That's where she's hustling — on the waste ground. No point getting your big notes out for her, chicken: it's five for a blowjob, ten for the real deal. And if she's in withdrawal, you'll get a discount.' The prostitute laughed joylessly. 'You'd better hurry — everyone knows she has AIDS and hep C. She'll be dead before long.'

Instead of returning to the office, Osama took a cab to the souk. The crush in this part of Kabul was unbelievable — it was where a large proportion of the city's three million inhabitants came to shop. Thousands of women in burqas were making their way through the busy streets, some on the back of a donkey led by their husband or brother. Merchants were scurrying all over the place. Osama walked deep into the souk, hailed by stallholders trying to sell him a new burqa for his wife, slippers, grilled pistachios, spices … He was a head taller than anyone else, and suddenly realised that the NDS informers swarming around the market would be bound to spot him. After pretending to check out a couple of shops, he paused in front of a big storefront shimmering with neon lights. The shop was called 'Parise-Kabul', and had a crude drawing of the Eiffel Tower next to the Dari lettering. Osama walked in and introduced himself to a shop assistant. A few moments later, the owner rushed over. He was one of the biggest merchants in the souk, and specialised in importing Western clothes and perfume. Strangely, his business hadn't collapsed under the Taliban — on the contrary, his fake Christian Bior and Chamel turbans 'from Paris' had sold like hot cakes.

The businessman asked Osama to sit on his best chair, and clicked his fingers for fresh mint tea, a rarity in Kabul. Osama had never been in Parise-Kabul before, and he was impressed. It was the biggest shop he'd ever seen — bigger even than Gum in Moscow. It had three storeys, unlike any other shop in Kabul. There was even a creaking escalator in the middle of the ground floor, proudly lit by a number of spotlights. Thousands of tchadors and burqas were hanging from the ceiling, along with all the provocative European clothing. Following Osama's gaze, the merchant said, 'Some women like to dress in European clothes at home. They invite each other around, put on make-up, and unveil their hair and much of their bodies, as they did under the shah. This is also the only place in the whole souk that sells burqas made from Italian fabric. Beautiful fabric, actually, from Modena.'

Osama took the sterile bag containing the shoe from his bag.

'I want to buy a pair of shoes like this to give to my son when he comes to visit. This is one of his favourite brands. Do you sell them?'

The merchant took the bag and looked at the shoe from every angle, through the plastic. His face clouded over.

'New Balance. No. No, qomaandaan Kandar. They aren't imported here. I can get you some, but they'd have to be brought over from the UAE. It would be expensive. Very expensive.'

'How much? A thousand afghanis?'

The merchant shook his head.

'Much more than that, qomaandaan, much more. These shoes are worth at least two hundred dollars. Once I've paid the middleman and the transport costs, plus an amount in case of theft, and my profit, that price will double. So twenty thousand afghanis, maybe more.'

Osama was staggered by the amount. The shahid was a poor devil, and could never have spent anything like that.

'Can't you get them in Peshawar?'

'You'd never find them in Pakistan — or only in the luxury boutiques of Islamabad, for even more than in the Persian Gulf.'

'What about a copy?' insisted Osama.

'It's not a well-enough-known brand. No one would copy them, because they wouldn't sell. And even if you did shift a few, it would be for less than Nikes or Cardins. So why take the risk of making them?'

Osama gave the bag containing the shoe back to the merchant.

'Look at this one again. Are you sure it's not a fake?'

'I don't need to look again, qomaandaan. I promise you that this shoe is an original — no copy would be as well made.' He waved at the clothes all around him. 'I sell a lot of fakes; I know what I'm talking about.'

Osama had initially assumed that the shahid had bought the shoes with the money he'd been given for the mission. He would now have to approach the situation from a completely different angle. His brain sifted through various theories as he struggled back through the market. Someone must have given the shahid the shoes to help him through security at the Hamad Café. There were two options. Either the shoes had been stolen from a Westerner — dead or alive — and given to Abdul Hakat by an Afghan. Or they had been given to him by a Westerner who was part of the operation. In either case, the person's fingerprints would be on the shoes.

NICK WAS DRIVING, his eyes red with exhaustion. This descent into the seediest parts of Zurich had tired him out. Everyone he'd come across had been both physically and morally ugly — futureless whores, punters starving for sex who treated them like objects, drug addicts, pimps with hearts of stone. Was this how he wanted to live his life, associating with the dregs of humanity? And all for this absurd investigation. He stopped at the first café he saw. He needed a beer, and flopped onto a bench at the back of a booth. He had brought a few documents from the case file with him. He wasn't officially supposed to take these kinds of papers out of the office, but he was starting to tire of the Entity and its security regulations. Even toilet paper was an official secret, according to them … he flicked through the documents for a moment, summarising what he knew so far. The fugitive had spent twenty years working for Willard Consulting, a powerful and secretive lobbying group that Nick had only heard of through this case. He'd often travelled to Iraq and Afghanistan, as shown by the dozens of flights he'd taken to the two countries over the past five years. He had betrayed his employer, but how and why, Nick didn't yet know.

The whole office was aware that Joseph was on assignment in Afghanistan with several of his men. Some of Nick's fellow analysts were looking into the affairs of a bizarre middleman who'd died suddenly a few days before. Nick was no idiot: he hadn't been told anything, but he knew that this could not be a coincidence. There was definitely some kind of link between the two cases. He suddenly realised that whatever progress he made with his investigation, it would at some point become necessary to find out what they were trying to hide from him. And, unfortunately, there was only one way to do that: he'd have to rummage through the Entity offices, with all the risks that entailed.

He finished his beer, staring into space. This case was making him more and more nervous. He felt as if he were travelling down a darkened tunnel. He wondered whether he'd be brave enough to go all the way.

9.

As soon as he arrived at police headquarters, Osama called a meeting with Gulbudin, Jihad, Rangin, and Abdul. Gulbudin looked absolutely shattered. He and Babrak had been very close, and the loss of his friend and colleague was a massive blow.

'From today, Gulbudin will take on all the investigative work Babrak was doing on the Wali Wadi case. I want everything else taken off his plate. Share out his other cases amongst you, please.'

'Yes, qomaandaan,' murmured his men in chorus.

Osama explained exactly what he needed from his team, while Gulbudin took notes in shorthand, with his good eye on Osama. At the end, he said simply, 'It will be done.'

'You will also all be helping with the investigation of the Hamad Café bombing; I want us to provide good support to the intelligence section.'

'This is a personal matter for the whole team. Where would you like us to start?' asked Jihad.

Osama gave him the bag containing the shoe.

'Put on some gloves, and make a complete list of all the fingerprints on this shoe. Take special care over the tongue and the sides, which would have been touched when the shoe was laced up. Then have as many reliable men as you need obtain files on all those prints.'

'What are we looking for?'

'I'll tell you later.'

Once he had read his mail and updated himself on all the investigations currently underway, Osama visited Babrak's widow for a second time. She received him surrounded by her family, who had arrived en masse from Zaranj to support her. The house's main room, whose ceiling was so low that Osama's head almost touched the ceiling, had been divided in two by a sheet, to create one area for the men and another for the women. The sideboard had been moved to bisect the two areas. The women were wearing brightly coloured dresses, and either little caps on their heads or a light veil that merely covered their hair. None of the men wore turbans or bushy beards. All were deeply distressed by the death of the young policeman.

A beautiful young woman with blue eyes and pencilled eyebrows insisted on filling Osama's plate. He nibbled the delightfully fatty lamb, and a little rice with spiced yoghurt. As soon as he had finished his yoghurt, another woman refilled his bowl. He wasn't hungry, but he ate dutifully so as not to upset her. He was surprised to see men and women occasionally talking together in the women's part of the room, without obvious regard for gender. He'd never attended such a mixed gathering: the general rule was that women should never be in physical or visual contact with men other than their fathers, brothers, or sons. But here, everyone, even the most distant of cousins, was hanging out together. Perhaps it was because most of the people in the room were Shiite.

A man slightly older than the rest came over to talk to Osama. His thick head of hair didn't conceal the scars on either side of his head. He explained to Osama that the Taliban had cut off his ears because they had thought him guilty of disregarding Sunni norms.

'I don't mind,' he added. 'I was lucky — some people had their noses cut off, or their throats slit.'

Osama nodded, but he was finding the morbid atmosphere oppressive. He took the widow to one side, to tell her that he'd decided to carry out his own investigation of the Hamad Café explosion, separate from the Anti-terrorist Squad.

'Will you find the Taliban who set off the bomb?'

'I'll find them,' said Osama. 'But I'm no longer convinced the Taliban were responsible.'

'I don't understand. Who did it, then?'

'I'm wondering whether the intended targets of the bomb weren't Babrak, Gulbudin, and myself. On account of our current investigation.'

Osama moved closer, while making sure to keep a respectable distance.

'The people who committed this murder will pay,' he murmured. 'I swear to Allah.'

'I've had enough of this violence. I don't want anyone else to die,' said the widow wearily. 'I just want my husband to rest in peace, and my country to become a normal country again.'

She walked over to a dilapidated Formica sideboard, opened a drawer, and took out a scrap of paper.

'Babrak made lots of calls before he went out. He was looking for a contact at the airport, for you. He finally managed to find someone, the husband of one of my friends. He seemed very happy about it.'

There was only one name on the piece of paper: Mohammed Taraki. Osama put it in his pocket. As he took his leave, the widow added, 'Babrak was a good husband and a good father. We loved each other deeply. I think I had just about convinced him not to take another wife.'

With that, she burst into tears. Osama paused at the door, but he had nothing to add — nothing useful, in any case.

Osama drove straight to the airport, after having made a long detour to the north, and another manoeuvre to shake off anyone on his tail. He started on Mir Bacha Kot, one of the two roads leading to the massive Bagram military base, but suddenly swerved off into a poor neighbourhood, and had his protective pick-up block the road behind him. He was aware that these manoeuvres were becoming more and more risqué, and that he wouldn't be able to avoid being tailed if his enemies were to approach the job professionally and with major resources. They could easily employ a whole team, with several men on motorbikes that he wouldn't be able to shake off. At least he was avoiding the biggest danger by leaving his mobile phone at the office, thereby thwarting their attempts at remote electronic surveillance.

Having weaved through unmarked lanes for half an hour, he finally came out on the other road to Bagram, which crossed the Shomali plain. It was a busy road. He did a sudden u-turn and sped off towards the city centre. A few kilometres further on, he took the airport road, rather pleased with himself: no one could possibly have followed him. He drove through increasingly heavy traffic, passing Coalition troop-transportation and military-supply trucks. Every three or four kilometres, a small group of Kabul's elite garrison troops, sometimes backed up by policemen, were observing the traffic in their immaculate uniforms and safari hats.

After two checkpoints, he finally arrived at the airport. A few forlorn taxis were waiting optimistically for a client next to the concrete suicide-car-prevention chicanes. A little further away, a couple of armoured 4x4s were parked in the VIP area, waiting for Western visitors or contractors rich enough to pay for decent protection. Osama parked his 4x4 in a space reserved for official vehicles, flashed his card, and walked into the airport building, which had recently been upgraded by the Japanese. It was empty, apart from a few travellers and the security services. There wasn't a single café or shop. It was clean, well organised, and well maintained — a model of what the new Afghanistan could do, with international support.

Osama didn't know anyone in the immigration department. All he had was the name Mohammed Taraki. He wondered whether the man was related to the Taraki who had co-run one of the two communist parties, the Khalq, in the 1970s. Osama wondered around the corridors for a while until he managed to identify Taraki. He was the airport cleaning manager! Furious at having made the journey for nothing, Osama decided to introduce himself anyway. Taraki worked in a tiny office cluttered with strong-smelling cleaning products. Through the window, Osama could see a German tank, and further away a plane about to take off.

'Sahib Taraki?'

'That's me.'

He was an old man who seemed worn out by life and its troubles, badly dressed in a ragged shalwar kameez. It was bitterly cold in his unheated office, and he'd wrapped a coarse brown patou around his shoulders. He spoke Pashtun rather than Dari, but was wearing a chitrali hat, like a Tajik. His speech was that of an educated man. As soon as he realised who he was talking to, he welcomed Osama warmly.

'I didn't know Babrak personally,' he began, 'but my wife works in the same health centre as his, and they are friends, even though Babrak's wife is Shiite. So there's a bond between us.'

'What kind of health centre is it?'

'It offers dental care to women. My wife runs it,' added Taraki with pride. 'Babrak's wife is the only one with any qualifications, apart from a Pakistani dentist. She's my wife's second-in-command. They are like mother and daughter.'

In Afghanistan, family was an essential component of social life. In the small villages of the countryside, second cousins often married each other, which reinforced the potency of the clan structures. Friendships between people of different clans or ethnicities were only possible in cities, where there was a certain amount of social mixing. Taraki asked for news of the investigation, and Osama told him that they were working hard but that nothing conclusive had emerged so far. Taraki nodded, as if he wasn't really surprised.

'I would be honoured to fulfil Babrak's request, especially now he's in the believers' paradise, *Insha'Allah.*'

'I asked him for a list of all the foreign passengers who arrived in Kabul in the three days preceding the 4th of March, and left between the 5th and the 7th.'

'That's right.'

'Do you know who at the airport could help me establish that list?'

'Me. I have the list.'

As Osama wasn't able to hide his surprise, Taraki added, 'I've one list of all the arrivals, showing their nationality, and another of the departures on those dates. You'll have to compare the two yourself.'

'How did you manage to get hold of this information?'

'My men clean the offices. They work at night, when there's no one here. Your colleagues in the border police aren't very careful,

Qomaandaan. They leave all kinds of documents in their rubbish bins.' Taraki shifted the sleeve of his filthy tunic to reveal a massive gold watch. 'Lots of people are interested in that information, as you can imagine. I keep it all. I usually charge — but not for you, in memory of Babrak.'

He opened a desk drawer and pulled out a roll of paper. It was a classic printout on perforated paper, at least two centimetres thick.

'Thank you,' said Osama.

He felt uneasy. From a purely legal point of view, Taraki was indulging in what could only be called spying. He should have stood up and denounced him straight away. By not doing so, he had become obliged to him.

'I don't have many friends,' said the man, as if he had read Osama's mind. 'But I'm loyal to them, as they are loyal to me. Can I count on your discretion?'

Osama realised that Taraki was too sure of himself not to have friends in every camp, probably including the Taliban as well as spies from neighbouring countries. And perhaps the Russians as well, which would explain his laid-back attitude.

'You can.'

He bowed to the man and left, carrying his precious list and wondering how many of them it had taken for Taraki to buy his gold watch.

As Osama drove away from the airport, he noticed a minibus tailing him. His car had been spotted. He was now being watched, by either the minister or his mysterious Western enemies. It was a good thing he'd been discreet; he didn't think they'd be able to find out whom he'd been to see. He drove straight back to the office. Gulbudin joined him immediately, resting his prosthetic leg on a second chair with a groan of satisfaction. Osama could never remember hearing him complain, not even when he'd been thrown, seriously hurt, into the back of a truck without so much as a mattress to lie on.

'We have the list of fingerprints. Four different sets, including those of Abdul Hakat, as confirmed against his police file. The other three are unknown. What do you want to do next?'

There was no automated fingerprint database in Afghanistan, although the Russians had started working on one before they left. The Americans talked about creating one, to help with their war against the Islamic fundamentalists, but it wouldn't be operational for years. The fingerprints might help Osama later in his investigation, but they would not lead him to a name. That was his job — and then he could compare the names with the prints.

'Did you leave traces of fingerprint powder on the shoe?' Osama asked Gulbudin.

'Yes.'

'Hide it carefully in one of our cupboards down in the basement. Then go to the hospital and give this letter to daktar Katoun. In person.'

After Gulbudin left, Osama sifted through his post. Reza had sent him the latest reports on the investigation. He read them avidly. The account of the interrogation of the shahid's brother was two pages long. The man hadn't changed his statement after a night in the police headquarters basement. It had been judged reliable. The man said that his brother Abdul was not very religious, and that as far as he knew he'd had no contact with fundamentalist groups since leaving prison. He confirmed that Abdul had participated in prayer groups, but claimed it was more for the free food than from any genuine desire to deepen his faith. Osama frowned. The document confirmed what he was thinking, but not irrefutably.

The second document was Katoun's autopsy report. Osama noticed that it was unusually short. He compared it to the document that Katoun had produced after Wali Wadi's autopsy. The font and type size were different, for a start. He suspected that it had been rewritten by the NDS. There was no mention of the lack of multiple layers of underpants, or of Abdul Hakat's unshaven pubic hair. Osama sighed and moved on to the next document, the technical department's bomb analysis. This confirmed that the explosive was indeed C5 — from the look of the chemical traces, probably a batch manufactured in Pakistan. No manual detonator had been found among the debris, but an antenna attached to a fragment of strap suggested that the explosive might have been endowed with a device allowing it to be detonated remotely. Osama read the document more closely. He was stunned that the NDS had allowed it to reach him untainted. The antenna was the same kind used by the Russian special services. The technician suggested that if this was indeed what had happened, the person activating the explosion would have been no further than a hundred metres from the Hamad Café.

Osama put down the technical report and started reading the intelligence department's account of their local investigation. The security guard, and also a neighbour, remembered having seen a black 4x4 driving away just after the explosion. The neighbour expressed surprise that it had moved so slowly, given that the café was already up in flames. He hadn't been able to identify the vehicle. Osama looked for the neighbour's name in the report, but couldn't find it. He decided to seek him out.

The area around the Hamad Café had returned to some semblance of normality, despite the continuing police presence. Two official vehicles were parked in front of the burnt-out building. The vegetable stall opposite was open, as was the butcher and the TV-repair shop. Labourers were at work on the most damaged shops and stalls, chivvied along by traders anxious to reopen as quickly as possible. It took Osama half an hour of chatting to neighbours to locate the person who had seen the 4x4. An old man whose turban and long beard made no secret of his affiliations, he invited Osama into his living room. A photo of him in front of the Kaaba at Mecca announced that he was a hajji. The photo occupied pride of place on the sideboard, the only piece of furniture in the room. Osama introduced himself as also having made the pilgrimage, and his host visibly relaxed.

'I'd like you to tell me about the night of the attack.'

The man was drinking tea and playing dice with two friends when the explosion took place. The windows had shattered, but no one was hurt. They heard bomb fragments clattering down on the roof. Later on, the emergency teams found bits of charred café furniture up there, as well as a human limb. The man and his friends immediately went out onto the street to see what was going on.

'Straight away, I think Hamad Café. They listen bad music and smoke hashish there. Some say they even sell alcohol, in secret.' He spat on the floor. 'Bad place, bad people. Bad Muslims.'

'What did you notice as you left the house?'

'I see Hamad Café burning. People running. Hurt people. A man on fire. He die right there.'

He pointed to a dark stain on the beaten-earth pavement, a few metres away.

'And then what happened?'

'I see car drive from next my house.'

'What was the car like?'

'Big. Black. Heathen car.'

An unbeliever's car. Osama thought of the armoured 4x4s used by government officials and certain members of the Coalition. Their Chevrolets and GMCs were often black, whereas the Japanese 4x4s driven by state employees, private companies, and NGOS tended to be white or grey. He suddenly had an idea.

'Did your friends see the car?'

The witness nodded vigorously.

'*Bala*. They see.'

'Do they live near here?'

'Bala. Not far.'

'Show me.'

The old man pulled on a tattered wool patou and Russian boots, and followed Osama out onto the street. They walked down winding lanes for about three hundred metres before coming to a stop outside a small two-storey house. The man knocked and walked in. The downstairs windows were broken, and the shutters had been closed to keep out the cold. A woman wearing an indoor veil that left only her eyes visible poked her head out and then vanished. The witness called brusquely to her in Pashtun; a few moments later, an old man appeared. Osama introduced himself as a policeman, without giving his name or unit. The interrogation didn't yield much. The man may have been a good dice player, but he didn't seem to understand anything; perhaps he was simple-minded. After a short while, Osama thanked him and asked to see the final member of the trio.

They set off on a new journey through the area's decrepit little lanes. It soon started raining, and the beaten-earth floor quickly turned into a muddy cesspit. A strong smell started coming up from the ground. Very few of these houses had sewers; and when the individual pits were full, human excrement was sometimes thrown straight out into the street. The rain thawed it and released its smell. Osama walked faster. The witness stopped in front of a building identical to the first, except that this one had windows. He announced their presence. A young woman appeared on the threshold, before scarpering to another room out of sight. Osama just had time to notice large eyes and a beautiful face.

'She my friend wife sister,' said the first witness, noticing his glance. 'My friend wife die in hospital. Friend marry last sister, she very young, much more pretty! She not want marry my friend, but he can. He pay parents and marry anyway. He very happy.'

At the end of his tirade he burst out laughing, as if this were the funniest joke in the world. Marrying the sister of one's dead wife was a matter of constant debate, with older and more modern people endlessly arguing for different interpretations of the Koranic verses. Osama, who was wondering what Mullah Bakir's opinion would be, suddenly found himself in a living room bizarrely decorated with posters of American cars. Corvette, Mustang, Cadillac … all the must-haves of the Detroit motor industry were displayed on the walls in glorious Technicolor. The third witness was hunchbacked, toothless, and hadn't been near a bath for a very long time. Osama felt sorry for the young woman who had had no option but to marry a monster like this. Life was undoubtedly no bed of roses for her. In any other country, a beauty like that would have married the attractive young man of her choice.

Osama was offered the best armchair, while the witness and the host argued over the honour of serving him tea. Eventually, Osama was able to start his questioning. This third man seemed much more intelligent than his two friends. He described the same scene as the first witness. Osama was champing at the bit, but he let him speak. Although he was only interested in the car, he didn't want the man to feel rushed.

'Then we saw the car drive off. It was a Grand Cherokee jeep, the latest model.'

'Are you sure?'

'Definitely.' The man waved at the posters on his walls. 'Latest model. I recognised the sound; it was equipped with a V8 engine. I'm sure it was armoured, too, because it sat a little low on its shock absorbers, and I could hear the axle grating as the wheels turned.'

'How far away from you was the car?'

The man indicated the distance to the end of the room. About four metres.

'Did you see the registration plates?'

'Yes.'

'Do you remember anything?'

'KBL first — it was a Kabul car. Then 7. There was a 7.'

'Concentrate,' said Osama. 'Close your eyes and think of the whole scene, not just the car. Try to relive the scene from the moment you came out into the road … try to gradually reassemble the scene.'

The man closed his eyes, frowning in concentration.

'I see 27, not 7. There were other digits, but I can't remember them.'

'Think,' said Osama, steadily.

'The last number — it's the same as the plates on the photo of the Mustang in here!' shouted the man suddenly.

'A 5, like this one?' asked Osama, pointing at one of the posters on the wall.

Osama continued the interrogation for another few minutes. Then he thanked the man, and left having casually found out his name. An address wasn't much use, as the road had no name, but he counted the number of houses that separated the man's house from the next crossroads. The small shop there might turn out to be a useful landmark.

THE NUMBER-PLATE DEPARTMENT at Kabul police headquarters was based in an old building that still bore scars from the 1996 battle of Kabul. The whole facade was scarred with long horizontal lines, where the attackers had swept the building from right to left with machine-gun and heavy-artillery fire. Osama showed his card to a surly policeman. The building wasn't heated, and the employees made their way around quickly, wrapped in the most extraordinary layers of clothes and blankets. Many were women — some unveiled, some wearing just a light headscarf. There was not a single burqa in sight. During the war, women had been thrown out of the entire public sector and forbidden from working; as soon as the Americans came along, they returned with a vengeance. Osama thought of Malalai. At this very moment, she was at a RAWA meeting in a secret location.

He waved a man over and asked him where to find the head of the number-plate department. The man pointed to the second floor. After a little trial and error, Osama found himself in the office of a woman who introduced herself as the new departmental head. She had pale skin, inky-black hair, and a very straight nose. She was wearing a rather token kind of veil, which covered her shoulders and only part of her hair. A stray lock fell on to her forehead. She was very beautiful, and gave the impression of being strong, too. Osama felt self-conscious, and found it difficult to look her in the face. The woman waited, comfortably, for him to explain the reason for his visit. He suddenly noticed that she was missing the index finger on her left hand. She saw him looking, and shrugged. 'A gift from the Taliban, when they decided that a woman with painted nails should be punished by removal of her finger. I was lucky — they only took one. It happened in 1999.'

The Taliban vice-repression and virtue-protection squads usually cut off all their victim's fingers, but they sometimes stopped at one or two, in a moment of leniency or because the victim agreed to sleep with them. He imagined this was what had happened with this stunning woman.

'I know what you're thinking, commandant. It was nothing to me; I would have done anything to save my hands. There were only three of them, luckily.'

Osama looked down, embarrassed by her candour. It wasn't the kind of thing that was usually talked about.

'Two of them were killed by the Americans in 2001, apparently. I bumped into the third two years ago, in the market. He was wearing a brand-new police uniform, and had cut his beard short, but it was him. I'll never forget. I'll remember the look in his eyes as he held those secateurs until the day I die. He seemed so happy to be mutilating me.'

She was shaken briefly by a sob. The victim bumping into her torturer — Osama had heard this story a thousand times. The woman soon returned to business: 'What can I do for you, qomaandaan?'

'I'm investigating an important murder, and I need some information.'

'Is it usual for the head of the Murder Squad to make enquiries in person?'

'On important cases, yes.'

'What do you mean by "important"?'

Osama couldn't believe a woman was daring to question him like this. He decided to reply honestly.

'I mean that high-level individuals seem to be implicated. I'm thinking of the security minister, for example.'

'I see,' said the woman, screwing up her face. 'So your boss has not approved your pursuit of this investigation?

'Not fully,' he admitted.

The woman ran her hand gracefully through her hair, under the veil.

'Corruption is a cancer. Unless we do something, it will bring those who amputate women's fingers back into power.'

Osama thought of Mullah Bakir. Whatever his libertarian ideas, Bakir had allied himself with the Taliban. Wasn't he being naïve to associate with a man whose allies committed atrocities like this?

'I'll help you,' continued the woman. 'Tell me exactly what you want: I imagine you need to know who a certain vehicle belongs to?'

'Yes. I have the make, but only part of the number plate. A Grand Cherokee jeep. The number plate starts 27, and ends with 5.'

'There aren't many Cherokee jeeps. They're all used by officials or foreigners.' She smiled, revealing a row of gold teeth. 'The Americans have installed some very effective number-plate-management software. Seeing as we have the make of the car, I can do a search on this computer here.'

She opened a tab on her computer and typed in a series of

instructions. Osama watched in fascination as her fingers flew over the keyboard. The movement of her arm periodically revealed a small henna tattoo on her wrist. Those pearly white, delicate wrists were a wonder to behold.

'Right,' she said suddenly. 'I have twenty-four Grand Cherokee jeeps. Do you know the colour?'

'Black.'

'Twenty-two. I'll print the list.'

Osama found what he was looking for in just a few seconds. *KBL 27645 SH.* Although the letters *SH* for *sharsi* indicated a personal vehicle, the owner was a firm — ASP or Aid Service Protection Afghanistan.

'The vehicle was bought and number-plated two years ago. I'll print out the address on the logbook. It's in the city centre, not far from the Serena hotel.'

Osama automatically held out his hand for the list. His head was spinning slightly. Assuming that their aim had been to slow down or even stop the investigation into Wali Wadi's death, his deputy's murderers had to be linked to Wadi's killers. And he had just tracked them down.

JOSEPH HAD FINISHED studying the GPS map tracing the cop's movements. The tag was working perfectly — he knew the whereabouts of the man's car at any given moment, and down to the last metre. He walked into the surveillance room.

'Nothing new?'

'There is, actually,' said one of the technicians. 'We've intercepted an interesting conversation between the superintendent's deputy and someone in their scientific department. Put on the headphones, and I'll play it to you.'

"Scientific police lab," said a man's voice.

"I would like to speak to Captain Kalandarish."

Joseph immediately recognised Gulbudin's gruff voice.

"Who's asking for him?"

"Inspector Gulbudin Heykmat, Murder Squad."

"One moment, I'll put him on the line."

A silence, and then a young voice with a strong Pakistani accent.

"Captain Kalandarish. I was about to call you."

"Have you made any progress?"

"Yes, one of my technicians has pieced together the Beretta series number. We tried all kinds of methods, but in the end it was the microscope that worked." He laughed. "The French renovated our whole building last month, and gave us new kit. You should come and see."

"I will. What have you found out about the number?"

"The weapon is not listed in Afghanistan. I called our military attaché in Italy. He spoke to Beretta and was able to trace the source of the weapon."

"So, do we know where it comes from?"

"Yes. It was manufactured under licence in the United States. It's a military model."

"In what way, military?"

"A 92F, a weapon the American army ordered from Beretta in the 1980s. This one is one of the earliest. They think it was probably de-listed and sold off to a collector. Or else stolen by a soldier."

"An American army weapon!" repeated Gulbudin.

"Why are you so interested in this Beretta?"

"An investigation. I can't say much."

Joseph pressed the stop button. There were millions of weapons in Afghanistan, tens of thousands in Kabul alone. The fact that Wali Wadi had been assassinated with a disguised pistol from American army stocks was not a simple coincidence, as he knew better than most: the contractor who killed Wali Wadi had spent seven years working for the CIA's National Clandestine Service. His opponent had just found the first major clue linking the assassination of Wali Wadi to the Coalition. Which was exactly what he had to prevent, by any means possible. He picked up his phone.

As HE DROVE BACK to police headquarters, it occurred to Osama that, for all their sophistication, the men he was pursuing were making unacceptable mistakes. The only possible reason seemed to be contempt for his compatriots. This made them careless, and they left traces that they would never have left in their own country. Using a car without changing its plates and giving a shahid shoes that weren't imported into the country were major errors, which could only be explained by a certainty that no serious investigation would be carried out. Osama thought of the security minister, who was doing everything he could to put a spanner in the works. He smiled. As soon as he arrived at headquarters, he headed for the intelligence department. His friend Reza was alone in his office. Osama shut the door behind him.

'Is your office secure?'

'We check it regularly, the last time about ten days ago. Sit down; we can talk — it's not tapped.'

'I need information on a Western structure here in Kabul. A company or an association, I'm not sure.'

'What's it called?'

'Aid Service Protection. ASP.'

Reza curtly instructed an orderly to bring him the file on them immediately.

'Don't you need to check that there is a file?'

'I have a file on *everyone,* Osama. Even you.'

'I doubt it's up to much.'

'That depends on who's looking … why are you interested in ASP?'

'I suspect them of blowing up the Hamad Café. To kill me. And my deputies, too. I think they were trying to prevent my investigation into the Wali Wadi case; I also think the minister is involved.'

Reza paled.

'Are you aware of what you're suggesting? Do you have any proof?'

'Some.'

Osama gave his friend an exhaustive report of his findings, not holding anything back. Then they waited patiently for the file, which was soon brought in by an orderly.

'It's a strange sort of company,' said Reza as he read the file. 'It was set up in 2007 with only five thousand dollars capital. For the first year it remained a shell, with barely any activity, and then suddenly lots. In the space of three days it rented offices, bought cars, and declared expatriate staff. That caught our attention. Must be a big customer.'

'What is its official business?'

'Security services, like everyone else. It's still a small company, and only employs ten people: two Germans, two Englishmen, a Spaniard, a South African, a Frenchman, and three Afghans, all Uzbeks. They seem to function as independents, on assignment, without a formal boss.'

'Do they have weapons permits?'

'Ten.'

'What weapons have they declared?'

'Since when are weapons declared in this country? No one respects the law. They must assume we take them for an NGO. They really do think we're a bunch of amateurs. Do you want to see our photos? I have a whole series.'

Osama looked at the snapshots — about one hundred of them, on three different boards. One set had been taken in the countryside, probably in some kind of combing operation by the company's mercenaries; the others were in Kabul city centre. All had been taken with a telephoto lens.

'Your men have worked well and fast. I didn't think your files would be as extensive as this. It's frightening.'

Osama wasn't kidding.

'You forget that my team was trained by the Stasi and the KGB. The KGB was really something in the 1970s and 1980s! As for me, I learnt from the Chinese, in Peking, and if you think back, you'll remember that at that time the CPC wasn't messing around. The guys who trained my team were the best in the world. We could give most Western cops a run for their money.'

Three or four of the snapshots showed a tall, young, arrogant-looking man getting into or out of a Cherokee jeep. The others used two battered Land Cruisers.

'Who is this guy?' asked Osama. He was the only one who had been photographed at the wheel of the suspect car.

'No little *askar.* He's the one who serves as head of this rabble.

He's a German. Look at him — what a peacock. He acts as if he owns the place.'

'What's his name?'

'Michaël Dortmund.'

'Is he the only one who drives that car?'

'Looks like it.'

Osama stared at one of the snapshots, in which Babrak's killer was grinning widely. He felt the rage rising up in him.

'Do you think he's the one who killed Babrak?'

'Do you have anything new on the investigation?' dodged Osama.

'Abdul Hakat's profile is still bothering me. It's the first time we haven't been able to link a shahid to a particular Islamic group. I also have the NDS report on the imam of the mosque he attended. He'd never attracted any attention. Didn't fit the profile of a martyr-maker.'

'Why do you say "didn't" — is he dead?'

'My men were a bit hard on him,' admitted Reza. 'He drowned in the bath during our interrogation.'

Osama shook his head. Another innocent man dead.

'You know how it is,' Reza went on. 'The minister put major pressure on me. For him, the investigation is over: we have a culprit, a motive, and he can ask the Americans for even more money to fight Kabul's Taliban groups.'

'Most of which will go straight into his or his colleagues' pockets. Yes, I know exactly how it is,' said Osama. 'What about the brother — what does he say?'

'He's been sent off somewhere, to a secret NDS prison. In Kandahar, apparently. Totally off the map. We'll never hear of him again. Quite possibly he's already been hung.'

'We have to do something. We can't let this sort of thing go unpunished.'

'I agree. What do you want to do?'

'Set a trap for these bastards. You can help me.'

10.

NIGHT HAD FALLEN — an icy, rainy, starless night. Nick was driving through a seedy suburban landscape of concrete, graffiti, and abandoned buildings. For him these were new discoveries, new sites of unhappiness, places he hadn't known existed until he started working on this case.

The cheese factory that the prostitute had told him about was less than half an hour's drive from Letten. If Letten was purgatory, this pocket of industrial wasteland cut off from the rest of Zurich was hell. Nick couldn't understand what would make a client come out here to brave desperate junkies, thugs, and AIDS-ridden girls. He parked his car under the only working streetlight, picked up his gun, and went looking for Yasmina.

It was a tedious process. Every five metres he asked the same question, 'Do you know where I can find Yasmina?', and got the same reply, 'No.' After an hour he reached the banks of the Limmat — the end of the road for druggies and drag queens. He could just make out a silhouette perched on a rock a little further on. As he drew nearer, his heart began to race. It was Yasmina. Up close, she was even more emaciated than in the photo. Drugs had completely destroyed her: her skin was covered in black patches and stretched tight across her cheekbones; her eyes were gaunt and bloodshot. She was dirty, and seemed at a very low ebb. As he came nearer, he saw that she was staring oddly into space. Then he noticed the tourniquet on her arm, and the needle stuck in a pockmarked vein. She'd just shot herself up. Horrible.

'Hello, Yasmina,' said Nick, forcing himself not to run away.

His greeting took a few moments to penetrate the prostitute's addled brain; eventually, she looked up at him with dull eyes.

'Hello, pet,' she replied slowly, in a rasping voice.

He looked around. A few shadowy figures had noticed his gun and were keeping a safe distance.

'What do you want?' she asked, very slowly. 'To make love?'

'No. I want to talk to you. I'm looking for one of your friends.'

Her laugh creaked in her throat.

'A friend? I don't have any friends, chicken. Apart from her.'

She jerked her head at the needle stuck in her arm.

'You had at least one. The man who came to see you in the Langstrasse squat. A former client.'

Her eyes softened. Nick thought he saw a flicker of something like melancholy.

'Oh! Leonard ...'

'Yes.'

'Were you with the bastards who broke that place up?'

'I want to find Leonard before they do, before they kill him.'

She laughed again.

'Leonard ... he was my best client. I was a pretty girl then, believe it or not: I read books, and wore make-up and lovely dresses. I took 700 francs a night. More, from some of them. I was Leonard's regular girl for six years. Until some bastard gave me a taste of crack. Now, it's five francs, and that's with the good ones. Sometimes I do it for two.' She began to cry. 'I'm going to die, like an old AIDS whore. It's awful, so unfair.'

Nick overcame his disgust to move closer to her. From here, the pustules on her face were even more repulsive.

'Do you know where Leonard is?'

'He took off when that commando group attacked the squat. I haven't heard anything since. And I won't.'

'Why did he come to see you?'

'He was being chased by some guys who wanted to bump him off. He didn't know where to hide. He didn't sleep for two days in the squat. He was terrified of all the junkies, but he had a gun. I was his look-out. No one gave him any shit.'

'What was he waiting for?'

'A new passport.'

'Are you sure?'

'Positive. He asked me to put him in touch with someone who made false passports. I knew a guy. Leonard gave me five thousand francs.'

She started sobbing hot tears again.

'I wanted to get out of this life. There's a clinic where they treat girls like me. I wanted to do one more trick, for ten francs. A junky. He fucked me without a condom, then beat me up and stole the five thousand francs.' She started crying again. 'I'm such a stupid old bitch.'

'Who sorted the passport for him?'

'A Greek. Stavos something. He used to be a client of mine. He hangs out near Unterstrasse.'

'Where, exactly?'

Yasmina sniffed. The tears had made her mascara run down her cheeks in long, dark lines.

'There's a café around there. The Istanbul. He's always in there. That's where Leonard found him.'

Nick stuffed a twenty-franc note into her hand.

'If you come back, I'll give you a discount!' cried Yasmina.

KHAN DURRANI was checking his post, as he did every morning. He reached for his in-tray. It was red, of course, to signify that it was only to be used for important documents. Everything in it was sensitive information. He had requested all the documents relating to the Hamad Café attack, and was reading them with the care they deserved. He started with the most recent NDS report. It was as he had expected: the police were floundering horribly, but it hadn't occurred to anyone that the attack might not be the work of the Taliban or Al Qaida. The NDS was suggesting a massive roundup of Islamist networks, to try and locate this new terrorist cell. The minister used his blue fountain pen to write on the document: *Agreed. Carry out a thorough combing. Keep me informed of any new developments. No need for kid gloves in the interrogations.* Then he looked through the technical report by the intelligence department, although he didn't usually bother reading that sort of thing.

An underlined paragraph in the middle of the second page drew his attention: *The shoes worn by the shahid were not bought in Afghanistan; they are a Western brand that is not imported here. This means that Abdul Hakat had been in contact with overseas elements. We do not think that these elements were from Pakistan, as these shoes do not seem to be sold there either. We think his contacts must have been Arab or even European. If we are able to pursue this line of enquiry, we will be in a position to take fingerprints from the shoes, and possibly point the finger at terrorist elements from the Arab states, or other countries.*

'What the hell is this?' grumbled the minister. 'What does it mean?'

He called for Dortmund to be brought to his office immediately, as a matter of utmost importance. The German arrived in less than an hour. He seemed very annoyed at having been summoned in this way.

'What's going on?' he asked, without so much as a greeting.

The minister silently showed him the file. He'd long learned to ignore the bad manners of unbelievers. With them, power and money were the only things that mattered.

'I don't speak Dari; you'll have to translate it for me.'

'Of course. My apologies.'

By the time Durrani finished translating, Dortmund was deathly pale. The minister was delighted. At last this arrogant jerk was stuck for something to say.

'Where did the shoes come from?' he asked.

'They were mine,' replied Dortmund tonelessly. 'And the T-shirt. That idiot wasn't wearing trainers, so we gave him a pair to make him look a bit more fashionable. We wanted him to sail through security. My explosive expert's feet are huge, so I had to give him my shoes.'

'It's a real pain. Your fingerprints will be on them, I suppose?'

'Of course they will! Whose prints do you think you'd find? Karzaï's?'

'It's a real pain,' repeated the minister, simply.

'I'm not on any files in this country,' said Dortmund.

'It seems that Kandar has visited the scene of the crime. We can't rule out the possibility that someone saw you, and that Kandar will manage to find out your identity. If that's the case, your shoes will incriminate you.'

'We'd better get them back right now.'

'I'll send my men.'

'No, I'll take care of it,' insisted Dortmund.

There was no way he was going to let any Afghans get their hands on something as explosive as that, and send him to prison for the rest of his life. Or worse.

Nick slept badly, haunted by nightmares. After the Limmat, he'd been to the Istanbul Café, only to find it closed. He had returned to his flat, exhausted and without the crucial information he was gradually inching towards.

He was closer to the fugitive than anyone else from the Entity. But that didn't help. It didn't solve any of his problems; any of the questions he was asking himself.

As he drove, he tried to think more calmly about the information he had gathered since the beginning of the investigation. Why had the fugitive deserted? Why had he suddenly decided to throw it all in?

Then Nick remembered something that Jacqueline had said during their conversation. He pulled over to the side of the road, rummaged in his folder, and found the Romance business card she had given him. A receptionist put him through.

'Jacqueline,' he asked as soon as he had her on the line, 'I would like to clarify something from our conversation. You said at one point that you hadn't had any news from your former client — don't mention his name on the phone, please — for a long time. What do you mean by "a long time"?'

'Since last November.'

He took a deep breath. Something was beginning to take shape in his mind.

'Had he ever disappeared for such a long time before?'

'No, he was very regular. He always took his holiday on the same dates, and I would usually see him a week before he left and the day after he returned. He would occasionally postpone our meetings, but for a few days at most; there was never a gap as long as six months.'

'Jacqueline, your client disappeared barely a few days ago. Before that, he was going to the office as normal. Nothing about his life had changed. Except with regards to you. The cessation of contact with you was the only major change in his life.'

'I don't understand.'

She seemed disappointed. As if she weren't a woman that men paid to use as they pleased … did she really think that a man could have genuine feelings for a prostitute, however charming? In that case, she was more naïve than her professional façade suggested.

'I'm sorry to ask again, but how was your client the last time you saw him? Was he different in any way?'

'Now that you mention it, maybe he was. He didn't want us to … you know … so we just chatted about various things over tea.'

'What did you talk about?'

'I really can't remember. I'm sorry. He seemed in a very good mood, whereas he tended to be quite cold.'

Nick put the phone down.

This was no coincidence, no unimportant piece of information. It was a vital clue.

He had just realised why the fugitive had broken off communications with Jacqueline. This opened fascinating new avenues. New trails. If only he could navigate them correctly.

THE CHEROKEE JEEP struggled to worm its way into Kabul's usual heavy traffic. Dortmund sat in the passenger seat, steam coming out of his ears. Suddenly, a delivery van stopped in the middle of the road, blocking their way. Two workmen got out to unload the contents — steel pipes for a building site. Dortmund was out of the car and waving his gun around before his men had had a chance to move. He whacked one of the workmen across the face with the butt, splitting his head open. Then he smashed the van windscreen and threatened the driver, who took one look at this madman and drove off, leaving his two workmen stranded. Twenty minutes later Dortmund parked right in front of the hospital, with no regard for any parking restrictions. He pulled the piece of paper out of his pocket. *Dr Katoun, medico-legal office.* He turned towards the Afghan in the back seat.

'Go and see this doctor. Tell him you've been sent by the NDS. Make sure your gun is visible in its holster. I want you to bring back all the Hamad Café bomber's personal effects. Tell him you're carrying out further tests. Make sure you have both the shoes; they are red trainers.'

'What if he won't give them to me?'

'Bash him up if you have to, but bring me back those shoes. Do you understand?'

'Yes, boss.'

The Afghan stepped out of the car, delighted to escape his angry boss. Half an hour later he was back. Alone.

'I had trouble finding him; he was in a surdery room.'

Dortmund didn't react.

'I don't give a damn where he was, you moron. Where are the shoes?'

'He's gone to get them, they're in an oderating theatre, and I'm not allowed in there.'

'Go back this instant. Just bring them to me, understand?'

Dortmund smiled sardonically as he watched the Afghan run off. "Surdery". "Oderating theatre". Christ! These guys were such morons. This country should just be torched and rebuilt from scratch.

Ten minutes went by. Then twenty. Why was his man taking so long? Just as Dortmund was about to get of the car, the Afghan appeared. He was carrying a see-through bag that he held up triumphantly. Dortmund could make out two red shoes inside. He sighed with relief. The Afghan slipped into the back of the car.

'The bag,' said Dortmund. 'Now.'

He opened it feverishly. When he saw the trainers, he thought he must be hallucinating. He took them out of the bag as if in a nightmare. These were not his New Balance trainers, but crappy copies sporting the usual 'Nike by Adidas' logo.

'I don't believe it,' he muttered.

He was trying to work out what might have happened when all the car doors were yanked open at once. Someone grabbed him and threw him to the ground. Lots of people were yelling 'police, police'. In just a few seconds, Afghans brandishing automatic weapons had handcuffed all his men. He was pushed into the back of a van. Standing in the road was a very tall man in a fur hat, with a grey-speckled beard and sparkling, snake-like green eyes. He walked slowly over. His stern face was inscrutable.

'Michaël Dortmund, I am qomaandaan Osama Kandar, of Kabul Murder Squad. You are under arrest.'

Before he could reply, Dortmund was whacked on the head with a police baton and shoved deep into the back of the van. The doors closed and the vehicle drove off, throwing him against the wall, his face dripping with blood.

When they arrived at police headquarters, Dortmund was removed from the van, and dragged rather than led to an interrogation cell. He started yelling: 'You have no right, you have no right, call the German Embassy.' The only reply was a fresh blow to the head, and several to the stomach. Jihad and Rangin handcuffed the dazed German to a chair. Rangin fastened the cuffs so tightly behind his back that he cried out in pain. Jihad frisked him thoroughly, putting the objects on the table one at a time: documents, a palmtop computer, a mobile phone, a BlackBerry, a Colt .38 calibre pocket revolver not found by the policemen who'd arrested him, a passport, and wads of dollars and afghanis. Spare cartridges. On the final search he also found a dagger in a calf sheath. He gave Dortmund one last slap and walked out with Rangin, leaving the German to his own devices. A few seconds later, Osama walked in, followed by Gulbudin. Osama glanced at Dortmund, and the prisoner shivered. He examined the weapons and wads of notes distractedly before picking up the passport.

'Take his fingerprints, Gulbudin.'

His deputy shouted something in Dari. Two uniformed policemen — great hulking Uzbeks — entered. They took off Dortmund's handcuffs. He tried to put up a fight, but it was no good; the Afghans were much too strong for him.

'Stop struggling,' said Osama. 'It's stupid — there's no point.'

One of the policemen forced Dortmund to straighten out his arm. Gulbudin picked up an inking-pad and smeared the ends of his fingers. Dortmund cried out and tried to pull his hands away.

'You're going to get your arm broken,' said Osama. 'Do you want to end up the only European in a cell with twenty-five Afghans, and your arm in pieces?'

That settled him down. Gulbudin took fingerprints from both hands. Then he wiped off Dortmund's fingers with a filthy rag and left with his precious prints. The German was reattached to the chair. Osama dismissed the two policemen with a jerk of his chin. Then he opened the passport.

'Your name is Michaël Dortmund. You were born on the 14th of December 1978, in Bonn, Federal Republic of Germany,' he began in his grating English. 'Officially, you are a security advisor, head of the company Aid Service Protection. You drive a black Cherokee jeep, with the number plate *KBL 27645 SH.*'

'Let me go, you piece of shit,' spat Dortmund. 'You have no right to arrest me. I have diplomatic status.'

Osama waved the man's passport under his nose.

'This is a normal passport. Where is your diplomatic safe-conduct?'

'At my office. Let me go, you bastard.'

'Stop insulting me, or you'll regret it. You'll be out of here very soon, I promise. But probably not as a free man.'

Osama leaned comfortably against the wall. His head almost touched the ceiling of the tiny room. Sweat was pouring down the German's face, and he was giving off a sharp, acrid smell that Osama would have recognised anywhere — the smell of fear.

'The vehicle you were taken from was seen next to the Hamad Café on the night it was bombed,' he continued.

'I don't know what the Ahmed Café is.'

'A café popular among young Kabulis, that some bastard blew up with three kilos of C5 strapped to the back of a poor idiot being passed off as a suicide bomber. That's what the Hamad Café is,' said Osama. 'You're aware of the sentence for acts of terrorism in Afghanistan, I take it?'

There was a knock at the door. Gulbudin came in, moving as fast as he could with his bad leg. He whispered a few words excitedly in Osama's ear. Osama turned towards Dortmund. His eyes had become even more intense.

'The fingerprints found in various places on the pair of shoes used by the shahid were indeed yours. So those were your shoes.'

The truth suddenly became crystal clear to Osama.

'But, of course, I'm so stupid! Who would have suspected a young man dressed in Western clothes with brand-new luxury trainers on his feet?'

'This is a set-up. I won't talk, you swine.'

Gulbudin swung his baton to whack the German over the head again, but Osama stopped him. A great hubbub was taking place in the corridor, with lots of shouting. A few seconds later, several plainclothed men burst into the room. One of them brandished his card: a colonel, from the security minister's staff.

'What are you doing?' he barked. 'Arresting citizens of NATO countries without informing us first? Are you out of your mind?'

Osama moved aside.

'We didn't know this man was German when we arrested him.'

'Liar! Let him go immediately. He's one of ours!'

'Let him go yourself, if he's one of yours,' retorted Osama scathingly.

He threw the handcuff keys on the floor, pushed past the secret agent, and strode out of the room. He was smiling. He had the fingerprints — formal proof of the German's implication in Wali Wadi's death. He had no further need of him.

Joseph finished his set of press-ups, and towelled off his sweat-soaked hair. It went without saying that Westerners didn't have access to any of the Kabul gyms, except the ones at the military bases and luxury hotels, so he'd decided to do an hour's worth of exercises every morning on the office floor. He towelled off, put on a clean shirt, and gave himself a sniff. Not great — he really should have gone home for a shower, but he didn't have time. He glanced at his emails, sighed in relief, and picked up his phone.

'Bring Peter and Marco with you.'

No greeting. No need for that. A few seconds later, Amin came in with his two colleagues.

Joseph reached for a dish of dried fruits and nuts. He picked up a handful of almonds and put them in his mouth. Amin and his colleagues could see his powerful teeth as he chewed. The sound was unpleasant and loud. The killer took another handful and ground them up like the first. The sound of chewing. Silence. The sound of chewing. Swallowing. At last he wiped his mouth.

'I've just obtained the general's approval for my new plan. Let's cause some chaos. This is our second attempt. It had better work this time.'

He flicked a business card across the desk at Amin.

'For you. Find him.'

There was only one name on the card — Abdullah Nassim Darani — plus an address, and a phone number starting with the Kabul code. Amin looked up at his boss.

'Who is this man?'

'An ex-mujahedeen. Runs a gang of hard-bastard criminals — kidnappings, extortion, drug trafficking. A member of his family was arrested in Lausanne last year for racketeering; he'd tortured a restaurant owner with a blowtorch. It was him who told the federal police about his charming uncle.'

'What does he have to do with us?'

'The general still doesn't want us to take care of Kandar directly,' said Joseph ruefully. 'We need locals to do the dirty work. Apparently this guy speaks Arabic. You can translate.'

'Yes, sir!'

Joseph took a handful of nuts.

'Take thirty thousand dollars out of the safe. We'll go over there now.'

Two vehicles were already waiting out front, their engines running. Joseph stepped into the first with Amin, while the other two Ks joined a couple of commandos in the second.

'What makes you think he'll be at home now?' asked Amin.

'We've been tapping his phone since yesterday. Berne told me that he's made several calls in the last two hours.'

The former mujahedeen lived in a Pashtun enclave next to the Tajik area of Karte Parwan, in north Kabul. They soon found themselves in a maze of little lanes, none of which bore signs. In the end, the driver stopped the car.

'We're lost, boss.'

Joseph turned to Amin.

'Knock on any old door. Find someone to show us the way.'

'No one will answer. It'll be dark in an hour.'

'I don't give a damn. Just sort it out — we're wasting time.'

Amin waved to a group of young boys. They spoke a hard-to-understand mix of Dari and Pashtun, but once a ten-dollar note was produced, one of them set off running. A K stepped out of the protective vehicle to stand guard. He wore protective sunglasses, a bullet-proof vest, and various handguns on his belt, and carried a black submachine gun. The Robocop gestured to indicate that he had the whole street under watch. The boy returned with a limping old man. In his same pidgin, the boy explained to Amin that the old man knew the street they were looking for, and could even speak a bit of English. Amin gave the boy another ten-dollar note; he took it delightedly.

'I'm looking for a house around here,' Amin said to the old man, consulting his Arab/Dari dictionary. Can you help me? *Ke maara koumak metonaa*?'

'Khou, farq namey kouna.'

'Which way is that? *Koudam taraf?'*

'I can show you the way,' said the old man at last, in very respectable English, as he opened the car door.

He got in next to Amin. He stank — a mixture of ancient grime, stale tobacco, garlic, and Rose cologne. Joseph silently opened the window. The two vehicles set off. They drove further into a slum of old adobe houses. The streets were strewn with refuse, broken-down machinery, the most unbelievable rubbish. There were no chitralis to be seen, but lots of beards: this was definitely a Pashtun neighbourhood. People glared at the two cars, doubtless taking them for Coalition soldiers. The old man seemed uneasy.

'We'll have to be quick,' said Amin. 'They don't like kafirs here. We could be lynched.'

At that very moment, a stone smashed against the windscreen of the armoured car.

'Just keep going, don't react,' said Joseph.

'Danger. They shoot us,' yelped the old man.

'You're starting to get on my nerves. Shut it.'

Fifteen minutes later, the old man tugged on Amin's sleeve and pointed to a house a little further on, squeezed between two small shops.

'If we all go, our man might think we're NATO soldiers and take fright. Just you and me, Amin,' ordered Joseph. 'The rest can provide protection, but from the vehicles.'

As soon as they stepped out of the car, the old man ran off as fast as he could. Amin was about to give chase when Joseph stopped him.

'Leave it. We don't need him any more.'

Joseph took out a long pistol and rested it on his thigh. It was fitted with a massive silencer. Then he nodded, and Amin knocked three times on the door.

'Who's there?' shouted someone from inside.

'We come as friends,' replied the Algerian in Arabic. 'To offer you work.'

'I don't need any work!'

'This job is worth ten thousand dollars.'

There was a few moments' hesitation. Then the door opened slightly, revealing a man in a pair of brown Afghan trousers and a vest. He was bald, with a moustache and the beginnings of a pot belly. He was aiming a gun at Amin's head, with a very steady hand.

'Fuck. Who are you? I don't know you!' he barked. 'What do you want from me? Are you American? Russian?'

'I'm a friend. I have money for you.'

Joseph appeared, his pistol held at hip height and aimed at the gangster's head.

'Tell him to lower his gun. That he doesn't need it.'

Amin translated. The gangster replied that he didn't believe them.

'Tell him that there are four commandos in those cars, so if we wanted to kill him, he would already be dead.'

Amin translated again. The man looked over to the cars, and hesitated a moment. Seemingly soothed by his visitors' calm attitude, he lowered his gun and asked them inside.

It was a large house by Kabul standards, and luxurious, despite the beaten-earth floor — a few trunks and carpets, an old-fashioned but new three-piece suite, and a home video connected to a stereo system with massive speakers. An RPG rocket-launcher and several Kalashnikovs were propped against a wall.

'Business is good, I see,' commented Joseph.

The translation provoked the first smile to appear on the gangster's face. He gestured his guests to the sofa, and sat down in the armchair.

'Women!' he shouted.

There was a great commotion in the room next door. Two shapes appeared in the passage, without entering the room — observing the usual stricture against the slightest contact between women and strangers.

'Tea,' ordered the man, without so much as a glance at his two wives.

The two subjugated shapes withdrew.

'What do you want?' asked the crook.

'Translate as I go along,' Joseph instructed Amin. He returned his gaze to the Afghan. 'We have a mission for you. To eliminate a government official. A cop. We'll give you five thousand dollars straight away, and another five when it's done. The target has bodyguards.'

'How many?'

'Between three and five.'

'That makes it more dangerous. Is his vehicle armoured?'

Joseph turned towards Amin.

'Do we know?'

'No.'

'Who is this cop?'

'Commandant Kandar.'

The gangster spat on the floor.

'That bastard. Son of a bitch has tried to arrest me three times, but never had anything on me, and had to let me go. His vehicle isn't armoured. I can do it, but I'll have to take all my men. Do you have his address?'

'Yes.'

'Where is it?'

They were interrupted by one of the women, who put a tray down in the doorway, making sure to remain out of sight of the unknown men, and quickly withdrew. The gangster stood up.

'So, this address?' he repeated as he brought over the tea.

Amin told him. The man shook his head.

'Not possible — there's a barracks there, and it's swarming with cops. Too dangerous.'

'What about if we give you more cash?'

'No. We wouldn't get out alive. Find someone else.'

This wasn't a negotiating strategy; his tone brooked no argument. After a moment's thought, Joseph asked, 'Could you do the job if you could get Kandar somewhere familiar?

'In that case, yes. But for forty thousand dollars.'

'Twenty.'

In the end, they agreed on twenty-five thousand, with half up front.

'How will I get him where I want him?' asked the gangster.

'Send a kid over with an anonymous note telling Kandar you have information about Wali, with a rendezvous. He'll be there, wherever it is.'

'Wali? Wali who?'

'Just say Wali. He'll come, I promise. You'll have to work fast. It needs to be done tomorrow or the day after.'

'It will be. How do I collect the second half of the money?'

'We'll know when you've acted. Someone will bring the rest of the money here when the mission is complete.'

'Are you joking? What makes you think I should believe that?'

'Nothing, my friend. But what choice do you have?

At a sign from Joseph, Amin tossed the wad of notes onto the table. The crook shoved it in his pocket. Joseph brought his face right up to the Afghan's. His washed-out eyes sparkled with an evil light.

'He better not try to con me. If he does, I swear I'll torch him, his family, and anyone else I happen to find. Ask him if he believes me.'

'Yes,' stammered the Afghan.

Joseph stood up.

'So, he'd better not screw up.'

THAT DAY, Osama came home early, to spend some time with Malalai. He knew that Khan Durrani would soon exert his influence to have Dortmund released, but he had already achieved his goal: to irrefutably link Dortmund with the so-called shahid. If he could find Dortmund's fingerprints at Wali Wadi's place, too, he would have come full circle and proven that the two cases were related. As he got out of his car, surrounded by bodyguards, he noticed that the policeman keeping watch over his house wasn't alone. Two other men were standing guard with him — soldiers, carrying powerful assault rifles. One of them wore a parachutist's tab, a rarity in Afghanistan. Their calm attitude, and the scarred face of one of them, suggested they were old hands accustomed to action.

'What are you doing here?' asked Osama, after the usual greetings.

'They told us to come,' said one.

'Who?'

'Our bosses.'

'Why?'

'To protect you, hajji. We would give our lives for you.'

'What clans are you from?'

'The Faizabad Sawak clan,' said one.

'The Jumm Alqiti clan,' said the other.

They were Tajiks. His enemies would have sent Pashtuns. Someone had realised the danger he was in and decided to protect him. But who? Osama walked into his house. Malalai was already at home, looking exhausted. He kissed her.

'Not a good day?'

'I treated two girls from Jalalabad. One of them, a twelve-year-old, had been doused in acid by Taliban because she refused to marry a fifty-year-old man. In revenge, her family kidnapped the man's brother's daughter, and cut off her nose and the tips of her breasts. Two innocent girls falling prey to the same barbarism! The men had used them instead of fighting each other directly. They were considered nothing — meat, worse than meat.' She began sobbing. 'I don't know if I can go on, Osama, life is too hard.'

Osama took her in his arms. She was trembling all over.

'The RAWA meeting couldn't take place,' she continued. 'There was suspect activity where we were due to meet — it seemed as if the Taliban were watching — so we decided to cancel. One of the girls has pulled out; she's too scared. I hope I won't crack.'

They stayed in each other's arms a long while. Then Malalai pulled away.

'I'll make you some dinner. This isn't for you to deal with.'

When he went to bed that night, Osama heard the throaty cough of one of the parachutists standing guard. He sounded unwell, but Osama knew he would remain there and defend him to the death. He thought about the American satellites spinning thirty-six thousand kilometres overhead, tapping all his communications, and the faeces-littered shantytown he'd walked through the previous morning. He thought about the TV programme he'd seen about a woman having her face remodelled by European surgeons, and the young girl from Jalalabad whose face had just been destroyed. He thought about the man who'd been tricked into blowing himself up, and the other men who blew themselves up of their own free will, to kill as many innocents as possible. He thought about his deputy, so full of life, who'd been assassinated as though he were nothing, or nobody. He asked himself why God allowed such things to happen.

Nick slipped into his car. It had been a long day, and he was champing at the bit for some progress on the case. He'd spent the last few hours allaying suspicion by working on spurious activities. Why wasn't he telling his employer the truth about his findings? He didn't know. Perhaps because he'd discovered that Joseph was in Kabul — something they'd been careful not to mention. For as long as they refused to explain the link between the two missions, he would have to remain on guard. There were too many deaths, too many mysteries, too much stuff being hidden from him and from others. He opened his briefcase to reveal an automatic handgun. It was an impressively heavy weapon, with a black butt made from composite materials, and the barrel elongated by an oblong silencer. He didn't like weapons, especially since the death of his friend. But he still stuffed it in his pocket.

The fairy lights strung across the entrance didn't stop the Istanbul café from looking like what it was: a squalid hovel, where alcoholics came to drink themselves into a stupor on a few glasses of cheap booze before staggering home. Nick parked a few metres up the hill and turned off the engine. For the first time in his life, he was alone in the midst of the action without a safety net. He stretched his hands in front of him and saw that they were trembling.

Let's hope I have the stamina to see this through, he thought, stepping out of the car.

Inside, it was just like every drinker's den the world over: a tired barman wiping glasses behind his counter, four or five sad customers nursing their drinks, background music emanating from an iPod hooked up to speakers. Nick didn't want to be overheard, so he walked around the side of the bar to speak to the barman. He quietly took out his federal department of justice badge, hoping the white cross on a red background would work its usual magic.

'I'm looking for Stavos,' he said.

'I haven't seen him tonight.'

'Where is he?'

'I don't know.'

'Listen, mate,' said Nick, 'I really want to talk to him tonight. I don't mean him any harm, but if I don't find him, various people are going to pay, starting with you. Pay heavily, if you take my meaning.'

The barman stared at Nick. He wasn't intimidated, although he didn't exactly relish being asked questions by a young guy in a cop uniform. On the other hand, the guy was flashing an official card, and those cards always spelled trouble. He looked into Nick's cobalt-blue eyes, which were shining with fierce determination. He began to feel even more uneasy.

'Right now, Stavos is playing cards at Hans' place,' he muttered quickly.

'Hans?'

'A bar, a bit further on — about a block away. There's a secret card-room out back. You knock on the blue door at the end of the main bar. Two knocks, then three.'

'Thanks,' said Nick. 'You made the right choice.'

Outside, it had stopped raining. He decided to walk. It was a poor neighbourhood, full of grog shops, little stalls, and foreign-run corner shops. It was pleasantly busy and chaotic, in sharp contrast to the usual calm of Swiss cities. More like France or Italy. He noticed a Hindi sign above one shop. Immigration into Switzerland had changed a lot recently: increasingly tight legislation meant that people from Bangladesh and central Asia had slowly but surely replaced the Africans and North Africans.

He stopped in front of the bar, which had no sign, looked through the window, and made out a blue door at the back. He walked through the room without a word, and tapped the code on the door. It opened immediately, to reveal a massive guy in jeans, vest, and heavy stubble. Behind him was a small, smoky room, with an even lower ceiling; there were five tables, all taken. Nick flashed his fake badge again. At the sight of the official logo, the porter seemed to shrink. The federal justice departments had a reputation for being even harsher than the district authorities.

'I'm looking for Stavos.'

'Not here,' said the hulk.

'I don't give a damn about the room,' retorted Nick, impressively cool. He was taking to this role. 'I just want to talk to Stavos. Give me any trouble and I'll have this dump closed down, and you arrested.'

The conversations in the room had stopped. Nick's heart was pounding, but the hulk didn't notice. He shrugged his shoulders and pointed to a man sitting at the nearest table — about thirty, narrow-shouldered. Nick noticed that his hands were ink stained.

'I haven't done anything. What do you want?'

'Come with me,' snapped Nick.

Stavos seemed resigned. He stood up obediently and put on his coat. The silence in the room was deafening. Then a man took out a cigarette and asked his neighbour for a light. As if responding to a conductor, the room returned to life. Conversations resumed; cards were dealt. Stavos left the room flanked by Nick.

'Are you really a cop?' he asked. 'Federal?'

'Shut up,' said Nick. 'You'll talk when I tell you to.'

All Entity vehicles had a hook embedded in the floor. Nick put a pair of plastic handcuffs on Stavos and pushed him into the back seat. As they drove away from the city centre towards the seedy industrial areas, Stavos became increasingly upset.

'Where are you taking me? I haven't done anything.'

'Shut it,' yelled Nick, taking out his gun and putting it on the passenger seat.

When he saw the impressive silencer, Stavos started blubbing.

'I don't want to die.'

Nick drove around the deserted streets near the cheese factory for a while, then headed for the darkest part, by the river. He parked on the riverbank and killed the engine. The rain, which had started on the journey, was now beating loudly on the roof. He unhooked the handcuffs, and pulled Stavos out of the car by his sleeve. He thumped him and sent him toppling into the mud. When he saw the gun aimed at his forehead, Stavos started sobbing in earnest. The front of his trousers were wet with piss.

'For Christ's sake, what do you want with me? Have pity, I haven't done anything.'

He seemed to have lost any semblance of resistance.

'A junky whore brought you a client. Her name is Yasmina — she was in the Langstrasse squat where that incident took place.'

'The smackhead squat?'

'Right. Her client wanted a passport. A man of about fifty, short, glasses, balding. Rich guy, not used to the underground life. We need to know the name he used for the passport. Then you can go free.'

'No. You'll kill me as soon as I've given you the name.'

'You'll go free. I just want the name.'

Stavos swallowed, and dried his tears. In the end, he cracked.

'Milton. I made him a passport for Lionel Milton.'

Nick took a deep breath. This was a massive step.

'There. That wasn't too hard, was it?' he said to the trafficker smoothly. 'Come on, I'll take you home.'

The stench of Stavos' piss in the Peugeot was almost unbearable. Nick wound down the window until they drew near to the shitty bar.

'Could you take a little further, please? A couple of streets?' asked Stavos nervously. 'I can't go back to Hans' place with my trousers like this. I'll have to change.'

As soon as he was alone, Nick started thinking about how to use the information. Since September 11, he'd had access to airline company lists: the companies were forced to give the SRS a complete list of all passengers entering or leaving Switzerland. The Entity had access to the computer that ran the programme, but if he logged in as himself he would leave tracks, and there was no way he was doing that.

OSAMA ROSE AT 3.00AM. He was still half asleep as he said his first prayer, begging Allah to help him in his search for truth. The floor beneath the prayer mat was hard, and when he stood up his knees were numb. With Malalai still asleep, he took care to make as little noise as possible — once she woke, she never dozed off again, as hospital duty had trained her body to be perfectly alert as soon as it was shaken from sleep. He stoked the stove so the bedroom would be warmer by the time she dressed. There was no shampoo in the bathroom, so he washed with a piece of rock-hard soap that smelled of rose. He hated the smell of rose on his own body, and cursed this Westernised city where it had become impossible to find the old simple soap that smelled of cleanliness and nothing else. He dressed quickly in the dark and left without slamming the door, carrying his rifle and his boots. The bitter cold froze his wet hair. He paused briefly to put on his boots, taking a deep breath and savouring the moment. This was his favourite time of year — the last days of winter before spring, followed by the stifling heat of June.

His 4x4 and the protective pick-up were waiting outside in the dark, engines off. The right-hand front door of the 4x4 creaked open and Gulbudin stepped out, wearing an old Soviet Army parka with a fraying collar. Osama could still see a patch where the red star had been removed.

'We're all set, hajji.'

Osama clapped his gloved hands together to warm them up before opening the hatchback. Two pots of fingerprint powder sat on the floor, as well as new brushes, gloves, and all the other paraphernalia needed to take fingerprints at Wali Wadi's place. Osama got into the passenger seat, and Gulbudin into the back. The driver was nibbling dried dates, his thermos wedged between the two front seats. The inside of the car was freezing — Osama had asked them not to disturb the neighbours by keeping the engine running. This was typical of the small selfless gestures that made Osama so universally liked.

The convoy set off. The streets were empty, with just the odd military truck driving around. It took them less than fifteen minutes to reach Wali Wadi's luxurious home. The lane was full of refuse, plus the corpse of a stray dog that no one had bothered to remove. Osama pushed aside the police ribbon blocking the door. The night watchman — a retired police officer — was sleeping soundly, wrapped in his *patou*. Gulbudin tapped him on the shoulder to wake him and let him know that they were going into the house. The watchman nodded and went straight back to sleep. They filed in. The gas central-heating was working — it was nice and warm. For a split second, Osama envied this kind of life. Despite the war, he was sure that Wali Wadi hadn't been cold for quite a few years.

'Where shall we look?' asked Gulbudin.

'On anything that Dortmund might have touched while he was here. In the study. The living room. The kitchen. Everywhere.'

The men took their brushes and fingerprint-powder sachets,

and set to work. Osama took the study. There were fingerprints everywhere. He sprinkled the possible surfaces with powder, and when a fingerprint appeared, compared it to the photo of Dortmund's. After an hour, he knew every furrow of Dortmund's finger by heart, and could immediately tell if a new print wasn't his. After two hours, he decided to focus on the safe. After all, it was surely what Dortmund had come for. Fortune smiled on him about six thirty in the morning, just as a pallid dawn started peeping through the windows: there was a print of Dortmund's index finger on the left inside wall of the safe. He must have made it while checking for any last documents left inside. Osama found a second print — of a thumb — on the inside of the door itself. Shortly afterwards, Gulbudin rushed in.

'We've found a Dortmund fingerprint in the loo!'

Osama followed him. The toilet was a large room, with over-ornate walls and a hand-painted ceiling. The loo roll-holder was shaped like a golden duck, and the water-fountain mouth like a swan.

'What is that?' asked Gulbudin, stunned.

'Foreigners use paper instead of a water fountain,' explained Osama, remembering his time in Moscow.

Wali Wadi came from a poor country background, the kind of place still inhabited by more than half the Afghan population. There were no bathrooms or loos in that Afghanistan: both men and women relieved themselves on the land around their houses, wiping themselves with sand or a flat stone. These grotesque toilets were Wali Wadi's revenge on life.

The walls were now dotted with powder patches. Gulbudin pointed to one of them, next to the golden, duck-shaped holder.

'There it is. Dortmund must have put his hand on the wall while he was sitting down.'

Osama had what he wanted — three of Dortmund's fingerprints, more than he needed to implicate him in Wali Wadi's murder. At 9.00am, he told his team that it was time to leave.

11.

OSAMA WAS IN ONE OF THE INTERROGATION CELLS, working on a man accused of having killed his neighbour with a pickaxe. The motive? A cart of vegetables, which the murderer coveted so he could start a corner shop of his own. He denied the crime, but blood had been found on him, as well as the pickaxe, which was hidden in his house. He should have thrown it away, but it had cost five hundred afghanis, so he wanted to keep it. Now he would spend thirty years in Pul e Charki — unless the courts decided to hang him instead. Osama let Rangin finish the interrogation: as far as he was concerned, the case was closed. He walked past the holding room. Another two men were waiting in handcuffs — one for having beaten his wife to death; the other, for murdering a peasant by shooting him in the head. Osama took the second man into his office, hands secured behind his back. Jihad sat him down on a chair and slipped out.

'This man you shot,' asked Osama, 'did you know him?'

'Na.'

'Never seen him in your life?'

'Na.'

'Why did you kill him?'

'To try out my gun.'

'Explain,' said Osama, taken aback.

'I bet a friend five hundred afghanis that, God willing, I could hit a target from three hundred metres with my old rifle — a 1925

Lee Enfield, a top-quality weapon. This man was standing there on a ridge, not moving. He was three hundred metres away. I couldn't find any other target at the right distance, so I shot him.'

'He was a shepherd, looking after his flock.'

'I didn't see the sheep, otherwise I would have shot one of them. The shepherd was a difficult target. I hit him right in the head on the first shot,' said the man proudly.

'His name was Nuredin Malkiour. He was forty-four years old. Now he's dead, and his wife is alone, with seven children to feed.'

'She still has the flock of sheep, so she won't starve to death, Insha'Allah.'

Osama stared at the accused to see if he was taking the piss, but he was perfectly serious. Osama couldn't find an ounce of remorse in his eyes. In the end, he called Rangin.

'Take him back to the cells.'

'What shall we charge him with?'

'Voluntary manslaughter. Call the prosecutor's office.'

The man would be lucky to escape hanging. An orderly appeared at the door.

'Qomaandaan! Someone at reception is asking for you.'

Osama went, still distressed by the interrogation of the rifleman. Kalkana the public scribe was sitting on a rickety bench in the reception area with a satchel on his lap, looking shy. Osama hugged him.

'I'm happy to see you. I've had a day full of nutters; it feels like the most moronic idiots in all Kabul have been conspiring to give me grief.'

'I have what you want,' said his friend, taking a parcel out of his satchel. 'Two powder tests, made in Turkey. Very reliable, apparently. The expiry date is more than nine months away.'

DORTMUND LAY in a squalid NDS cell, somewhere in the sprawling basement beneath headquarters. He stretched, and took a sip of water. He had been relatively well treated since the intervention by the minister's policemen: no more beatings, no handcuffs, food, and even bottles of mineral water instead of the dysentery-producing stuff from the tap. He wasn't too worried — he'd done good work for the Americans, the French, and the English, and then those strange Swiss guys: he knew too much to be left to moulder in an Afghan cell.

A key turned in the lock.

'Go, you free, go quick,' said the NDS cop who'd got him out of police headquarters, in his rough English.

There was nothing to sign, no counter-interrogation, never mind a lawyer. They returned his stuff, minus the wads of cash that had disappeared somewhere between police and NDS headquarters. He pocketed his passport and found himself on the steps of the building. Two black 4x4s were parked out front. One of them flashed its headlights, and the two vehicles drove up to him. The passenger door of the second opened from the inside. He got in.

'You look quite fresh, for someone leaving an Afghan jail,' commented Joseph from the back seat.

His lean, muscular body was sheathed in close-fitting black fatigues, and a pistol in a holster was strapped across his chest.

'Right, what's happening now?'

'Our friends in Berne don't see many options. You'll have to leave the country.'

'I thought there was still work to do on this job.'

'Aren't the cops on your case enough? You keep leaving incriminating evidence. There's no option but to send you back to Europe. My company will pay your airfare on behalf of Willard Consulting. You should be grateful we're getting you out of this mess.'

'I don't have any work in Europe! I make more than eight thousand dollars a month here. All this is that bloody cop Kandar's fault.'

'I know.'

'What are you going to do about it?'

'We're going to kill him. Your friend the security minister will help us. But it's no longer your job. Your job is to go back to Europe and lie low for a while.'

Two men were shouting at each other on the side of the road —

something about right of way. Joseph sighed. This city disgusted him. The 4x4 pulled up to the pavement.

'Go and pack. Then one of our men will take you to your office — we want to be sure that your papers are left in good order. I'll collect you myself this evening to take you to the airport.'

'What about my fingerprints? The prints taken by that dirty cop will have to be destroyed.'

'I said, "Go and pack."'

THE ORDERLY put the note on Osama's desk.

I know what case Wali was working on, it said. *You'll find what you're looking for in his office, in the furthest room, under the fourth floorboard.*

'Orderly,' called Osama.

The cop returned and stood to attention.

'Qomaandaan.'

'Who left this note?'

'A child. I took it from him myself.'

'Describe him to me.'

The child didn't sound like the one that Mullah Bakir usually sent. Osama wondered what this mysterious note could mean. It might be a trap. Or not. He was suspicious of his enemies, but if he could find out what Wali Wadi had been up to, his investigation would be a done deal. He decided to go. In the corridor, he called to his deputy.

'Gulbudin, I need to go to Wali Wadi's office. Gather a few bodyguards.'

'The thing is …'

'Is there a problem?'

'Yes. The deputy secretary-general of the UN is visiting, and our men are on duty. Rangin and Jihad are out investigating. Mohammed is on British-run target training.'

'Too bad — we'll have to go on our own.'

Osama slipped into the passenger seat of his 4x4. The driver was new.

'Who are you?' asked Osama.

'I was working in the 6th district. They transferred me to headquarters this morning.'

Gulbudin hopped into the back, along with one of the few team members still at headquarters. The driver set off. Osama fondled the grenade in his pocket. He was also carrying a pistol. Gulbudin and the cop each had a Kalashnikov; the driver, an old American rifle. Osama wondered whether either the driver or the policeman knew how to shoot. He turned on the radio, and a swaying rhythm came on. The driver and the young policeman started clapping their hands in time. Osama turned around. He immediately noticed an old 4x4 behind them — a Volga from the Soviet era. The windscreen was so dirty that he couldn't make out how many men it held. A delivery truck was blocking the street, so the driver turned into a side road. They drove down it for half a mile, until they weren't far from Wali Wadi's offices. Osama noticed that the driver was nervous; he kept licking his lips as he looked in the rear-view mirror. Osama gripped his pistol.

'What makes you so uneasy?' he asked in a loud voice.

The driver didn't reply. He sped up, and suddenly turned right into a dead end. He opened his door and jumped out of the moving car, which continued for a few metres before coming to a halt.

'Out! Quick!' yelled Osama to Gulbudin and the other cop.

The Russian jeep that had been following them had just stopped at the entrance to the dead end. Seven men stepped out, all armed, and then a hail of bullets hit Osama's 4x4. Gulbudin responded with a burst from his Kalashnikov that floored one of the attackers, while the young cop cowered behind the engine next to Osama, firing blindly. Osama raised his pistol and shot a few rounds, forcing the attackers to take cover. All the Volga's windows shattered, but no one was hit. One of the attackers fired back. Osama recognised the hoarse sound of an AKM — short, precise bursts of fire, showing that he was a pro, used to preserving his ammunition ... The young cop fell, hit in the head; Osama stretched out on his belly to grab his rifle. The breech remained open, so he frisked him for a spare magazine. Nothing.

'Got any spare rounds for me?' he asked Gulbudin.

'No, only three rounds in my rifle, and one magazine in my pistol.'

'Same here.'

Osama assessed the situation. Their attackers were blocking the lane. There were still six of them, with formidable weapons. They shot well, like professionals used to combat. If they climbed onto the adjoining roofs they'd be able to snipe at them and kill them from a distance, without him or Gulbudin being able to hit them with their less-powerful handguns. Gulbudin had fought in the war; he grasped the situation perfectly. He turned a pale face to Osama.

'We're fucked, boss.'

'Not yet.'

Osama pulled the pin out of his grenade. He murmured a short prayer and threw it as far as he could. It rolled under the jeep that the attackers were using for protection. Osama tensed his muscles in anticipation of the blast. Five seconds passed, and then ten, but the grenade didn't explode. Gulbudin shook his head.

'Shit. Is it Paki?'

Osama nodded. This sometimes happened with bad-quality grenades made in Peshawar. Several thoughts flew through his mind. He hadn't had time to say goodbye to his wife or his children, Nita and Ramazan. Who would protect Malalai if he weren't there? Would she be forced to marry someone from Osama's family against her will? His brother, or one of his older cousins? No, she would emigrate or kill herself rather than submit to a man she didn't want. His thoughts jostled against each other. As in a dream, he watched the men start to fan out — weapons cocked — in small successive movements, like commandos, covering each other with short, precise bursts of gunfire. There was no way that he or Gulbudin could move without being killed on the spot. It was all happening with a sort of crystalline purity. He knew he was going to die in this squalid lane, under enemy fire. Gulbudin fired four shots that bounced off the wall near one of the attackers' heads but didn't hit him. Osama came out of his daze to fire two shots, with no more success. Suddenly, he glimpsed movement on a roof up to the left. Several men dressed in long tunics and black turbans had just appeared, brandishing folding

Kalashnikovs. A storm of bullets rained down on the attackers. Two fell immediately, followed by a third. Two more tried to flee; they were felled by several prolonged bursts of fire. The sixth managed to escape, but had barely reached the end of the lane when two turbaned men jumped on him. The fugitive gave a strangled cry as one of the unknown men took a curved dagger from his tunic.

'*Allah U Akhbar!*' he yelled in a hoarse voice.

He slit his prisoner's throat with a fluid movement. Then the turbaned men disappeared, as suddenly as they'd arrived. Gulbudin waited a few moments before standing up, clutching his pistol. Sirens were blaring in the distance.

'By the grace of Allah,' he exclaimed. 'Who were those men?'

'Friends of a friend,' replied Osama, thinking of Mullah Bakir.

An American tank screeched to a halt in front of the entrance to the dead end. Several helmeted marines strapped into thick bulletproof vests leapt out, and aimed their assault rifles at Osama and Gulbudin. Osama threw down his pistol, immediately copied by his deputy. There was no point getting killed by accident after the event.

'Whatever happens,' said Osama, 'don't mention that those men were wearing turbans.'

Joseph was shut up in his office, re-reading the tapped phone script. A hysterical Gulbudin had called police headquarters as soon as the shoot-out was over, to request support. Joseph soon realised from the disjointed conversations he'd had with three or four different police officers that the Afghan gangsters had botched the job, and that Kandar and his deputy had escaped without a scratch. All the attackers had been killed, which wasn't a bad thing — at least they couldn't blab. A mixture of luck and presence of mind had saved the lives of Kandar and his deputy. To say nothing of the unexpected arrival of the mysterious saviours, whom Gulbudin barely mentioned on the phone. This commandant was becoming more impressive by the day — Joseph couldn't deny his fascination, despite the professional hatred he felt for him.

Joseph made himself a coffee as he tried to think about what had happened. Then he called the Tajik translators to tell them to speed up their work. He had asked for the very latest NDS reports — available thanks to Echelon's formidable listening capabilities — to be sent from the Entity database. This rescue was intriguing. According to the NDS, about ten men had appeared out of nowhere. They'd wiped out the attackers — experienced ex-soldiers — in a matter of seconds. Who were they? Witnesses said Afghans. Ten armed men couldn't be a coincidence — this was a planned bodyguard. But who? Baloch from Kandar's clan? Hazara from his deputy's? Or a more disreputable bunch altogether?

A beep informed him of the arrival of a new translated report. He skimmed it, pausing thoughtfully at one of the witness statements. A shopkeeper had mentioned that Kandar's rescuers wore turbans and at least two of them had long beards. An idea began to form in Joseph's mind — a new way to dispose of Kandar.

The one-legged man showed Osama into Mullah Bakir's office. It had been a little over two hours since the assassination attempt. The room was almost entirely dark, with a single small oil-lamp burning on the table. Mullah Bakir was lying on his bed.

'Forgive me not rising to greet you, brother Osama,' he said in a whisper. 'I'm not very well.'

'Would you rather I came back tomorrow morning, Mullah?'

'No, on the contrary, your presence is precious to me. I'm sorry not to be able to serve you tea; it would have been an honour.'

'The honour is all mine,' said Osama.

He brought a glass over to the mullah. As he drew nearer, he saw that the man's forehead was clammy and that he was trembling with fever. Dysentery.

'I drank some water at a destitute brother's home this morning,' he explained. 'It was stagnant. I'll be better tomorrow.'

Tiredness made his voice sound even more strange than usual, as if he were reciting. They drank, the silence broken only by their sips and swallows. The muezzin at the local mosque began the evening prayer in a melodic voice, and the mullah sighed with pleasure.

'I'm glad you escaped the attack.'

'I'm presuming my rescuers were sent by you.'

'They took a huge risk to intervene like that, in the middle of Kabul. They are all wanted by the Coalition for their links to the Taliban.'

'They saved my life.'

'*Allah U Akhbar,* you were not hurt. Who were your attackers?'

'Ex-mujahedeen, from the elite troops that fought at the battle of Kabul. It's a miracle we escaped.'

'Where did they come from?'

'Kabul, mostly, and one from Kandahar.'

'What about the driver?'

'He's the brother of one of the commandos. He really is a police officer.'

'An operation like that would cost money,' said Mullah Bakir softly. 'A lot of money.'

'We found a little over twelve thousand dollars at the commando leader's house.'

'An Afghan would have paid in afghanis. So it must be foreigners.'

'Good deduction, Mullah. A neighbour told us that some foreigners came to see the man yesterday. They arrived in two cars. Armoured 4x4s.'

'That confirms what I'd heard. One of my spies tells me that Minister Khan Durrani has met with a particular foreigner several times this week, both at home and at work. He has also made a great many international phone calls in English.'

'This foreigner — was he Russian, American ...? Do you have any more information?'

'No. My informer doesn't have access to that level of detail. Phone calls aren't listed in the diary, and the minister has his timetable destroyed at the end of each day. He's as careful as a snake.'

Osama hid his disappointment. He had come up against a brick wall.

'Thanks to my source, I knew without a shadow of a doubt that there would be an assassination attempt on you,' continued the mullah. 'The minister talks about you all the time; it's becoming an obsession. That's why I organised a watch. My commando has been hanging around police headquarters constantly. You were lucky they managed to tail you without you noticing. I also installed additional security outside your house.'

'Those soldiers guarding my house last night? I thought that was courtesy of the justice minister.'

'It was me. The head of their unit owes me a big favour. And yet he's an ANA colonel, a heathen Hazara who never prays and has killed many of our Taliban brothers.'

'I don't understand. Why do you maintain relations with someone like that?'

'I'm a … flexible man. This colonel is an honest professional. We respect each other. I anticipate a role for him in the future. We'll need real soldiers running the army — competent men, not imams who may have been toughened up by life underground but still don't understand military strategy.'

Osama sighed. This conversation was surreal.

'The only good news in this whole business is that the failed attack will give me a few days' grace.'

'I wouldn't bet on it. The minister is already talking about a new plan. The people who want you dead are preparing another strategy. I don't know what it is yet.'

'I'm going to ask the justice minister for protection. If things get really hot, that will be more discreet than your men. Can you withdraw your arrangements?'

'As you wish.'

The mullah coughed, and suddenly threw up into the large bowl at the foot of the bed. Osama took it without a word, and went off to throw its contents into the toilet.

'That's what I like best about Afghanistan,' said the mullah, as Osama returned. 'Who knows what tomorrow will bring? Men seemingly devoted to Karzaï and his cronies proffer goodwill to people like me, so as to assure their future should we return to power.'

'If you return to power, this country will go back to the stone ages.'

'The trend I represent doesn't support the banning of music, brutality towards women, summary justice, or certain other ... excesses of our movement. You forget that we re-established order in this country, and abolished poppy farming.'

'And supported Al Qaida. And massacred tens of thousands of innocents. And introduced an absurd and tyrannical Sharia. Would you like the two of us to draw up a list of your crimes and mistakes? You mustn't be too quick to pass over what the Taliban has been responsible for.'

'Not the whole movement, brother Osama — just some of our excessively pious and gullible members, manipulated by a few cruel leaders. At the beginning, there was a genuine balance in the Taliban leadership between the hard-line followers of Mullah Omar and the moderates who gathered around me. It was the unforeseeable seizing of power by the most violent wing, from the *Deobandi* school of thought, that led to the bad habits with which you are familiar. The Taliban government I dream of will not resemble the one that preceded it. There will be no space for ignorant men like Mullah Omar. Still less for the cruel and fanatical Arabs of Al Qaida. I dream of a new Afghan movement — *national, liberal and Islamic.* A new order in which faith will raise men up, in which tradition will be respected without renouncing progress, and in which human dignity will be protected.'

'I'm not sure a vision like that is compatible with the Sharia you plan to reinstate.'

'Sharia, but what Sharia? There are so many interpretations of the holy book! In my view, Sharia isn't an absolute written law, brother Osama. I don't subscribe to the traditional view that it is something *uncreated,* which should be taken literally. That is an obscurantist and foolish view of the dogma. Sharia is an *interpretation,* which necessarily changes with time, place, and who is administering it. Understood like that, I believe a modernised Sharia is possible. And that is the heart of my vision for Afghanistan: the invention of a *21st-century Sharia.*'

'That vision is far removed from what is envisaged by the Taliban.'

'Again, Mullah Omar doesn't have exclusive rights over Taliban thought. He is charismatic, of course, but underneath he's no more than a dull brute.'

'I am not able to discuss these subjects properly with you — my political education is too basic,' replied Osama.

'I'm not asking you to make speeches. Just staying alive would be a good start.'

Osama took his leave of the courageous mullah. As he drove back to the office, he wondered what on earth he was going to tell his bosses to justify the unexpected help he had received. If the mysterious Westerners trying to kill him realised that he, the head of the Kabul Murder Squad, had been rescued by Taliban, he would be tossed right into the eye of the storm.

Joseph tapped in the security code and instructed the Cube to connect. A few seconds later, the general's face appeared on the screen.

'How did Kandar get away?' The general had no time for niceties.

'I don't know yet,' admitted Joseph.

'Who rescued him?'

'The minister is making enquiries. Witnesses are talking of bearded men with turbans.'

'Taliban?' asked the general icily.

'It's possible. The thought had occurred to me. It doesn't exactly seem to fit his character, but in this country …'

'I don't give a damn. We'll have to find another way to wipe him out.'

'I want him dead, too. But let's stop trying to hide in straw houses. That's twice now we've used external contacts instead of my own team, and twice we've failed. Let me and my Ks take care of it — I'll have that cop dead within three days.'

'No, Joseph.'

'He has to die — you've said so yourself. And now that decision has been taken, we owe it to ourselves to execute it professionally. Have I ever failed? I've had enough of working with these useless outsiders. Let me and the Ks have done with it, once and for all.'

The general checked nervously that the room's electronic protection was on. Talking about this stuff could entail a jail sentence, regardless of the protection enjoyed by the Entity. The general was aware he'd crossed every red line a long time ago.

'It's out of the question. I cannot implicate you directly, Joseph. The risk of you being seen or arrested is too great.'

'If I do it myself, I can give you a 100 per cent guarantee of success,' repeated Joseph.

'No way. Not in Kabul; we're not familiar enough with the territory. There are too many secret services. The Pakistanis. The Russians, listening to everything. I cannot let you act directly.'

'What's going on, general? I don't recognise you. Isn't acting when no one else is able to precisely what the Entity is for? Our *raison d'être*?'

'I said "No".'

Joseph surrendered.

'In that case, we'll have to rely on the most effective technology there is. When I heard that Kandar had been rescued by men in turbans, I had an idea. You know I've had his personal vehicle tagged? That means we know its precise location at any given moment. Let's use the NATO method for disposing of Taliban chiefs.'

'A drone?'

'Yes. A single missile — job done.'

'In Kabul? You must be out of your mind!'

'We can find a way to get him out of the city. It'll be a clean, tidy job. This tag will continue working for a few more days, so we can hit him when we like, how we like. And it won't leave any traces.'

'Only the US army possesses attack drones; I'm not authorised to ask it for help.'

'I'm not so sure about that,' replied Joseph. 'I've heard people talking about phantom drones — machines that were apparently destroyed in accidents, and are then used for undercover operations.'

'Hmm. You're right,' admitted the general after a few seconds' thought. 'I know Blackwater has carried out some covert operations in that way.'

'You see!'

Drones were used on a daily basis in Afghanistan and Pakistan, for reconnaissance and intelligence operations, but also for targeted attacks on Islamist strongholds — in which case they were equipped with bombs. The Israelis had used this strategy successfully against Hamas, and the Americans had copied them, thus greatly increasing the number of drones in circulation. Drones allowed the US to kill 'cleanly' without using ground troops. A missile obviously wasn't as precise as sniper fire, but the collateral damage was judged acceptable, given the advantage of not using American ground troops directly to eliminate people.

'I've changed my mind. Using a phantom drone is a good idea,' conceded the general finally.

'Can you get me one without going through Nellis?'

Joseph was referring to the massive US Army base in Nevada from which most drones were controlled.

'I think so, but I'll have to do some research.'

With that, the screen went dark.

Nick decided to wait outside the general's office until he deigned to see him. He had been there a good half-hour when the door opened. He jumped.

'Come in.'

Nick had barely sat down when the general asked him about the latest progress in his investigation. He described the conversations he'd had with the prostitutes, but didn't mention his discovery of the false passport. As long as they were concealing things from him, he would play his own cards close to his chest. The general didn't seem particularly interested in his account of his interviews with Jacqueline and Yasmina.

'Do you have anything new on his character?'

'Not really. I feel a bit stuck. But I'm working hard.'

The general looked downcast. Nick was waiting for the right moment to ask the question that was burning him up. Sensing that the general was about to put an end to their conversation, he took the plunge: 'I understand there's another investigation taking place in

Kabul. Can you tell me the link between what's going on in Zurich and in Afghanistan? It might help with my investigations.'

'No,' said the general, definitively.

'But I only know half the story. How am I supposed to get anywhere!'

'I think I've been very clear, Nick. What's going on in Kabul is outside your remit. End of conversation.'

Nick took his leave, disappointed. He would have to return to his original plan — if they wouldn't tell him the truth, he'd have to find it out himself. Instead of returning to his office, he went to see Margaret. She had gone to lunch, but there were two other translator-analysts in the office — women who worked from Russian and Arabic. He sat down to chat with them, keeping one eye on the glass partition. As they talked, he saw that Margaret had a photo of him on her screen saver, along with a spaniel and a beautiful sunset. He felt ashamed. He'd split up with her a few months before, for no real reason except perhaps that they got on so well it was starting to seem natural to move in together. He'd preferred to return to his selfish little life, he told himself sadly. The events of the last few days had made him grow up. He was realising the importance of things he'd previously thought irrelevant — like being able to fully trust another person. *Margaret and I deserve a second chance*, he thought.

He'd been in the women's office about ten minutes when a tall figure walked past, behind the screen — the slim, elegant general, with his shaved head and immaculate black suit. Nick waited a few moments and then strolled casually over to the window. He saw the general slip into his Audi and drive off.

This was the opportunity Nick had been waiting for.

He took his leave and made for the general's office. He knew that his secretary always took her lunch at the same time as him. The door was closed — a heavy, intimidating hardwood door, protected by the impressive iris-recognition system used for all Entity offices.

Except that Nick happened to know that the system had been disconnected because the general wasn't happy with it. The door took a while to release, and he found that annoying. It was being replaced that same day by a simpler and faster fingerprint system;

with a bit of luck, the job hadn't yet been done. Nick said a silent prayer, and pushed the door handle.

A few seconds later, he was sitting in the general's chair. He smiled. How easy was that!

The computer had been left switched on and logged in — another breach of the ferocious Entity security protocol, which required everyone to set up their computer so it automatically logged off when the keyboard hadn't been touched for sixty seconds. The general was clearly one of those men who believed that the rules applied to everyone except them.

The email inbox opened with a single click. It required encrypting at log-in and log-out, but seemed straightforward enough to read. Nick decided to focus on messages between the general and Joseph — they were the most likely to shed light on the relationship between the Afghan investigation and what was going on here in Zurich.

He gave himself ten minutes; not a moment more.

His heart was hammering in his chest, but he opened Joseph's messages calmly, one at a time, with the most recent first. Reading them was like a dagger in his heart:

> Kandar and his two deputies gathering in a public space in two days time. Possibility of intervening to eliminate the whole team in one hit. Await your green light.

> Minister ok in principal but rejects military operation. Suggests suicide bomb. Risk of major civilian losses. Confirm absence of Western nationals in the location. Mule and logistics seem ok. Await your green light.

> Suicide bomb missed its target. Kandar not hit. 30 dead for nothing. Await your instructions.

> Wali Wadi investigation continuing. Kandar seems to have understood Dortmund's role. You'll have to warn our clients.

> Preparation of a new mission to eliminate Kandar. Use of local elements confirmed. Await your green light.

Dortmund must be eliminated. Have prepared drone solution. Await your green light.

Michael Dortmund stepped into the passenger seat of the car, carrying his travelling bag. He was stunned that they'd come to collect him at dusk: Westerners always avoided the airport road after 6.00pm, on account of the increasingly violent terrorist attacks. Several bomb-experts linked to Al Qaida had come over from Baghdad to teach the Taliban how to make IEDs, the remote-control bombs that were spreading terror throughout Iraq. Over the last few months there had been more and more explosions. Second surprise: Joseph, sitting in the back seat.

'You again?'

'I told you earlier that I can't get enough of you,' quipped Joseph.

Dortmund noticed that the killer's pale-blue eyes were even colder than usual.

'I'm taking you to the airport,' continued Joseph. 'The general wants you protected, in case the Afghans start screwing around.'

Dortmund muttered his response: 'I can still manage to catch a plane on my own.'

Amin started the car. It slipped into the traffic, zigzagging deftly between the other vehicles. Amin took Cinema Zaina, and then continued along the Sarobi road instead of turning left towards the airport.

'Am I leaving from Bagram?' asked Dortmund in surprise.

'We ended up putting you on a military flight to Europe. More discreet that way.'

They drove along. Dortmund relaxed. He had no time to be afraid. He felt a cold object on the nape of his neck, and then he lost consciousness.

Joseph put down the Taser he had used to stun Dortmund. The man would be knocked out for about a minute, which was plenty. He removed a case from an inside pocket of his safari jacket and took out a prepared syringe. He stuck it straight into Dortmund's neck, right up to the hilt, and plunged in the piston. Twenty centilitres of aqueous solution containing ten grams of potassium chloride entered the jugular vein. Ten seconds later, Dortmund's heart stopped beating. Joseph put the syringe back in its case.

'Done?' asked Amin.

'Done.'

They drove on for another half-hour. The landscape out here was barren, with just the odd hovel appearing in the headlights. Amin turned right, down an unpaved track.

'You're sure it isn't mined?' he asked nervously.

'I had the track checked by an army Buffalo this afternoon.'

As if to echo his words, they passed a series of red-painted stones indicating mines on the side of the road. After three hundred metres, the red stones stopped. The 4x4 drove deeper into the massif, following the track that weaved its way among the rocks. Joseph had chosen this place because the Russians had destroyed the only two nearby villages, where Katyusha rocket launchers had been based, twenty years before. All the inhabitants had been massacred: no one lived around here anymore. When NATO had launched a search for stray Taliban four years ago, they hadn't even found the tiniest hamlet. He'd read the reports.

'It's madness, coming here this late at night, boss,' repeated Amin.

'Shut it. What do you want us to do with the body, you moron? DHL it to lost property?'

He looked at his mobile phone: no signal. After another half-hour, they finally came to a stop. Amin took out a shovel and began digging a hole to one side of the track. When it was ready, they rolled Dortmund's body into it, naked.

12.

THE NEXT MORNING, OSAMA ASKED TO BE TAKEN to Shafakhana Emergency Hospital on his way to the office. There was a massive crowd in the main lobby, even though it was seven thirty in the morning. A bus full of passengers had toppled into a ravine on the outskirts of Kabul; there were dozens dead and more than fifty wounded. A row had erupted between families of the wounded and the medical staff — a male nurse had been beaten with a stick before two security guards dispersed the families with the aid of their truncheons.

Osama noticed a woman lying on a stretcher in a pool of blood. A man, apparently her husband, stood next to her shouting loudly.

'What's going on?' Osama asked a man he'd recognised, a lecturer from the university of Kabul.

'This woman is losing a lot of blood. She was in the bus. She's dying, but her husband won't let the male nurses anywhere near her. Two female nurses were found from a different part of the hospital, but another family stopped them coming in here on account of not being adequately veiled … they went to put on burqas, apparently, but haven't been seen since. No one knows what's going to happen.'

Osama looked at the growing pool of blood under the stretcher. He continued on his way. A woman rushed after him.

'*Dokter, Dokter,* is my son going to survive?'

He stopped. The woman was wearing a heavy burqa; he could barely hear her voice through the fabric, and couldn't make out her eyes at all. Three terrified young children were hanging on to her — a rural Pashtun woman who didn't know the Dari word for doctor.

'I don't know. Sorry, *bakhena ghuarum,* I'm not a doctor.'

He continued walking. This time she didn't try to follow him. The basement was calmer, despite the wounded laid out on stretchers outside the operating room. Osama made his way to Katoun's office. It was empty. He waved down a passing nurse and showed him his card.

'Find me Dr Katoun.'

'He's with the director.'

'I need to see him anyway.'

The nurse obeyed. Osama felt a little ashamed for insisting, in the current circumstances. Katoun appeared a moment later in his surgeon's gear, with blood on his apron. He took off his mask.

'Hurry up, Osama. I was in an emergency meeting. We've got to look after the wounded from the bus.'

'Sorry. Did you do the powder test on Wadi's body?'

'Yes. It's negative.'

'There's no possible mistake?'

'No. My report is somewhere on my desk. Take it — it's for you.'

Osama took his friend's hand.

'Tashakor.'

He soon found the report, amid an indescribable mess of documents. It was exactly what he'd hoped for. As he left, he noticed that the stretcher on which the injured woman had been lying a few minutes earlier was now covered with a sheet.

'What happened?' he asked a witness, aghast.

'She lost all her blood; no one could agree on who was allowed to carry her …'

The husband was crying hot tears. Two stretcher-bearers appeared, picked up the body, and took it away.

'You let men come near her now, then?' Osama couldn't help asking, horrified at the man's attitude.

'Now she's dead, it doesn't matter if a man comes near her,' he replied between two sobs.

Osama didn't know what to say to this madness. He left the hospital, wondering what Malalai would have done.

Nick ran alongside the lake, lost in thought, alone. It felt like the world was collapsing around him. His world, in any case.

First, Werner.

Then the discovery of the emails between Joseph and the general. He'd done some research on the Wali Wadi character they mentioned — a few discreet searches through various databases, using Margaret's log-in. She was still unaware of the cover she was providing. He hadn't found much, apart from evidence that the fugitive and the middleman had met regularly, almost once a month, in Europe or Pakistan. They worked together, that was for sure, and had done so for at least five years. But what was their business? He still had no idea.

He flopped onto a bench. It was very cold, but he was steaming after a 20k run. Usually, the stunning scenery calmed him down, but not today. When he got home, he'd searched the Internet for information about the suicide bomb that Joseph had referred to: thirty dead, eighty wounded — many of them seriously. These were innocent people crippled and blinded for nothing. Because of the Entity. Because of his *colleagues.*

He stared furiously at the landscape. He could understand and even accept that it was sometimes necessary to take violent action against elusive enemies. But exploding a bomb in a café full of civilians? No. His choices were limited now — either fight or flight. Fighting meant finding out the truth. Understanding the relationship between Wali Wadi and the fugitive. Determining the contents of the Mandrake report. And finding the fugitive.

He promised himself he would go all the way, whatever the cost.

Osama was back at police headquarters with Katoun's report in his pocket. The technical aspect of his investigation was complete; he had all the proof he needed. There was only one thing left unresolved, and it was a big one: why had the Westerners assassinated Wali Wadi? He wrote a brief report, setting out the results of the new powder analysis, along with the bundle of supporting evidence that allowed him to conclude it had been murder disguised as suicide. His principal suspect was a German citizen, Michaël Dortmund, whose fingerprints had been found at the site of the incident. After a moment's hesitation, he added a paragraph in which he suggested that Michaël Dortmund had also been responsible for the Hamad Café attack, whose main target had been his deputy, a Kabul Murder Squad inspector, and whose only credible motive was to slow down the investigation into Wali Wadi's death. He was therefore requesting a warrant for the arrest of Michaël Dortmund on charges of murder and plotting a terrorist attack, and also access to the state resources necessary for his capture. Before signing the report, he showed it to Reza. His friend read it quickly, groaning every now and then.

'You're not pulling any punches, Osama!'

'What do you think of the report?'

'There's no getting away from the facts.' He shot his friend an admiring glance. 'You've worked hard, you old bugger. And I happen to share your conclusions regarding the Hamad Café.'

'Are you prepared to put that in writing?'

'Hmm. Do you really want me to lose my job?'

'I'm not joking. Tell me.'

Reza leaned back in his chair.

'The security minister is powerful. I'm Pashtun, I know, but from a very small clan. What's more, Durrani has Karzaï's trust. Your story implicates a Westerner, which will be very awkward for the Coalition. Don't forget that the Germans assure the security of the airport: hundreds of soldiers, super-modern tanks, electronic countermeasures … The last thing Karzaï wants is to fall out with a big European country like Germany. Since the last "elections", he has no credibility and no constituency. The Coalition is the only thing keeping him in power — the day they no longer like him, he'll be out of there, simple as that. If you think that Karzaï is going to support you against Westerners, my dear Osama, you're more naïve than I thought.'

'I don't yet know who is implicated in this business, and who isn't. If we followed your argument to its logical conclusion, Westerners would be untouchable.'

'And isn't that the case?'

'Dortmund isn't a state employee — he's independent. Nothing proves that he was in contact with officials or working to anyone's orders when he committed the murder.'

'And my mother's name is Mullah Omar? Don't treat me like an idiot, Osama. Your case stinks like a dead dog. You're being followed and listened to by powerful people. They have access to communications satellites and teams of Russian and Dari translators. They are capable of hiring ex-mujahedeen and destroying a heaving café just to wipe you out. They can obtain C5, and equipment from the former Red Army. Don't you see what all this means? Dortmund is just a puppet. There's clearly a large organisation behind all this.'

'For the moment, only one foreign individual is implicated. I'm just at the start of my investigation,' said Osama.

'You're fighting people more powerful than you. Germans. Swiss. Since when do Swiss individuals intervene in war? It's a neutral country. These guys work for someone else; it's obvious. Someone influential. Haven't you wondered whether it's the Americans?'

'No — for the moment I only have something on Dortmund.'

'Think a little.'

'I don't know *why* Wali Wadi was killed, or why certain people are so determined to stop this investigation. I don't know what Wali Wadi's safes contained, either, although I suspect that is the key to everything. I have to find out what was in that safe.'

'Well, I suspect that this attack on you wasn't the last, and that you're going to get yourself killed sooner than you think.'

'The justice minister will help me finish the investigation. He will protect me.'

'It wasn't him who appointed us, plus he's a Tajik. Look how Karzaï fired Amrullah Saleh. Like a dog. I'm sorry to say so but, in this country, Pashtuns are the only ones who count.'

'I hear what you're saying, Reza, but I'm going to pursue this, whatever the cost. As for you, you're only on the fringes of the investigation. And anyway, you can assure your own safety with a protector even more powerful than the justice minister.'

'Oh yeah? And who is this mysterious treasure? I hope you don't mean Abdullah Abdullah — he's nothing since he lost the election.'

'I'm thinking of the minister of commerce. He's a Ghilzai,' said Osama quietly. 'I know you saved his life last year by warning him of a bomb with his name on it. Without you, he'd be dead. He's indebted to you.'

'How do you know that?' grumbled Reza.

The Ghilzai Pashtun tribe were as powerful as the Durrani, and the minister of commerce was the rising star of the Karzaï government. He wasn't corrupt. The money that he, like everyone, skimmed off, went to supporting his village, clan, and henchmen. His own lifestyle was simple. Seeing his friend still hesitating, Osama added: 'Haven't you wondered what I thought about the fact that your own technical department released a truthful report on how the bomb was detonated?'

'Hmm.'

'Come on, tell me.'

'The security minister's game is sometimes excessive,' admitted Reza. 'There were too many deaths in that attack. My men pretended to hush it up by modifying the autopsy report, but they knew exactly what they were doing when they allowed the technical report to go out uncensored.'

'"They" doesn't mean a thing. You're the boss. You did it on purpose, to help me. Didn't you?'

'Hmm. I'm just doing my job. Our friendship has nothing to do with it.'

Osama put a hand on his friend's shoulder.

'You did the right thing, and I'm grateful. Enough of this cynical-cop persona.'

'I'm not a *good* man in this case, Osama. Do I need to remind you that I made sure not to touch a line of the phoney autopsy report on Abdul Hakat, for example?'

'I don't give a damn about the autopsy report. All you need to do is specify in your own report that the shahid was wearing a single pair of underpants, and that he hadn't shaved or washed. Everyone will understand.'

'Yeah.'

'Does that mean you're going to put something in writing for me?'

'OK, OK,' sighed his friend. 'I'll write what I think: that the shahid wasn't a shahid. He was just a poor guy manipulated to unwittingly blow himself up. But I'm not mentioning Dortmund.'

'No need, that'll be plenty,' said Osama, delighted.

Reza sat in front of his computer. It didn't take long. He printed his report, stamped it, signed it, and called an orderly to make several copies.

'What are you doing now?' he asked Osama.

'I'm going to pay a visit to the justice minister. If he'll help us, they won't be able to bury the investigation.'

'And Dortmund?'

'He must have left the country. I'm going to ask for an international arrest warrant to be issued. I'll go and see the head of European police cooperation myself.'

'Hmm.'

Reza seemed suddenly ill at ease. Osama wondered if it was fear of indirectly defying the security minister. He returned to his office with this question unanswered, but satisfied with the meeting. He called the justice minister's secretary and obtained an appointment for late afternoon. Around 6.00pm he put on a clean shirt — he always kept a few at the office — and a jacket, and left discreetly.

THE MINISTRY OF JUSTICE was one of the few impressive buildings in Kabul. It had been built out of freestone about fifty years before, and then was more or less abandoned by the Taliban, who had their own, more summary notion of justice: stoning for adultery, hand amputation for theft, and additional forms of maiming or simply execution for other crimes and misdemeanours. The sentences were decided by imams, and applied by anti-vice and virtue-protection squads. The new government had struggled to re-establish a justice system worthy of the name, with judges, clerks, police officers, and everything else that makes up a state judiciary. The Americans and Italians had funded a renovation of the ministry, thus giving the legal authorities a place to carry out their work.

Osama left his bodyguards outside and climbed the stairs alone. The central staircase was impressive. There was still a massive red star engraved in the ceiling, along with a stylised hammer and sickle. The designs had been shot at with Kalashnikovs, but the damage was minimal. Osama was shown straight into the minister's office, without even seeing the waiting room. The minister stood up to greet him and took Osama's hand in both of his.

'I'm so glad you escaped that attack, Qomaandaan.'

The justice minister was small and trim with twinkly eyes. His light hair was starting to go white, and he wore a short beard. He was one of the new government's token Tajiks, and was often put forward as a symbol of the country's newfound unity. Osama quickly explained the case, before giving the minister both his report and the one written by the intelligence department. The minister pressed an intercom button.

'I am not under any circumstances to be disturbed for the next forty-five minutes.'

He put on a pair of small, round glasses and started reading the two documents. Every now and then he jotted a note in his attractive, compact script. Osama noticed that he wrote from left to right, using a non-Arabic alphabet. He'd spent twenty years in exile and had retained the Western style of writing from his years in London and America. When he'd finished, he took off his glasses and rubbed his eyes. The look he gave Osama was solemn.

'First of all, I must congratulate you on this remarkable investigation. What an impressive piece of work.'

Osama scratched his neck uneasily. He always felt suspicious of this kind of compliment.

'How do you see the continuation of the case?'

'I'm not sure there is a continuation, qomaandaan.'

Osama paled.

'Could you explain what you mean by that?'

'We'll try to arrest Dortmund, of course. But you'll agree that he has probably left the country by now. As for issuing an international warrant and officially interrogating the German authorities, I'd have to ask President Karzaï about that, but I can guarantee he would refuse.'

'Why?'

'Because this is a sensitive topic, qomaandaan. My colleague in the Ministry of Security is nervous; people close to the president are nervous. This case is making a lot of people nervous. Too many people.'

'I see,' said Osama.

'Actually, I'm not sure that you do, qomaandaan. It's not in the best interests of anyone for too many government officials to be nervous right now. Not the international community, not NATO, not the UN. Nor, probably, the Afghan people.'

'The logical conclusion to that argument would be to close down this ministry,' retorted Osama. 'The purpose of justice, its *raison d'être*, is to make criminals "nervous", as you put it. My job is to continue this investigation to its rightful end, whoever becomes "nervous" as a result.'

'I didn't say that your investigation had to stop,' remarked the minister gently.

Osama thought about what he'd just heard.

'Let's imagine that I continue working on the case. Am I to understand that I won't have official support to investigate foreign nationals?'

'No official support doesn't mean no unofficial support.'

'Will the prosecutor's office agree to reconsider the investigation as that of a crime?'

'Not at the moment. But if you obtain more information, then why not?'

'What kind of information?'

'What Wali Wadi was up to. For as long as you haven't found out what he was doing and who with, your intellectual conception of the case will remain weak, despite the impressive body of evidence you have compiled. You need the *whole* system.'

The minister stood up and shook Osama's hand.

'Continue with your investigation. I will make sure you are protected, by reliable men. But there will be no international arrest warrant, and no intervention at the German embassy. Let's forget Dortmund and anything else that might annoy the Coalition, for the time being. Oh — you'll need money to see this investigation through. There'll be people to buy, and possible travel to undertake.' The minister held out an envelope. 'This contains five thousand dollars. From the secret funds given to me by the Coalition. Use it well.'

Osama put the envelope in his pocket. The minister walked right up to him, and murmured, almost in his ear: 'I trust you. Keep working on this, but at the proper pace. Find out Wali Wadi's secret.'

'We'll have to see if *my* pace and *my* ways of working can fit with yours,' said Osama, looking the minister in the eye.

'I hope so with all my heart, qomaandaan. Most of all, be careful — your life is hanging by a thread.'

Osama thought about this conversation all the way back to the office. The justice minister probably had his own interest in the case. Although he was Tajik, he was known to be favoured by certain Pashtuns because he'd never seen eye to eye with Massoud. He was pro-Western, but had fought for lenient sentencing of the most moderate Taliban, going so far as to argue for dialogue with Mullah Omar. It was even rumoured that he'd helped certain Taliban escape, while demanding the death penalty for those who'd favoured the arrival of the Arab Islamists. His power would increase if leading members of the Karzaï government were dismissed on corruption charges. He might then put forward his candidature at a forthcoming *Loya Jirga,* aiming for the post of prime minister, or even president. Osama sighed. He'd always hated politics, and here he was, up to his neck in it.

13.

NICK STARED AT THE LOW CLOUDS covering Berne. His recent discoveries hadn't exactly lifted his mood. He now approached all his colleagues with suspicion, wondering who knew the truth about the Entity, about the monstrous secret that bound them together. He was aware that, having made such fantastic progress, his investigation had now reached a ceiling. He knew the fugitive's false identity, but that wasn't enough.

He munched on a croissant as he read the various reports. The only unexplored trail was that of a pastor who'd provided spiritual guidance to the fugitive over the past few months. The man who'd interrogated him was ex-Special Forces, so not exactly a master of psychology, and the conversation had not gone well. The pastor might yet be a mine of information.

Once he'd drunk his coffee and rinsed out the cup, Nick got into his car. He was becoming very familiar with the Berne–Zurich road. The parish was in Saatlen, a suburb to the north of the city. Pastor Kingston Dana was a former delinquent whose criminal record by the age of fifteen included dozens of crimes of varying degrees of severity: insulting a police officer, graffiti, theft, attempted burglary, burglary, assault ... when he was sixteen, Kingston Dana had been banged up for the armed robbery of an off-licence on the outskirts of Lausanne. He was given five years, reduced to two on account of age and good behaviour. It was in prison that he discovered his faith, and also his true vocation. He left Lausanne for Zurich, where a Protestant church took him in. He performed very well at the seminary, was welcomed into the profession, and had led his own church for the last ten years. Like other churchmen from minority backgrounds, he tried to help struggling young people reintegrate themselves into society. The Entity report advised investigators to treat him with kid gloves; he had easy access to the media, and was no great fan of the police.

Nick parked in front of a whitewashed concrete building surrounded by a sparse little garden, with low-grade housing and dilapidated high-rise estates all around. He pushed open the door of the church. Inside it was dark.

'What can I do for you, brother?' boomed a deep voice.

A man was standing behind him, wearing a black suit buttoned up to the collar. He was tall, probably **six foot six**, with a massive paunch. His face was jowly with fat. He must have weighed **over one hundred and forty-five kilogrammes**. And yet he gave off an incredible physical strength, as if the seminary hadn't completely effaced the convict in him.

'Father Kingston Dana?'

'That's me. And you, what's your name?' he asked brusquely.

'Nick. Please excuse me, this is my first time in a Protestant church; I'm a Catholic. How should I address you? Father, or brother?'

'Let yourself be led by your heart. What are you doing in our church?'

The pastor seemed a solid and trustworthy man. Nick decided to just to tell him the truth.

'I'm looking for one of your flock.'

'Which one?'

'Leonard.'

The pastor's facial expression didn't change, but several years in intelligence had made Nick highly perceptive. Dana had reacted, almost invisibly, to the mention of the name.

'He was one of my flock, but he's disappeared. You're not a friend, are you?'

'Not really.'

'I didn't think so. I have a highly sensitive cop radar, wherever they come from.'

'I'm not a cop, and not an enemy, either. Could we have a proper talk somewhere?'

'What about? I don't think I have anything to tell you.'

'But I have things to tell you.'

Dana hesitated a moment, then motioned Nick to follow him. They sat down in the sparsely furnished little presbytery — an old recycled sofa, a wooden table, plastic chairs, a few simple posters in German and French. None of it was beautiful, or matching, yet Nick immediately felt at ease.

'I'm listening.'

Without mentioning his employer's name, Nick told the entire story since the shoot-out in the squat.

When he finished, Dana walked over to a small bar, took out two bottles of French beer, and put them on the table.

'Thirsty?'

'Yes, thank you.'

'You're playing a dangerous game. You must be brave. Or else just reckless ...'

'I've done worse. The north face of Mont Blanc, in the middle of November, alone.'

'This isn't sport, it's politics. You're still young, probably too young for a case like this. It doesn't seem to me that you understand all the implications of what you're doing.'

'That's something I'll ask myself once I've found out the truth. At the moment it's too far off.'

'What will you do when you find Leonard?'

'I don't know yet. I want to find out the hidden side of all this. I don't want my friend Werner to have died for nothing.'

'Do you think Leonard would be willing to help you?'

'He can't stay in hiding for the rest of his life,' said Nick. 'The best thing for him to do would be to reveal everything he knows. Once the truth is out, no one will need to track him down and kill him.'

'You're kidding yourself. Leonard is an extremely intelligent man. No one will *ever* find him.'

The giant took a gulp of beer.

'Your colleagues are powerful but stupid,' he continued. 'A man came to see me, trying to pass himself off as a Lausanne cop. I knew he wasn't. He was an ex-soldier, with a killer's eyes. He was playing soft, but I've spent enough time inside to recognise a real bastard when I see one. After all, I was one myself, once.' He took another gulp. 'Leonard was frightened. He came here to see me after he fled. He even slept in this room for a night, but he didn't stay long — he knew that son of a bitch would come here looking for him. I offered to introduce him to people who could help, but he knew someone, although he didn't tell me their name. He left that same day, and I haven't heard anything since.'

'I know who it was — Yasmina, his ex-prostitute. I found her.'

'You're sharper than your little mates.'

'I also know the false name that Leonard is using. But that's not enough.'

Dana finished his can, crushed it as if it were paper, and lobbed it into a bin. It hit the bottom, which made him smile.

'What else do you want?'

'The thing that's missing in your story.'

'What?'

'The woman.'

A glimmer flickered in Dana's eyes. Nick saw that he'd hit the jackpot. There was a woman, and the pastor knew her! The pastor was staring at the ceiling, as if weighing up the pros and cons.

'Yes, there's a woman,' he finally admitted. 'How did you know?'

'Because of the change in Leonard's behaviour, just before he disappeared. He'd been seeing the same call girl for several years, an arrangement that suited him perfectly. He wouldn't have stopped seeing her without a compelling reason — a reason linked to whatever he was up to, because their "split" happened several months before he fled. Also, why stay in Zurich, when it was so dangerous for him? That makes no sense. I've thought hard about these two inconsistencies. It seems to me that the only valid reason is the existence of a third person. Leonard had no child, so it must be a woman.'

The pastor smiled.

'A woman, not a whore?'

'A woman, full stop. A heart for a man who'd never shared anything with anyone. A man who'd had enough of his life.'

'You're clever. I'm impressed by how you've pieced things together.'

'I'm on the right track, then?'

'You are. Leonard did indeed meet a woman. They fell madly in love,' admitted Dana. 'She was much younger than him and married to a stupid, violent man who made her life a misery. A simple story, you see, one that's happened over and over since people first started walking the earth.'

'So they fled together.'

'With Leonard's secret. His report. The one your friends are looking for.'

'Do you know what's in it?'

'No, and I'm glad not to. Leonard told me the contents were enough to break a fair few governments. Here and overseas. Perhaps that's why they'll do anything to find him.'

'What about Leonard's girlfriend — what's she like?'

The pastor smiled ironically.

'She's not someone you forget. I've never seen eyes like that. She has a soft face, and smooth, almost velvety skin. A remarkable body, of European, Asian, and Middle Eastern ancestry. I can say without hesitation that she's one of the most beautiful women I've ever seen.'

'What was she doing in your parish?'

'She discovered our religion last year. She was actually planning a secret baptism. She and Leonard met by accident. Love at first sight. A few weeks later, she persuaded him to meet me. He agreed for her sake. At that point, Leonard was a materialist who no longer believed in anything or anyone. He had worshipped the god of money until it devoured his heart. When he came to my little church, he met Jesus. It doesn't matter whether you're a high-flying financier or a street dealer, the day sometimes comes when you stop believing in what you're doing — when you want to give your life some meaning, to stop thinking only of yourself, and the money you're going to make.

Leonard had come to that point in his life. I knew it before he did. Leonard and I enjoyed true mental communion. He called it "fate". The poor black man and the rich white man — two bastards who happened to meet God and open their eyes to the reality of their bastard lives. And she was the trigger for his awakening.'

Nick finished his beer. All this was fascinating, but not enough to help him catch the fugitive. He needed more — names, contact details.

'What is the girl's name?'

'Her first name is Zahra. I don't know her surname.'

'What! She's Muslim?'

'Of course she's Muslim. Her baptism was to convert her to the Christian religion. Zahra is Afghan.'

Osama went straight home, rather than via the office. The two parachutists who'd appeared yesterday were still there. He pushed open the door. It was nice and cosy; Malalai must have been burning the coal stove on full. The wonderful smell of *shorwa* and crusty *nan* made his mouth water. Malalai was wearing a multicoloured peasant dress made out of pseudo-rough cotton.

'Where did you buy that dress? It suits you so well.'

'I was given it today. At RAWA.'

'Your meeting finally took place?'

'Yes. I was elected unanimously to the governing council. This is my welcome present.'

Osama tried to hide his concern.

'What did you decide?'

'We're going to start our recruitment campaign, as planned. I was put in charge of selecting the educators. The first interviews will take place at the end of this week.'

Osama shook his head.

'I've stopped trying to persuade you against this, because I've realised it's futile. Can you at least promise me to be careful?'

Malalai threw herself into his arms.

'Don't you worry, my big qomaandaan. I'll be *very* careful.' She put her hand on the wide strap of her dress. 'I went for a wax this morning. Shall we celebrate?'

Osama tore off her dress like a twenty-year-old.

Later, they lay on the bed enjoying this moment of peace. Osama listened to his wife's heart beating against his chest. He felt vaguely ashamed for being so happy. He had a beautiful, clever wife who loved him and had chosen him personally, rather than as a result of family pressure. He had work, a reputation, a kitchen, and enough money to eat well and buy water for two showers a day, when most of his compatriots ate meat once in a blue moon and didn't wash for the whole winter. Both his children had good jobs and were safe overseas; he'd only lost one, who'd died bravely in combat, whereas entire families had been destroyed by the war. Then he heard Malalai sob next to him.

'What's the matter?' he murmured.

'I'm so lucky to have you,' she said. 'I don't know how I would live without you. Perhaps in a village with no electricity, working the fields, sharing an ignorant and dirty husband with three other wives.'

Deeply moved, Osama held her even more tightly. They fell asleep wrapped in each other's arms.

NICK PARKED in front of the heaving terrace of a small café just off Grossmünsterplatz. He needed to take stock of his recent discoveries, but who with? Unused to working alone, unable to share his thoughts with anyone, he felt oppressed by this solitude, especially since the strain of Werner's death. He was almost tempted to call Margaret, but decided against it — there was no point putting her in jeopardy. He ordered a grilled-chicken salad and a glass of red wine, and was served by a gorgeous, tall, slim girl, with blonde hair tumbling to her shoulders, in a tight top and miniskirt. Not long ago he would certainly have chatted her up, but today he didn't feel up to it. Again, he felt the weight of the last few weeks on him, a major shift in his way of seeing the world — a need for seriousness, depth, stability.

He sighed. This was the perfect place to reflect on what he'd discovered. He looked at his watch; he would wait until the Entity employees had gone home to connect to the federal Transport

Ministry's database, using Margaret's secret log-in details. He might be lucky enough to find traces of an aeroplane ticket, but then again he might not: the fugitive could well have decided not to use his false passport in Switzerland. He could have driven to Eastern Europe, and flown from there with a company that didn't send its passenger lists to NATO countries. Some of the airlines from ex-USSR, Middle Eastern, and African countries that weren't buddies with America and the EU were indifferent to the sanctions threatened if they refused to share their databases.

He massaged his neck, and realised he was extremely tense. But the cooking smelled good, and he felt reassured by the sounds floating in from the street: a woman walking her dog; a council machine cleaning the pavement. This was normality — far removed from K troops and the murky underground world of the Entity.

He couldn't stop thinking about Zahra, the new girlfriend of the man he was looking for. Who was she? Apostasy was punishable by death in Afghanistan, as in most Muslim countries. This woman must be very brave, as well as possessing the stunning looks dwelt on by the pastor.

He ordered an apple tart for dessert, but was too keyed up to savour it properly. There had to be hundreds of Zahras in Switzerland — although, he suddenly thought, if she was as beautiful as the pastor said, he might be able to find her through the federal Immigration Department databases. They always included photos.

Joseph and Amin slipped into the old, dented Zhiguli. The Paykan's brand-new engine had broken down, leaving them with this unarmoured car. Their Afghan dress — *shalwar kameez,* brown kalpan, and chitrali — and four-day beards made them unrecognisable from a distance as Europeans. Joseph had wedged an assault rifle equipped with a rocket launcher between the two front seats. They entered the heavy Kabul traffic and soon found themselves at a standstill. Joseph shut his eyes, as if asleep. Amin was impressed by his serenity. He'd never seen Joseph betray the slightest anxiety amid all these vehicles driven by fierce-looking bearded men, whereas he could feel his own fear rising, and the sweat running down his back. Every pedestrian was a possible shahid; every vehicle might contain Taliban troops.

'Relax,' said Joseph with his eyes still shut, as if reading his mind. 'You're safe with me. Calm down, and drive carefully.'

'How do you manage to stay so calm? Don't you ever get scared, or what?'

A slight smile appeared on Joseph's face. His eyelids opened, startling Amin with the lifeless grey eyes, two liquid pools.

'Fear is a state of mind.'

'That's what the head of my ninja unit in the Aurès used to say. You're telling me! He ended up with his throat slit like a pig.'

'It's good to be afraid, Amin. All good soldiers are afraid. The ones who aren't die sooner.'

They drove past the first set of traffic lights in Afghanistan, at Charahi Pul Artan. There was a group of peasants gathered around it, staring and admiring, and a light tank making a show of guarding it. Joseph turned left into a less-congested avenue. Half an hour later they were in the road where commandant Kandar lived. Joseph took out his camera and started snapping furiously, capturing every detail. The house was more closely guarded than he'd expected — by a 4x4, a pick-up loaded with a 12.7mm machine gun, and several men in brand-new fatigues bearing Kalashnikovs. He'd need a whole squad to storm it. In the event of a shoot-out, the invading team would have a hard time escaping. There was also a police station at the end of the road, about one-third of a mile away. They would respond to a shoot-out in two minutes, max, leaving a single escape-route, in the opposite direction. He grimaced. This wasn't at all promising. He examined the immediate surroundings. The roofs were a possibility — all the houses were low to the ground. He noted all this on his palm top, thinking that a flyby might be necessary to check all the ways in and out of the house.

'We're going to be spotted,' Amin suddenly remarked, tense. 'Lots of the neighbours have been staring at us. We're too visible here; I have the impression everyone knows everyone in this neighbourhood.'

'OK, let's go.'

They'd driven about six hundred metres from the superintendent's house when they noticed a long wall — an ANA barracks. That ruled out the escape route.

'Did you see that?' asked Amin, indicating the watchtowers overlooking the barracks.

'Of course I did. Storming his house would be no picnic, that's for sure. I can see why that gangster wasn't up for it. This cop is a clever guy.'

'Are you cancelling the operation?'

'You don't really think we were going to fire a missile *within* Kabul? I just wanted to check whether there was an alternative solution to a drone.'

'And?'

'You saw for yourself. He's too protected — we'd need dozens of men with heavy weaponry. The answer is no.'

'If you can't attack within Kabul, then what are you going to do?'

'Wait for him to leave the city. Or provoke him to, if necessary.'

'How are you going to draw him out without making yourself vulnerable?'

'I don't know yet. But I'll think of something.'

THE GENERAL WALKED slowly up to his contact. They met once every six months, here on the banks of Lake Geneva where they wouldn't be spotted. As always, the man had come directly from the airport, without bodyguards, in an ordinary, unmarked car, having crossed the seas in a private jet. They shook hands without warmth.

The man was tall and fat, with a thick mop of doubtlessly dyed black hair, and bushy eyebrows. Many would have killed their own grandmother for the power he possessed, but he was an honest man, with little taste for plotting; a man who had spent twenty years negotiating the tortuous corridors of power, in parliament and now government, out of a simple desire to serve his country. The new president had appointed him to look after 'special affairs,' and incidentally clean up after his predecessor's highly controversial tenure. Since coming to the post, he'd discovered many sensitive files, but the Mandrake File was of another order entirely. He prided himself on being unafraid of anything or anyone, but he was scared of the Mandrake File. He had accepted the notion that the fugitive was in hiding somewhere, and likely to stay there. After all, the man could die in hell for all he cared. On the other hand, he found the knowledge that a copy of the Mandrake File was floating around quite unbearable.

'Hello, general.'

'Hello, Robert.'

'So, where have you got to?' asked the man in his distinctive Southern drawl.

'Nowhere,' admitted the general. 'A copy of this bloody report is missing, and we still don't know where Wali Wadi hid it.'

'That is very annoying,' said Robert, with characteristic understatement.

'For the moment, we've plugged the gaps. We've sorted what needed sorting, despite the many challenges that you're aware of. We'll collar our man the day he pops up anywhere. So, as soon as we find the file hidden in Afghanistan, the case will be settled.'

'You're presenting your mediocre results in Afghanistan as triumphs, and the principal purpose of your assignment as a foregone conclusion, when actually we're at a standstill. Have you managed to put a stop to the investigations into the deaths of the middlemen, at least?'

'We have in Iraq; the file is definitively closed. In Afghanistan, we're working on it.'

'So am I supposed to understand that the investigation into Wali Wadi's death is still ongoing?'

'Yes. The cop in charge is a force of nature.'

'That is *very, very* annoying,' repeated the man. 'I'm starting to regret having employed your services.'

'None of your official services have been any more successful at finding the fugitive, despite the massive resources at their disposal. With regards to Kabul, I'm doing my best to remedy the situation, without leaving tracks. I bear no responsibility for the fire you've asked me to put out. There are still some smouldering embers, certainly, but no longer any flames. That's what you wanted, isn't it?'

'I want the report. Every copy, every single copy.'

'We shall be forced to act very brutally, given the situation.'

'You have carte blanche. That's why the Entity was created, why it exists, and why we pay it so handsomely. You're the boss, so act like one.'

'That's what I'm doing.'

'So where is the bloody report?'

The man had barely slept since discovering the contents of the Mandrake report. He was an honest, practising Christian, and had had nothing to do with creating this situation, but his task now was to clean it up and sort it out, whatever the cost. If he'd known about it *before* the elections he wouldn't have taken the job, but it was too late now. He put his hat back on.

'Goodbye. I don't want any more smouldering embers, to use your expression; I don't even want cold ash. I want the whole business to disappear completely. Do you understand? And do me a favour, in future: spare me the yellow-bellied fireman analogies.'

The man returned to his car, leaving the general by the lake, staring into the water, alone and bitter. As a soldier, he still couldn't believe how people so powerful and supposedly intelligent could have been this careless, thus forcing him into a scorched-earth policy. For the first time since the start of the investigation, he asked himself whether the Entity — his baby — would survive this.

OSAMA LEFT HIS HOUSE only to find that Gulbudin was waiting for him in his car. His protective pick-up had changed: this one was a new Ranger equipped with a massive anti-aircraft machine gun, a Russian Dushka mounted on a tripod. An ANA soldier was strapped into position, wearing a bulletproof vest and an American army safari hat. Three impeccably uniformed soldiers stood next to him, laden with ammunition.

'These men were there this morning,' announced Gulbudin.

Osama walked over to the pick-up.

'*Salaam Alaikum, manda na bashi.* Peace be with you. May you not be tired. May you have long life.'

He greeted each soldier this way, receiving a traditional greeting in return. When all greetings had been exchanged, he asked the first, 'Where are you from, brother?'

'Tutachi. My name is Abdul Khorosan. I will fight to the death for you.'

'And you,' he asked the other two. 'Where are you from?'

'Mari Chaq.'

'Bala Marghab. We, too, will fight like lions for you.'

'I killed four Russians during the war,' said the first.

'I killed three Taliban,' said the second. 'Two I beat to death, and the other I slit his throat.'

'I haven't killed any yet,' said the last, who was very young, 'but I'm not afraid to die.'

He proudly produced his sights-equipped rifle, as proof of good faith.

One Baloch and three Turkmen. Osama had guessed that none were Pashtun after seeing one of them zipping up his fly when he arrived, having probably urinated against a wall — something completely forbidden by Pashtun code. The justice minister had sent him ethnic-minority soldiers, who would be impervious to any pressure from the Pashtun clans. Very clever. It was also proof that he really did want Osama alive to complete his investigation. For now, at least.

They started driving. The massive machine gun on the pick-up worked magic on the traffic — other vehicles pulled over immediately to let them past. Not out of respect for authority, but because the men working on these kinds of government-protection vehicles were known to be both trigger-happy and untouchable. The journey to the office was fifteen minutes shorter than usual. On the other hand, this highly visible protection might cause jealousy within police headquarters, so he got out as soon as possible. He waited at the bottom of the stairs for Gulbudin, who was walking more slowly than usual, with a limp.

'What's up?' asked Osama.

'I was attacked in the street yesterday,' admitted Gulbudin. 'A gang. Five of them waiting outside my house. They whacked me on the head with a stick, and stole my prosthesis. It's worth ten thousand afghanis on the black market. I didn't have time to draw my pistol.'

He was on the verge of tears. Now Osama understood why he was wearing his chitrali so low. He wanted to hide his humiliating injury.

'If we solve this case, I'll ask them to buy you a new prosthesis,' said Osama.

He helped him up the stairs. Without his Western prosthesis, Gulbudin's limp made him seem badly handicapped. They settled in Osama's office, and were soon joined by Jihad and Rangin.

'Did you put out the warrant against Dortmund?' Osama asked Jihad.

'Yes, last night, as soon as you left the minister's office. I spoke to immigration. He hasn't left the country. Not by plane, at any rate. I sent a team to his home around midnight, but he wasn't there. His papers and some of his stuff were missing. The night watchman opposite told me he'd seen him getting into a 4x4.'

Osama pulled a face.

'He's skedaddled, on a false passport. Did you alert the customs posts at the borders?'

'Yes. He hasn't been through any of them.'

'The whole case seems like a set-up,' said Osama. 'The justice minister was very clear. We have to return to our starting point: understanding what Wali Wadi was up to.'

'So we put all the teams back on to Wadi?'

'Yes, we'll start again from scratch. Re-interrogate the witnesses. Find out who's on the other end of the phone numbers we identified in Switzerland, Baghdad, and here in Kabul. We'll do another search of Wali Wadi's house and office, using as many men as necessary. Gather a team — we'll start at his home. We'll finish our meeting on the way.'

GULBUDIN DROVE Osama's car, with Jihad, Rangin, and Abdul in the back. Osama, riding shotgun, turned towards Gulbudin.

'Tell me about the numbers listed on Wadi's phone bill.'

'We have eight interesting numbers in Kabul. Wali Wadi was in touch with the ministries in charge of military ordering, which was a new departure for him. He called the defence and security ministries every day. He would call the switchboard rather than a direct line, so I don't know who he was speaking to.'

'I went to see the receptionists last night,' said Jihad, 'and played them Wali Wadi's voicemail message, but none of them recognised his voice.'

Osama filed this information in a corner of his brain.

'What about the Iraqi number?'

'Impossible to identify.'

Osama put his pen down.

'Remind us how many calls Wali Wadi put through to that number?'

'Thirty-six in two months,' replied Gulbudin.

'They were working together,' commented Osama. 'All we have to discover is what on.'

'We've reached an impasse with the Swiss number. I ended up calling it myself, and was asked for a code. It's a secure server that redirects the call to the target number once a security code has been entered.'

'Curiouser and curiouser,' remarked Osama. 'These people are powerful, but doing their utmost to remain in the shadows. Good job, Gulbudin.'

He turned towards Rangin on the back seat.

'What do we know about Wadi's recent business deals?'

'According to the intelligence department, he played a part in various defence ministry munitions contracts, as well as contracts for major civil amenities, but the whole thing is extremely mysterious. He was a very private man. We don't really have a precise picture of his business.'

Something occurred to Osama when he heard the word munitions. The number of bullets actually shot by soldiers was impossible to count. Those contracts were a perfect opportunity for misappropriation. He caught Gulbudin's eye.

'I see what you're thinking, but I'm not convinced,' said his deputy. 'Munitions fraud would be small-time — not something serious enough to justify such a violent reaction on the part of the security minister.'

'There's something else we still haven't spotted,' commented Jihad.

'This is beyond our sphere of activity. I don't see what more we can do,' said Rangin.

'We have proof that what was presented as a suicide was actually a murder,' replied Osama. 'We've identified the direct culprit, who is now on the run. That's not bad going. Our mission now is to find out who gave the order, and what the men pursuing us are so determined to recover.'

'What makes you so sure there's still something to find?'

'Our enemies are putting too many resources into tripping us up. They're afraid of us, although we know nothing.'

'Whoever was pulling Dortmund's strings was an unbeliever,' commented Rangin. 'Do you think we're powerful enough to take this on? Sorry to be blunt, qomaandaan, but all the cops at headquarters are convinced you're going to be sidelined before we solve the case.'

Inside Wali Wadi's house, it was still nice and warm. The boiler had been left on. They walked straight over to the main study. Everything was exactly as they'd left it. There was a smell of sweat in the air, from all the technicians who'd worked in the room. Gulbudin headed for the library with an inspector in tow. The others went off to search the rest of the house. After three hours, they broke off. Osama glanced at his deputy, who nodded. Osama made for the bedroom. His men had turned everything upside down, but he began his own search anyway. At a certain moment, his gaze fell on a wooden box sitting on a gold-leaf pedestal table. It was the kind of object you might find in any Afghan home — ordinary, badly painted, nothing like the ostentatious decoration of the rest of the house. He looked at it, intrigued. It was empty. He was about to shut it when he realised that something wasn't quite right. The inside was smaller than it should have been. And yet the weight seemed perfect.

'There's nothing in there,' said Jihad. 'I've already checked.'

'And me,' added Rangin.

Unconvinced, Osama continued to examine it from every angle. One of the sides was too thick, which made the inside smaller — as if it contained a hiding place.

'Jihad,' he called out eventually. 'Do you have a knife?'

The wood was soft, and cut easily. Osama suddenly felt something click, and the over-thick panel opened. Osama smiled triumphantly. He wasn't surprised that previous searchers hadn't found it — a Westerner would never have spotted this trick, because the object looked so normal, and weighed right. Even his deputies had been fooled ... He used the tip of the knife to lift the panel completely out, revealing a cylindrical hiding place hollowed into the wood. Inside was a slim cigar case with a screw-top lid, containing a rolled-up sheet of paper.

He pulled on gloves and unrolled the document, surrounded by his men, who looked at it in dead silence. The paper crackled. It contained two lines of writing:

Mandrake File.
31"10'50.15'N. 66'11'06.92'E'.

Osama showed it to Gulbudin, his heart pounding. 'Looks like GPS coordinates. That's a latitude and longitude, isn't it?'

'Absolutely,' confirmed Gulbudin. 'It's in this country, I'm sure. Towards the end of being a gunner for Massoud we had highly precise South African mortars, which we fired using a laser rangefinder into which we entered the longitude and latitude coordinates. They were exactly like these. Shall I check the coordinates on Google Earth?'

'Yes, but discreetly,' replied Osama, who didn't know what Google Earth was.

'"Mandrake File." Do you know what it means?'

'Absolutely not. But it's important enough for Wadi to have stashed it away in this hiding place that has survived two consecutive searches. We're getting hot!'

They looked at each other excitedly. What if this was the treasure that the men who'd emptied Wali Wadi's safe were looking for?

They stayed another two hours, dismantling the entire house without finding a thing. Then Osama signalled it was time to leave. The name was churning around his brain. *Mandrake File.* What could it possibly mean?

14.

THERE WAS A STRANGE ATMOSPHERE at police headquarters. NDS men had been prowling around the place more or less openly since early that morning, making the cops nervous. Someone had already mentioned Osama and his team's visit to Wali Wadi's home. On the return journey Osama had been warned that a squad of secret police agents were heading for Wali Wadi's office, to secure the site and prevent any new incursion on their part. He didn't care. He had a lead at last.

'What's going on?' he asked one of his men, in the corridor. 'Everyone's looking very strange.'

'The central heating has broken down, qomaandaan.'

Osama suddenly realised it was horribly cold in the building — no more than 10 degrees. The men had huddled stoically into blankets, but their hearts weren't in it. Osama had installed a coal stove in his meeting room, run from a common pot contributed to by all the officers in his squad. He went in and found most of them camped out in there.

'I see the meeting room is popular today,' he joked as he came in. 'I'm afraid we need to discuss a confidential case. Please let me have it for half an hour.'

The men went out grumbling, leaving Osama with Gulbudin, Jihad, Rangin, and Abdul. The document they'd found at Wali Wadi's home was running around and around his brain. He was itching to search the Internet for the meaning of the word

'Mandrake'. Jihad rushed over to the computer.

'I'm connecting to Google.'

He typed in 'Mandrake'. To their great surprise, tens of thousands of results appeared. They were mainly articles on an American comic strip about a famous magician. Neither Osama nor any of his men had ever heard of the character, but the number of results suggested he must be extremely popular. Jihad narrowed his search to 'Mandrake + Wali Wadi'. Then he tried various combinations, with various different words.

'Always the same references — to this comic strip character!' he ended up saying, vexed. 'What shall we do, qomaandaan?'

'Find an online copy of the comic strip, Jihad, and print it out for me. Perhaps it has a secret meaning that will become clear once we've read it.'

'Consider it done.'

'Rangin, we need to find the location of these GPS coordinates. Then at least we'll know where to look, even if we don't know what we're looking for. Can I count on you?'

'Yes, boss. I'll look on Google Earth right away.'

Rangin soon found what they were looking for — a spot about eighty kilometres south of Kandahar, and south of the Quetta road, too, on the edge of Helmand province. This semi-desert region was a Taliban stronghold, right next to the southeast border with the region of Pakistan sometimes known by Westerners as the Tribal Areas. It was mainly populated by the most regime-hostile Pashtuns imaginable, but there were also a few Baloch and Bruhui communities in the extreme south.

'Hardly the perfect spot for a holiday,' remarked Gulbudin.

'We need more detail,' said Osama. 'Is it a village, or a base? Rangin, go over to military headquarters. Come back with some maps. We need to find out exactly where we're going.'

'I'll go and prepare the vehicles,' said Gulbudin. 'We can't afford to break down out there.'

JOSEPH'S EYES were closed. A nervous tic played on his right eyelid, and from time to time he would grimace.

'Boss! Boss!'

He opened his eyes. It was one of the Tajiks from the surveillance team.

'What's the matter?'

'We've intercepted a message that you'll want to hear. Come and listen. I think it's very important.'

Joseph entered the control room. The Tajik gave him a pair of headphones, and pressed play.

'Garage?'

Gulbudin's voice, unmistakeably. Joseph felt as if he knew the man intimately, having listened to his voice over and over again. He even knew the name of his favourite restaurant in Kabul.

'Yes. Who's calling?'

'I am Commandant Kandar's deputy.'

'And I'm second in command to the garage manager. Ahmad, from Almitia village. Do you remember me?'

'Of course. Peace be with you, my brother.'

After the usual greetings, Gulbudin came to the subject at hand.

'Several of us, including the commandant, are leaving the city tomorrow. Can you check the vehicles over — the commandant's 4x4 and the protective Ranger with the 50-calibre machine gun?'

'We'll take care of it. Are you going far?'

'Far enough. We'll need spare petrol cans, and water. A hundred litres.'

'We have all that. What about weapons — do you want us to get you some from the armourer?'

'Could you?'

'For the commandant, yes. What do you need?'

'One short- and long-wave radio, some defensive grenades, AK74s equipped with grenade launchers, a sniper rifle with its telescopic sights, and spare cartridges for the Kalashnikovs and handguns. And fifty boxes of three hundred cartridges for the 50 cal.'

'Are you going into a Taliban area?'

'I'm counting on you to be discreet.'

'Of course. No one will know a thing, I swear to God.'

'Thank you, my brother.'

The recording stopped after another series of bowing and scraping.

'Interesting, don't you think?' asked the technician.

'Very,' confirmed Joseph. 'Thank you.'

He returned to his office, carefully closed the door, and let himself collapse on the sofa. Here, finally, was the chance he'd been waiting for. Kandar was dead.

Osama knew he'd have to wait at least two hours for the maps, so he decided to plunge into the many other cases requiring his attention, rather than go crazy waiting. The most recent case his men were working on concerned a young woman who'd supposedly committed suicide. As usual with the suicides of very young girls, Osama suspected rape by a family member, or some sort of family vengeance: mostly, the girls were sprayed with petrol and burned alive by their parents because they'd refused an arranged marriage to a much older man. The young woman in question had died in hospital, with 90 per cent burns. Osama had imprisoned the father, older brother, and mother, but so far none of them had confessed. Osama gave instructions to check for traces of ethanol on the girl's dress, and to have an experienced inspector — Gulbudin, in this case — take over the interrogations.

With a sigh, he moved on to authorising a pile of expense claims from his men, and then to a complaint from a trader regarding a young inspector from Osama's team, who'd extorted eight thousand five hundred afghanis from him. Osama hesitated for a moment. The inspector was a valuable asset, who'd only recently joined police headquarters. But eight thousand five hundred afghanis was a hell of a lot of money when an ordinary policeman earned barely three thousand five hundred per month. The report prepared by the justice ministry said that the cop had threatened to kill the trader's entire family and to rape his eight-year-old daughter. That settled it. Osama signed the suspension order. A final glance at the report showed him that the man was a Pashtun from the same region as President Karzaï. He checked the place of birth: the same town, even. If he belonged to the same clan, the Popalzaï, then a suspension would be no use at all — the man would just be urgently transferred to another police station, and his file discreetly purged of any compromising information. Osama added a handwritten note requesting that the policeman be immediately imprisoned until further investigations had taken place — a decision that would attract even more new and powerful enemies …

He checked his watch. Jihad had left just over an hour ago, meaning that Osama still had a little time to wait. He used it to check over the document transferring Babrak's pension rights to his widow. He hated paperwork, but he needed to take care of this; otherwise, the request would be lost in the maze of Afghan bureaucracy. He put himself down as the widow's legal guardian, just in case an ill-meaning member of her family decided to try to hijack her pension, or force another marriage on her. He added a request to the head of general services to find the widow an administrative post, which would pay her better than the charity she currently worked for. Finally, he wrote a letter to the Ministry of Social Affairs, so that the widow would receive a one-off payout for the death of her husband. The mechanism for this was in place but it was never used; instead, unscrupulous bureaucrats skimmed off the money. Osama planned to make sure it was applied this time.

Jihad and Rangin burst into the office just as he was placing a final intercession on top of his pile of outgoing mail. Rangin was weighed down with several paper scrolls.

'OK, qomaandaan. I have the maps.' He put them down on the desk. 'Sorry, they're heavy.'

'Go and find Gulbudin. We'll look at them immediately.'

The maps weren't in order, and the Cyrillic text on the ends was so faded that they had to unroll them all in order to find the one relating to the exact area they were looking for. Eventually, Gulbudin called out, 'I think I've found it.'

The coordinates referred to a nameless village. Osama wasn't sure if it was Pashtun or Bruhui, but he knew he wouldn't be welcome in either. Luckily, the names on the map showed that there was a Baloch area a little to the west. He'd be able to establish some support there; but in this kind of remote region, every valley was its own unique territory. He closed his eyes to think more deeply. First he'd have to pass unnoticed through Kandahar, an area infested with government-hating Taliban. The Americans had launched several major military operations to the west of the area; he'd have to hope the most recent was still underway, so that the American troops would be occupied far from his own destination. After that, he'd have to take the Quetta road through an area crawling with would-be martyrs. He'd probably have to finish his journey on the back of a donkey, doing his best to avoid landmines, and all without the aid of the Coalition or the Afghan army. This was no joke. He'd need to take several men and plenty of provisions, and sleep in villages rather than guest houses, so as not to advertise his presence. The journey would take at least two, possibly three, days — and the same on the way back. The only good news was that it was a relatively flat region, none of it higher than fifteen hundred metres.

'What do you want to do, qomaandaan?' asked Gulbudin.

'I don't think we have any real choice. We must go. Jihad, Rangin, and Abdul will come with us. I'm also going to bring my nephew and one of his friends, to operate the Dushka machine gun on the pick-up. Gather weapons from the police armourer, and have the 4x4 looked over. We'll also need a high-frequency military-campaign radio, in case we have to call the army to our aid.'

'I saw to it earlier. The weapons and vehicles are being organised as we speak,' said Gulbudin.

'When will we leave, qomaandaan?' asked Rangin.

'As soon as possible. Tomorrow morning at dawn, if the 4x4 is ready. 4.30 departure.'

'The Coalition's anti-mine vehicles won't have been past, at that time!'

'I know. But we can't wait till 9.00am. I want us to have left Kabul before anyone realises what we're doing. We'll take the risk.'

Gulbudin bristled, but nodded in silence.

'I don't know quite what we'll find, or what kind of place we're going to,' added Osama. 'The only thing I know is that Wali Wadi hid a document critical to this case there, and took steps to ensure that someone would be able to find it in the event of a problem. I hope the document will be the key to everything. If we find it, then Babrak won't have died in vain.'

'I'll take care of all the travel arrangements, boss. We'll be ready tomorrow morning at 4.30.'

'We must keep our destination secret. Don't say anything definite to your wives. In fact, give them the impression we're heading north.'

Osama opened the drawer of his desk and took out the envelope full of dollars that the justice minister had given him. He would probably need it on this journey. After a moment's hesitation, he also picked up all the maps from military headquarters. No point letting anyone guess where he was going.

On the other side of the world, a silent alert flashed on an operator's console at Entity headquarters in Berne. As soon as he saw it, the operator opened the file. The computer informed him that an Afghan IP address in Kabul had just connected to the Internet and carried out a series of Google searches on a word that had been put on 'Red Alert'. The operator read the file carefully, wrote a short report, and sent it to his boss marked 'urgent', not realising he'd just triggered a crisis. The Entity's internal security director was quickly woken, and within a few minutes was reading the report.

He wasted no time picking up his encrypted phone.

'Sorry to bother you, general. Could you switch on your jammer?'

He could hear voices in the background — the joyful hubbub of a cocktail party. A few seconds later, the reassuring ambient hum of the jammer reached his earpiece.

'What's going on?' asked the general.

'Someone at Kabul police headquarters has been searching the Internet for the word 'Mandrake'. We've just received the alert.'

He could sense his boss's silent anxiety, and hear his breathing.

'General?'

'I'm thinking. What were the exact terms they used?'

There was no possibility of it being either a mistake or the work of a comic-strip enthusiast. The general put down the phone and immediately dialled Joseph's number.

'Switch on your jammer,' he said, when Joseph picked up.

As soon the hum reached him, he shared the news.

'That could fit with what I've just discovered,' remarked Joseph. 'Kandar's deputy is making arrangements for a trip out of Kabul. He's asked for the petrol tank to be filled and the engine checked over, and he's ordered ammunition and extra fuel. I was about to ask for permission to fire a drone, but this changes everything.'

'It would seem they haven't yet found the CD,' commented the general. 'They just have the location. They're leaving Kabul to go and find it.'

This thought soothed him a little. The situation was less dreadful than he'd imagined on receiving the alert.

'Does the phone recording give us their exact destination?'

'No. They weren't at all precise. But you should be able to persuade your contacts at NSA to train a satellite on them,' suggested Joseph. 'The tag my mole attached to Kandar's car functions in all terrain, even mountainous, and has a reach of thirty kilometres. We'll follow them at a distance with an unarmed observation drone, and wait for them to collect the CD. Then my Ks and I will intervene. We'll take possession of the CD, and kill Kandar.'

The general thought for a moment. In theory, Joseph's suggestion was excellent. Exactly what he would have done, in any civilised country. But Afghanistan was different. The country was a powder keg, seething with terrorists. In order to attack without being seen they'd have to use several observation drones, and helicopters. The Afghan terrain was difficult, and infested with terrorist groups that could appear out of secret caves or hiding places at any moment. What would happen if the team missed Kandar? If it was attacked by Taliban? The CD ending up in the hands of their enemies would be even worse than the worst possible scenario he'd yet envisaged.

'General, sir? What should I do?'

'Let's not take unnecessary risks. At the worst, the CD will remain hidden where it is. It's time to abandon the old position, Joseph. Let's hit Kandar as soon as he's left Kabul.'

'Good.'

'You mustn't leave any traces. The attack mustn't arouse the slightest suspicion.'

'It's all sorted. I've already taken care of it.'

'I'm counting on you.'

THAT EVENING was the last that Osama and Malalai would spend together before his trip. Malalai was worried about her husband travelling to an area renowned for such savagery — because in a country like Afghanistan, that was really saying something. Osama lay against her, savouring her warm body. He felt good, strangely; not at all afraid. This journey would be the culmination of all his hard work. Malalai's hair smelled of honey, along with a wonderfully subtle aroma of dried fruit that he couldn't quite place. Suddenly, she started trembling.

'What's going on?' he asked. 'Don't tell me you're afraid for me?'

'Of course I am. The region is overrun with Taliban. They're such beasts. Have you forgotten how they recently cut three men into pieces in front of Abdullah Abdullah's election monitors? The monitors went mad, apparently.'

'You mustn't worry. There'll be several of us. At least we won't be high up in the mountains. We may come across some Taliban, but I'm less frightened of them than of the snow. And I'm taking my most trustworthy men.'

'Don't talk rubbish, Osama Kandar! Those Taliban are insane, and you're entering the heart of their stronghold.'

'What I'm doing isn't all that dangerous. No more so than working for RAWA. Why don't you tell me how it's going with those mates of yours, instead?'

'The pressure on us is increasing,' she said. 'The men who killed Meena are still at large, and I know they'll never be caught. One of our representatives was stabbed in the middle of the street this morning, in Faizabad market. She thought she would be safe in a Tajik area, but the Taliban found her anyway. She was saved by the traders, but the soldiers did nothing to stop her two aggressors from fleeing.'

Osama breathed in the aroma of the fresh flowers that his wife had crushed against her skin before they made love — a tradition that Reza Shah's mistresses had helped disseminate among educated

Afghan women.

'Our daughter phoned this afternoon,' continued Malalai. 'I'm sorry to have to tell you this, but she wants to file for divorce.'

'Divorce? But … what happened?'

'It's not that Charles has done anything particularly bad. More a case of boredom. She doesn't love him anymore.'

'This is very serious. They've only been married three years! A woman can't reject her husband like that when he's done nothing wrong. She has no right! This is absurd!'

Malalai snuggled up against him.

'Young people aren't like us anymore, Osama. Staying together for a lifetime isn't what they're after, these days. And anyway, life in Montreal is different — things move faster, the women are independent and live their lives as they see fit. Divorce has become the norm.'

'I am scandalised,' exclaimed Osama. 'What will happen to our granddaughter?'

'She will stay with her mother. For the next few months, Charles is going to rent an apartment near Nita, but after that I don't know. He's always wanted to live in Asia rather than Canada. I'm not sure if he'll stay in Montreal to be near his daughter.'

'What a waste.'

'You weren't happy she married a Christian. You ought to be glad, now.'

'That's not the issue. He's her husband; she shouldn't be rejecting him without a good reason.'

'And yet she has. She has her own reasons, and they are enough.'

'And how is she going to support herself? What will she live on?'

Malalai giggled deep in her throat, the way Osama adored.

'Our daughter has just been promoted. She's a fully fledged university lecturer now. If you add in the jobs she does for the private sector, she makes a lot of money — much more than our two salaries combined.'

'What about our son? Have you had news of him?'

'Ramazan is doing well. He received a raise recently. He's off to work on a hydroelectric factory project in southern Australia.

Tasmania, I think. He's happy.'

'Still no plans to marry?'

'Osama! He's barely thirty years old. Let him enjoy life a little.'

Osama grumbled an inaudible reply — something about these young people not knowing how lucky they were. Then he stretched out his hand for a glass of water. The movement knocked over the gun he'd placed by the bed. Malalai cried out. Osama sat up on the edge of the bed, and picked up the gun.

'Is it our daughter's news that's upset you?' asked Malalai.

'Do you think I ought to be glad? That's not how a young Muslim woman should behave. It's not right.'

'Don't be so harsh. Our children live carefree lives, like all young Westerners — no more, no less. They have the liberty to think about themselves, rather than always worrying if they'll be alive tomorrow. That's why they're lucky. They've forgotten the horrors of this country, and assume that everything they have is a given. That's how life should be for all Afghans, don't you think?'

'I don't see things the way you do. Our children have been perverted by the West — they've forgotten the precepts of our religion. I think they're behaving badly. They make me feel ashamed.'

'No. They are young and free.'

'You're free, too.'

'You must be joking! Free to live in a house guarded by armed men, under threat from those crazy Taliban who want us back in the dark ages? You see,' said Malalai with sadness in her voice, 'some people dream of luxury cars, marble bathrooms, cruises to the other side of the world ... when all I want is to be able to sleep with my husband without a gun or grenade by the bed.'

'Not in this lifetime,' replied Osama. 'But it's not my fault.'

'I know.'

Osama folded back the cover.

'I'm going to pray,' he said.

Malalai cuddled into his back and held him tightly.

'Don't go, Osama! Please, tonight is our night. Perhaps our last. You can pray tomorrow morning, before you go.'

Osama hesitated a moment, then lay back down. Later on, when sleep hadn't come and the room's silence was filled with his wife's regular breathing, he thought back to her phrase. 'Our night.' He wondered whether he'd still be alive at the end of his journey, if he'd experience other nights like this one. He murmured his prayer in the darkness, begging Allah to help him fulfil his mission.

15.

At the heart of the American base at Bagram lay a protected zone inaccessible to regular soldiers. Only certain officers from the Special Forces, the CIA, or other spy services — if they'd obtained explicit permission — were allowed through the barbed wire-topped double-concrete wall. The only way in was a door equipped with a fingerprint-recognition system, guarded day and night by heavily armed Rangers. Inside the zone was an unremarkable building covered in sand-filled panels and bristling with antennae. Inside, a very small number of handpicked operators watched over the secret operations of the Predator reconnaissance and interception drones. Some of the drones only carried surveillance cameras, while others were equipped with one or two sophisticated Hellfire missiles, capable of destroying a tank. An operator in one of the command-centre rooms had been following a single vehicle for the last two days. He didn't know what kind of vehicle it was, or who was driving it, and he'd never heard of Qomaandaan Kandar; for him, this was simply vehicle number AXX 74. He glanced at the clock on the wall. He was sure he'd be able to fire a missile from a phantom drone at this hour of the morning without causing any collateral damage. What a treat. He called to the other person in the room, a young man of about twenty with a shaved head.

'Bryan, is Vega 31 ready for take-off?'

'On standby for emergency procedures. As always.'

'Launch it.'

At that very moment, the door opened. Joseph entered, followed by Amin. Joseph took a piece of white paper bearing a series of numbers and letters — the secret code for the operation — out of his pocket. The operator checked it before looking up at the two new arrivals.

'I'll call my manager. Have a seat while you wait.'

The operator picked up his telephone. They could hear him murmuring quietly.

'Sir, I'm asking for authorisation to launch a missile on a Top Priority target, in a non-military operation. I've received a signed executive order to this effect from a higher authority. Two civilians have just come in with an authorising code.'

'Give me a minute,' said a man's voice.

A few seconds later, the manager was in the room. He was a rather stout forty-year-old African-American, dressed in fatigues, with a shaved head and bushy moustache. His uniform bore no distinguishing mark or indication of rank. He nodded at Joseph and Amin before taking an enquiring look at the attack order. It came from his direct boss, an ex-colonel who was perfectly authorised to activate a *wet operation*, as targeted assassinations were called. The document was what was known as a 'blank' — an instruction that wasn't on official headed paper, wasn't stamped, and didn't have the indispensable archiving number. He immediately understood the deal: this document would be destroyed after the firing, which would apparently never have taken place.

'Which drone is being used?' he asked the operator, sure of the answer.

'Vega 31. It's just taken off; I've put it on a waiting path.'

This was an attack drone that had supposedly crashed several months before. He was now in unfamiliar no man's land, on one of the phantom operations that agents sometimes spoke about with a quaver in their voice.

'Do you know who the target is?' he asked Joseph.

'An Al Qaida mole in the Afghan security system. A real swine. We've been waiting to get him for ten days now.'

The manager calmly put the document in his pocket.

'Well, let's not miss the chance to wipe him out. I confirm the instruction to fire. Divert the Predator, and position it a half a mile behind the vehicle, at minimum speed.'

'Yes, sir!' said the operator.

Joseph discreetly led Amin over to one of the consoles. It was a sophisticated machine — microphone, headphones, camera, and two additional five-inch screens just above the main one. A series of numbers and letters appeared, followed immediately by real-time images taken by the Predator. The infra-red cameras allowed them to see two vehicles, a 4x4 and a pick-up, driving along at a lively pace. Joseph was stunned that the resolution was good enough to show every detail, down to the carriage of the machine gun mounted on the back of the pick-up. Intent on his job, the operator gestured at them in a friendly way.

'Here they are. Are you ready?'

'Yes,' said Joseph.

'How do you propose to bury an operation like this?' whispered Amin. 'Drone fire is easily recognisable. And the Afghans will be able to analyse the debris.'

Joseph turned his dead eyes towards Amin.

'We're using Russian missiles — Vikhrs — instead of the usual Hellfires. They are extremely powerful anti-tank devices. They fly at six hundred metres a second, and contain a very particular type of explosive produced only by the Russians. Which means that in the event of an investigation, no one will be able to incriminate us.'

'Aren't you afraid of journalists?'

Joseph smiled distantly.

'We'll clean up all the traces. I've organised everything already. We're paying thirty members of the Albanian contingent. They have heavy-lifting equipment. I've rented the men and the machines — two thousand dollars per soldier, thirty thousand for their captain, and seventy thousand for the colonel in charge of the regiment. All in cash. Enough to make them do what I want, but not enough to indicate the importance of the operation. They will be supervised by the five Ks you saw leaving earlier. We're going to remove the bodies and the remains of the vehicles, and then clean up the road with a high-pressure hose. No one will ever know.'

He glanced at the big clock on the wall.

'They left an hour ago. The vehicles transporting the lifting equipment travel much more slowly than Kandar's convoy, but they will still be at the location in less than forty-five minutes. The operation is immaculately planned, Amin. Take a leaf out of my book.'

'Yes, boss.'

'Target locked,' said the operator suddenly. 'Fire imminent. I can see a Dushka mounted on the back of the second vehicle. It's a protective vehicle. The official must be in the 4x4 at the front. Are you certain of the target?'

'The target is confirmed. We've had a tag on that car for the last ten days,' replied Joseph tersely.

'Arming of the two missiles,' instructed the manager.

'Vikhrs armed,' announced the operator.

'We can now set the active phase in motion,' said the manager. 'Can you confirm?'

The screen showed the two vehicles stopped at the side of the road, signing their own death warrant.

'Fire the missiles,' ordered Joseph.

'Vega 31, armed, locked on. I confirm the firing of the two Vikhrs, simultaneously,' announced the operator in a neutral voice.

He lifted a plastic valve at the top of his firing console. Beneath was a simple commutator made out of shiny metal. Joseph noticed the drops of sweat on the man's forehead, and the fixed gaze that made him look almost hypnotised. The operator, like him, knew that his act would release the flight of a missile packed with deadly explosives that would transform the steel packaging into thousands of white-hot, razor-sharp fragments. The operator nodded at him slightly, as if asking for forgiveness. Then he pulled down the commutator.

'Missile fired,' he announced in a voice now coloured by a certain excitement.

It was like a Hollywood film. Two trails of smoke enveloped the Predator. The Russian missiles were now heading for their target.

Osama was dozing in the passenger seat of the 4x4. Jihad, being the team's best driver, was at the wheel. Gulbudin and Rangin were deeply asleep in the back, holding their guns. The protective pick-up was just behind them, with Abdul and a policeman in the cab, and in the back two of Osama's cousins, former Northern Alliance mujahedeen. Suddenly, Jihad swore in Dari.

'What's going on?' asked Osama.

'The front left wheel is spinning.'

Jihad pulled up at the side of the road. Rangin and Gulbudin had woken. Osama got out, followed by his men. The 4x4 was tilting heavily to one side, the tyre completely destroyed.

'We must have driven over something metallic,' grunted Jihad. Then he noticed the carcass of a Russian tank a little further on. 'Those caterpillar pieces always cut through our tyres like butter.'

Osama stretched.

'I'm going to pray. We won't have many other opportunities this morning. Who's coming?'

Abdul and the three Hazara declined, on the pretext of having to help Jihad change the tyre. Osama walked off, followed by Gulbudin and Rangin. He started to unroll his mat a few metres away from the two vehicles, but then thought again. The sound of men changing tyres was hardly conducive to prayer.

'I'm going a little further away. Watch out for mines,' warned Osama. 'Stay close to me, on the road.'

Fifty metres further on he stopped, as did both his companions. They'd only just bent down when a massive explosion rang out. The burning blast swept them off their feet, and the pressure seemed to burst their eardrums. Osama's *shalwar kameez* was catching fire. He barely had time to put it out by rolling on the ground before he lost consciousness. When he came to, both vehicles were on fire. There were dismembered, bloody, blackened bits of body all over the place. He shook Rangin, who opened his eyes.

'What happened?' he groaned.

'We were attacked,' said Osama. He stood up, grimacing. The surroundings were empty; no one was coming to finish them off. This wasn't a Taliban ambush. They'd been stationary, so a landmine or IED was also out of the question. Suddenly, he understood. They'd been targeted by a missile, fired from a drone or helicopter. Dozens of Taliban had been assassinated like that. Osama felt a surge of fury. He was just doing his job, and they'd targeted him like a common terrorist. He bent over Gulbudin and shook him.

'Gulbudin. Wake up.'

His deputy didn't move or respond, so Osama turned him over. Gulbudin no longer had a face: a shard of metal had ripped through his head, taking out the jaw and one eye. Osama dropped the body, horrified.

'What do we do now, Hajji?' cried Rangin, totally lost.

Both vehicles had been destroyed. The 4x4 had been directly hit, and was nothing but a smoking shell. The protective pick-up had been hit by fragments, and was burning like a torch. Rangin limped over.

'Qomaandaan! What do we do?' he repeated, panic-stricken.

Osama looked over the scene. Pieces of human body littered the road and surroundings for dozens of metres. Two black shapes inside the pick-up were suddenly consumed in a roar of flames, punctuated by an explosion of burning plastic. Suddenly, he heard a kind of barely perceptible rumbling — the drone, on its way back!

He threw himself on Rangin, pinning him to the floor.

'Don't move,' he ordered. 'They're coming to check we're dead.'

'Who?' yelled Rangin.

'Shut up, or we're done for.'

At the command centre, the operator turned towards Joseph.

'Confirming that both missiles hit the target. Shall I call the drone home?'

'No, I want it back there, to make sure everyone is good and dead.'

'OK, sir. It has plenty of fuel.'

The operator moved the joystick, sending the Predator around in a large circle. Two minutes later, the drone was hovering above the carcasses of the two vehicles. The intense smoke made for poor visibility.

'I can't see a thing,' grumbled Joseph.

'It's always like this. I can see enough to confirm that both vehicles were hit. They are completely destroyed.'

'Can you see the bodies?'

'Not really, with all this smoke. They were probably carrying spare petrol cans. I can see bits scattered around the place,' said the operator. 'Look, those are legs. And that's a torso.'

'Hmm.'

The Predator made another loop, crossways. The smoke had diminished slightly.

'I have three bodies in front of the first car, about fifty metres ahead.'

'Are they moving?'

'No, they're dead.'

'Fly lower,' ordered Joseph. 'If they're alive, they'll panic.'

The operator pushed the joystick. They watched the drone slow down, and go into a nosedive. Its massive shape passed a few metres above the bodies, and then looped around again so as to shoot more film.

'They haven't moved,' announced the operator. 'Nothing — no movement at all. They must have been killed outright.'

'OK, they do seem to have had what was coming to them.'

'We need to bring the drone back, right now,' said the manager suddenly. 'We can't risk someone seeing it.'

For the first time, Joseph looked anxious.

'Negative. It must stay there until the ground team arrives.'

'The Russians and Chinese are watching the area. The French possess two aircraft carriers with interception capability. This machine isn't supposed to exist. It must hedgehop back to the base before someone spots it.'

'We can't take the risk of an injured person escaping. Let's wait for my teams to arrive — they'll be there in half an hour.'

'It's the procedure, sir,' replied the manager. 'I have to apply it. Even with phantom operations, there is a procedure.'

'It's an absurd procedure,' muttered Joseph angrily.

'There's nothing I can do about that.'

Joseph could tell the man wasn't about to change his mind. He turned on his heels.

'There will be no official report, as agreed,' cried the manager as he left. 'You can tell that to your superiors, whoever they are.'

Amin followed Joseph. The manager was ostentatiously tearing the firing order into small pieces, and watching as the remains fell gracefully into the bin.

Osama released his grip on Rangin. The young policeman had panicked and tried to jump up and run off as soon as he heard the Predator approaching, but Osama had contained him with his powerful arms. And a good thing, too: he was sure the drone would have sent back images of them lying still, as if dead. He got slowly to his feet. They both looked terrible, with torn clothes and their faces covered in blood and soot.

'You're not hurt, Rangin?'

'No, qomaandaan.'

'We don't have any weapons. Go and see if you can find a gun.'

Rangin came back a few moments later, empty-handed.

'They've all been either burnt or smashed to pieces, I couldn't find anything intact. What are we going to do?'

All Osama had was his little brown-leather travelling bag, which had somehow survived the explosion. The envelope containing the justice minister's dollars was still in his pocket. He noticed a small track leading up the hill.

'Let's go up there. It might lead to a village. I don't want to stay on the road.'

The biting cold didn't make the climb any easier, and nor did the burden of having just lost their loved ones. A few hundred metres up, Rangin collapsed in tears.

'Jihad — he was like a brother to me. He didn't deserve to die, and I don't deserve to live!'

Osama picked him up.

'We'll weep for our friends later, Insha'Allah. Right now, we've got to take cover. Come on.'

Osama's green eyes were sparkling with unbelievable intensity.

Rangin could feel his boss's fierce determination, and it inspired him to tackle the steep climb. After half an hour's exhausting effort, they reached the top of the hill. Osama paused for a moment, struck by the grandeur of the landscape in front of them — ochre mountains as far as the eye could see, gradually acquiring a purplish tinge as the sun rose. He pointed out a trail of lights in the darkness of the valley, a few kilometres away: a convoy of about a dozen vehicles.

'Soldiers arriving. Quick, we need to be on the other side.'

As they reached the far slope of the hill, they spotted a wretched village made up of a few clay houses and a tiny mosque. Subsistence farmers and shepherds must live here. Then Osama noticed an old Zhiguli — they might be able to drive it to Kandahar, where they could hire a 4x4 to reach their final destination. They walked faster, energised by rage and the need to take shelter from their pursuers. After about twenty minutes almost at a run, they reached the village. Osama was barely out of breath, but Rangin was struggling, unused to mountain conditions.

Osama made for the biggest house, no more than a hovel itself. A woman was relieving herself nearby, a pile of flat stones within reach. When she saw them, she covered her head with her veil but didn't stop her business. This was already mountain country. Osama had once read an English diplomat who stated that in this Afghanistan, the Kalashnikov was the only sign of the modern age. It was a harsh, violent world, a million miles from the modernity of Kabul, and this woman defecating on the ground outside her house was a useful reminder of that. Osama knocked on the door. Three minutes later, it inched open to reveal a hostile face.

'*Salaam Alaikum. Manda na bashi.* Peace be with you, may you not be tired. May your body be strong, and your family robust,' began Osama.

The man responded, his hand on his heart. When they'd finished their greetings, he opened the door a fraction more.

'I'm from Kabul,' explained Osama. 'I'm the qomaandaan of a police department. A missile was fired at my vehicle, killing my men.'

'Why did they want to kill you? Are you Taliban?' asked the man.

He wasn't hostile or friendly, just neutral.

'No. I'm just a policeman trying to do his job. They want to stop me, but I've nothing to do with the Taliban. Or the Karzaï government.'

'Will the unbelievers come here?'

'They might.'

The head of the village let them in, and they followed him into his living room. He snapped his fingers; a child appeared, and was instructed to bring them tea, bread, and salted yoghurt. The man gestured to Osama and Rangin to sit down.

'If the soldiers come here, we'll hide you in a secret room under the kitchen,' he said. 'Many men sheltered there during the Russian occupation.'

They drank their tea, and ate the bread and yoghurt they'd been given. Some colour returned to Rangin's cheeks. Osama relaxed a little. The furnishings were very poor: rough, un-dyed, unlined wool rugs; a chest; some threadbare cushions; and a few badly painted wooden boxes to hold the Koran and other precious possessions. There was a single photo on the wall, showing two young men in traditional Afghan dress with Kalashnikovs on their shoulders, alongside soldiers sitting on a tank. All were smiling at the camera.

'My sons,' said the head of the village, noticing Osama's glance. 'Both dead.'

The soldiers on the tank were white men, and wore the Russian uniform. Osama made sure not to comment: who was he to understand? An hour after they arrived, a man appeared and whispered in their host's ear.

'Were the two vehicles burnt by the side of the road yours?' he asked.

Osama nodded.

'Some men are inspecting them. They have several trucks, a crane, and 4x4s. They're Westerners, but not American soldiers — they're wearing the same kind of fatigues as the Russian Specnaz. Some of them are heading for the village. They'll be here in ten minutes — you'd better hide.'

Their host took them into the kitchen. They all pushed aside the boiler, which was fuelled by dried cowpats. The pungent smell was almost unbearable. Under the boiler was a trap door. Osama went down first, followed by Rangin. The secret room was tiny — no more than five or six square metres. It contained musty, threadbare blankets, an old Kalashnikov, and two grenades inscribed with Cyrillic writing. Rangin knelt down with a grimace. The trap door closed on them, and the boiler scraped across. They were in total darkness. A little later, they heard noises in the house — people speaking English with a foreign accent that Osama couldn't recognise. The sound of boots became very loud over their heads. Three or four soldiers were searching the house. Then the voices faded, and disappeared. A little over two hours later, the boiler was noisily moved and the trap opened. The head of the village's face appeared, beaming.

'You can come out.'

'Have they gone?' asked Rangin.

'They're looking for you in the surrounding area. They say that two terrorists have fled.'

Osama thought about the drone. It had sent back images of them both lying flat on the floor. When they didn't find the two intact bodies, their killers must have realised that they were alive and had escaped.

'Did they tell you our names?' asked Osama.

'No, they just talked about two Taliban.'

Osama dusted himself down. The killers wouldn't know who had survived, because the bodies down there were too damaged for identification. But if they were professionals — as they had proved they were — they would search for them relentlessly. If he and Rangin continued along the road, they'd be bound to encounter roadblocks, which they'd have no chance of handling unarmed. They would have to try another route. It would take longer — two days rather than one — and they'd be more likely to step on a landmine, but they had no choice. It was a risk worth taking.

'I need to get to Kandahar,' said Osama. 'Would you be able to rent me your car, and someone to drive it? I'll pay you for the petrol, and a fee on top.'

The head of the village cried out indignantly — he wasn't expecting any compensation, he was proud to help his brother, he didn't need anything in exchange. He instructed his son, who had a driving licence and was the owner of the car, to take them. They left straight away. The son told Osama that he worked for a Kabul meat wholesaler; his job was to travel around the local shepherds and buy meat for less than it sold for at the livestock markets. He was a shrewd-looking man of about forty, with two wives. He explained to Osama that he'd bought the second with his salary: fifteen hundred dollars and only two goats, as she was second-hand, limped, and was missing five teeth.

After half an hour of travelling along stony tracks at twenty kilometres an hour, they came to the tarmac road — well before the site of the attack, which they soon reached. Osama was stunned to see that the two vehicle carcasses had been removed. He asked the driver to stop, and got out. The road had been washed down with a power hose, and the body parts removed. That only thing that had escaped the soldiers' attention was a single piece of blackened iron, a little further on. He knew one of the main ANA headquarters was under a hundred kilometres away, but only NATO possessed this kind of sophisticated lifting equipment, and especially the capacity to intervene as quickly and effectively as this. And yet the soldiers who'd been looking for them spoke with an accent, and weren't wearing official uniforms. Who were they? Special Forces operating incognito, or mercenaries? He heard a noise, and saw an old truck appear around a bend. He jumped back into the car and gave the order to drive off. The site of the drama was soon out of view.

'How long to Kandahar?' he asked.

'It's less than five hundred kilometres away — eight or nine hours by the usual road, but the secondary road is very bad, especially at the beginning,' replied the head of the village's son.

The journey along the potholed earth road was even worse than expected. They stopped several times to pray and eat, and around 6.00pm the son asked if they'd like to sleep in Qalat. Osama wasn't keen to enter the city: it was too close to the site of the attack, and they might be awaited there. Better to find an isolated village. They were in the heart of an entirely Pashtun area, but the Pashtun had a well-deserved reputation for being the most welcoming of Afghans, for whom hospitality was no empty concept. In the end, they couldn't find a village by the side of the road, so Osama decided they would all sleep in the car. He slept badly. He hoped his wife hadn't been told of his death. Before he left, Osama had warned Malalai and Reza that he wouldn't be in touch for four or five days, so as not to give his enemies any sense of his whereabouts.

They continued their journey the next morning at dawn.

First they came to Qalat, an important city thanks to the big army garrison, and then Jaldak, still a sleepy kind of town, despite the Taliban having made it one of their pre-2001 command centres. It still bore the scars of the savage fighting that had taken place there. After three hours' drive, they finally entered the former Taliban capital of Kandahar just after 2.00pm. There were soldiers everywhere, and almost no women. The few they could see hurried about in pairs, heads down beneath their burqas. The city was still the haunt of hard-line Islamist militiamen; nothing had really changed, despite the millions of dollars squandered on reconstruction. Osama wondered how much of it had ended up in the pockets of the security minister and the other corrupt politicians who were shamelessly looting the country. They drove into the city. You could feel the tension — the inhabitants were either hostile or rushing about looking frightened. Brutish Taliban types kept staring at them. Osama hadn't been in an atmosphere like this since 2001. The Taliban had already won in Kandahar: the city belonged to them, despite the government flags dotted around the place.

'Where do you want to go?' asked the driver.

Osama didn't really know. He'd never seen so many bushy beards. His enemies were everywhere. He suddenly realised that no women were driving. Kandahar was the most rigid city in the country, the one where the most conservative brand of Islam held sway. He would never manage to hire a car discreetly here. Suddenly, he had a brainwave, inspired by a recent conversation with Malalai.

'Let's go to police headquarters.'

'But you said to avoid it,' protested Rangin.

'I've changed my mind. Trust me.'

The young policeman scowled. With his Western haircut, clean-shaven face, and tucked-in shirt, he felt like a foreigner in this crowded city that was hostile to the slightest modernity.

'Untuck your shirt,' said Osama. 'I'm going to get us some turbans.'

He went into a stall on Herat Sarak, the main road running through the middle of the city, and bought two blankets, some strings of prayer beads, and two turbans. Eventually, the Zhiguli drew up outside police headquarters. A brand-new sign on the wall announced the ANP/Afghan National Police, in English. Osama noticed that someone had opened fire on the sign, riddling it with bullets. Lovely ... He walked inside.

'I'd like to talk to Captain Kukur.'

'Who's asking?'

'The husband of Malalai, her friend from Kabul.'

Kukur was a woman, the only one in the Kandahar ANP. She'd escaped the clutches of the Taliban several times; they wanted to kill her as a lesson to others. When the Taliban was overturned she'd been able to return to her job, even being promoted to her current rank of captain. She still carried a truncheon and pistol, but like all women in Kandahar was obliged to put on a burqa whenever she left police headquarters. She was known throughout the country for her stand on women's rights. Malalai had told her that she was a member of RAWA; they'd spoken several times, and had the greatest respect for one another.

Osama was shown into a small office, where Captain Kukur was sitting behind a tiny wooden desk. Osama noticed a pistol lying next to the computer, which was connected to a wifi router. The Coalition's money wasn't only reaching Kabul, then. The captain was wearing a simple hijab and a loose dress that concealed her figure. Her fingers were laden with rings, and one hand bore a henna tattoo. She appeared dynamic, courageous, and intelligent — but then she'd have to be, to brave the Taliban like this in the heart of their stronghold.

'Can we talk?' asked Osama softly. 'It's very important.'

She stared at him, surprised, before replying. 'Yes. I have many enemies, but they aren't sophisticated enough to tap my conversations. And in any case, what I do or say doesn't matter to them, because I'm just a woman, an inferior being. The only thing that matters is that I'm here, which is why they'll end up killing me.'

It was true, of course, and Osama had often thought it, but he was stunned to hear her so clear-headed about her own fate. Not wanting to be overheard, he pulled the door slightly towards them, but couldn't close it completely because an unmarried man and woman weren't allowed to shut themselves in a room together. He sat down on a rickety chair.

'You're Malalai's husband?' she murmured.

'That's right. Osama Kandar, qomaandaan of the Kabul Murder Squad.' He replied so quietly that she had to lean forward to hear what he was saying.

'Malalai told me you were the most handsome man in Afghanistan. I must say, she wasn't lying.'

Osama felt himself redden. Captain Kukur burst out laughing.

'What do you need? And why the secrecy?'

Osama carefully explained the situation, without revealing exactly where he was heading. As soon as he finished, he knew that this woman would help him.

'You like danger, qomaandaan.'

'I don't really have a choice.'

'I understand.' She waved her hands at the empty office in which she worked. 'Perhaps another Afghanistan will emerge from our efforts. A free country, inclined towards modernity, saved from the fundamentalists, incorrupt.'

'Now you're the one who's talking dangerously!'

They both laughed. Then she grew serious again.

'I imagine you want a 4x4, a driver, and one or two bodyguards?'

'You imagine correctly.'

'The car is no problem; you can take mine. The driver and bodyguards will be more difficult. No one is quite trustworthy here. But I do know a young man who might be able to help. He's totally reliable, and he's a Pashtun.'

'Who is he?'

'My son.'

Osama raised an eyebrow. 'What I'm doing is very dangerous', he said. 'I was attacked without warning. Your son would be risking his life. I don't think it's a good idea.'

'My son is in constant danger from the very fact that he's my son. Several Taliban groups would kill him just to get at me. Helping you wouldn't be any more dangerous for him than simply living in this city.'

'What is his work?'

'He's a baker.' Kukur smiled. 'He makes the best flatbread in Kandahar, and possibly the whole region. There's almost always a queue outside his bakery. He's a good boy, who's never touched a gun in his life. He has just one wife — a teacher — and two lovely children. I'm proud of him.'

'I will accept your help. Let me tell you where I'm going.'

She took out a military map of the region that was almost as detailed as the one Osama had used in Kabul. Osama noticed that the place names were in Cyrillic script.

'It was used by the Russian Special Forces,' she explained when she saw him looking. 'It dates from just before they left, 1987 perhaps, or '88. Almost nothing has changed since then — no new roads have been built, the villages are all the same. Which says a lot about what's happened in this country over the last twenty years: nothing likely to feature on a map …'

'It's this village,' said Osama. 'Pamni Lilou. Do you know it?'

'No. It looks tiny. It's right in the tribal area.'

'Does the army control that area?'

'The army controls *nothing* beyond the parking lot of this barracks. And yet …'

'Do you think I can go there?'

'It's dangerous. Even with my son, you might get murdered. Your beard isn't bushy enough — they'll soon take you for an unbeliever.'

'I can't go back now,' he said. 'I have to take that file back to Kabul, whatever the cost. But I don't want to put your son in danger. Just lend me a car — Rangin and I will be fine.'

'You won't find it on your own. Also, you speak Pashtun with a Kabul Dari accent, so it'd be immediately obvious that you're not from around here. You need a local guide. I'll call my son, and he'll meet you here in an hour. Please.'

Osama didn't offer her any money — she would have been mortally offended. But he did ask her where he could buy guns and a sniper rifle.

'To do what?'

'For me. I was a sniper in the Northern Alliance.'

'Malalai never told me that.'

'I don't boast about it. Having killed people isn't something I'm proud of.'

'This country forces us all to do things we aren't proud of,' she answered immediately.

She wrote a name and address on another piece of paper.

'This man will supply you with all the weapons you need. He works with the Taliban as well the army, so be wary of him — he's a real snake.'

Osama thanked her from the bottom of his heart, and left. Rangin was waiting for him in the café opposite, drinking a Coke, which had been the fashionable drink among the Taliban ever since a Coca Cola factory had opened in Pakistan. Osama decided to leave Kukur's 4x4 at police headquarters, preferring to reach his contact by taxi, as he didn't know Kandahar. The city was true to its reputation — ugly, dull, noisy, and dirty. It took them more than forty minutes to reach the address that the police captain had given them, even though it was just under five kilometres away. The taxi stopped in front of the entrance to a small market.

'Where is it?' asked Osama.

The taxi driver gestured contemptuously at the market. The atmosphere was very bizarre — Osama felt as if the traders were pretending not to see him. When he turned around, he saw that Rangin had put his chitrali back on his head. The chitrali was a traditional Tajik hat, and the southern Pashtun hated the Tajiks almost as much as they did the Americans.

'Put that hat in your pocket,' he ordered, furious. 'You're a Pashtun. What are you doing wearing a Tajik hat in a Taliban stronghold? What have you done with your turban?'

'I left it in the café,' admitted Rangin. 'I'm not used to wearing a turban. Sorry, Qomaandaan.'

Things felt a little more normal once Rangin was bareheaded. Several traders called out to them to buy fruit, burqas, ammunition, and sexual tonics. You could find anything you wanted in this market, however disreputable. After several minutes wandering through the maze-like lanes, they finally found the shop whose name they'd been given. Osama instructed Rangin to wait outside.

The shop sold saucepans and ammunition, as well as surplus military stock, including American, Russian, and Pakistani army fatigues. Also plenty of *keffiyehs,* meaning that Arab Al Qaida fighters must shop here, given they were the only people in Afghanistan to wear the keffiyeh. Osama wondered why the NDS tolerated a business like this in central Kandahar. The owner approached, with a great show of respect. He barely reached Osama's shoulder, and seemed very impressed by his visitor's stature.

After a series of convoluted Pashtun greetings, the man asked Osama what he was looking for.

'I'd like two rucksacks, two water bottles, gloves, hats, two sleeping bags, two torches, and a shovel,' said Osama.

'I have Russian army sleeping bags, but they're not the best quality. I do have better ones, but they're more expensive.'

'Show me.'

The businessman came back with two sleeping bags in their protective sacks. One of them had a hole right through it.

'Italian army equipment, from Herat,' explained the businessman. 'These are the best on the market, better than the American army ones — they're used by the Italian alpine chasseurs.'

Osama pointed at the hole.

'Is this a bullet hole?'

'I don't know, noble visitor. Perhaps the Italians didn't want to hand over their sleeping bags? Perhaps they were killed by Taliban? Nobody knows. Three thousand afghanis for them both.'

Osama negotiated a price of one hundred and twenty dollars for all the supplies.

'I need something else,' said Osama. 'Something that isn't for sale on the open market.'

The businessman looked at him craftily.

'I can get hold of many things that others don't have. What are you after?'

'A folding-stock Kalashnikov. A Dragunov sniper with ammunition. And grenades.'

'That can be done. How will you be paying?'

'In dollars,' replied Osama, blessing the justice minister for his foresight.

'That will make it 20 per cent less expensive. Five hundred dollars for the Dragunov, a hundred for the Kalashnikov, and fifty dollars for ten magazines.'

They came to an agreement at three hundred and eighty dollars for the lot. Osama held out the notes, which the businessman took solemnly. Then he disappeared into the back, and returned a few moments later with a blanket that he unrolled in front of Osama. The Dragunov wasn't a recent model, but it was in good condition. Osama checked the firing pin, the breech, and the sights, which were made by Zeiss, the best in the business. The previous owner of the weapon must have been a true professional. The grenades were a Russian design, made in Pakistan. He would have preferred originals, but that was probably too much to ask here in Kandahar.

'That's perfect. Could I have a more discreet bag?' asked Osama.

Weighed down by their packages, Osama and Rangin didn't see the young boy that the businessman had instructed to follow them as soon as they left the shop.

16.

NICK TOOK ADVANTAGE of Margaret having been called out of the office on a secret assignment to spend a few hours on the immigration databases, using her log-in codes. The lack of reaction to his recent searches proved his initial hunch: the Entity's internal security was watching his communications via his personal log-in and passwords, but they couldn't watch all the computers all the time. He therefore opened two windows concurrently — one on his own computer using his log-in, and the other, using Margaret's, on the computer that had belonged to Werner.

Try as he might, he still hadn't found the slightest trace of the woman he was looking for. There were just too many Zahras. It was maddening. He possessed potentially explosive information, but on his own he was unable to make use of it to find the people he was after.

In the end, he switched the computers off. Rather than keep going around in circles, he decided to return to the fugitive's house in Zurich. He still had a sense of having missed something on his first search.

At Rue Klein, nothing had changed. He spent three hours rummaging around, without finding anything new. Eventually, he flopped down on the office sofa, opposite the desk. He wasn't getting anywhere. It was driving him nuts: he'd made so much progress, so many discoveries, and now this!

He glanced absently around the room. Suddenly, something

caught his eye — a mark on the wall, around the painting that concealed the safe. He approached, fascinated. Close up, it was obvious: the paint on the few millimetres of wall surrounding the edge of the painting was a little darker than the rest, as if it had previously been protected from the sun. The painting was slightly smaller than it should have been.

He touched the signature with his finger. A Manet. A painting like this had to be worth millions of dollars. He started searching for the receipt, and eventually found it: the painting had been bought from Christie's of London, in 2002, for fifteen million pounds.

Interesting, he thought. The fugitive had bought this painting several years ago. *Why move it here now ... to replace something else?* He decided to see where this one could have hung before. He looked around the whole house without finding a suitable spot. What could it mean?

In the end, he couldn't think of anything better to do than to make a systematic search of the house. He started with the cellar, which he hadn't previously paid much attention to. It was protected by a double-locked, reinforced door and a sophisticated alarm system that was, fortunately, disconnected. Behind the reinforced door was a vaulted room of about three hundred square metres. Air conditioning kept it at around twelve degrees. Nick shivered. The walls were covered with shelves of wine, laid out unconventionally, the bottles upright rather than horizontal, their labels visible. Quite a collection — about two thousand bottles, and only the very best. He ran a finger over the labels: Mouton Rothschild, Latour, Pétrus.

He noticed an empty shelf at the back and walked over. This was the first time he'd paid it any attention. The shelf was not the slightest bit dusty, as if it had recently been swept. There were only three bottles on it, out of the four or five hundred it could have held. He took one down: Chateau Talbot 1952. There was very little liquid in the bottle; it was unlikely to be drinkable. He pulled down the next: Chateau Palmer, 1943. Same thing — too little liquid, well below the shoulder of the bottle. The third was a Chateau Margaux that had, again, lost much of its liquid. He put it back on the shelf, and went upstairs to look for the receipts.

Leonard had spent an absolute fortune on French wines over the last few years. Two thousand bottles, costing an average of five hundred Swiss francs each — Nick soon worked out that that made more than a million Swiss francs. And this was before you counted the three hundred Pétrus 1982s, one hundred Cheval Blanc 1947s, and two hundred Romanée Contis that he'd bought separately at auction, for a similar sum. Nick was quite sure those bottles weren't in the cellar. So where could they be? The Entity's report had specified that the fugitive hardly ever went out, and never entertained at home. Surely he couldn't have drunk six hundred bottles all by himself? For a moment, Nick wondered if he'd been robbed. Then he realised the truth.

It was so daring that he burst out laughing. No wonder his colleagues hadn't noticed!

'Leonard, you're a genius!' he murmured.

He walked straight over to the painting and took it down.

Captain Kukur's son was waiting for Osama and Rangin in the police headquarters garage, next to a dusty old Toyota 4x4. His name was Abdullah. He had the features of an eagle, and a large potbelly. His tousled hair and thick red beard made him look very young.

'My mother explained your mission to me,' he began. 'I'm aware of the danger, and I'll help you, as much as I can.'

'Thank you. Do you know the area we're going to?'

'A little. When I was just starting out I used to sell bread there sometimes, but the villagers didn't really have cash and I didn't like being paid in kind. I haven't been there for about ten years. It's worth knowing that the closer you get to Quetta, the deeper you are into the tribal areas. Neither the army nor the police ever go there — only smugglers and Taliban are brave enough.'

'How will they receive us?'

'I don't know,' said Abdullah. 'It will depend on the village chiefs. Some of them are very welcoming, but others can be aggressive, even vicious ...'

'We'll be as careful as we can. Let's leave now,' decided Osama. 'There's no need for us to hang around here.'

They piled into the jeep. It was so old that it didn't even have air conditioning. The seats and dashboard were in tatters, but the motor seemed to work fine. They were soon out of Kandahar. They passed Takht-e Pol, still a Taliban stronghold, and then turned off onto an unpaved road. In the southwest the mountains (much smaller than in the north) sloped down gently, creating a semi-arid region on the Iranian border. And yet the track was in such bad repair that Abdullah soon had to slow down. Nothing grew in these bleak plateaux that continued for huge stretches at a time. Everything was beige — the same constant beige colour. They passed several ruins, villages that had been destroyed by the Russians or the Coalition forces. The potholes, along with the deep ditch running down one side of the track, kept them to below thirty kilometres an hour. But at least it wasn't snowing. On the contrary, the sky was blue and it was warmer than in Kabul — maybe thirteen or fourteen degrees. Around seven in the evening, Osama realised that they'd be likely to plunge off a cliff if they continued after nightfall. He reluctantly instructed Abdullah to stop the 4x4 in the middle of the track. They locked their doors, ate, and rolled themselves up in their sleeping bags to face the night.

The trader who'd sold Osama the gun listened carefully to the report from the boy he'd instructed to follow them. The man who'd bought the sniper rifle had rejoined his companion, and then another man, in front of police headquarters. They'd driven off towards the south in a dented 4x4. The boy was accustomed to tailing clients on behalf of the trader, who was a keen informer to both the Taliban and the NDS. He'd flagged down a motorcycle, and paid the driver a few afghanis to discreetly follow the 4x4. They'd lost it at the start of a desolate dirt track, thirty kilometres south of Kandahar. The boy swore to the trader that the track led into a deserted area. The trader took out his map. He was surprised at where his client was headed — the area was an absolute black hole. It contained nothing but villages, often so tiny and insignificant that no one had even bothered to name them. Travellers were on their own there. They were usually following instructions from former inhabitants, something like, 'Take a path after the fourth blue mountain, behind the gorge to the left of the track. After twenty hours' walk, you'll pass a ford. The village is on the right, on another path, after another three hours' walk.'

He wondered again what those men could be up to in an area like that. It was obvious from his icy stare and haughty manner that the big guy who'd bought the sniper rifle was used to giving orders, and unlikely to take no for an answer. He had the authority of a Taliban chief, but his beard was short and tidy. He didn't seem comfortable in his turban, as if he'd put it on specially. The trader didn't think he was an NDS officer — he didn't have their unbearable arrogance — but he was probably a government official. His clothes were clean and his hands weren't calloused. A smuggler? Didn't seem like it. Also, he spoke Pashtun with a slight Dari accent, like someone from Kabul. The trader had a decision to make: keep the information to himself, denounce the man to the NDS, or warn the Taliban. Three very different choices. He thought about it. He'd denounced a lot of people to the NDS recently — one more or less wouldn't make any difference. On the other hand, the Taliban's influence in the region was rising daily, and doing them a favour would stand him in good stead.

He thought some more. If this mysterious man wasn't a smuggler or an NDS man, he might be a Coalition spy. The Taliban would be delighted to slit the throat of a traitor like that, once they'd ripped out his eyes and genitals as an example to others. The trader pulled on a patou and turban, and strode over to the little mosque nearby.

The mullah who received him was very young, with strange blue eyes, white skin, and blondish hair, making him look like an Englishman. The resemblance stopped there, however: the mullah was a half-crazed fanatic. Everyone in Kandahar knew that he'd personally committed atrocities towards the end of the Taliban reign, slitting the throats and mutilating the bodies of those requiring Islamic punishment. Like many, he hadn't been investigated after 2001, and had simply taken refuge in his mosque. Aware of his fierce reputation, the police and military avoided him, and government officials turned a blind eye to his inflammatory preaching.

The trader told him what had happened, emphasising the visitor's smart appearance and detailed knowledge of weaponry.

'How did he pay?' asked the mullah. 'Afghanis or dollars?'

'Dollars.'

'Show me the notes.'

The trader reluctantly took out the wad of money. The mullah examined it with care.

'Look,' he said. 'These notes are crisp, almost new, and the numbers are consecutive.'

'What does that mean?'

'They've come straight from the bank that printed them. These notes must have been provided by the American authorities. They're the only ones who have access to such new money.'

'Do you think he's a spy, Mullah?'

'Of course he's a spy. What else could he be? Tell me again which road your boy saw them take.'

The trader took out his map. The mullah wrote a few laborious notes on a grimy sheet of paper. He was almost illiterate, something most of his congregation didn't know. When he'd finished, he pushed the map back to the trader, but kept the money.

'You did the right thing coming to see me, *Allah U Akhbar.* I'll keep these notes, because God wouldn't like you enriching yourself selling weapons to an enemy of the true faith, don't you think?'

'Of course,' stammered the trader, cursing his rashness.

'We will never forget what you have done today, my brother. I will immediately let our brothers in the mountains know. We will catch these men, and interrogate them.'

ACCORDING TO NICK's brief Google search, Joseph Stipowitz & P. Golan was one of the top Zurich galleries for old paintings. It was protected by a reinforced double-entrance security door. A stunning young woman with hazel eyes and auburn hair led Nick and his roughly wrapped painting through to the back of the shop, where she sat him down at an inlaid desk.

'What can I do for you?' she asked.

She was wearing a fitted suit with a white blouse, and a pearl necklace and earrings. Nick produced his fake card from the federal Justice Department.

'I'd like your opinion on a painting.'

He unwrapped it. She looked excited.

'A Manet! Show me.'

'It's an important work. Don't you think it would be better to ask Mr Stipowitz?' asked Nick. 'Or Mr Golan?'

'There is no Mr Golan — only Miss Patricia Golan, which is me,' replied the young woman icily. 'I hold a doctorate with distinction in history of art from the University of Zurich, as well as specialised qualifications from the Sorbonne and the London School of Art. Will that be enough, do you think, or must I really call my colleague?'

'I'm so sorry,' stammered Nick. 'I do apologise.'

The specialist took hold of the painting, but put it down barely two minutes later.

'It's a fake.'

'Are you absolutely sure?' asked Nick, as a matter of form.

So his hunch had been correct. The fugitive had gone off with his wine and his favourite painting, leaving a forgery behind. Which meant everything must have been organised, probably well in advance. The Entity was searching for a desperate man, when they were actually dealing with a very shrewd operator.

'To tell you the truth, it's a very good copy, and yet the paintwork doesn't have the exactitude or sheen of a real Manet. Even natural pigment is nothing like the paint that French artists were using at the time. Ours is slightly glossier. The frame is modern, but has been artificially aged with acid. The wood is a little too light; it's not the solid oak that was used in France. The signature is fairly close to the original. Overall, I must admit it's a pretty good job.'

'I see,' said Nick. 'And how much would a copy like this cost?'

'At least twenty or thirty thousand francs, maybe more. The forger is very talented.'

'Would the original be worth as much today as it was around the year 2000?'

'More or less. The price of unique works of art hasn't dropped with the economic crisis. There's an increasing number of Asian buyers.'

'If someone had the original, would he need an authorisation to export it?'

'No. The owner can legally do whatever he likes with his painting, as long as he has the certificate of authenticity, which Customs might well wish to see on departure from the country. He would, however, have to insure it for the journey, using an experienced specialist, as there's an extremely high risk of degradation.'

Nick felt his heart begin to race.

'Are there many specialist insurers?'

'Not as many as one might think, and not all are reputable. If you're talking about a commodity like a one-off ancient painting, there are really only two companies in Switzerland. One is in Lausanne, and the other is here in Zurich. If you need to export a painting, they take care of everything: wrapping, secure transportation, specialist removal men, insurance ... Would you like their contact details?'

Nick was thrilled. So the fugitive had been preparing this for a long time. He'd anticipated everything before he left ... except for his employer, Willard Consulting, attempting to bump him off, forcing him to flee before he'd sorted out his passport.

This was a new angle on the case: whatever secrets the fugitive held, he had decided to burn all the bridges to his former life and start afresh with his new love, probably far from Switzerland. If Nick could just find out where the fugitive had sent the painting, he'd have cracked the case. With a place as well as the name the fugitive was living under, the manhunt would soon be over. Nick smiled: he hadn't done badly, for a solo act — and in a short space of time, too. Tough luck for the Entity that he had no intention of telling them what he'd discovered.

He visited the first brokers, but they had no trace of such a case. He'd have to go to Lausanne, then.

He parked his car in front of a large stone building — the Bel Air tower, Switzerland's first skyscraper. It was impressive, if nothing like its American counterparts. The brokers' office occupied the entire fifteenth floor. Through the glass partitions, Nick could see smartly dressed young people working hard at their computer screens. He presented his card at reception, and asked to see someone in charge. He was soon shown into the office of the managing director, Michel Louvin — a well-built man with crew-cut hair, who looked more like an ex-soldier than a haulier. Nick liked him immediately. He asked to see Nick's business card again, looked at it carefully, and offered him a seat.

'I've already spoken to your colleagues at the Geneva police department about the importation of stolen works of art,' he began. 'Are you working with them?'

'This investigation is strictly at a federal level,' replied Nick. 'We're up against a network of money launderers that operates between Europe, America, and Asia. It doesn't steal works of art; it uses dirty money to buy them.'

'I see,' said the man, relaxing. 'How can I help you?'

'There's one man in particular, a Swiss financier, whom we suspect of laundering drug money by buying old wines and works of art, and then re-exporting them outside Switzerland.'

The man looked doubtful.

'We sometimes see stolen paintings that have been bought by collectors, but laundering … that would be difficult with paintings, because it's hard to buy many or important ones in cash. Theoretically, you could buy in cash from private brokers, outside the auction rooms, but it's not as common as one might think. People who make their money selling drugs tend to buy villas or yachts, rather than works of art. Wine would obviously be less complicated, but the total amounts wouldn't reach anything like the same level. Which shipment in particular are you interested in?'

'A Manet painting and almost six hundred bottles of superb French wine. Sent a few weeks or months ago, to an unknown destination. The name of the man who sent them is Milton. Lionel Milton. He has a Swiss passport.'

'A Manet and some great old wine — yes, that does ring a bell. We dealt with that not very long ago.'

He tapped at his computer for a few minutes.

'Here we go … I have it. We carried out a high-security shipment for your guy. Lionel Milton. Five hundred and seventy five bottles of great French wine, worth two and a half million Swiss francs. Very rare bottles, hard to get hold of even in France. The painting was a Manet, insured for fourteen million pounds sterling. We automatically priced it below what he'd paid at auction, on account of the economic crisis, and he didn't argue. The title of the painting is 'Baignade au bord du lac.'

'When and where did you send them?'

'The twenty-fifth of February this year. To Perth, Australia. Addressed to a certain Zahra Kimzi, with instructions to leave the package with a guardian, as Ms Kimzi had not yet arrived in Australia.'

The next morning, Osama and his two companions continued their journey. They drove across a windswept plateau before coming down a hillside into a wide, shallow valley. Here they found a running stream that seemed to have emerged from nowhere, along with a few willows and elms. The temperature had increased again with the sun, and despite the dust they soon had to open their windows to avoid roasting in the car. After about ten kilometres, they came to a village. As they slowed down, Osama noticed that the vehicle was tilting to the right.

'There's something wrong with one of our tyres,' he said.

The front tyre was going down. Some children turned up as they were changing it. One of them chucked a stone, hard, hitting Rangin right on the head. He yelped with pain, and reached for his gun. Osama stopped him.

'Don't do anything. We don't want these villagers on our backs.'

They put the wheel back on, and took the opportunity to drink some water. Just as they were about to leave, Osama saw a group of turbaned men approaching. Their clothes may have been wretched, but they all carried Kalashnikovs over their shoulders. Abdullah paled. Osama put a hand on his shoulder.

'Stay calm. I'll talk to them.'

There were at least fifteen men — all with long, bushy beards, dirty turbans, and a hostile attitude. Osama and his companions were clearly not welcome here. Their leader was in the middle of the pack. He was missing part of his face, half his nose had been reattached at a skewed angle, and in place of his right eye there was simply a fold of burnt skin. He was horrible to look at.

'*Bakhena Ghuarum,*' began Osama diplomatically in Pashtun. 'May your life be long, your body robust, and your family strong'.

'Who are you?' asked the man abruptly. 'What are you doing here?'

'We need to get to a village. It's five hours' drive from here, over the hills towards the south. We need to cross your land to reach our ultimate destination.'

'That's not possible. No stranger may do that. You must leave immediately. Or else come to the mosque garden with us, and we can discuss things in peace.'

With these threatening words, some of the armed men accompanying the leader spread out in a military formation. Osama no longer had any doubt that he was face to face with a Taliban commander. He looked over to the place that the man had mentioned. The mosque was a small, square building, the largest in the village. Strangely, there was no house on its right side — instead, a kind of tree-planted esplanade. As if the inhabitants wanted to avoid that particular space, even though they'd built houses everywhere else.

'We don't intend to come to the mosque garden,' he replied. 'On the contrary, we want to head in the other direction, to the top of that hill there, and down into the valley beyond.'

'The mosque garden is very pleasant.' insisted the leader. 'It's cooler over there. It'll be nice.'

Osama somehow sensed that the Taliban leader's suggestion was a trap, and that they should remain all together, near the car. He replied severely, 'Is this how a leader applies *melmastia*? Have the Pashtun around here forgotten the old ways? Has the hospitality due to travellers disappeared? Have foreigners made you forget the rules of our culture?'

These words clearly disturbed the leader. Melmastia — the duty to welcome any visitor, whoever he might be, with dignity, and help him with his troubles — was at the heart of Pashtun tradition. Being reminded of it by this giant with the strange green eyes seemed to reverse the power balance, while putting him in a difficult position with regards to his men.

He hesitated.

'I need your help,' said Osama. 'You must help your Afghan brother with his troubles.'

'You can go,' decided the leader. 'I see from your attitude that you're a man of truth. Would you like to drink tea with us?'

'I thank you for your hospitality, brother,' said Osama, 'but we have a long journey ahead, and there are people who would be only too pleased to catch up with us before we reach our destination. It will be more prudent, both for us and for you, that we continue our journey without delay.'

'As you like,' said the leader. 'May you have long life.'

He personally accompanied Osama back to the 4x4. As he opened the door, Osama asked, 'What exactly is in the mosque garden? Why has no house been built in that space?'

The Taliban burst out laughing.

'That's where we execute our enemies, on the side facing away from Mecca. We've slit the throats of Russians there, but also corrupt army officers, two foreigners, and even a tax inspector. Lots of people have died there. If you'd gone just then, you'd probably be dead by now. You did well to refuse, *Allah U Akhbar!*'

Osama stepped back into the car. It smelled acrid. Of fear.

AFTER EIGHT EXHAUSTING HOURS, they reached a new valley. They had passed dozens of identical bare hills, and taken paths so narrow that their chunky 4x4 could have toppled into the abyss at any moment. The further south they went, the lower the altitude, and the more bleak the landscape: round, arid, windswept hills without any sign of life. They hadn't seen a tree since early that morning. Eventually, they came around a bend and Osama spotted an ill-assorted bunch of mud houses clinging to the side of the mountain. No electricity, of course; not a single sign of modernity. Osama stopped the 4x4 in the middle of the village. Children ran up shouting, desperate to see what was going on. A few women in burqas appeared, too, but vanished as soon as three men stepped out of the car. In a little while, a man approached. His trousers had been cut off at the ankle, and his filth-blackened feet were visible through shoes without laces. Three more men followed him at a respectful distance. There were no Kalashnikovs here; only old repeating rifles. Osama recognised some Lee Enfields — English guns a hundred years old, which the mujahedeen had used at the very beginning of the war against the Russians. Even Kalashnikovs hadn't reached this village, and that was saying something. Osama introduced himself to the village elder as a friend of Wali Wadi, come to collect a parcel that had been left for him. The elder frowned in concentration.

'I'm sure I don't know any Wali Wadi,' he said. 'That's not a name from around here. Is it Tajik?'

'Uzbek,' replied Osama, his hopes dashed — surely they hadn't made this whole journey for nothing?

'Your friend, this Wali Wadi, he's never been to the village,' stated the man. 'There are only Pashtuns here.'

Osama thought. He was certain that the coordinates pointed to this village. Wali Wadi wouldn't have hidden the map for nothing.

'Wali Wadi lived in Kabul,' he insisted. 'Perhaps he knew someone in the village, to whom he gave these documents. A friend, who left them here on his behalf.'

The briefest glimmer appeared in the man's eyes.

'I don't think your man knew anyone in the village. We are very poor,' he said. 'We don't have anything. Do you think we'd be living like this if we knew someone from Kabul?'

Osama realised that the man was trying to make a little money. He felt sorry for him, and pulled out a wad of dollars.

'I've travelled far for these documents. I would be very happy to reimburse you for your help.'

He immediately stuffed the notes into the village elder's hand. The man counted them carefully. A hundred and fifty dollars — enough to feed the village for several days, and buy some new goats as well. He said, 'One of our young people left for Kabul seven years ago. He returned a few weeks back, very ill. Perhaps he knew your friend.'

'Can you take me to him?'

'Yes.'

The head of the village led them to a little house slightly apart from the others. He entered without knocking. A woman was sitting on the bare ground, next to a shape laid out on a rug. As he approached, Osama saw that the shape wrapped in blankets was in fact a young man. He was bedridden and skinny, but still very beautiful, with a face like a wild animal's — pale eyes, and black hair stuck to his forehead with sweat. He was in the throes of a high fever.

'What's the matter with him?' asked Osama. 'He must be taken to hospital.'

'He's been like this for days', said the woman. 'There's nothing we can do for him. He caught a disease in Kabul. *Deveney Naroghey.'*

A blood disease. Osama bent over the boy.

'Can you hear me?'

'Yes,' said the boy faintly.

'What's wrong with you? We can take you to Kabul.'

'It's too late. I'll be dead soon.'

'What is wrong with you?' asked Osama again, sure of the answer.

The emaciated face, the fever, the general state of the young man reminded him too closely of the way Malalai had described some of her patients.

'*Eydz,'* breathed the young man.

AIDS. The boy caught his breath, and grabbed Osama's hand. He was unbelievably strong for someone so ill.

'I got it in Kabul. It's all over for me.'

Osama kept the boy's hand in his own. It was boiling hot. Homosexuality was strictly forbidden in Afghanistan, as in every Muslim country, and yet was practised by a great many boys, given the difficulty of meeting girls before marriage. Heroin use, which had rocketed since the fall of the Taliban, hadn't helped matters. The transmission of the virus was facilitated by the fact that nobody admitted to these risky behaviours. As for condoms, the mullahs thought them an evil object brought in by unbelievers, and fiercely opposed their sale as well as their use. Instead, they preached chastity, which wasn't very popular amongst the young.

'What do you want?' rasped the young man.

'What Wali Wadi gave you.'

'Where is he? Why doesn't he come and get it himself?'

'He's been assassinated. I'm in charge of the investigation. He was killed for the document that I've come to find — the Mandrake File.'

'Wali is dead?'

'Yes. I'm sorry. I don't think he suffered — it seems to have happened very fast.'

The young man remained frozen for a moment, as if struck by lightning, and then began to weep softly. His hand trembled in Osama's. Between sobs, he said, 'Wali told me that if he died, I must publish the information on as many Internet sites as possible, all over the world. He told me once that it was his life insurance, but I don't know any more.'

'What kind of file is it?'

'It's on an encrypted CD-Rom. It can only be read using very sophisticated software that I've never had access to — it's not available in Afghanistan.'

'What did you do, before?'

'I was a computer programmer. That's how I met Wali — installing his office network.'

The young man began to cry again.

'Where is it?' asked Osama, gently.

'In my bag, over there.'

Osama found it easily. On the sleeve, in Western script, was written *Elements of the Mandrake File*.

'Is this it?' asked Osama.

'Yes.'

'Do you know what's in it?'

'No. Like I said, it's encrypted, and I don't have the software to read it. See the code on the back?'

He was referring to a series of at least twenty numbers and letters, in no apparent order.

'Yes.'

'That's the code. You'll need it to read the CD.'

'Thank you. Lots of people have already died trying to obtain this.'

The young man's tears flowed faster.

'Have the people who killed Wali tried to kill you, too?'

'They've killed both my deputies and several of my men.'

'That CD,' breathed the young man, 'it's all I have left of Wali, along with a few photos. Don't lose it.'

'I promise you I'll use it well.'

The boy closed his eyes. It seemed to Osama that he had fainted. He put the CD and the piece of paper into his inside pocket, squeezed the young man's hand one last time, and stood up. As he reached the door, he heard a weak voice ask, 'Wali? Was he infected?'

Osama thought back to the HIV test carried out by his friend Katoun.

'No. He was healthy. It wasn't him who infected you.'

He thought he saw a smile form on the dying boy's face. Outside, the sky was darker than it should have been. Abdullah and Rangin walked up, tense and restless.

'So?'

Osama took the CD-ROM out of his pocket.

'We've found what we were looking for.'

'What is it?'

'I have no idea,' admitted Osama. 'Seems like an electronic report. We'll need a computer to read it. We'll do that at Kandahar, at your mother's place.'

'Shall we go?' asked Abdullah. 'We shouldn't stay here too long.'

Osama looked up at the sky, which was starting to fill with stars. It would be madness to drive back the way they had come in this dark.

'We must sleep in the village,' he announced. 'We'll leave at dawn.'

The head of the village was overcome with joy when Osama told him of their decision to stay the night in his house. They waited a little way off as two women cleaned the reception room, and a third heated water. They were served boiled eggs, bread, and sour yoghurt with herbs. The flour had been milled very roughly, probably with a stone, leaving tiny pebbles in the bread. It was also full of weevils that crunched between their teeth, but Rangin and Abdullah were starving and gobbled it up to the delight of their host. Osama barely touched his plate, preoccupied by the young man dying a few houses away. They were brought sweet cakes, but he still wasn't hungry. As tea was served, a man arrived and whispered in their host's ear.

'The boy has just died.'

When Osama stood up, the head of the village asked, surprised, 'Where are you going?'

'To pay my respects.'

Their host burst out laughing.

'That wasn't a man. Let the women deal with him.'

Osama left the table. It had rained during the meal, and the path leading to the isolated house was terribly muddy. The young man's mother seemed surprised to see him. She scrambled to hang up a sheet, to screen off the women who sat with her.

Osama knelt down by the bed. He recited several verses of the Koran. What would Wali Wadi have thought of this wretched house, on the edge of this village in the middle of nowhere — he who lived in his ridiculous palace, with his sports cars and grotesque golden duck toilet-roll holder? Did he have the faintest idea what kind of place he was sending his former lover back to? Why didn't he send him to a private clinic, in Russia or Pakistan?

Osama rejoined his companions after an hour with the body, weary and depressed, despite his find. They went to bed around nine in the evening, huddled together against the cold. Osama paid silent homage to the courage of Rangin and Abdullah, and fell asleep.

JOSEPH WAS BARELY FATIGUED by the training session he'd just completed in the dojo, a vast room within the Entity complex. He was back in Berne, and not unhappy at having left Afghanistan. He'd immediately returned to his usual routine — an hour's match against the best sportsmen on his staff, followed by a second hour in the gym. He'd put himself through the same regimen ever since he was twenty. This continued effort, along with the experience accumulated over hundreds of assignments, had kept him at the top of his game when most fighters his age were already on the decline, weakened by fat, pain, or a taste for comfort. He towelled himself off carefully and put on his suit and the lace-up shoes with the nonslip rubber soles. As always after an intense session, his adrenalin was flowing. He felt sharp, excited, on the alert.

He loved that feeling.

His tiny office was next to the general's. He switched on the light and went in. A few documents were waiting on his desk, so he started looking through them. Suddenly, there was a knock at the door.

His visitor was the Entity's head of internal security, Johannes Gobler. A particularly twisted individual, bordering on the paranoid, he had been head of security at one of Zurich's private banks. Joseph trusted him completely. He had a double role: making sure that Entity offices and communications were watertight, and managing the staff to avoid potential defections. Joseph looked at him questioningly.

'What's going on?'

His subordinate sat down opposite, his face blank. Small steel glasses, tidy grey moustache, hair shaved around the ears, straight back, impeccable posture. He put a laptop on the desk and turned it towards Joseph to enable him to see the screen.

'Do you remember the security cameras I installed in all the offices last year?'

'Of course,' muttered Joseph, wondering what Johannes was getting at.

'They're linked to movement sensors. In accordance with your instructions, in the general's office and your own they are only activated outside work hours, from 8.00pm to 7.00am, and over lunchtime. I'd like you to watch what camera number three recorded a little while ago.'

He clicked on the keyboard. A video started playing. It was the general's office. Today's date was shown on the right of the screen, along with the time — 13h12. The seconds rolled past. Suddenly, the door opened. Nick walked in. He appeared anxious. He looked around, then sat down in the general's chair and immediately began to tap away at his computer. The seconds and minutes were still rolling past on the right of the screen.

'How did he get in?'

'The general had deactivated the door's security system that morning. It had been annoying him for a while.'

'Stupid. How can we take risks like that?'

'I did underline the risks we were taking, but he's the boss, so what could I do? He promised to lock his door. He didn't.'

'Absurd! What about the computer log-in — how did Nick get that? Only the general is supposed to know it.'

'The general probably didn't follow my parameter guidelines,' said Johannes. 'I think his computer session was still open. You know what he's like with computers.'

'What a cock-up! Do we know what Nick was up to?'

'No. I don't have a camera on the general's computer.'

The film continued. Nick seemed fascinated by what he was reading. After ten minutes, he stood up. The camera caught his inscrutable face, and then he disappeared. Johannes Gobler stopped the computer.

'Ten minutes would be enough for a pretty good look at the general's email. Or a detailed rummage through his electronic files. I thought this might interest you. Do you want me to get Nick in here?'

'Are you insane? Let me talk to the general first.'

Joseph's icy tone belied his fury. His employee nodded slightly, and left. Joseph headed straight for his boss's office.

'General, we have a problem.'

NICK DROVE ABSENTLY through a depressing light rain, both fearful and excited at what he was about to discover. Everything was grey. He asked himself why he put up with such a leaden, cloud-heavy sky, with this stifling, cramped landscape moth-eaten by rampant urbanisation. He came from the mountains, and loved nothing more than rock climbing and skiing. This wasn't the life for him.

He stopped at a traffic light, behind a thirty-tonne lorry. Soon, he'd know. With an address in Australia, the fugitive's false name, and his girlfriend's real name, they wouldn't be able to elude him much longer.

He found a parking spot in the narrow street that ran along the back of the building where the Entity was based. It was night-time, and the roads were deserted — just two or three pedestrians striding past, heads down, rushing to escape the rain and wind. The entry hall was depressingly generic, a big square room with marble walls and floors, brightened up by a few anaemic houseplants. He said hello to the night watchman and fed his card into the card reader, causing the Plexiglas gates to open. The Entity's offices were on the fifth and top floors. Here, security was of a whole different order — opaque double doors made of reinforced glass, with cameras at both entry and exit. Nick stepped through the first door and put his hand on the glass plate. The second door opened with a thud to reveal furniture, carpets, lithographs on the wall, all very bland and businesslike. The receptionist looked up from his magazine.

'Good evening, Arthur,' said Nick.

'Good evening.'

He walked into his office; but instead of sitting down at his own desk, he used the one that had belonged to Werner. As he'd often done recently, he started one session using his own code and another on Werner's computer with Margaret's. Connecting to one specialised database after another was a tedious and tricky business — despite government promises, they weren't really interconnected. After half an hour, however, he was convinced that Zahra had not yet officially entered Australia. Unofficial arrival by boat was in theory possible, but seemed very unlikely given the effectiveness of the Australian immigration service. A man as careful as Leonard would never take the risk of his girlfriend being arrested and then deported for illegal immigration. So they must still be together, somewhere else. He just had to find out where.

An hour later, Nick suddenly came across what he was looking for in an email exchange on one of the immigration databases. The Australian immigration minister wanted his Swiss counterpart to provide various pieces of information concerning Zahra Kimzi. All Afghan citizens applying for long-stay visas in Australia were subjected to a special security procedure that required particular documents as well as references from the governments of the countries in which they had previously resided. The Swiss minister replied in another email that he didn't have all the documents requested by the Australian authorities, which didn't surprise Nick in the slightest. Immigration controls had toughened up — it would be much harder for Zahra to obtain an Australian visa today than a Swiss visa in 1999. September 11th had had its impact, even in Oceania.

Another document attracted his attention — a handwritten letter from Zahra to the Australian authorities, explaining that the Afghan consulate in Geneva couldn't provide the documents they were asking for. This was down to an administrative issue, as confirmed by the Swiss minister after an exchange of letters with the Afghan consulate. The Australian response was brutal: without these documents, no visa could be supplied. It was up to Zahra to obtain them as best she could, and anything else was outside their remit. It was the perfect bureaucratic response.

From this, Nick understood that the fugitives weren't in Australia, as Zahra could not yet be there legally.

She needed official documents for her visa — papers she didn't have with her — an official family record book and, most importantly, an original birth certificate from when she was under six months old, which could only be acquired in her country of origin. The conclusion was obvious: that's where she was. In Afghanistan. In the lion's jaws, with her lover.

This was the moment of truth. He had found the fugitive. A good soldier would now present his general with the information. The Entity wouldn't take long to get their hands on Leonard and Zahra, his bosses would be grateful, and that would be the end of the story, as far as he was concerned. He'd be celebrated, and perhaps promoted.

Except that …

Except that his bosses had been lying to him since the very start.

He still had no idea what it was that had freaked them out so much that they'd committed vile acts such as assassination attempts on government officials from a friendly country, and a bombing in central Kabul. How could Nick trust such cruel and cynical men? He wanted to stop this madness. He wanted to destroy them.

The door to his office burst open.

'Margaret! What are you doing here?' he exclaimed.

Her eyes were red, and she looked upset. As no one was watching, she graced him with a kiss on the mouth before pulling away to look at him as if seeing him for the very first time.

'I've just overheard a conversation in the corridor. They seem to be looking for you.'

'Who are "they"?'

'Three Ks. Joseph wants to see you. They look armed and dangerous. What have you done?'

'Nothing. Nothing serious, anyway. Are you sure there were three of them?'

'Yes.'

Nick was petrified. Joseph had no reason to suspect him; he'd left no traces of his investigations. Why were they after him? His forehead beaded with sweat, and he quickly hid his hands under the table so that Margaret wouldn't see them trembling.

'You don't look well. Are you ill?' she asked.

'No, I'm scared,' he admitted. 'Listen, everything's going to be all right, trust me. But don't tell anyone you've seen me here. Can I count on you?'

'Yes, but …'

'It's important. Promise me?'

'You're scaring me, Nick.'

He walked calmly towards the exit. His mind was whirling. He could see the entrance hall at the end of the corridor. The receptionist had been replaced by a hard-faced young man he'd never seen before. He swerved into the kitchen before he was noticed. It was a huge room where staff met up for coffee at all times of day and night. Two men and a woman he knew slightly from the economic analysis department were sitting around a table, chatting. They greeted him warmly. He could feel his heart beating in his thorax, and tried fruitlessly to calm himself down. He could leave the building by the back stairs, but then what? If he fled, he'd never be able to return to Switzerland. He suddenly realised that he had reached an impasse. If the Entity suspected him, they would hunt him to the ends of the earth. His only option was to flee to London where his father lived, and request official protection from the English.

He returned to his office. No one was waiting for him. He opened his desk drawer. His work pistol had disappeared. Luckily, his bosses didn't know he had another gun in his briefcase, the chunky automatic handgun he'd used when looking for Yasmina. He checked that it was loaded, and stuffed it in his jacket pocket. The main exit was now being guarded by a K, so he couldn't use that. He headed in the opposite direction, towards the emergency exit. Even the Entity had to respect Berne's safety regulations, and the city regularly sent fire inspectors to check the buildings. And here was the flaw: the security mechanisms had been devised to stop people entering the Entity floor, not leaving it. He opened a door onto the emergency stairs, and found himself on a small landing. There was a camera just overhead, the movement sensor sending it whirring into action. Nick didn't have much time. There was a reinforced door in front of him. He knew that the other side didn't have a handle or a lock. He hoped it wasn't alarmed — just one of the things he'd never been told about. He slid the bolt. No alarm sounded. He ran down a first flight of stairs, and a second, before coming to a sudden stop at a familiar sound. Someone was running up the stairs below him. He clumsily grabbed his pistol, flipped off the security catch, and continued downwards. Almost immediately, he found himself face to face with two men: forty-year-olds with short hair, hard faces, and dead eyes. Ks. He pointed his gun at them.

'Don't move,' he screamed.

'We're looking for you, Nick,' replied one of them calmly. 'Joseph wants to talk to you. Put away your gun and come with us.'

'Get stuffed!' shouted Nick.

The men didn't seem flustered by the situation, just irritated. As if none of this was any of their business.

'What's got into you?' asked one of them. 'Come on, let's go.'

He took a step forward. Nick pressed the trigger. Two shots rang out. The bullets lodged in the ceiling. Pieces of plaster and broken neon light rained on the Ks. Nick had deliberately aimed over their heads.

'Hands on your head. Now!'

'Chill out, man,' said one K, as he complied. 'They don't want to harm you, just talk to you. The general has some questions.'

'Get stuffed. On the floor. Come on, on the floor right now!'

The two men looked at each other. Nick fired another blind shot. This time it hit one of them in the thigh, spattering blood over the wall. The K collapsed.

'Bugger. I'm hit.'

He hadn't cried out, and barely even grimaced. The other killer looked at Nick. There was no trace of fear or emotion on his face. Nothing. Nevertheless, he lay down on the floor, still watching Nick.

The landing was fairly large, but Nick could see that he'd have to pass very close to the killer to get down the stairs.

'Move up against the wall,' he said more firmly. 'Your face against the wall. Come on, faster.'

He tried to remember what they'd taught him on that training course when he first joined the SRS. He was amazed by how quickly it all came back.

'Now, move your arms away from your body. Further. Bring them up behind your back, above your body. That's it, keep going. Now, turn your palms to the outside.'

The Entity agent found himself lying on his belly, arms facing backwards, palms turned out — a very uncomfortable position that made movement of any kind extremely hard. It was only then that Nick moved forward, the butt of his gun held tightly to his chest to stop it from being grabbed. The two killers had seen what he was doing and realised they wouldn't be able to take the gun. He passed by them, his heart beating a hundred miles a minute.

As soon as he reached the stairs, he started running. He heard the unhurt killer stand up. Two shots rang out, but the staircase was too narrow for the killer to get a good angle, and the bullets went wide.

Another shot rang out. This time, the bullet brushed his arm. He didn't want to retaliate — he knew he was no match for a K, and that if he revealed himself enough to shoot, the K would definitely hit him. He flew down the stairs and flung open the ground-floor emergency exit. It thudded against some cardboard boxes stacked up against a brick wall. He found himself in a sort of narrow alleyway, between two buildings, and started sprinting towards the road. He could see the front of his car, parked outside the grocery shop. Two shots rang out, muffled by a silencer. He turned around and fired a shot himself, hitting the K right in the chest. The man collapsed, but not before he'd fired another shot. Nick felt as if he'd been hit in the leg with an iron bar. He fell, knocking over a dustbin of rotten fruit. When he finally made it to his car, he scrambled inside. No one was following him.

Christ, it was agony. He'd been hit; he was bleeding. The car seat was already all sticky.

Half a mile down the road, he saw a parking lot. He drove up to the second-highest storey and killed the engine. Grimacing, he pulled down his trousers. The bullet had merely skimmed the skin, creating a long, shallow furrow. The wound was bleeding heavily, but was superficial. Only a .22-calibre bullet would have made such a tidy, delicate wound. He realised that the K hadn't wanted to kill him — only to wound him in the leg.

The wound would heal fast; it just needed disinfecting and bandaging. He tried to start the car, but his hands were shaking so much that he couldn't turn the ignition key.

'Come on, calm down,' he muttered to himself.

He managed to start his car in the end. But where to go? They must already be waiting outside his house. They'd be bound to know the names of all his ex-girlfriends. He drove slowly, making sure to obey the speed limit. A few minutes later, he stopped in front of a brilliantly lit shop window with a group of young people waiting out front, carrying sports bags. His gym.

He put on his hazard-warning lights. He could feel the pistol barrel still hot in his jacket pocket. There were only four or five bullets left — not exactly enough to fight off a determined commando. A few minutes later he re-emerged, limping. He'd hidden a fake passport in his gym locker a few months before. At the time, there wasn't much reason to do so, except perhaps as a general precaution: in job like his, you never knew what tomorrow might bring. He'd started out at the Entity on an internship in the technical department, and knew how to create government documents. He'd simply lifted one of a batch of Belgian passports. The official stamps and everything else were available in the office, so it had been child's play. Those were the days.

17.

Osama woke first, around six in the morning, and slipped silently out of the house. The sun still hadn't come over the mountains, but a pinkish dawn was breaking in the East. He picked up his prayer mat, taken by a sudden desire to pray at the top of the hill above the village, where he'd have a stunning view over the whole area. The sun came out as he reached the top of the hill, shining its rays over the bare mountains, lighting them up in oranges and greys, dotted with patches of fog. The landscape was spectacular, and he looked at it quietly for a long moment, his heart full of a sense of plenitude. Allah had created this beauty; what a shame that the Afghan people couldn't just enjoy it, in peace. Soon he would go back to Kabul and read Wali Wadi's CD. He wouldn't be able to keep information like that to himself without putting his life in danger, so he would give it to the Ministry of Justice, or even publish it on some kind of website: once the information was in the public domain, he would be safe. He thought of Mullah Bakir, who wanted this information, and of the Westerners who had tried to kill him. The truth was, he couldn't decide anything before he knew exactly what was in the CD, and who was implicated.

He was just about to kneel down and pray when he noticed something moving in the distance. He screwed up his eyes for a better look. He knew that movement by heart; he'd seen it hundreds of times when he was fighting with the mujahedeen, and also later, when he'd joined the Northern Alliance. It was a group of men walking through the mountains. He counted about twenty — some on foot, some on horseback. A few more, even, maybe twenty-five. He thought of the men they'd encountered the day before: there hadn't been that many of them. The Westerners would have come with helicopters and drones. Only Taliban would travel like this, on foot and horseback. One thing was for sure: if he and his men stayed where they were, they'd be dead. Their only option was to flee while there was still time. He sprinted back down the hill to the village.

Rangin was rinsing his face from his flask. 'What's going on?' he asked when he saw Osama's alarmed face.

'A group of armed men, under an hour's walk from here. They have horses. We must flee. Where's Abdullah?'

'He's sleeping.'

'Go and wake him — we're leaving immediately.'

Osama looked for the head of the village. He was peeing crouched down, in the scree.

'The road to the east isn't safe,' announced Osama, 'I've spotted a group of men. We'll have to leave another way.'

Osama thought back to the map he'd examined in Kandahar, with Captain Kukur. There was a Baloch area to the southwest of this place. Pashtun Taliban wouldn't follow them there.

'How do we travel to the southwest?' he asked. 'To the Baloch area. Is it possible in a vehicle?'

The head of the village thought for a moment.

'There is a track; it leaves from bottom of the village. Follow it for two hours. You'll reach the top of a hill, the tallest hill around. Instead of continuing down into the valley, take a track along the crest of the hill, to the right. That track might be good enough for a vehicle, or it might not. After half an hour's drive, you'll reach a new crest, even taller this time. You'll see it — we call it the blue hill. Watch out for mines; the Russians left hundreds of them in these mountains. Leaping mines and toy mines. They've killed many men, women, and children. After the crest, you come to a plateau. That's where the Baloch live, but be careful; they're not hospitable like the Pashtun — they don't have our traditions. People say they slit the throats of stray visitors.'

'We'll manage,' said Osama.

They left immediately. The track was even worse than the one they'd come in on, and the Toyota was confined to walking pace.

'What exactly did he mean, when he warned us to watch out for leaping mines?' asked Rangin. 'And toy mines? I thought all mines worked the same way.'

'Leaping mines are special devices that the Russians dumped here at the end of the war,' said Osama. 'The wind covers them with dust and sand, but they remain active for a very long time. If you step on one, a spring projects it into the air, where it explodes. Instead of blowing your leg off, the fragments hit you in the head and chest. Horrific. Toy mines are pocket-sized mines made out of coloured plastic, designed especially for children, who are attracted by the bright colours. When a kid picks one up, he sets off the arming plunger and it detonates. They've blown off the hand or arm of plenty of children around here.'

Rangin looked shocked at Osama's explanations. He was a young man from the capital, an urban kid who wasn't yet familiar with all the atrocities that had been committed during the campaigns, by the Russians as well as the Taliban. Osama envied his indignation. Like all old-timers, he'd long become accustomed to all kinds of horrors — those inflicted on the country as well as those it had inflicted on itself.

'I'm scared they're going to catch us up. Are we going any faster than a man on foot?' asked Rangin anxiously.

'Barely,' admitted Osama.

At the top of the hill, Osama looked back through his binoculars. The Taliban were almost at the village — in fact, those on horseback were entering it as he watched.

'They won't kill everyone, will they?' asked Rangin in a frightened voice.

'No. Even in these campaigns, melmastia must be observed. They could not harm these villagers for having respected the Pashtun code of honour, by welcoming other Muslims.'

Osama was interrupted by the sound of gunfire. He paled, and took up the binoculars again. He saw men driving the villagers out of their houses and shoving them to the ground. Shots rang out; the shapes on the floor shuddered under the impact, and were still. A little further on, another group of men were leading away the women — some in burqas, some still in house clothes.

'My God, the bastards are massacring them,' cried Rangin. 'We've got to help!'

'There are three of us, and more than twenty of them. We'll only get ourselves killed, too.'

Osama hoped that the women would be shot immediately, like the men, but he knew that they'd have their throats slit after being raped by several men. After the murders, the Taliban would set fire to the houses, and burn the bodies with petrol they'd found in the village. Then they would portray it as a Coalition blunder, a botched bombing by Allied forces. Some journalists would believe them, some wouldn't, but they would definitely report the news, because a war that doesn't kill innocent people is of no interest to anyone. Plenty of massacres carried out by the Taliban had been blamed on American bombers in this way, increasing the resentment of an ill-informed population always quick to believe in atrocities committed by the occupying forces.

They continued for two hours without incident, at the same frustrating pace. From time to time, Osama checked behind them with the binoculars. They had barely increased their lead on the group. They were at the mercy of a breakdown or any kind of problem with the track. As if echoing his thoughts, Abdullah let out a curse.

'What's the matter?' asked Osama.

'We've got a flat.'

They frantically changed the tyre. The bolts were too tight; they thought they'd never manage to detach the wheel. After a stop of more than thirty minutes, they finally set off again. The pass that the village elder had told them about became visible above them. Two figures appeared at the top: men in turbans, carrying guns. Abdullah swore.

'Stop the car,' ordered Osama.

He got out, carrying his Dragunov. The gun felt strangely

familiar, with its sturdy wooden stock and the big sights on the top. He had lived with one for several years, fought with it, held it at nighttime, felt its roar against his cheek each time he fired it. He'd vowed to himself that he'd again never use a sniper rifle, he thought bitterly, as he loaded a cartridge into the chamber — but what good were vows in Afghanistan? He cursed the Taliban as he put the rifle on the roof of the vehicle, balancing it on a blanket to give himself a better firing position. He could see the figure of the first man very clearly, thanks to the remarkable magnifying power of the Zeiss. He adjusted the dials. The man was over half a mile away, the wind was strong, and his targets were moving. He used a powerful cartridge. It was a remarkable shot, which only a tiny number of snipers could have pulled off in such conditions. The shot reverberated like a canon in the silence of the valley. One of the figures reared up, flung backwards like a puppet. Osama didn't give the other Taliban time to think before he pulled the trigger a second time. A new shot boomed out three seconds after the first. The head of the second figure disappeared, blown off by the bullet.

'*Al Hamdullilah,* you got them both. From half a mile away!' exclaimed Abdullah admiringly.

'Let's go,' said Osama simply, not keen to comment on his prowess.

When they reached the summit they came across the two Taliban fighters lying on the side of the track. The Dragunov's supersonic bullets had finished them off immediately. They were frozen in grotesque positions, arms and legs spread as if doing gymnastics, covered in blood. Rangin stepped out of the car to take their guns — old Pakistani Kalashnikovs — and, most importantly, their radio, which he stuffed into the car. One of the men had also been carrying a curved dagger, the Taliban's weapon of choice for slitting their enemies' throats. Rangin threw it into the ditch and got back into the car.

'If they're waiting for us at the top of every hill, we'll never get out of here alive,' said Rangin.

'This region is almost deserted; I don't think they can mobilise men that easily. We've got a chance,' said Osama.

Suddenly, there was a great crash. The 4x4 lurched violently forward, as if pushed by a giant hand, and then ground to a halt with a screeching of metal. They got out to check the damage. The track had collapsed, and the Toyota was stuck in a hole, its rear wheels in the air. Abdullah bent over the vehicle, horrified.

'The front axle is twisted. We'd need a winch to get it out of here. The car is fucked.'

'We'll continue on foot,' said Osama. 'We're not very far from the Baloch plateau now.' He pointed to the top of the mountain. 'It's after this pass. Less than three hours' walk; maybe only two.'

They took as much water, provisions, and ammunition as they could manage, and started walking. Suddenly, Rangin yelped.

'Look!'

Osama turned around. The cavalrymen had split off from the foot soldiers and were galloping towards them. At that speed, it wouldn't take them long to catch up. Osama gave the CD to Abdullah.

'I'll hold them off with the Dragunov. You're Pashtun — they might let you go. If you get out of here alive, give this CD to your mother and tell her to give it personally to the head of the intelligence department at Kabul police. He's my friend, his name is Reza, and he'll know what to do with it. Go and see my wife — tell her I love her, and that I'm sorry not to live out my life with her.'

He hugged both men, moved into position with the rifle on a rock, and waited. He had to let his pursuers approach until they were close enough to shoot. The sun warmed his face, and he soon felt a bead of sweat drop into his eyes. After about fifteen minutes, he decided they were close enough — just over half a mile away. He checked on his companions. They were running more than walking towards the crest of the hill; they'd soon reach it. He moved into firing position and shot down the first horseman. The bullet went straight through his face, and a purplish cloud surrounded the back of his head as the shot rang out across the valley. He aimed at the second horseman, and brought him down like the first. The third turned hastily, but he didn't have a chance. Osama's third bullet hit him square in the back, sending him flying off to one side.

Osama stood up, gripping his rifle. The three horses had stopped, anxious. Osama couldn't leave them alive for the other Taliban to use, and if he walked all the way over to catch them, he would risk finding himself face to face with the foot soldiers. He killed all three horses with well-placed bullets. What did three animals matter, when so many men had died? And yet killing these splendid beasts saddened him deeply. He slung the Dragunov over his shoulder and rushed to catch up with his friends behind the crest of the hill.

He reached the crest after fifteen minutes' brisk walk. The sight warmed his heart. A massive plateau unfolded before his eyes, many miles wide, dotted with scrub and a few scrawny trees here and there. A little further on, less than an hour's walk away, was a town, with the minaret of a mosque towering above it. These were the Baloch people, his own tribe. They were saved! His two companions had noticed him and were waiting. Osama sped up. Suddenly, he saw young Abdullah leave the track and head for a big rock a hundred metres away. He screamed, 'Abdullah, no! Stay where you are!'

Hearing his shouts, the young man stopped, but he was too far away to understand. He gave Osama a friendly wave and carried on walking, unzipping his trousers as he went. Osama frantically shook off his rifle strap. He'd have to shoot in the air, to get Abdullah's attention. At that very moment, there was a dull crack. As in a nightmare, Osama saw a sort of grey disc shoot up from the ground, above Abdullah's head. It exploded, hitting Abdullah at point-blank range. The young man made a macabre pirouette as pieces of his flesh flew off in every direction. Rangin was about to go to his aid, so Osama fired twice in the air. The shots stopped him. Osama put his hands in a cross shape over his head, instructing Rangin not to move. He ran to reach him.

'Was that a leaping mine?' asked Rangin, white as a sheet.

'Yes. Stay here. I'll walk in Abdullah's footsteps to reach him.'

The body wasn't a pretty sight. One leg lay fifteen metres from the body, the head had been blown off, and the other limbs had been mutilated. The body, riddled with mine fragments, was cut all over. Osama covered himself in blood searching Abdullah for the CD. When he found it, he felt a pang of anguish. The CD had been hit, and the plastic had melted. He hung his head. No more CD; no more leads. He had lost.

A group of men from the village was coming to meet them. Osama looked at Abdullah's blood flowing from his body. His own hands and clothing were stained with it — as they had been with Gulbudin's, and Babrak's before him.

Osama wept, for the first time since his son had died.

Part II

18.

THE OLD 4X4 CREAKED INTO THE PARKING LOT at Torkham border post. It was a flat, dirty town, the houses made of cob and raw concrete. It was also quite frightening, on account of the Kalashnikov-bearing Pashtun militiamen. Everyone seemed to be carrying a weapon.

'Let's have a drink before we cross the border,' suggested Nick's guide. 'I'd rather wait for the lunch break, when there'll be fewer ISI agents around to ask questions.'

'OK,' said Nick.

He was exhausted by the journey, and by the continuing pain from his leg wound. He'd fled by driving across the Italian border, and then taking a bus to Milan, where he obtained medical treatment by passing the wound off as a domestic accident. He got on well with the young Senegalese surgeon, a recent graduate of Dakar University who spoke perfect French. He'd probably never seen a gun wound in his life, and treated Nick without fuss. Once he'd been patched up, Nick caught a flight to Dubai on his false passport, and then another to Islamabad.

It was a standard journey for businessmen, journalists, and aid workers based in the area; nothing that might draw the attention of his enemies.

Nick had bought Pakistani clothes and hadn't shaved in two days, but he still looked like what he was — a young Westerner slightly lost in a country he didn't know. People were eyeing him in a surreptitious and often hostile manner. Luckily, the Kalashnikov slung over his guide's shoulder discouraged the asking of any awkward questions. At Islamabad, he'd hired a taxi all the way to Peshawar, the capital of western Pakistan. It was driven by a halfwit who didn't speak a word of English. Nick got out in the middle of town to change taxis and find a guide to accompany him on the final leg of his travels. He'd had to buy a special government permit in order to enter the tribal areas. Actually, the permit was free, but since the Home Department of Tribal Affairs was as corrupt as the rest of the Pakistani government, it had cost him almost two hundred rupees to acquire it immediately. He'd taken the precaution of making five copies of both the permit and his passport, and slipping a hundred-rupee note in with each. These photocopies had worked wonders at all four roadblocks between Peshawar and the border: the Pakistani soldiers had pocketed the cash and let him through, no questions asked.

He admired the panoramic view at Michni check post. The area was dangerous, but his armed guide (a necessity for Westerners after Peshawar) seemed reliable. He belonged to Khyber Political Agents, the government outfit that had a monopoly on official guides for Westerners. Nick had presented himself as a Belgian doctor working for a humanitarian organisation. The guide seemed to believe this, although he had insisted on taking Nick to buy a gun at Peshawar market, probably the biggest open-air arms market in the world. Everything you could imagine was made and sold there, from homemade pen guns to rocket launchers. He seemed disappointed when Nick refused to buy anything at all to defend himself.

Nick drank his tepid Coke in silence, enjoying this moment of peace before the final leg of his journey. Between Torkham and Kabul was at least ten hours of motorway, assuming that all went well. On the other side of the border, dozens of taxis waited for the Afghan and Pakistani merchants who used this important route. In spite of his exhaustion, Nick was impressed to be driving along the famous Khyber Pass, a route travelled by generations of adventurers through the tallest mountains in Afghanistan, the Hindu Kush.

'Do you think the whole journey will be this smooth?' he asked the guide, when they'd finished their drinks.

'This road is very dangerous,' replied the guide in his jerky English. 'We wait for a military convoy.'

This was a government-hostile Pashtun area, in which Taliban moved around freely on both sides of the border. The Peshawar–Jalalabad–Kabul axis was one of the most important in the country, strictly controlled by the Pakistani army to the east, and the Afghan army plus NATO to the west. But this didn't prevent frequent attacks. You would only have to stray a few miles to find yourself deep in enemy territory.

They waited two hours, and then several white 4x4s bearing the UN initials drove up. Nick's guide went off to talk with them. He came back a few minutes later, smiling broadly.

'They're going to Kabul. I've told them you're a doctor, and they're happy to take you. Wait for them on the other side.'

Nick said goodbye to his guide. Then he slung his bag over his shoulder and walked to the border post, avoiding the puddles of melted snow as best he could. The border post on the Pakistani side had been renovated, and there was some semblance of order. He paid five hundred Pakistani rupees to two raggedy customs officers, who let him through without a single question. On the Afghan side, the chaos was appalling. Soldiers were asleep on the bare floor, wrapped in blankets against the cold. The place was teeming with Pashtun merchants waiting resignedly for permission to cross; others, preferring to speed up the process with a few hundred afghanis' baksheesh, negotiated quietly with sinister-looking Customs officers. Nick slipped two twenty-dollar bills to one of the officers, and was immediately given a three-month humanitarian visa. Ten minutes later, he found himself in a stony parking lot.

Since his return, Osama had spent most of his time shut up at home. He'd been forced to make a detour of about sixty miles to the west through bleak and hostile territory, escorted by a group of Baloch warriors, and it had taken him five days to return to Kabul. He and Rangin had stopped at Kajaki Dam and then in Kandahar, where he'd personally informed Captain Kukur of her son's death. This woman, who had unflinchingly faced death threats, assassination attempts, and general intimidation for years, had collapsed and burst into tears, and he'd been unable to console her.

When he thought about it, he wanted to vomit. In any other country in the world, the return of two policemen previously declared dead would have provoked a huge emotional response from the population, a massive outcry of public opinion. His testimony would have been on the front page of the newspapers. But nothing happened. The security minister had planned for it all with his usual duplicity. During Osama's absence, he'd conducted a highly effective brainwashing campaign: the staff at police headquarters were all convinced that Osama and his men had been attacked by a group of Taliban who'd stolen their vehicles and then abducted the wounded to torture and kill them. Their return was a massive shock — everyone had been sure they were dead. Hoping for a miracle, Osama gave the remains of the CD destroyed by the leaping mine to the police technical department, but of course they couldn't do anything with the fragments. In the end, they were destroyed on the personal instructions of the minister. Osama pleaded his case, explaining that the attack had been from a drone and not the Taliban, but it was a lost cause: he was unable to substantiate his claims. The remains of the two vehicles destroyed by the missiles had disappeared, probably sold for scrap by now.

Osama was up against a powerful politico-military machine; it was a David-and-Goliath fight. He had, of course, done everything he could, but his investigation just didn't look good: he'd lost his five best men, including both deputies; many innocent people were dead; and the Mandrake File no longer existed. In other words, he'd failed.

Totally.

And, as if that wasn't enough, the minister had opened an investigation against him for disobeying a superior. He had no doubt that he'd soon be suspended.

He was pondering all this when there was a knock at the door. A young man — Mullah Bakir's messenger — stood on the threshold, holding an envelope. Osama walked into his living room to read the letter, noting the elegant handwriting and good-quality paper.

Qomaandaan,

My informer in the minister's office has just told me that his boss is about to sign an arrest warrant on you, to be served in the next few hours. The minister has been preparing this for a few days now. He waited to set the procedure in motion until this morning, when his counterpart in the Ministry of Justice left for Europe. One of his pet public prosecutors will sign off your imprisonment. The official charges are many. You are accused of departing Kabul with your men, thus leaving your area of competence without orders, and on a road that hadn't previously been secured by the army; you are also suspected of being in league with the Taliban, which would explain why you were the only one to escape alive, along with your young colleague Rangin.

You will be imprisoned secretly at Bagram, without the slightest possibility of legal representation. Two new deputies have been prepared, to replace Babrak and Gulbudin. One is a Kandahar touran friendly with the minister, the other a police headquarters bredman Pashtun who detests you. Their instructions are to 'rid the department of vermin'.

Trying to resist or to proclaim your innocence would, in these circumstances, be utterly futile.

I advise you to go into hiding, until things become clearer. Send your wife to the countryside. If your networks let you down, I can provide you with all the help you need, including weapons and money.

Don't waste any time. You're more useful to this country alive than in the sordid jail they're intending to send you to, where you are bound to meet with an 'accident.'

There is still hope. Fight on!

Your friend,
Mullah Mohammed Bakir.

Osama was accustomed to heavy blows, but this letter knocked him for six. He didn't exactly need such overwhelming news after his defeat in the mountains, but he soon pulled himself together. He packed a few things — a pistol, several spare cartridges, some grenades, his faithful Kalash, his Koran — and collected all the money hidden in various boxes around the house. He didn't have much else. Then he unlocked the door to the storeroom. He pushed aside a pile of cardboard boxes blocking the back wall, and used a knife to cut away the crude mortar concealing a hiding place in a hollow brick. Inside were two Uzbek passports he'd bought from a smuggler in 1998, when the Taliban seemed invincible. The first was for a certain Hamid Kadenis; the second, for Malalai Kadenis. He looked thoughtfully at his wife's passport. He'd never mentioned it to her; he'd stolen a photo from her desk, had the document made in secret, and hidden it away. She still didn't know that he'd contemplated the two of them fleeing the country. He'd felt ashamed of it at the time, and still did now, even though in the end he'd decided to leave Kabul and fight the Taliban in the mountains rather than running away. He took the two documents, closed up the hiding place, and returned to the house.

He was ready to go.

It was just then that somebody knocked on the back door, which gave out onto a narrow lane that no one ever used. Osama picked up a rifle, intrigued but not overly concerned. NDS henchmen would have bashed down the front door. The discreet camera he'd installed on the roof of his neighbour's house and trained on the back door showed just one man, in jeans and a jacket. Osama opened the door, holding his rifle. He squinted at the visitor, sure he'd never seen him before.

'Commandant Kandar?' asked the man in a gentle voice.

He was young, Western, with very blue eyes and slightly overlong curly hair.

'Yes. Who are you?'

'My name is Nick Snee. May I come in?'

'What for?' demanded Osama coldly, gripping his rifle a little tighter.

'I'd like us to talk about Mandrake.'

At first, Osama was speechless. Then he opened his door properly, and showed Nick into the living room.

'We have very little time. I need to leave this place.'

'Are you fleeing?' asked Nick, surprised.

'That's none of your business. Who are you and what do you want?'

'I used to work for a Swiss agency that's hired for highly sensitive missions — a clandestine outfit by the name of the Entity.'

'I don't know that name.'

'I wouldn't expect you to. And yet it's responsible for all your troubles over the last few weeks — the bombings and the other attacks. Minister Khan Durrani is merely a pawn. The suicide attack at the Hamad Café; the mujahedeen on the way to Wali Wadi's office; the drone — that was us.'

Osama stood up, white as a sheet.

'You bastard! How dare you come here and mock me? Leave this instant!'

'I had nothing to do with those atrocities! I'm just an analyst. I burnt my bridges with the Entity as soon as I found out what they'd done. I want to help you. That's why I've come here — so we can fight these killers together.'

'I don't understand any of this gibberish. I'm asking you again: what exactly do you want?'

'For us to work together.'

'Work together? On what?'

'Finding Mandrake.'

Osama laughed bitterly.

'So you haven't heard the most recent news. My trip was a failure; the Mandrake File was destroyed; my bosses are after me. It's all over. I'm sorry. You'd better go back to your country and forget this whole thing. For me, it's over. Done and dusted.'

'Mandrake isn't only a file. It's also the name of a man on the run — the author of the file that bears his name. It's Leonard Mandrake that I'm trying to find. And I know he's hiding here, in Afghanistan.'

Mandrake ... Osama had never imagined that Mandrake could be a person. It was yet another flaw in his investigation. He'd certainly missed a lot — too much. He looked carefully at Nick's dusty face.

The young man looked exhausted, but his eyes were candid and his attitude sound. Osama's judgement had been sharpened by all his years at war, as well as with the police. He'd often been forced to bet his life on a sudden alliance. He knew immediately that he could trust this boy.

'What makes you think he's in this country?'

Nick explained.

'We'll talk later,' said Osama when Nick had finished. 'We have to go. I'll be arrested in a few minutes if I stay here.'

'But … why?'

'I'll explain. You and I have a great deal to tell each other.'

Joseph sat in his little office, waiting for his team to track down Nick. They'd been working flat out for the past two days, with Joseph trying to remain as calm as possible. His totally neutral face would have given anyone who didn't know him the impression that he was bored. And yet thoughts were clanging around in his brain. Nick's escape had revealed several important things. First, it was clear that he was completely aware of how he'd been manipulated. More importantly, he'd also realised that the Entity had seriously broken the law in trying to wipe out Superintendent Kandar. Joseph wasn't exactly sure what Nick had found on the general's computer, but he could imagine: enough to cause a massive scandal, and put them all in prison.

He had to find him, and kill him before it was too late.

How could an analyst with no experience of practical operations have disappeared like this? Joseph didn't currently know, and that was disturbing, too. In his job, the greatest disasters often stemmed from these kinds of tiny details — minute things that, put together, led to total loss of control of the situation. A man knocked at his door and put a sheet of paper on his desk; a colleague was summarising the acquired information for him on an hourly basis. So far, they hadn't found much. They knew that Nick had gone to Italy, because his 307 had been found in a long-stay parking lot on the other side of the border. There were traces of blood inside it. The technical team had done a DNA test on the stains, and would have the results in the next two hours. The car might be a false trail, of course, a specially designed decoy, but Joseph doubted it. Just in case, a K team had been stationed in Milan with a helicopter, giving them access to most of Italy. The thought that Nick had outwitted him put Joseph in a cold fury, close to rage. He detested failure. He took a deep breath. Now their job was to find him. Their only trump was that it would be impossible for Nick to catch a flight without being noticed. That thought gave him an idea. He called one of his men.

'Where do we keep the blank passports?'

'In the safe.'

'In the technical department?'

'Yes, boss.'

'Nick worked in that department for six months when he first joined the Entity. Go and see if any are missing.'

The man came back twenty minutes later, carrying a box.

'There are twenty-four passports. I don't know if that means any are missing.'

'You cretin! It's all listed on the computer system.'

They went over to one of the analysts — a tall, rather plump blonde — and asked her to connect to the Entity's main server.

'There should have been twenty-five passports in that box,' she announced.

'Look for the missing passport,' Joseph instructed.

'It's passport number 5678XV79,' she said a few moments later. 'Belgian.'

'Check whether it's been presented to an airline company.'

On a new tab, she accessed the central computer of the federal Transport Department, which was connected to the databases of most European countries. She got an immediate result — a record of a departure from Italy, on a flight to Dubai.

'Is that a mistake?' asked the K, looking over Joseph's shoulder.

'No. No, it's not a mistake!' said Joseph. 'Show us the photo.'

The analyst obediently clicked on an icon to download the national-entry case file pertaining to that passport. The new biometric systems had turned this into child's play. Soon, a photo filled the screen. It was definitely Nick.

'Find me all the flights taken on this passport. Create a link with Nick Snee's official passport, triangulate them, and see if you can't find links to companies that don't automatically declare their passenger lists.'

The blonde began tapping busily at her keyboard. After about ten minutes, she turned the screen towards them.

'I've only one connection: a flight from Dubai to Islamabad on a low-cost local airline, FlyDubai.'

'What the hell's he doing in Pakistan?' asked the K.

'He's only passing through, you idiot. It's Afghanistan he's headed for. He'll cross the border by the Khyber Pass.'

'But … why?'

Suddenly Joseph understood. It was so massive. So unexpected.

'Kandar! He's gone to find Superintendant Kandar. He wants to work with him to destroy us.'

It felt very strange to Osama to be hunted in Kabul by the same police departments that he'd served faithfully for years. There were even more keyed-up soldiers and policemen at all the crossroads than usual. The radio had just announced that a barracks had been attacked: twelve shahids had blown themselves up in sequence, allowing three insurgents to enter the barracks through the gaps and fire their automatic weapons at anything that moved. The Taliban were continuing their gruesome little game of cat and mouse.

'Where are we going now?' asked Nick.

Osama put a finger to his mouth: he was sure that their taxi driver understood English, although he had said he didn't. He asked to be dropped at a small café near the hospital where Malalai worked. When they'd sat down, Osama asked Nick to give him a detailed description of his investigation and findings, and only interrupted occasionally to ask a question.

'You haven't discovered anything more precise about the relationship between Leonard Mandrake and Wali Wadi?'

'Nothing more than what I've told you. Mandrake travelled to Pakistan a lot — several times a year — and I imagine that he met Wadi there. They also met up secretly in all sorts of other locations around the world. When I was ferreting through various databases, I found flight bookings for Wadi to Paris, London, and Frankfurt, and they corresponded to reservations made by Leonard Mandrake for the same destinations on the same dates.'

'So Mandrake possessed some very sensitive data and, somehow or another, Wali Wadi had access to it,' said Osama. 'Had he stolen it, or was it an exchange?'

'Nobody knows. The only thing I'm sure of is that the directors of Willard Consulting panicked when they realised that secret information was being leaked. They tried to clean up the mess on their own.'

'Dortmund was given the job of assassinating Wali Wadi in Kabul, while another team took care of Mandrake in Zurich,' continued Osama. 'When these efforts weren't wholly successful, the Entity was brought in, and you with them.'

'I think we've understood what happened, in what order. But now I must ask you an honest question, given that you're on the run, and that your bosses have put a price on your head. Are you still in a position to help me find Leonard and Zahra?'

Osama smiled sadly.

'My situation is what it is, but this is my country. I have networks of friends all over the place. Wherever they're hiding, we'll track them down.'

Osama left Nick sitting at the back of the café, and crossed the road. Malalai's department was empty. He flagged down a nurse and introduced himself. She sat him down in her tiny office and went off to find his wife. Malalai turned up ten minutes later.

'Sorry, I was in the operating theatre — a labour. Sweet of you to come and see me. Hey, I've got a surprise for you, too.' She rummaged in a drawer, pulled out a piece of soap the colour of Turkish Delight, and waved it triumphantly. 'Look,' she said with pride. 'I went to the market, and found some rose-scented soap. It's your favourite, isn't it?'

Osama smiled as Malalai took off her theatre headgear.

'By the way, a Taliban insulted me, on account of my wearing only a hijab and not a proper burqa. The charming man called me a whore and the spawn of the devil. He threatened to scar my face with his scissors. I told some policemen, but they just laughed! They didn't even pretend to give chase, when they could easily have caught him.'

'He didn't hurt you, did he?'

'No, if you think it doesn't "hurt" to be insulted while you're out shopping. I discussed it with my RAWA colleagues yesterday. Did you know that in this country there's no provision in the law to punish men who insult women?'

Osama didn't know. Noticing his solemn face, Malalai leaned towards him.

'What's going on, Osama? You look shattered.'

He explained the situation to her.

'You think you can hide from the NDS in Kabul?'

'For a little while, yes. I don't even know if Mandrake is in Kabul. I may have to leave the city to find him.'

'Would you like me to go into hiding, too?'

'It would be better. Tell them you're sick.'

'I'll ask a friend to put me up. That'll be safer than my family. I'll go later, after my shift.'

'Leave your phone here. They can use it to find you. I'll do the same. If you want to talk to me, leave a message with your most trustworthy nurse. What's her name?'

'Amina. And what about me — how will I be able to find you?'

'Through Mullah Bakir.'

She kissed him.

'Will this young Westerner give you a better chance of finding the bastards who killed your men?'

'I think so.'

'Find them, Osama, and when you've found them, punish them.'

OSAMA HAD TEARS IN HIS EYES as he left his wife. He went back to Nick in the café.

'What do you want to do now?' asked Nick. 'See your friend Reza?'

'No.'

'Why?'

'He has an important job, and people know we're friends. I don't want to complicate his life for no reason. I'd rather rely on less visible sources.'

He needed time to think. Time, and caffeine. He ordered a double Turkmen coffee. 'We'll go and see someone who can help us,' he said, after downing it in a single gulp. He was thinking of Mullah Bakir. 'But I'm warning you, he's an imam — a man who's been in your enemy camp.'

Nick paled.

'A Taliban?'

'Moderate. But still a Taliban, yes.'

'Don't you have anyone else?'

'I have plenty of trustworthy friends, former mujahedeen or people from police headquarters, but I fear they may be being closely watched. The NDS is very impressive. Mullah Bakir is easier to talk to. He saved my life when your cronies sent a group of killers to assassinate me.'

'Why would a Taliban, even a moderate, want to help us?'

'I don't know. You can ask him yourself.'

They flagged down a taxi. Overwhelmed by exhaustion and the seriousness of the situation, they didn't speak on their way to the mosque. Shortly before they arrived, Osama caught sight of a small shop on the side of the road, whose owner was pulling down the metal shutters. He ordered the taxi to stop.

'What are you doing?'

'You can't go to the mosque dressed like that. There might be NDS spies hanging around. You need a disguise.'

'But I'm wearing Afghan clothes!' protested Nick.

'You look about as much like an Afghan as I look like a Wall Street trader,' retorted Osama. 'You need to become invisible.' He nodded at the burqa stall. 'Put on one of those, and you'll be fine.'

'Oh no,' groaned Nick.

Osama left him on the pavement and went to buy a burqa and all the trimmings: tunic, trousers …

'Go and put this on in one of those little lanes. It's dark; no one will see you.'

Nick found it hard to navigate the bumpy ground in his burqa.

'So?' asked Osama wryly. 'Comfortable?'

'It's stupid,' protested Nick, 'I can't see anything with this net in front of my eyes. How can they force people to dress like this? It's inhuman.'

'The women here manage fine. You'll get used to it,' said Osama, thinking of Malalai's objections.

He'd never put one on himself, not even to experience what it felt like to be rigged out like that.

They continued their journey on foot, with Nick struggling to keep up with Osama, like a submissive wife following behind her husband. The mosque was almost empty — just a few believers praying in silence, kneeling on threadbare mats. The one-legged man recognised Osama. He went to prevent Nick from following him in, but Osama stopped him with a wave of the hand.

'She's coming in with me.'

Mullah Bakir was working at his computer. When Osama came in, his face brightened with a huge smile of absolute sincerity. He rushed to greet him.

'Brother Osama. Delighted to see you safe and sound. Really, it's a great joy.'

They hugged. Then the mullah turned towards Nick.

'Your wife, Malalai? And yet she's known to be allergic to the burqa.'

'You can take off your disguise, now,' said Osama.

Mullah Bakir was stupefied to see Nick appear, his face all red from the heat.

'Who is this?'

'A Swiss friend. I saw English magazines here when I first visited, so I imagine you speak it.'

'Absolutely. Welcome to Afghanistan,' said the mullah to Nick. 'I studied in Geneva and at Cambridge in my youth.'

He spoke perfect English, with the posh accent of a former public schoolboy.

'What did you study in Europe?' asked Osama.

'Cellular microbiology. I'm afraid I even have a PhD.'

'But then ... why did you become a Taliban?' asked Nick incredulously.

'The Taliban of 1995 were not the Taliban of 2001. In 1995, we were supposed to be a movement of intellectuals. It is true that Mullah Omar — who I suspect may be unable to read — and I have had a rather more difficult relationship of late. But please, take a seat, I will serve you some tea.'

Osama let him pour. They allowed their drinks to cool in silence.

'You did well to come and see me quickly,' said Mullah Bakir. 'The minister has announced that you left your men to be massacred while you skedaddled into the mountains in the most cowardly way.'

'That's disgraceful! A horrible lie!' cried Osama, losing his temper. 'Me, a mujahedeen, fleeing combat?'

'Anyone who knows you will know that — your staff, most of all. But what are a few honest policemen against the word of the state? And, in any case, I'm well placed to know that there haven't been any Taliban attacks on that road over the last two weeks.'

'My friends will help me.'

'People will silence them.'

'What do you mean, people?'

'People close to the Coalition,' replied the mullah, peering at Nick. 'Americans, French, English ... we may find out one day. Whatever, I'm sure Westerners are involved in this. Charming people, and so civilised ... of course, assassinating someone with a five-hundred-thousand-dollar missile, shot from an ultramodern drone, is far more politically correct than the throat-slitting favoured by my Taliban friends. Those unbelievers, especially the Americans, adore technology. They can't help it. Killing with a high-tech machine somehow doesn't seem like killing, to them ... but is it in fact morally preferable? I will leave you to ponder that very *interesting* question.'

'Why are you helping us?' asked Nick.

'What makes you think I'm going to help you? You're only an unbeliever, after all.'

'Stop playing with words.'

A small smile appeared on Mullah Bakir's chubby face.

'You're right. I have nothing against unbelievers; they can worship whichever God they like, or even no god, which seems to be the latest trend in Europe. I respect everyone's beliefs, so long as they let us live as we please, as good Muslims respecting the Book. What do you know of the relationship between Westerners and the Taliban?'

'You took in Bin Laden and his cronies. You helped him prepare attacks against the West, including the one on September 11th that killed thousands of Americans. That's what I know about the relationship between Americans and the Taliban.'

'Is your friend just pretending to be stupid, or is it for real?' Mullah Bakir asked Osama.

'The September 11 attacks made Westerners very nervous,' said Osama. 'And not everything he said was rubbish.'

'That's true,' admitted the mullah. 'You're young, and you don't know much about the local situation. You might like to know that before Mullah Omar committed the unpardonable mistake of giving a warm welcome to Al Qaida and its Arab friends, our regime was completely accepted by the West, and our relationship with it was very cordial. We were even financed by Washington, until 1997. Didn't you know that? At the beginning there was definitely a honeymoon period with the United States. We were putting things back in order, you see. We almost completely wiped out opium production — and, incidentally, this country is now, thanks to the Coalition troops and President Karzaï's corrupt regime, responsible for almost 80 per cent of worldwide production. We were in regular contact with Western government officials as well as various multinational corporations with big plans for our country. Our revolution re-established order in a country devastated by general negligence, warlords, illiteracy, and drug trafficking.'

'Re-established order by reducing women to slavery, and taking the country back to the stone ages ... ' retorted Nick.

'This country was in the stone ages well before we took power ... ever since the Mughal emperor Babur was chased out, namely in the 15th century of your ungodly calendar. As for the excesses of our regime, it was a revolution — and all revolutions have their excesses.'

'Not as many as yours!'

'Ours was one of the least bloody of recent centuries. Think of the French *colonnes infernales.* Or the thirty or forty million deaths of the Chinese Cultural Revolution. That doesn't stop your governments from embracing the Chinese leadership with open arms. Yet are the men leading China today so very different from those in power forty years ago? No. So study history, of which you know nothing, young man, and spare me your simplistic moralising lectures. The fact that I wear a turban doesn't make me narrow-minded. Things are always more complex than they seem, in this cruel, multipolar world, as the Western commentators like to call it …'

After this great speech, Mullah Bakir selfishly and triumphantly served himself more tea, leaving their glasses empty.

'Nick, Mullah Bakir is our friend. You can trust him. I'll vouch for that.'

'OK,' grumbled Nick.

'What do you need?' asked the mullah, serving them more tea now. 'I can help you hide, and get you information. Or weapons. Whatever you need, in fact.'

'In Kabul, we don't need anything,' decided Osama. 'But I'll keep your offer in mind, because if we have to travel to the Pashtun areas we will need your help. Thank you, Mullah, for the tip-off, without which we might have been arrested.'

Osama stood up and embraced the mullah. He looked tiny, clasped against Osama's massive frame. He ceremoniously shook Nick's hand, and then, with an odd sort of smile on his lips, watched them leave.

'WHAT DO YOU MAKE of that?' asked Nick, as they reached the street.

He'd put the burqa back on, and was finding it even harder to walk now that it was almost dark.

'He wants to know what's in the report. We'll have to wait to find out why.'

'To harm NATO, of course,' exploded Nick.

'Not necessarily. Mullah Bakir is not so much an Islamist as a revolutionary, a nationalist who believes in God. He thinks the current regime is going to collapse, and when that happens, he hopes to play a major role in the return of a more moderate Taliban government. Having information on the Americans and other important NATO countries could help him acquire their support when that moment comes.'

'Switzerland doesn't belong to NATO, or the Coalition.'

'This case goes far beyond Switzerland. It wasn't Switzerland that lent the Entity a drone to kill me. Only the Coalition countries possess drones.'

'So that's it? Mullah Bakir wants us to help him put together a file so he can blackmail NATO?'

'We'll see when the time comes. For now, we have to prove our innocence. Once the Mandrake File is in the public domain our names will be cleared, and we'll be able to prove the crimes of those who've tried to destroy us.'

'If you say so ... Where are we going now?'

'To see a friend of mine, Adbul Dost. He's retired now, but we worked together for years. He was the head of Kabul Drugs Squad. He's an honest man, and was a great cop, highly respected.'

Osama flagged down a taxi to take them to the Karte Parwan neighbourhood. The lack of street lighting was compensated for by a mass of street hawkers' braziers. An unbelievable number of people crowded the pavements. They drove for another half-mile or so, into a rather poor area where it was almost completely dark. Osama asked the taxi to stop in front of a house still scarred with bullets from the battles of 1995–96, although smoke rose from a chimney on the roof. The door was opened by a chubby Afghan with a bushy grey moustache.

'You? Osama! Come in, quickly.'

Nick followed them into a tiny hall, and then a smoky room that functioned as both living and dining room. The man gestured for them to sit down on the cushions.

'Would you like my wife to come and look after yours?'

Nick took off his burqa.

'A Swiss friend. We're in trouble,' remarked Osama. 'We need to sleep here.'

'I know. The NDS came round asking after you. They know we're friends, and they posted a lookout in front of my house all day. It's lucky you came at night. Tomorrow morning, we'll go out the back.'

Osama stiffened. Adbul Dost was an old friend, but they hadn't seen each other for almost a year. The fact that the NDS had targeted him would mean that all his close friends and colleagues were being watched.

'It's going to be hard to avoid them,' remarked the cop, as if reading his mind. 'If they're watching me, they must be watching everyone who might be able to lend you a hand. You're going to have to leave Kabul. Hide out in Farah or near the Iranian border, in Baloch country. Out there, NDS spies would be lynched for asking about you.'

'I have a mission to complete first. We're looking for a couple, in hiding here in Kabul — a Swiss man and an Afghan woman. Can you help me?'

'I can find them if they're in a hotel or a guest house. If not, my networks are no longer very active. I'd need more time, and money.'

'They don't know anyone in Kabul, so they're bound to be at a hotel. The man is fifty-two years old; the woman, about twenty-five. She's come to collect the official documents she needs for an Australian visa application.'

'Do you have their names?'

'We think the man has a false passport in the name of Leonard Milton. The woman is probably using her real name, Zahra Kimzi.'

The former cop seemed encouraged by all this information.

'I'll pop out now, to see a few friends who might be able to help. I'll have what you need by the end of tomorrow morning, latest. In the meantime, you need to stay hidden. Just use Hamid's room for the night.'

Osama knew that Dost was referring to his only son, killed by the KGB twenty years earlier for fighting in the mujahedeen resistance. Neither Dost nor his wife had ever recovered. The small room that the former cop led them to was like something out of a time warp, with its posters of long-forgotten Afghan singers, its mini Russian

Migs, and even Hamid's clothes folded carefully on the shelves, as if he might return at any moment.

'I'll sleep on the rug on the floor,' said Osama.

'No, let me,' protested Nick. 'Take the bed, you'll be more comfortable.'

The retired policeman put his hand on Nick's shoulder.

'You're a brave young man, and I feel proud that you're fighting for us at Osama's side. Take my son's bed — it's an honour for someone like you to sleep in it.'

Nick was so exhausted that he fell asleep almost immediately, but not Osama. He felt hunted in his own city. Even when he'd joined the resistance to fight the Russians, and then the Taliban, he hadn't had this awful sense of being caught in the clutches of a hugely powerful machine, combining human networks with the most clandestine technologies.

THE JET LANDED on Bagram runway at 4.30am. It was a trijet, capable of carrying twenty people from Zurich to Kabul in a single flight. It was registered in Panama to a bogus company, but it actually belonged to the Entity. The plane taxied down the runway and parked a little way off. At this hour, the airport was quiet; only drones and reconnaissance planes were flying, and a C-130 Hercules gunship was idling, waiting to take off. The jet's airstairs unfolded and the men stepped out, Joseph first. As well as the two K troops of seven killers, all of them carrying two big bags of weapons, there were two analysts and three IT experts. Five 4x4s were lined up nearby. The men climbed into the vehicles, which drove off immediately. An Entity agent had booked a safe house just off Charahi Massoud. The men who stormed into it had slept on the flight and were ready to start work immediately, if necessary. Inside the building, everything was ready: fifteen computers on a secure wifi connection, encrypted mobile phones, mountain gear …

Joseph immediately began allocating his men to various missions. One team would connect to the databases of every hotel and guest house in Kabul, and check the details of all the foreigners staying there. Another would make contact with the NDS, to obtain a list of all the people whom Osama Kandar would have been likely to contact on his return, and to check out the surveillance on him. Joseph looked at his watch. If Nick was hiding in this city, with or without the Afghan cop, he was certain to find him. He couldn't wait for dawn to break.

Abdul Dost didn't have a secure wifi connection or a computer, never mind a team of men, but he was fast and effective with his old-school methods. He began by visiting the city's best hotel, the Kabul Intercontinental, perched on a hill twenty minutes out of town with a panoramic view over the city. The disadvantage of this relative isolation was lack of security, so three armoured cars guarded the road, supported by dozens of heavily armed soldiers. Several of the receptionists here had worked as informers for Abdul when he was still in post. One of them recognised him immediately, and rushed over to greet him. Even retired, Abdul could have anyone involved in drug trafficking sent straight to prison, and that was most of the hotel staff. He soon obtained the list of guests — no Leonard Milton, and the only people fitting Mandrake's description were journalists and businessmen.

The cop drove to the Golden Star, known to every Kabuli because it occupied the only tall building in the city. Abdul was lucky there, too — one of his former contacts had become assistant manager. His research took longer this time, as there were three couples and two apparently single men whose descriptions fitted the one given by Osama. But he only had to search their rooms to realise he was on the wrong track. Abdul didn't lose heart. His next stop was the Safi Landmark, a stylish hotel, though with a poorer reputation than the first two. A suicide bomb had destroyed part of the façade a few weeks back. He drew a blank there, too. He then spent four hours making the rounds of the more humble hotels and guest houses, but without success. Several establishments had been attacked over the last few months and had closed down, if they hadn't actually been razed.

Around midday, he looked at his watch. He'd exhausted all the possibilities. Suddenly, he realised that he'd forgotten one hotel, the smartest of the lot — the Serena, by Zarnegar Park. Formerly the Kabul Hotel, it was now owned by the Aga Khan. People said that its suites were the most luxurious in Kabul, and that some even had their own private saunas. A suicide squad had attacked the hotel several months earlier, almost killing the Australian ambassador. Had it reopened? Abdul Dost had recently spent several weeks with his family in the countryside, where newspapers were a rarity. He might have missed the news. He got back into his ancient, decrepit Toyota, and drove to Mohamed Jan Khan Wat, a busy road on the other side of the Kabul River that led to the Serena. There were chicanes on the road, guarded by jumpy policemen. When he reached the hotel he could see from the furore of activity that it was certainly open: taxis, limousines, bodyguards, masses of ANA soldiers, and even a few Western mercenaries with earpieces and M4s slung over their shoulders.

It took him several minutes and a great deal of charm to get through the armoured anti-suicide-bomb double doors, and then the metal detectors. The entrance hall was stunningly beautiful, a blend of traditional Afghan architecture, ancient works of art, and modern materials. Adbul whistled, impressed. He was astounded that such a luxurious hotel existed in Kabul. Several men in black suits lingered in the hall, jackets bulging around their weapons, not doing much for the atmosphere. Fortunately for Abdul, most of the staff from the Kabul Hotel had been re-employed, and he soon saw someone he knew. The man was still a porter. Adbul had helped him out of a tight corner once, so he was bound to cooperate. In any case, he greeted Abdul with a big smile.

'As-Salamu Alaykum, degarman. Welcome, Kouch aamadeyn.'

'Greetings, greetings,' said the cop. 'But I wasn't a degarman — a lieutenant colonel, just a captain. You're too kind.'

'I heard you'd retired; are you back on the job?'

'Just for one case. I'm looking for a couple who may be hiding here — a Swiss man and an Afghan woman. They arrived together from Europe. He may be using a passport in the name of Lionel Milton.'

The porter frowned.

'Milton … rings a bell.'

He checked his computer.

'Milton, yes. Suite 308. He arrived five days ago, and hasn't been out since. I haven't seen him, not even once. He eats in his suite. I don't have anything on a woman; she isn't registered.' He looked up from his screen. 'The foreigner probably slipped the receptionist a big tip when he signed in. Some clients do that when they bring a mistress.'

Abdul nodded; he was very excited. He slipped the man a two-hundred-Afghani note and made him promise not to say a word. Then he leapt into his car.

The porter went back to work, not realising that one of his assistants had overheard the whole conversation. The man was a young Pashtun recently returned from London. He worked some nights, and had been on duty when the Swiss man by the name of Milton had checked in. The man had given him five hundred dollars to let him know if anyone came asking for him. He slipped out of the porter's lodge.

'I'll be back in five minutes.'

He bounded up the emergency stairs to the first floor. Then he took the lift up to the third floor, ran to the door of suite 308, and knocked.

'Who's there?' asked a man's voice in English.

'The porter, the one you saw the day you arrived.'

The door opened. The Swiss man looked at him anxiously. He was wearing a plain pair of jeans and a polo shirt.

'What's going on?'

'Someone came asking for you. A cop.'

The man went white. He opened the door wider. The porter caught a fleeting glimpse of an exquisite young woman as she disappeared into the bedroom.

'Tell me what happened.'

'It was a retired cop, someone the head porter knows. He was asking if you were here, you and this young woman.'

'Did he know my name?'

'Yes, he mentioned your name, Lionel Milton. When my boss

confirmed that you were staying here, the cop gave him two hundred afghanis to keep his mouth shut, and left. Running.'

Mandrake shoved a wad of dollars into the porter's hand and slammed the door shut. Zahra came to the bedroom door.

'What's going on?'

'We've been found.'

She raised her hand to her mouth, horrified. Mandrake put his hands on her shoulders.

'We can't stay here — we've got to leave.'

'When?'

'Now.'

'But I'll have my papers in five days!'

'I know, but if we wait five days we'll be dead.'

'Shall we try another hotel?'

'No way — they have my false name. We've got to leave Kabul.'

'Where will we go?'

'I don't know! Let me think. We need to find a solution. Fast.'

After a few seconds' silence, Zahra spoke up.

'I'm not registered at reception, so they don't know my name. We could take refuge in my village.'

'Where is it?'

'A hundred and twenty-five miles from here, in the northeast, near the Pakistan border. From there, we can go even further north, towards Tajikistan and the other ex-Soviet countries.'

'Will we be safe? What if the police phone your family for information?'

Zahra walked up to him and put her hand on his.

'There's no phone there, my love. No Internet, no electricity. Nothing. It's in Nuristan, the most primitive part of Afghanistan. Neither the police nor the army ever go there. No one will find us there.'

'What about the Taliban?'

'Last time I visited, it was one of the few districts where the inhabitants had chased them out without any help from the Americans.'

'That sounds like a possibility, then,' admitted Mandrake, with a trace of hope in his voice. 'But the country is at war. Won't the journey be dangerous?'

'I don't know. But with money we should be all right. My mother and I managed it alone, before she was killed.'

Mandrake nodded.

'OK, we'll try. We have no choice. I'll find us a car. We need to leave right now.'

JOSEPH WAS PACING like a caged lion around the overheated room where the analysts were based. The minister had personally informed the NDS that Kandar was on the run, probably in Kabul. The city was swarming with informers. Kandar was too tall to stay hidden long; they'd find him in a matter of days. Joseph's analysts had been working hard all day, checking every detail of every foreigner on the hotel lists, looking for anyone who could possibly be Nick. They weren't sure if he would have checked in under his real name, so they were examining each file individually. When they'd gone through all the available accommodation in Kabul, they would move on to other Afghan cities, with the help of the NDS. It would take as long as it took.

'Sir!' cried one of the analysts suddenly. 'I think I've found something. But it's so unbelievable that I'd like you to come and see for yourself.'

'Nick?'

'No, sir. Mandrake. He's checked in under the name of Lionel Milton. Hotel Serena, Kabul, Suite 308.'

'What's this? Leonard Mandrake? Here, under a false name?'

'Yes, sir. Come and see for yourself.'

Joseph looked at the file. He knew Mandrake's face by heart, and there was no question it was him. What the hell was he doing here in Kabul, under a false name? This was the last place that Joseph would have looked.

'That's him, isn't it, boss?'

'Yes.'

'What the fuck is he doing here?'

'I don't know. He's been trading with this fucking country for ten years — maybe he has friendly contacts we don't know about.'

'What will we do?'

A wave of life-giving warmth ran through Joseph's body, as it did every time he found a man on the run. It was the hunter's instinct. Everyone had been looking for Mandrake — in Europe, Asia, and America — but he'd found him first.

They'd come full circle: Mandrake would die at the same time as Nick and the Afghan cop. The death of these three would put a stop to all his worries. A full stop.

'Put on your gear,' he told his men. 'Weapons, bullet-proof vests. Time to go to work.'

OSAMA GOT OUT of the car first, followed by Nick. They had to leave the guns that Abdul Dost had lent them in the car, at the end of the road. You weren't allowed to park in front of the hotel, never mind bring in a weapon — no chance, not even with a police ID. The hotel was surrounded by a high, stucco-covered concrete wall. The main gate was a double barrier against suicide attacks, reinforced with massive concrete chicanes. Osama showed his card at the first security check, where the guards carried assault rifles. The guard gave him a military salute and let him through.

Inside, they had to pass through an x-ray machine before they could enter the paved, tree-lined courtyard. They walked past the reception desk as if they were hotel guests, and then into a hall containing two lifts up to the suites.

'Let's take the stairs,' suggested Osama.

There was a guard on every landing. The third-floor corridor had a white marble floor embellished with a thick rug, the walls were covered with hardwood panelling, and you could hear birdsong from the garden. Nick was staggered by the luxuriousness of the place. Eventually, they came to door 308. Osama knocked lightly.

'Room service.'

No one replied, so he waved his card at a chambermaid.

'Police. Open the door, please.'

Looking terrified, she obeyed and then ran off as fast as her legs could carry her. They entered the suite.

'Empty,' said Osama.

There were still some clothes in the wardrobe, and a few newspapers lying around, but it was obvious that the two fugitives had left in a hurry. Nick pointed to the safe.

'They didn't even bother to close it. There's still some money here.'

'Someone warned them that there'd been enquiries,' said Osama.

'We've had it,' said Nick.

'Not necessarily. Come on, let's get out of here.'

As they got into their car, Nick noticed a convoy of three 4x4s bristling with antennae stopping just in front of the hotel. Several Westerners in fatigues got out, carrying assault rifles. Osama started the car immediately. The group of men rushed towards the hotel entrance, but then one stopped at the side of the road and stared at them. It was Joseph.

'Quick, let's go. That's an Entity man.'

'Did he see us?'

Osama's question was soon answered, as two of the 4x4s roared towards them.

'They've recognised us! We're done for, in this wreck,' cried Nick, white as a sheet.

Osama accelerated. With a squealing of brakes, he did a U-turn on Charahi Pashtunistan, and veered hurriedly into a street cluttered with vans and motorbikes.

'They're gaining on us,' said Nick.

'I know.'

Osama took two screeching right-hand turns, narrowly missing the cars parked along the pavement. Nick noticed the dome of a large mosque.

'That's Id Gah mosque. We're not far from Shor Bazaar,' said Osama. 'We'll lose them there.'

He turned again, this time into a potholed road. The car started careening wildly. At that very moment, they heard a dull crack. A hole appeared in the rear windscreen.

'They're shooting at us!' screamed Nick.

'Looks like it,' replied Osama soberly.

He drove fast and well, lips clenched, focussed, getting the most out of the old banger.

'Get the Kalashnikov,' he ordered. 'Empty the magazine on them.'

Nick grabbed the gun clumsily. He leant out of the window, trying to aim. The wind filled his eyes with dust. He pulled the trigger, feeling the scorching cartridge cases hit his face and clatter into the car. The 4x4 behind them didn't even falter — in fact, it accelerated.

'I missed them. The magazine is empty.'

'We're nearly there.'

Osama jammed on the brakes, and swung the wheel hard. The car turned almost ninety degrees, hitting a mud wall with its fender and knocking it over in a cloud of dust. The passenger window shattered on impact. Osama swung the wheel again, and put his foot down harder. The lane was only just wide enough for the little Toyota. Both wing mirrors were torn off on the walls of houses as they passed. The 4x4s were right on their tail, bashing down walls with an apocalyptic roar, sending debris flying through the air. In the chaos of dust and noise, only the radiator grills could be seen, a little closer every second.

'They're catching us up,' cried Nick.

'We're going to be OK.'

There was a dull roar. The first 4x4 took off, then came back down and sank into the ground, as if sucked up front-first. The bonnet disappeared into the road, leaving the back wheels more than a metre in the air. The second 4x4 smashed straight into it with a thunderous crash. The impact pushed the first vehicle almost vertical. There was a kind of explosion, and water spurted out sideways. Flabbergasted, Nick saw two men drag themselves awkwardly out of the second vehicle, their faces streaming with blood, brandishing pistols equipped with silencers — Joseph and one of his Ks. Then Osama turned into another, equally narrow lane, and their pursuers were left behind. He burst out laughing.

'Three years ago, two cops and I were chasing a man, and he got away from us like that. He had a little car and we were in a Ford Ranger. The pipework around here was done by a corrupt businessman who knew Karzaï's brother. He wanted to save money repairing the road surface, so he slipped the pipes under planks of wood, and poured the tar straight on top of that. But because the earth is soft, the road surface collapses whenever a big vehicle drives on it. The council wanted to put it right, but the money was stolen.' He laughed again. 'I said to myself that if I was ever being chased, I'd ditch my pursuers here. To be honest, I didn't think it would ever happen.'

Osama seemed very pleased with himself, and completely unfazed by the fact that he'd just escaped death. Nick closed his eyes, his heart still beating at two hundred miles a minute. They drove for quarter of an hour down unmarked streets, and then Osama parked the car. He hid the keys under the carpet, and flagged down a taxi.

'Are we going back to your friend's place?'

'No way. They have the licence-plate number, so the NDS will already be on their way there.'

'Where are we going then?'

'Right now, I can only think of Mullah Bakir. We'll see where we stand later on.'

19.

Osama lay on the mattress that Mullah Bakir had lent him. The mullah had gone to give his three o'clock sermon, and Osama was thinking hard in the soothing half-light of the room. He tried to imagine Leonard Mandrake, forced to flee in an unknown country in the middle of a war. Where could he go? The fact that his false identity had been discovered meant that he wouldn't be able to take a flight without acquiring a new passport, which was impossible in Kabul. Iran was unthinkable, and Pakistan extremely risky: its secret services were very powerful, and couldn't refuse anything to the Coalition. But yet all was not lost. Mandrake had millions of dollars in secret bank accounts. He could use the name of a bogus company to rent a private jet from Tajikistan or Uzbekistan. Central Asia's former Soviet republics were like sieves: with money, he'd be able to buy new passports from the local mafia. For now, Mandrake's most sensible plan would be to hide out somewhere for a week or two, while he organised his departure properly. So where would a man who knew nothing of Afghanistan hide? Osama considered his girlfriend, Zahra. She still had family here — in 2002, after the Taliban fell from power, she and her mother had visited their home village. She must have registered herself with the police authorities. There was a chance she might have given the address she was heading for, in the village, rather than a hotel. At the time, she had no reason to be cautious. Osama waited for the mullah to come back from preaching and went over to talk to him.

'I need your help. I want to search border-police records for a woman who came back to the country in 2002 — Leonard Mandrake's girlfriend.'

'That was a long time ago, brother Osama. Do you think the records still exist?'

'Yes. The Russians supplied the border police with computers before they left. As early as 1980. I know my colleagues; they are KGB-trained, so they keep everything and discard nothing. That information will be stored somewhere. It just needs finding.'

'In that case, we'll find it. Give me the young woman's name.'

The mullah called over a small boy, gave him the piece of paper, and whispered a few words in his ear. The child ran off.

'We will have your information soon, Insha'Allah. In the meantime, make yourselves completely at home.'

THE INFORMATION CAME two days later, in the morning, by way of another small boy, carrying a note folded into a Koran. Mullah Bakir opened it eagerly.

'Zahra Kimzi did indeed visit Afghanistan in May 2002. She arrived on May 14th with her mother, and left again on June 2nd, alone. Her mother was killed in an ANA bombing near her village. A misfired mortar. Did you know that?'

'Yes.'

'She did give an address — a village in Nuristan called Kir.'

'Do you know it?'

'No. But at least now I understand why the girl's surname seemed unusual. She's a Nuristani.'

Osama pulled a face. The Nuristani were a controversial ethnic group. They were traditionally pagans, and had only converted to Islam at the end of the 19th century. Ever since, they'd practised the most rigid form of Islam in the area. They were a sort of lumpenproletariat akin to India's untouchables, mistreated by Pashtuns and Tajiks alike. It might seem strange that one tribe could remain untouched for more than a thousand years, despite the gradual Islamicisation of the rest of the country, but less so if you were familiar with that part of Afghanistan. Nuristan was one of the wildest regions in the world, a desert-like place on the fringes of the Hindu Kush. The average altitude was more than three-and-a-half thousand metres throughout, with plenty of plateaux at over four-and-a-half, and alarming differences in height even for a mountainous country like Afghanistan. The road network was practically nonexistent, and almost impassable in winter. In one sense, it was the perfect place to hide.

'Going to Nuristan in late March is no picnic,' remarked the mullah. 'Wait a moment, I'll find a map.'

It was odd, to say the least, that an imam would keep military maps at home, but then nothing surprised Osama when it came to Mullah Bakir. The map was at least six metres square, so they unfolded it on the table. It featured hundreds of villages, some annotated with a handwritten note in Russian. Osama noticed a red line underneath Wama, where a major Taliban attack on the ANA had taken place two years earlier ... A bit of searching revealed Zahra's village, Kir. It was in the middle of nowhere, about a hundred kilometres northwest of the Pakistani town of Arandu. The exact altitude wasn't listed, but there were four-and-a-half-thousand-metre peaks immediately to the west, and also the north.

'The place is a living hell. No roads; huge mountains. It would take a serious expedition to get there. What's more, the area is infested with Taliban.'

'Zahra and her mother managed to get there without protection.'

'That was in 2002. The Taliban weren't welcome there then. But since the Coalition operations, thousands of Islamist fighters have converged on the region, precisely because it's the most difficult to access — even more so than the mountains of Tora Bora. The situation has done a U-turn: these days, it's definitely one of the most dangerous parts of the country.'

'Zahra must not know that,' said Nick soberly. 'They are hurling themselves right into the mouth of the lion.'

They digested the bad news for a moment.

'We have to go. We don't have any choice.'

'You're crazy,' replied the Mullah.

'Osama's right,' added Nick. 'I'm going, too.'

'I don't want to meddle in your business, but I don't see how you'll get through. Even you don't have the slightest chance, qomaandaan. And as for your charming friend … the local fighters will eat a little blonde like him for breakfast. Also, it's not only the Taliban you have to worry about. You'll be driving on tracks that are still covered in snow, in a totally hostile natural environment, in temperatures between minus fifteen and minus thirty degrees, with new snowfall, crevasses, landslides, and avalanches. No Westerner ever goes there — even the French doctors avoided it during the war against the Russians.'

'I'm familiar with the mountains.'

'Nick, we're not talking about the Alps here. We're not going skiing.'

'I was born in the mountains. I didn't come all the way here, to the end of the world, to hide out in a mosque. I'm going all the way, and you needn't try to change my mind. There's no point.'

'That's absurd,' retorted Osama.

'I'm going to come, too,' announced the mullah. 'On your own, you'll be massacred.'

'It's too dangerous!' protested Osama. 'You've no reason to take such risks for us.'

'The two of you might just manage the journey on your own. But once you're there, how do you think you're going to come across to the villagers, who hate the government? With your looks and your urban Dari accent, they'll take you for a Baloch lord or, worse, a government stooge. You won't last two hours. Not to mention your friend. Whereas I'm known to all Afghans. Everyone knows I used to be on the secret Taliban Council. People aren't aware that Mullah Omar hates me — that by the end of the Taliban reign he wanted to imprison or kill me. Everyone thinks we're still buddies. And they adore him in those areas near the Pakistan border.'

'The journey will be very physically arduous. Do you think you'll manage?'

The mullah gestured around the room they sat in.

'I'm getting soft here. I'm coming.'

'In that case, I'll go and find the equipment we need,' said Osama.

'Let's meet here in two hours.'

He borrowed two thousand dollars from Nick and went straight to a car dealer near the Maulana Abdul Mateen mosque. The dealer was a sly but trustworthy Hazara. Four years before, Osama had cleared him of a murder charge brought by his brother-in-law, a crook who wanted to take over his business. A corrupt judge had already thrown the car dealer into a collective prison cell populated only by Pashtuns, so Osama had in fact saved his life. The dealer welcomed him with open arms. After the usual greetings and the inevitable scalding *chai,* Osama told him why he was there.

'I have to go to the mountains, in the north. I need a robust 4x4 that can manage steep, snowy slopes. Can you rent me a Volga jeep, or a Kamaz?'

The dealer frowned.

'How many people are travelling?'

'Three on the way there; maybe five on the way back. I can't use a government vehicle.'

'I know you have enemies, qomaandaan. An NDS informer came to see me yesterday, asking me to let them know if you came here looking for a car. They know what you did for me.'

'I see,' said Osama, gravely.

'You saved my life, qomaandaan,' continued the man warmly. 'You can trust me; I won't say a word. I have a Volga and a Cherokee, but I can't rent them to you. You need something more powerful, especially if the NDS is after you. I have an almost-new Toyota that belonged to a warlord who was brought down by the Americans. It's armoured, and the V8 motor is in perfect condition. Come and see.'

The long-chassis land cruiser was certainly impressive, with its bull bars, tinted windows, and special snow tyres. Two fat aerials went up from the roof into a sort of metallic mast welded to the front bumper.

'An ultra-modern radio device, to scramble remote-control bombs.' The dealer knocked on one of the windows. It made no sound at all. 'It's B7, you see. The windows and doors are both armoured — they'd withstand a volley of Kalashnikov shots. It can top a hundred kilometres an hour, despite its weight. The warlord had a special winch fitted to the front, so it can be extricated if it falls into a snowy crevasse. There's a fifty-metre cable in the boot. This is the vehicle for you.'

He opened the boot to reveal extreme-cold equipment: jackets, gloves, hats … all the gear you'd need to brave the mountains in winter. It was standard stuff for drug traffickers. Osama also saw two folding-stock Kalashnikovs, and even an AKM rifle, wrapped in a blanket, plus a box containing dozens of cartridges and several grenades.

'I picked it up the day after the owner was arrested, and haven't touched a thing. I thought I'd be selling it to another warlord.'

'Why did the NDS leave the car for you?'

The dealer smiled slyly.

'They just took the drugs, and replaced this car with another one, an old Lada, which they registered on their list of confiscations. As for this one, I have an arrangement with the head inspector, who's related to my second wife. He takes 50 per cent of the sale.'

Osama nodded. Typical baksheesh, of the kind he'd always refused for himself.

'I don't have all that much money. How much would it cost me for one week?' asked Osama, sure of the reply.

'Qomaandaan, I am indebted to you! I would be deeply hurt to charge you even a single afghani for this car. Keep it for two weeks, if you like.'

Osama shook his hand, moved. The man hugged him, as was the Hazara custom.

'Good luck, qomaandaan. May Allah help you to kill your enemies and the friends of your enemies. May you come back from your journey even stronger. I will pray for you.'

When he returned to the mosque, Nick and Mullah Bakir were ready. They were wearing brown woollen coats, and had plastic bags full of bottled water and tinned food piled up at their feet. Mullah Bakir sat in the passenger seat, and Nick in the back. Neither commented when they saw all the weapons and other equipment in the boot. They left Kabul just as the sun was disappearing behind the mountains, fringing the crests of the hills in purple. Osama switched on the headlights and took the Kunduz road for the last leg of his mission.

Osama was concentrating hard on the driving, so he managed to avoid a flock of goats that had decided to stop in the middle of the frozen road. He braked, and the 4x4 skidded to a halt without crashing into any of them. He'd already killed two goats in less than three hours, and each time a shepherd had appeared with his hand out. It was enough to make you think that the animals had been left there on purpose … They'd been driving for five days, and their supplies of food and water had long been exhausted. To start with, they'd taken the big road towards Kunduz, crossing the Panjshir valley, which neither the Russians nor the Taliban had ever managed to take from Commandant Massoud. Then they turned off onto a small potholed road that ran along the side of the mountain near the Khawak Pass, almost almost four thousand metres above sea level. This took them to Atiti, a humble mountain town, and then to the city of Nuristan, which gave the region its name.

Twice, villagers had confirmed that they'd seen a foreigner and a woman in a big 4x4 with Kabul plates. Osama saw now that he hadn't been particularly wise to choose such a visible car for this kind of region, but it was too late. And, in any case, the armoured Toyota was reassuring, although they'd seen enough Russian tank carcasses along the Panjshir valley, and then on the Kamdesh road, to remind them that armouring only provided a certain degree of protection in areas as rough as northern Afghanistan. The road itself was particularly dangerous — a narrow ribbon of badly damaged tarmac and frozen earth, scattered with snowdrifts and patches of black ice that had to be broken up with a pickaxe. When a truck came the other way, they had to slow down to walking pace and edge past it with millimetres to spare so as not to tumble into the ravines on either side, some of them hundreds of metres deep. The dozens of carcasses rusting at the bottom of the abyss were testament to the risk.

Osama was no stranger to living rough, but he was still struck by the destitution of the area's inhabitants, the poorest in the whole country. They came across very few vehicles — the odd ancient Toyota or Zhiguli, some old cars held together with bits of string, a few ramshackle lorries, but no modern 4x4s at all. Everything was covered in snow, and as cold as one would expect for late March — sometimes as low as minus twenty-five. The villagers they passed were muffled up in incredible layers of clothes and blankets to protect themselves from the cold, but had retained their dignity, and cut proud figures with their green or blue eyes and thick red hair. The Nuristanis' geographical remoteness and pagan culture meant that they hadn't mixed much with other Afghans. Mullah Bakir told them the legend that the Nuristani were direct descendants of the Macedonian soldiers of Alexander the Great, the founder of Kabul, who'd taken refuge in the north of the country after the collapse of his empire. It was, however, hard to imagine the army of the world's greatest military figure ending up in these poor valleys at the end of the world.

Shortly before Kamdesh, they stopped at a pitiful village where they were due to turn off the road. Osama went to talk with one of the inhabitants.

'May Allah be with you, may your body be strong,' he began. 'How is the road?'

'It's passable,' said the villager.

'Are you sure?"

'A truck came through last week. It fell in the ravine and everyone died, but the road is fine — you'll get through, Insha'Allah.'

'What about security?'

'Good, although there are many armed groups.'

'Taliban?'

'Gangs originally from Pakistan and from Kabul. They were kicked out of the army and have taken refuge here.'

'Taliban, then?'

'Yes, Taliban. Very bad,' confirmed the villager.

Osama wondered if the man was just stupid, or whether it was local custom to avoid giving straight answers to questions. Another villager was walking towards them, so Osama asked if they could buy any food.

'No, no food. Nothing here.'

'No eggs?'

'No, nothing. No eggs, no meat, no cheese, nothing.'

Osama took out two notes.

'We have eggs, cheese, and meat,' announced the villager. 'Come with me.'

Osama went to tell his friends that they'd be able to eat in the village. They were both at a very low ebb. The refined mullah had altitude sickness, and was aching all over from the thin air. He crept painfully out of the vehicle, taking tiny steps like an old man. As for Nick, he'd caught dysentery, and it wasn't responding to medication; they had to stop every hour for him to relieve himself by the side of the road. Nick grimaced at the grotty little houses. For the last two nights they'd slept in tiny, badly heated rooms, containing up to ten villagers huddled together for warmth. The air was almost unbearable — most of these poor wretches hadn't washed since the end of the previous summer, and Nick's sense of smell was being severely tested. And yet he handled all these inconveniences without the slightest complaint. Osama was impressed by the changes in the young man over the last few days, the way he'd toughened up — something he would never have thought possible in a Westerner of his generation.

Paradoxically, Mullah Bakir was finding it harder to deal with the primitive living conditions, the rotten food, the strong smells. Between his studies at Cambridge and living the high life in the Taliban government, the refined imam had forgotten what it was like to live rough ... Having said that, he was trying to put on a brave face, and whatever the circumstances retained his sense of humour, made even more darkly ironic by his conscious peppering of his speech with flowery vocabulary and an inimitable Oxbridge accent.

'Oh, marvellous,' he said when he saw the mud houses covered in dirty snow. 'This particular *holiday destination* will surpass all others, I feel sure.'

The villager showed them into his house. A woman had placed several dishes straight on to the filthy rugs on the beaten-earth floor.

There were no individual plates, and of course no knives and forks; in these remote areas you ate from a communal dish with a simple wooden spoon or with your fingers. They started with the traditional boiled eggs — every Afghan villager's staple diet.

'I don't think I'm ever going to be able to eat a boiled egg again,' said Nick, already green.

Mullah Bakir knelt down painfully, assisted by an awed villager to whom Osama had revealed the visitor's identity. Flatbread and yoghurt were soon served. The yoghurt was sharp and sour, despite the cold. To tell the truth, it was inedible, although Osama swallowed it down graciously. Nick spat out his first spoonful. He rushed outside holding his belly, but couldn't help soiling his trousers. One of the men burst out laughing, revealing a toothless mouth. His neighbour soon joined in, and then all the other men. Mullah Bakir was laughing loudly, too.

'The food is disgusting; the place, squalid; the people, savages. We really have come to the end of the world. Did you know that some Nuristanis still secretly practise idol worship? Which is even more peculiar, given that their believing brothers are often the most obtuse people one could imagine.'

'I didn't know a mullah could consider believers obtuse,' remarked Osama as he finished his yoghurt.

'Faith shouldn't be a once-and-for-all thing. It must include a kind of existential scepticism towards the dated and often obscure rules that make up the precepts of the Koran. In my opinion, everything in the Koran is open to interpretation, except of course the existence of God and the Prophet. My fellow imams at the University of Cairo have popularised my theory under the title 'The reasonable doubt of the informed believer', but I fear these sophisticated concepts will struggle to penetrate a shack like this.'

The mullah swallowed a mouthful of yoghurt, and pulled a face.

'For example, the people of these remote regions have never accepted the new marriage code I was able to introduce, at a time when Mullah Omar still paid some attention to what I suggested. These people are worse than the Pashtuns!'

Over the course of the journey, Osama was gradually finding out just how important Mullah Bakir had been at the beginning of the Taliban revolution. The development he'd just referred to was one of the only Taliban reforms to favour women. Basically, the Pashtun code totally excluded women from inheritance, whereas the Koran traditionally granted them half of what a man would receive. The Taliban had therefore imposed the compulsory granting of a half-part to women, something strongly opposed by many ethnic groups. Osama had read in the paper that the real break between the Taliban government's moderates and hardliners had dated from that reform.

'I didn't know it was you who initiated that law. My wife wasn't in favour — to her, imposing the right to a half-part was tantamount to accepting that a woman is worth half as much as a man.'

'Malalai is wrong, brother Osama. Half of something is better than all of nothing. Public acceptance of reform is not easy to obtain, in this country. The reactionaries are always more determined to stop reforms than the forces of progress to carry them out, and often more organised, too. I would never have been able to ratify equal treatment for men and women.'

'But would you have wanted to?'

'What I wanted was totally irrelevant, if the chances of obtaining it were nil. In politics, the only thing that counts is effectiveness: it's better to have no debate and a small move in the right direction, than a big debate and no movement at all.'

They fell quiet, because a new round of boiled eggs had arrived. Also Nick had returned, wearing a fresh pair of trousers. He managed to gulp down three boiled eggs, along with a bit of mouldy bread. He coughed; the air in the room was hard to breathe, on account of the cowpats fuelling the stove. And yet the villagers were bestowing an honour on them — the smelly cowpats were rich in energy, and both rare and expensive.

'Has a foreigner in a big car accompanied by an Afghan woman driven through here in the last two days?' asked Osama when the meal was finished.

The head of the village burst out laughing, and his friends followed suit.

'Yes. He very sick. Always in ditch. Always say *'Tachnaab da koujaas? Tachnaab da koujass?'*

'Where are the toilets?' So Leonard Mandrake's stomach hadn't stood up to the journey any better than Nick's. The exchange made Mullah Bakir smile.

'Do you know where they are heading?'

'They go Kir. But Taliban looking for them. We say not go. Danger. We say *Khaana bourou,* go back home, but they no listen. They big problems if go on.'

'Have the Taliban kidnapped them?' asked Osama, devastated.

'*Chaayad.*' Maybe.

It was impossible to get anything else out of them — either they didn't know, or they weren't saying.

THE NEXT MORNING, the surrounding mountains were covered with an immaculate layer of fresh snow. The landscape was extremely grand — a raw, wild environment well beyond the scope of man. Osama went to pray a little way off, where he could enjoy the view. By the time he returned, Nick and Mullah Bakir were ready to go. Nick's dysentery had abated slightly during the night; the medication was finally working. The villagers refused the five hundred afghanis they tried to give them, claiming it was an honour to host Mullah Bakir in their home. At the mullah's insistence, the head of the village finally accepted the money.

'I'll use it to buy two sheep, for my future wife,' he said, smiling.

In many villages, if you wanted a second wife who was a virgin, you had to pay for one or two horses and several sheep, as well as hand over several thousand dollars. The poorest villagers would emigrate to Iran or the Gulf States, and bleed themselves dry to pay these absurd dowries worth several years' wages. When a husband was disappointed in his wife, having paid so heavily, he would burn her or throw acid at her, and demand the dowry back. No one in Kabul, apart from the Taliban, was really committed to abolishing these customs.

'The dowry economy is the only thing in this country that works, apart from suicide bombings and baksheesh,' quipped Mullah Bakir, still in sparkling form.

They spent the whole day in the car, driving at an average of fifteen to twenty kilometres an hour, dodging snowdrifts and crevasses. Osama drove as well as he could, but the 4x4 wasn't easy to handle on account of the armouring. They fell into two crevasses, and only re-emerged thanks to the winch. That night, they stopped in another village, even poorer than the last. When the head of the village heard that Mullah Bakir was among his guests, the house went into overdrive. They ate boiled eggs, re-cooked rice, and a sort of stew made of stringy bits of meat floating in a putrid stock. The head of the village seemed very proud to be offering them meat. It was clearly high, but to refuse it would have been a sign of contempt, so Osama wolfed it down along with the foul-smelling rice. Mullah Bakir and Nick could barely manage a mouthful. The epicurean mullah's expression faced with this awful sustenance was a thing to behold. They finished the meal with sweet condensed milk in cartons printed with the American flag — one of the goodies that the Coalition was distributing in the villages. Osama was surprised that aid was reaching this far. The head of the village drank the condensed milk, crushed the carton with his foot, and spat on it.

'American,' he said. 'Bad.'

Osama wasn't about to copy him. In his day, real mujahedeen didn't accept presents from the Russians they were fighting.

They woke early the next morning, around five. Osama would have happily slept for another couple of hours, but the head of the village was intent on performing his first prayer with the famous Mullah Bakir before sun-up. Outside, it was bitterly cold, probably minus twenty. Osama nevertheless insisted on visiting the well. He stripped off to his underpants and washed in the freezing water with a small piece of soap that the head of the village had lent him. He felt much better for it, and put on clean underwear and a clean shirt. When they came to leave, Nick had to burn some petrol under the motor to get it warm enough to start.

They continued their exhausting journey — another night, another wretched village, a dismal morning marked only by the crevasses they had to cross and the patches of black ice that blocked their way. Empty jerry cans rattled around in the back of the 4x4.

Osama had worked out that they had three days' worth of petrol left. Around three in the afternoon, just after they'd crossed a snowy pass, Nick pointed out a black shape on the banks of the ravine, a few metres from the road. A new Land Cruiser with Kabul plates was lying in the ditch.

THE 4x4 wasn't looking good, on its back, covered in snow. One of the doors was still open, revealing the empty airbags hanging down. The axle was completely twisted. Osama turned off his engine. Silence enveloped them immediately, an impressive silence interrupted only by the howling of the wind. There was not a tree, not a house, not a bird, nothing alive, in sight — just black rocks, snow, and glaciers.

Osama scrambled a few metres down into the ravine to inspect the vehicle. The two rear tyres were torn to shreds. He ran his finger along the scraps of rubber, examining the rims.

'They were shot at with a hunting rifle or a shotgun. There were at least two gunmen — the bullets came from both left and right.'

Osama struggled to climb back up, on account of the frozen rock face. Nick had to give him a hand.

'Someone had blocked the road,' continued Osama. 'Mandrake must have tried to force his way through, and they were shot at from the back. The vehicle tumbled towards the ravine, and luckily came to a halt almost immediately on account of the flatter ground. They were lucky that the ambush didn't take place further up the hill, or they would have fallen two or three hundred metres.'

'Do you think they were hurt?'

'The vehicle is OK, and I didn't see any blood inside. The windscreen is intact; no one was thrown against it when it turned over. They're probably in good health, unless they've been slaughtered since their capture.'

Nick looked around. The same grand, hostile, deserted landscape lay in every direction.

'Where could they be?' he murmured.

They continued their journey, driving even more slowly now that the threat had become reality. The road coiled interminably around the mountains. After about half an hour, Osama suddenly braked. The 4x4 skidded, slid on a patch of black ice, and came to a stop across the road. A dozen men were barring their way, brandishing weapons. They looked determined and dangerous, aiming rusty old Kalashnikovs and repeating rifles from the early twentieth century, but also hunting rifles and grenades. Although they were protected by the armoured vehicle, Osama decided to switch off his engine and go and speak to them.

'Don't leave the car, whatever you do,' he ordered Nick. 'Lock the doors as soon as I'm out. If there's a problem, try to turn the car around and get away.'

He stepped out of the 4x4, his hands clearly visible.

'May Allah be with you,' he said, greeting the man who seemed to be the leader, 'and with your men. I greet you in the name of Allah the powerful and the merciful.'

'May Allah be with you,' replied the Taliban chief.

He was young, with bright blue eyes outlined in Khol, and a face that would have been handsome were it not for the bushy, hennaed beard. He spoke Dari with a heavy Pashtun accent.

'Soldiers and infidels are not allowed in these mountains. Why have you come?'

'We are neither soldiers nor infidels. We come in peace.'

'Your car is too good — only infidels and traders in Karzaï's pay can buy a vehicle like that,' replied the chief, ominously.

'Al Hamdullilah, I have come here with the great Mullah Bakir, friend and confidant of Mullah Omar. He is in the car. You may greet him — he will consent to talk with you — but put down your gun, because no one threatens Mullah Bakir, except infidels, and Allah will punish them for their crimes,' said Osama loudly.

A murmur ran through the group. Seizing the moment, Mullah Bakir opened the car door and stepped out grandly, belly first, wearing his turban. He proffered his hand, which the chief hurried to kiss.

'Mullah Bakir! Mullah Bakir! Allah U Akhbar!' squealed the Taliban, crowding around the mullah.

When things had calmed down a little, Osama spoke to the

Taliban chief.

'We have a Westerner with us. He's a *dhimmi,* an inferior Christian, but also a friend of Islam and the soldiers of God. I ask you to welcome him as well.'

He motioned to Nick that he could get out of the car. The chief glared at him, and then lost interest.

'What are you doing here?' the Taliban chief asked Mullah Bakir. 'Can we help you?'

'We're looking for a Christian and his companion. NATO is also looking for them, to kill them. I have come to bring them back to Kabul.'

'We captured them yesterday morning, at first light! They had a vehicle with Kabul plates, like all regime collaborators, and a lot of money in the car. We took their dollars and their afghanis. They also had blankets, and boots, and food — rice, lamb, flatbread, sugar, tinned food — and a compass and a gun. We took everything for our warriors, *Allah U Akhbar.*'

'What about them — where are they?'

The chief looked obstinate and didn't reply. Foreseeing disaster, Osama repeated, 'Where are they?'

'At the village. But we have sold the infidel.'

'Sold?' exclaimed Osama. 'Who to?'

'A group of great warriors from around here — Herb Kalit a Islamia.'

Osama noticed Mullah Bakir pale at the mention of the name.

'Why did you sell them, for the love of God?'

'We are not powerful enough to negotiate a ransom with the Coalition. Herb Kalit e Islamia is used to taking hostages. They promised us five hundred dollars, five horses, twenty sheep, and two hundred kilos of onions.'

'Are they already at the village?'

'Maybe. We'll see when we get back, Al Hamdullilah! The deal won't be closed until my return.'

'We need to speak with that foreigner,' said Mullah Bakir. 'He is worth a great deal to us. We will give you more money than Herb Kalit e Islamia. Much more.'

'And the girl?' asked Osama suddenly. 'What have you done with her?'

'Going with a Christian is a crime; she is a pervert! I spoke with the village imam, and he has given his verdict, Allah U Akhbar. He's a wise man — he can read and count to ten!'

'What did he decide?'

'The imam says that the girl has betrayed Islam and our laws by going out with a man with no father or brother present. And that our sacred book, the Koran, forbids the marriage of a Muslim to an infidel unless they convert beforehand. This girl has committed the worst of crimes. So she had to be punished.'

'What did you do with her, for the love of God?'

'The Imam in his great wisdom decided that the girl must undertake a Muslim marriage before dying, and satisfy the warriors fighting the infidels for the glory of Sharia and the sacred book. There are thirty of us warriors, all brave, all having given much to Allah. The girl was married to each of us before being punished according to the sacred book.'

'You all raped and stoned her!' cried Mullah Bakir, horrified.

'Not raped, Mullah, consummated, according to the laws of Islam, may Allah be praised. She liked it a lot — we are all strong and healthy. I consummated my marriage first, in the early afternoon of yesterday, and again before five o'clock prayers, and again after prayers. I consummated my marriage all evening; with Allah as my witness, I was in good health, as strong as a ram. Then Abdul consummated, and Muhammad after him, and then Hazrat, and Younous. All night. Abdullah, Zalmay, Bismullah, Wahid, Sebghatollah, Jarollah, Zarar … each of them honoured her with their fervour which, as Allah is my witness, was great. The girl may not yet have been stoned — some of the warriors may have taken their time to consummate their marriage, as I did.'

'Let's go,' ordered the mullah. 'Show us the way to your village. I will talk to your imam.'

His face inscrutable, the chief clapped his hands, and his troop began walking. Mullah Bakir's authority was such that it wouldn't have occurred to the chief to demur. The group had been joined by a child with three donkeys. The chief and two of his men rode on the donkeys, followed by their warriors, with the Toyota bringing up the rear. The thick snow slowed the donkeys' progress, so they couldn't have been doing more than three or four kilometres an hour.

They were horrified. Osama had experienced moments of extreme violence during the war, but that was war, and Kabul was still a large, relatively civilised city. Here, he was gradually coming to the realisation that his country wasn't what he'd recently thought it was. He had spent too long cut off from the reality of rural Afghanistan. Here in Nuristan, as in Kandahar, none of the rules of civilisation that he believed in existed. He thought about Malalai's struggle for women's rights. She would never achieve it!

They continued at walking place, and then the men turned off on a path across the mountain, signalling to them to continue along the road. Osama accelerated.

'You paled when the Taliban mentioned Herb Kalit e Islamia,' Nick said to Mullah Bakir. 'Do you know it?'

'Unfortunately, yes. It was created by my worst enemy.'

It was terrible luck. Osama felt as if everything was conspiring against them. How had they offended heaven to deserve such fury?

'Tell us about it,' continued Nick. 'At least then we'll know what to expect.'

'There is an Afghan warlord called Gulbuddin Hekmatyar. Along with Massoud and Dostom, he was the main architect of the struggle against the Red Army, and one of the people who allowed us to overthrow the communists. When we Taliban began our conquest of Afghanistan, in 1996, Hekmatyar betrayed Dostom and Massoud to come over to our side, and this helped us gain power. The two of us sat on the secret Taliban Supreme Council together. He is an ardent Islamist, and in favour of Sharia, of course, but his crude and literal interpretation of Islam is not that of an educated man. Hekmatyar recommended the eradication of all those who didn't practise 'proper' Islam. He was one of those pushing for the massacre of the Hazara because they are Shiites, for example. I opposed him from our earliest days in government.

Hekmatyar had a right-hand man called Emir Beg. Emir Beg

was so cruel that everyone was afraid of him, even among the Taliban. For instance, he cut off dozens of peoples' arms for using toilet paper instead of flat stones. The Koran doesn't mention toilet paper, he would say, and therefore anyone who uses it is ungodly, and committing a crime against the Koran. The same for people who shave their beards — the Koran never mentions any shaving by the Prophet, may He be praised, so anyone who shaves is, according to Beg, guilty of a crime. Emir Beg is illiterate — I don't think he's ever read the Koran — but he was very charismatic, and people were seduced by his strength. I tried to stand against him, at first by arguing in front of Mullah Omar that the Koran doesn't mention Kalashnikovs either, or 4x4s, or electricity, and we used them — so therefore the Koran was surely not to be taken literally. They didn't listen. So I decided to rally other imams on the Taliban Secret Council who were also horrified by the violence of Hekmatyar and Emir Beg. We were helped by the atrocities they were committing in the areas they controlled. Mullah Omar didn't dare take on Hekmatyar, but we did manage to disgrace Emir with the case of the coffin.

'What did he have to do with that?'

'He was visiting the Customs offices that day. It was he who ordered the flogging.'

Osama knew the story only too well. In 2000, a rich émigré had asked for his body to be repatriated after his death. The Taliban had opened the coffin when it came through customs, in case it contained forbidden substances. The Westernised man was clean-shaven. When the Taliban saw that the corpse was beardless, in opposition to the prescriptions of the sacred book, they became furious and ordered for it to be given eighty lashings as punishment. When the affair was made public, it contributed to the discrediting of the regime by emphasising and caricaturing the absurdity of the Taliban laws.

'I see. What happened after that?'

'The day Emir Beg was due to be arrested, he was warned, and he fled into the mountains. I knew he was Nuristani, but I thought he was hiding much further north, beyond Barg e Metal.'

'Are you sure that he holds it against you? You weren't the only one to make the decision, after all.'

'I was the driving force. I destroyed his career, and forced him and his men to flee like dogs. He had power; he had the ear of Mullah Omar; he had a big house in Kandahar, bodyguards, young dancers, and various women he could marry for a single night, with the help of obliging imams. So to answer your question, yes, I think he does hate me. If he catches me, he will impose the special punishment he reserved for his personal enemies.'

'Which is?'

'He will gouge out my eyes, cut off my fingers, nose, and tongue, and sever my genital organs. Then he'll let me die slowly. Apparently, it takes two or three weeks to die of the infections, sometimes more.' The mullah laughed joylessly. 'My *friends,* brother Osama, dear Nick, if we fall into his hands, I fear this fate may be yours, too.'

As soon as they reached the village, the leader strode over.

'They're down there, in the orchard, with the imam — about to start the stoning!'

They followed him at a run. As they rounded the last house, they saw the villagers gathered on a snowy plateau. A woman in a torn tunic sat on her heels, her hair loose, attached to a sort of hemp leash. Osama recognised Zahra. This woman huddled in the snow with her tangled hair and glassy eyes didn't look much like the beauty in the photo. A burqa-wearing woman tugged on the leash, but Zahra didn't react; instead, she collapsed in the snow, as if catatonic. A child raised his arm and threw a stone at her. Another soon followed. In the next few seconds, a dozen stones hit Zahra, without her reacting at all.

'*Estaad Cho,*' yelled Osama. 'Stop this!'

The hands raised to throw more stones fell back down, surprised. Osama put his rifle on the ground and knelt by Zahra. Her forehead was ripped to pieces, and she was wounded in several places. Horrified, he saw that blood was also running down the insides of her thighs, which were reddened with drying scabs. The soldiers had torn her open as they'd raped her.

'We've come to rescue you,' he murmured in English.

'It's too late,' she replied, eyes rolling in her head.

While Osama helped Zahra to her feet, Mullah Bakir scolded the crowd.

'Unbelievers must be punished, true, and also Muslim women who have relations with infidels. But this woman never had sex with the foreigner, as you could not have known. Also, that foreigner is an enemy of Bush and Obama, an enemy of the little devils, a friend of the Afghan people. You must free them both.'

'Who are you, to tell us what to do?' demanded an old man suddenly, his hennaed beard reaching almost all the way to his belt.

'And you, brother, who are you?'

'I'm the village imam. I say what's right.'

'Do you know how to read?'

'No, but I've learnt the holy book — I can recite it by heart, from the first to the final sura. And you, who are you?'

'I am Mullah Bakir, friend of Mullah Omar and former member of the Taliban Secret Council.'

On hearing these words, the imam threw himself to his knees, and a murmur spread through the crowd.

'Mullah Bakir, glory to you! May you kill many unbelievers,' shouted a man suddenly. 'Death to the Jews, death to the Christians!'

'We'll obey your orders, because you're a friend of Sheikh Bin Laden, the holy man!' cried another.

For a few minutes, all they could hear was the villagers' jubilation as they crowded around Mullah Bakir to touch his clothes or kiss his hand.

'Mullah, may you help Sheikh Bin Laden destroy all Jews and Crusaders!' roared the imam.

Mullah Bakir extended a magnanimous hand.

'Stand up — for all Muslims are brothers, and no imam need kneel before anyone but Allah. And now, my brother, take us to the foreigner.'

Osama stopped to help a still expressionless Zahra into the car, and then ran to catch up with Mullah Bakir, the imam and the leader of the troop. The villagers scattered out of his way. He'd noticed that his stature and sniper rifle caused a certain frisson among these people, who'd never seen such a tall man in their lives. The leader stopped by a mud hut, its path cleared of snow. Two armed and bearded men were guarding the door.

'Go on in,' suggested Mullah Bakir to Osama in English. 'I'd better stay outside with these *charming, sophisticated,* and *welcoming* gentlemen.'

A stove was giving out a little heat. A man was crouching at the back of the shadowy room with a chain attached to his wrist. The other end of the chain was fixed to a hoop embedded in the wall. He was hanging his head, and his breathing was laboured.

'Leonard Mandrake?' asked Osama.

The man looked up, surprised. Osama's first impression on seeing the two fierce eyes was one of astonishment, at the fight still in them. Mandrake had scabs on his face, his nose was broken, and his lip was split. He'd clearly been badly beaten, but he'd retained all his dignity — a legacy of the powerful man he'd once been. Osama had been expecting to find a terror-stricken fugitive, but this man was calm, still trying to master a situation beyond his control. Mandrake stared intensely at Osama.

'Who are you?'

'It's complicated. I'll explain later, if we manage to get out of here alive. My name is Osama. I'm a policeman, and I've come from Kabul to rescue you.'

'Rescue me?' repeated Mandrake. 'Zahra — how is she?'

'We rescued her just before the villagers began stoning her. We weren't a moment too soon.'

'Did they … well, you know …'

'Yes, I'm afraid so. She needs medical treatment, but she's alive — that's the main thing.'

Osama undid the padlock, and helped Mandrake to his feet. He stumbled, and Osama had to support him.

'Sorry. I'm not used to high altitudes, and I caught dysentery.'

Osama put an arm around his shoulders.

'Come on, I'll take some of your weight.'

'My bag, over there.'

'We don't have time.'

'It's important.'

'Your report?'

'Yes.'

Osama picked up the leather satchel. When they both came out, closely entwined, an angry murmur spread through the crowd. Sensing it was time to intervene, Mullah Bakir thrust a wad of notes into the leader's hand, before waving his own in the air.

'My brothers, I have given your leader many afghanis, money that comes from Mullah Omar himself. One hundred thousand afghanis!'

A new murmur spread. This was an enormous amount of money for such a poor village.

'With this money,' continued Mullah Bakir, 'you will be able to buy horses and sheep, chickens and goats, onions and garlic, and many, many eggs. Al Hamdullilah!'

'Allah U Akhbar, Allah U Akhbar,' chanted the men in response.

They returned to the vehicle, surrounded by the exultant crowd still raucously praising God, Bin Laden, and the glory of the Taliban. Nick leapt out of the car to help Osama. Even the sight of another Westerner didn't dampen the villagers' excitement, and their cries became even louder.

'We'd better hurry,' said Nick. 'We need to get out of here before the Islamists arrive.'

Nick gently installed Mandrake in the back of the Toyota. Suddenly, he heard a dull rumble in the distance, growing louder with every second. He stood up, alarmed.

'What is it?' he called to Mullah Bakir.

Osama had already understood. He'd heard that noise many times when he was fighting the Russians. Helicopters were approaching along a valley, concealed by the surrounding mountains.

'Our enemies,' he said.

At that very moment, a massive transport helicopter appeared, followed by a second, and a third. The three machines hovered over the village like giant dragonflies before coming gently to land. The rotors hadn't even stopped when all the side doors opened and soldiers sprang out, rifles shouldered and ready to shoot. Over the deafening roar of the engines, Nick could hear the officers encouraging their men. One villager brandished his gun, and was immediately hit in the chest by a flurry of bullets. Another met the same fate. Several more scattered with their weapons, but well-aimed gunfire sent them sprawling to the floor. In just a few seconds, the site was clear. It was then that Nick noticed the soldiers weren't wearing Afghan army uniform. They were dressed in black fatigues, with no identifying logo. Two men were coming down the steps of one of the helicopters — an African–American colossus, and a white-haired man in a smart black suit, incongruous in this environment.

'That's Joseph, head of the K troops,' whispered Nick to Osama. 'We're fucked.'

'Don't move,' replied Osama. 'There's no point getting shot like rabbits. There are too many of them.'

A new noise above made them look up. A low-flying drone passed by. It circled them, and rose back into the clouds. Meanwhile, the Entity killers were rampaging through the village with their weapons. There was the odd burst of gunfire. Joseph examined the scene with a critical eye. Suddenly, he noticed Nick and Osama. He nudged his neighbour and pointed to the 4x4. They saw a smile spread across the giant's face.

'What's going on?' asked Mandrake, from inside the Toyota.

'We're fucked,' muttered Nick. 'They've found us again.'

'Who?'

'My old colleagues from Switzerland, who were employed by Willard Consulting.'

'They don't work for Willard,' murmured Mandrake. 'They work for the CIA.'

Joseph was approaching, followed by the colossus, who carried an impressive black pump-action shotgun. Joseph stood in front of them. No emotion was visible on his face; just a vague irritation.

'Well done, Nick. You nearly had us, again.'

'How did you find us?'

'Through the car-hire guy who supplied the 4x4 to your friend Mandrake. A satellite found it in the end — a brand new 4x4 isn't hard to find on these mountain roads. Then we asked for NATO's help, and they sent dozens of reconnaissance drones. An operative noticed the unusual levels of activity in this village, and I realised Mandrake must have been taken prisoner here. We missed the arrival of my dear colleague and his Afghan friend, but I'm delighted to have you all here for the final party.'

He smiled joylessly.

'Final, in all senses of the word, for you all and for you too, Nick. It's a shame you couldn't help ruining everything.'

'Ruining everything? You're accusing me of ruining everything? You're insane!'

Joseph shook his head.

'You don't understand anything, you cretin. And that's why you're going to die.'

'You're a killer. You boast about fighting for democracy, but you're just as evil as the people you're fighting.'

'If you think that, you must really be naïve.' Joseph shook his head. 'You've no idea of the world we live in. No idea what's festering behind the scenes. Your comfort, your petty little life — you owe it all to guys like me.'

'You've killed dozens of people for this bloody report. Why?'

'It's not only the report, Nick. Also the others looking for it.'

'Who?'

At that moment, something strange happened. For a fraction of a second, it seemed as if the face of the shotgun-wielding black giant was losing its shape, dissolving. The next instant, his head exploded, and a loud blast rang out. Two other soldiers collapsed. Joseph instinctively flung himself to the ground, and then ran for cover.

'What's happening?' screamed Nick.

'We're being attacked,' said Osama. 'It's the Taliban.'

Turban-wearing Afghans yelling mysterious slogans suddenly appeared on every side. They fired on the Entity troops, who responded with their assault rifles and grenade launchers.

'These are Herb Kalit e Islamia men,' announced Mullah Bakir tonelessly. 'Look over there. That's Emir Beg — I'd know him anywhere.'

They saw a man walking majestically down the snowy mountain, surrounded by warriors who were spreading out over the entire village. They were a proper army. A rocket hit one of the helicopters, destroying it instantaneously. Soon combat was raging between the Islamist fighters and the Entity men — fewer, but much better trained. About twenty Taliban corpses hit the ground in the space of a few minutes.

'Let's get out of here,' yelled Nick. 'It's our only chance.'

'Whatever you do, don't stand up — crawl to the car,' ordered Osama.

A bullet bounced off the vehicle's armoured bodywork just as he was opening the door for Mullah Bakir. Joseph was aiming at them, using a gun equipped with sights. Inside, Mandrake cried out in pain as a spray of blood spattered against the window. Osama shut the door with a cry of rage. The killer shouldered his gun once more, aiming at Osama this time. Osama rushed around the car and jumped in from the other side, protected by the armoured bodywork. He span the car around and managed to get it back on the road. Several dozen bullets crazed the windows without any of them shattering. They were being shot at by the Taliban, as well as Joseph. The second helicopter exploded. Then the road curved around, and they could no longer see a thing.

'How's Mandrake?' asked Osama.

'He's been hit in the chest, on the heart side. He's blacked out. There's a lot of blood.'

'Shit, shit, and shit!'

Suddenly Nick, who was bent over Mandrake, announced, 'That's it — he's dead. Zahra is haemorrhaging massively. She's going to die very soon, too, if we don't do something.'

'I have no transfusion equipment in the car, no morphine, nothing. We're two days' drive from the nearest city.'

'She's fucked.'

Osama opened his window. They could hear the rattle of gunfire in the distance, still going strong.

'There were almost two hundred Taliban, and I only counted twenty fighters, max, for the Entity. They've no chance,' said the mullah.

'Don't be too sure,' objected Nick. 'Those Ks are all ex-commandoes, top of their game. They aren't dead yet. Your friend Emir Beg still has something to worry about.'

'Those Taliban are crazy — they're going to lose dozens of men, maybe more. Aren't they afraid of dying?'

'Emir Beg would like to get his hands on me more than anything in the world,' replied Mullah Bakir. 'He must have heard I was in the area, and decided that the foreigners were here to capture us. Then he ran all kinds of risks to capture us himself instead.'

Osama accelerated, despite the snow and the black ice.

'There was a drone. It must have circled high above us for a couple of hours. How come its infra-red cameras hadn't picked up the Taliban?' asked Nick.

'Perhaps they spotted it with their binoculars. They probably used a trick we used to play on the Russians, years ago. You advance beneath a blanket covered with snow and icy water — it makes your body heat undetectable to the drone's infra-red sensors. I've done it several times, and the Russian helicopters never caught me. We mujahedeen learnt that from the French commandoes who trained us.'

Later on, Nick took Zahra's pulse.

'Nothing. She's dead.'

Osama squinted at the bag that Mandrake had given him.

'Open it,' he ordered.

Nick took out two CDs and a thick file, protected by a thick plastic cover.

'The Mandrake File,' said Osama. 'At least they didn't get everything.'

Epilogue

Osama, Nick, and Mullah Bakir were resting on threadbare rugs at the back of the house owned by Kalkana, scribe to the poor. Osama had assured his companions in misfortune that no one would come looking for them in the heart of this slum. And in fact they did feel safe in Kalkana's pitiful house, despite the constant blackouts, the lack of running water, and the foul stink of the whole neighbourhood.

The drive back to Kabul had taken them five days. They'd put a blanket over the bonnet of the 4x4, and stopped every fifteen minutes to cover it with icy water. That blotted out the heat of the engine so they could escape detection by the surveillance drones sent after them by NATO. They buried Leonard Mandrake and Zahra in a makeshift grave at the side of the road: Mullah Bakir conducted a short ecumenical service, even reciting a Christian 'Our Father' for the foreigner. They piled a few stones on top of the grave. Now they were waiting. Nick had done what the three of them had decided. The die was cast.

Early the next afternoon, a private jet landed at Bagram. Two men in suits stepped down the stairs, accompanied by a dozen more in fatigues. They rushed into armoured 4x4s, and set off for Kabul. One of the suit-wearing men immediately connected to the Internet using his encrypted BlackBerry, and sent a short message to the address that Nick had provided. It said simply, 'I've arrived.' A few seconds later, he received a reply, made up of digits only — a telephone number. He dialled it.

'Nick, this is the director of the CIA,' he said. 'I've just arrived in Kabul.'

'I'll give you the address', said Nick. 'No need to tell you that if you mess us around in any way, the report will be online within two hours.'

'Stay calm!' cried the director of the CIA, his voice betraying a hint of panic. 'Please, do nothing at all to compromise the situation. I gave you my word last night that nothing will be attempted against you. I've personally read, in its entirety, the Mandrake file that you kindly sent over, and have informed the highest state authorities of its contents. I have come in person to make sure that we take care of this problem without any more bloodshed.'

'Is my father with you?'

'I'll pass him over.'

Nick had suggested to his companions that they make a deal with the new director of the CIA — an experienced man appointed by President Obama, and portrayed by the media as honest. The presence of Nick's father was their surety: before becoming a lawyer, he'd been a British Foreign Office diplomat, and for about ten years an important agent for the British secret services. Nick had often asked himself how much his own decision to join the Swiss service had been influenced by the secrecy surrounding his father, and by the gossip about his exploits. Was it continuity, or the desire to impress or even outperform his father? He'd often wondered about that.

He stifled a smile. What better life insurance could he have obtained? It would be impossible for even the Entity to wipe out a well-known and respected English citizen, former MI6 agent, and lawyer for the Crown. For the first time in several days, Nick relaxed. He gave Osama and Mullah Bakir the thumbs-up.

'Everything is going as planned,' he said.

Three quarters of an hour later, the two 4x4s entered the narrow lanes of the shantytown. They drove through a tortuous maze of alleys before coming to a stop in front of Kalkana's house. The drivers hadn't even had time to switch off their engines when the door opened, revealing Osama and his Kalashnikov. One of the bodyguards made to get out of the car, but was stopped by the director.

'No. Just Mr Snee and me.'

He stepped out of the car, followed by Nick's father. Nick sighed with relief when he saw his dad. Finally, they were safe. They hugged.

'It's all over now,' said his father.

Osama was wearing his astrakhan hat, and a blanket over his shoulders, making him look like something from another century. A few moments later, the five of them were sitting around the table. The tension was palpable. The director put a bag on the table, and took out a large, square metal box. It was crackling.

'This machine produces intense electronic signals to prevent any surveillance of our conversation. It's indispensable. Is that OK?'

'Yes,' said Osama.

The director turned towards Mullah Bakir.

'We have a very detailed file on you, Mullah. We don't consider you an enemy, but someone acceptable to negotiate with.'

'I'm glad to hear it. Am I to understand that you won't be sending your drones after me the next time I leave Kabul?'

For the first time since the beginning of the conversation, the director of the CIA cracked a smile.

'We continue to support the legitimate government of President Karzaï, while also working towards national reconciliation with the moderate members of your movement. If things change, please know that America will not forget you, to the extent that you are able to curb the suicidal urges of your friends this time.'

'I couldn't ask for more,' said the mullah, bowing slightly. 'The moderate wing of the movement has learnt its lesson. We will keep ourselves in check.'

'The conversation we are about to have is confidential in nature. I have every trust in you, but …'

'I think I've already proven my loyalty in this matter,' interrupted Mullah Bakir. 'May I remind you that, without me, Commandant Kandar and Nick would be dead. Surely you don't expect me to wait in the street while you discuss these serious matters between yourselves?'

The director didn't immediately respond. Nick's father placed a friendly hand on his arm.

'We have no choice.'

'OK. Gentlemen, various individuals have committed serious mistakes. Inexcusable errors. Powerful people have made money in scandalous circumstances, using the power conferred on them by ordinary citizens — particularly the citizens of America. They have stolen, lied, and killed. Before I came here, I spoke to the president of the United States. He is devastated by the affair, all the more so because one of his esteemed colleagues thought it necessary to authorise the Entity to consider itself exempt from all legal constraints in its efforts to track down Leonard Mandrake. The president has asked me to put an end to the unbelievable levels of carnage created by this case. My mission is to resolve the situation as best I can. This will entail punishment, but without unleashing the scandal that would destroy us all. I have been given every power to accomplish this.'

'We're listening.'

'Every individual who has personally enriched themselves will have to return the money they have stolen. The president was very clear on this point. If they do not, there will be no investigation by the FBI or the secret services in the relevant Western countries, but a direct and final intervention.'

'What do you mean by a direct and final intervention?' asked Osama.

'The money or their life. The president has signed an executive order to the effect that every action be taken in retaliation, including termination with extreme prejudice.'

'That's what the CIA calls it when someone has to die,' explained Nick to Osama, in case he hadn't understood the subtleties of the language.

'Our NATO friends who are also implicated are as keen as us to avoid a scandal. The issue will be resolved in exactly the same way in all the capital cities concerned. Only the Dutch government hasn't been informed, because they are not ... *equipped* for the necessary kind of decision. We will act on their behalf. These individuals will resign over a period of eight to ten months, to ensure that the media doesn't pick up any link between them.'

'The punishment is weak,' commented Osama.

'These precautions are clearly not sufficient for Patrick Willard. He died in his sleep last night.'

'How?'

'There are a few experts particularly talented at this kind of thing. The doctor who examined him concluded it was a cerebral haemorrhage. There won't be an autopsy. The cremation has probably already taken place. In the absence of an heir, the company could be sold ... but we have had a discreet word with the Swiss government. Willard Consulting will be dissolved, and its archives destroyed. It was a company founded on secrecy; no one will be any the wiser.'

'The bankers are the missing link in this discussion,' said Mullah Bakir. 'They only profited indirectly, of course, but I'm sure you will recognise that the eight billion dollars that moved through Switzerland will have made a lot of money for the banks. How could they not have realised that these deposits might be illegal?'

'You're right in theory, but it can't be proven. Hundreds of billions of dollars pass through Switzerland every year; they will argue that they acted in good faith. And some of them probably did. Sorting the wheat from the chaff would be impossible without an in-depth legal investigation, and interrogations of the relevant bankers at every level. And that investigation could not be carried out in secret. I'm afraid that, on that front, there is nothing to be done.'

'No change there, then ... Your compatriots are certainly impressive, Nick.'

'What about the companies that profited from all this?' asked Osama, his tone still icy. 'The ones that provided the fake documents? What will become of them?'

'The American and relevant European governments have contacted the implicated individuals to obtain resignations from their boards,' replied Nick's father, pre-empting the CIA's director.

'The four chairmen who profited personally from the situation are going to hand over in the next few weeks, in exchange for no criminal investigation. They will have to give back the personal profit made on their thefts. As for the other chairmen, we've been assured that they won't be continuing beyond their current terms of office, which range in length from six months to three years. Finally, in anticipation of your next question, Nick, the Entity was dissolved last night. And please be assured — though I'm sure you guessed as much when you read the Taliban's victory statements — that all the K troops pursuing you were killed in the Afghan mountains. We have managed to recover their corpses; fourteen, to be exact. We think they wiped out more than a hundred Taliban, including Emir Beg, but none of them survived. Except the man called Joseph. His corpse was not found.'

'Do you think he's still alive?'

'It's possible. To tell you the truth, we know nothing about him — not even his real name. It will probably remain a mystery.'

'What about the general?'

'He threw himself off a bridge over the Aar at three o'clock this morning. He drowned.'

'Was he helped, I wonder?'

'It wasn't necessary. The general had his faults, but he was perfectly aware of the seriousness of the acts he was concealing. He simply felt that he had no choice; he had to accomplish his mission — to protect the security of the West, whatever the cost. That relentlessness was mistaken, but I respect his courage. His suicide is merely the natural outcome of his attitude.' The director of the CIA looked back at Osama. 'Do you have any more questions about the organisers of the cartel?'

'No,' said Osama after a moment's hesitation. 'But I don't think the measures you have detailed are equal to the problem. I was hoping for justice, but this is a farce.'

'We've made the right decisions, if you put the case in its proper context.'

'What context? The context is very clear.'

'Oh really? Are you sure? Do you think your involvement in

this investigation was a matter of chance? We ourselves aren't at all convinced.'

As Osama didn't reply, the director of the CIA insisted.

'I repeat my question. Was it in the normal way of things for you to be personally involved in this investigation? Certain elements have suggested to us that individuals seemingly exterior to the case actually had a great interest in your investigations.'

'You think I was playing a double game?'

'No. We wonder if you might have been manipulated, without your knowledge. Who put you on the case?'

'I don't know,' admitted Osama. 'I was warned by a policeman I didn't have the time to track down. But I don't see what that has to do with all this.'

'How old was this policeman?'

'Young, under thirty.'

'Any distinguishing characteristics?'

'For the love of Allah, what is the point of all these questions?'

The director's face brightened. He passed a photo to Osama.

'I think I can answer some of this. Do you recognise this man?'

The photo showed a young Afghan male walking down the street. The scar on his left cheek was clearly visible.

'Of course!' exclaimed Osama. 'That's him — the orderly who told me about Wali Wadi's suicide.'

'Are you sure? It was he who sent you to the scene of the crime?'

'Absolutely. Who is this man?'

'His name is Abdul Muhammad Kantor. He works for the NDS, as a member of the electronic counter-espionage department, with the rank of captain. But in this case, Kantor wasn't working for the NDS. We think he is also the secret head of a foreign power's Afghan network.'

Several more photos followed the first. They showed the 'orderly' sitting at a café table with an Asian man.

'Who is the other man?' asked Nick, intrigued. 'A Hazara?'

'His name is Zhao Lin. His official title is Cultural Advisor to the Chinese embassy, but in fact he's a colonel who is regional head of the Chinese secret service, Guoanbu.'

'I don't understand. Where do the Chinese come into all this?'

'The Chinese are more and more active in Afghanistan and Iraq — not in the fight against terrorism, but in order to build up information against us. They know that all wars give rise to financial blunders and to embezzlement. They actively support the search for compromising information, in the context of their underground battle against the United States and NATO to claim the lithium and other precious mineral deposits that have been discovered in the Afghan subsoil. By publishing the Mandrake report, they would have entirely destroyed the legitimacy of our activities here. They would have chased us out of the country and got their hands on what they are after: the mineral resources desperately needed by Chinese industry. We picked up a major increase in the intensity of electronic traffic between the Chinese embassy in Kabul and the Guoanbu headquarters shortly before Wali Wadi's death, and in the days immediately following. We concluded from this that they were somehow or other aware of the case. Wali Wadi probably approached them at the same time he approached Willard, thinking he'd be able to obtain the best price for his information by having them bid against each other. Luckily, he didn't have time to conclude the deal. The Chinese knew they couldn't carry out an investigation here without being noticed, so they needed a gifted and incorruptible local investigator, likely to take on the security minister, but whom they could control from a distance without his knowledge. And that's where you came in, Commandant Kandar.'

'I'm not a puppet. I would never have given foreigners information about this investigation!' cried Osama. 'And anyway, how would they have thought of me? I don't know this Abdul Muhammad Kantor. Or the Chinese.'

'You don't, but your colleague who heads up the intelligence department of Kabul police does.'

A new photo appeared — his friend Reza sitting in the same bar, talking with the Chinese colonel.

'You know him, don't you?'

An intense astonishment appeared on Osama's face, mixed with something else. Disgust. Sadness.

'When you were training in Moscow, he was in Peking.'

Osama looked lost, suddenly. As if dealt a fatal blow by the betrayal of his friend, the man he'd counted on throughout this investigation.

'He was only there for twelve months, but that was enough for them to remember him. For the past few years, your friend has received a monthly deposit to a discreet account with the Bank of China, in Macau. In exchange, he helps them out. That's how he has recently acquired a pretty seaside villa, just south of Shanghai. He's planning to retire there one day with a beautiful lady. Reza was Guoanbu's secret weapon. We're sure it was he who had the idea of bringing you into the game, without your knowledge, and he who was charged with keeping an eye on the investigation. If you had found anything, the Chinese would have known straight away. They would have made sure they got hold of the report, or a copy, through Reza. Objectively, it was a lovely stunt, one of the best they've nearly pulled off in recent years.'

Too shocked to reply, Osama watched the spy pick up the photos and put them back in his satchel, as if nothing had happened.

'That's the big story behind the little one. I'm sure you'll understand that we aren't keen to allow those guys to reap the benefits.'

Nick and Osama looked at each other. Osama had already pulled himself together, with rage replacing despondency.

'What do you intend to do about Reza?'

'Nothing.'

'What do you mean, nothing?'

'We'll keep a close eye on him, so we can follow Guoanbu's activities more easily. Unless you want to intervene yourself, Commandant. Morality isn't really our field. If you want to punish him, go ahead; we would understand perfectly. It's up to you.'

Osama nodded impassively. There was no way of knowing what he'd decided.

'It goes without saying that all the charges made against the two of you have been lifted. Commandant Kandar, you will return to your duties tomorrow. President Obama has already called President

Hamid Karzaï to ask him to dismiss the security minister and to ensure that all investigations against you are dropped. As for you, Nick, come and work with me. I need people like you in this agency.'

'I'm sorry, but I don't want to work for the intelligence services anymore. Not any of them. That's not the life for me.'

'I understand,' replied the director.

He looked disappointed. There was a few moments' silence.

'I know that all these decisions don't add up to a perfect whole, that they won't obliterate the suffering you've been through. But in real life there are no rose-tinted endings. The ending is always grey. Sometimes it's pale grey; sometimes, somewhat darker.' He sighed. 'This was the neatest way we could think of to bring this affair to a close. Once and for all.'

Nick's father put a hand on the file that sat on the table, and looked into Osama's eyes.

'The world is what it is — we cannot change it. I would have preferred another outcome, but this is the only one we could envisage. This is not cynicism, but realism. We also know that you will all be able to keep this case to yourselves That is a necessity, over which none of us has any choice. Now, can we take this ... thing?'

Osama stared at him, his eyes shining. Thoughts were whirling around his brain. He would have liked another outcome, but he couldn't change the world. The plotting between the great powers, China, NATO, the secret documents and bank accounts, his friend's betrayal, the traps — it was all too complex for him. He was just a cop, trying to do his job as honestly as he could. He pushed the CD towards the director of the CIA.

Then he stood up, and went to find Malalai.